Praise for *Slippage*

"The short fiction of Harlan Ellison defies labeling. Mixing tropes from various genres and investing them with a healthy dose of his own larger-than-life personality, Harlan Ellison creates fictions unlike anything else in the marketplace today. Ellison's stories are in a class all their own."
— *San Antonio Express News*

"Ellison writes with a relish for gutter slang, veins-in-the-teeth violence and brand-name pop culture, and his work hums with a relentless narrative drive."
— *New York Times Book Review*

"Complex in form and thought — humorous, witty, wise, even a bit sad — one of Ellison's best fictions."
— *Bloomsbury Review*

"As one of our finest short-story writers in any genre, Ellison demands and deserves close attention. By turns funny, angry, rueful and horrific, *Slippage* finds him in fine form."
— *San Francisco Examiner and Chronicle*

"With *Slippage*, Ellison provides fresh evidence of why he has pleased so many readers and won so many awards."
Cleveland Plain Dealer

"Tough and hard-boiled or as lyrical as a poem, *Slippage* is jam-packed with passionate, entertaining and excellent writing from one of America's finest living writers."
— *St. Petersburg Times*

"Twenty-one outrageous, inventive stories that celebrate the fortieth anniversary of Ellison's career."
— *Playboy*

"His tales seem to take place in the gut. *Unsettling* is a key word when discussing Ellison. He most decidedly does not want his readers settled: He disturbs things, shakes them up badly; he makes you *feel*."
— *San Diego Union Tribune*

"This is one of his finest pieces of fiction. Even after more than forty years, Ellison remains one of America's most passionate, entertaining and provocative writers."
— *Des Moines Register*

"This is such stuff as dreams are made of. Or nightmares."
— *Memphis Flyer*

SLIPPAGE

PRECARIOUSLY
PREVIOUSLY POISED,
UNCOLLECTED
STORIES

HARLAN
ELLISON

HOUGHTON
MIFFLIN
COMPANY
BOSTON
NEW YORK
1998
A Mariner Book

COLLABORATIONS:
PARTNERS IN WONDER COLLABORATIONS WITH 14 OTHER WILD TALENTS [1971]
THE STARLOST: PHOENIX WITHOUT ASHES (WITH ED BRYANT) [1975]
MIND FIELDS 33 STORIES INSPIRED BY THE ART OF JACEK YERKA [1994]

NON-FICTION & ESSAYS:
MEMOS FROM PURGATORY [1961]
THE GLASS TEAT ESSAYS OF OPINION ON TELEVISION [1970]
THE OTHER GLASS TEAT FURTHER ESSAYS OF OPINION ON TELEVISION [1975]
THE BOOK OF ELLISON (EDITED BY ANDREW PORTER) [1978]
SLEEPLESS NIGHTS IN THE PROCRUSTEAN BED ESSAYS (EDITED BY MARTY CLARK) [1984]
AN EDGE IN MY VOICE [1985]
HARLAN ELLISON'S WATCHING [1989]
THE HARLAN ELLISON HORNBOOK [1990]

SCREENPLAYS, ETC:
THE ILLUSTRATED HARLAN ELLISON (EDITED BY BYRON PREISS) [1978]
HARLAN ELLISON'S MOVIE [1990]
I, ROBOT: THE ILLUSTRATED SCREENPLAY (BASED ON ISAAC ASIMOV'S STORY-CYCLE) [1994]
THE CITY ON THE EDGE OF FOREVER [1996]
"REPENT, HARLEQUIN!" SAID THE TICKTOCKMAN [1997]
(RENDERED WITH PAINTINGS BY RICK BERRY)

RETROSPECTIVES:
ALONE AGAINST TOMORROW A TEN YEAR SURVEY [1971]
THE ESSENTIAL ELLISON A 35-YEAR RETROSPECTIVE [1987]
(EDITED BY TERRY DOWLING, WITH RICHARD DELAP & GIL LAMONT)

AS EDITOR:
DANGEROUS VISIONS [1967]	NIGHTSHADES & DAMNATIONS: THE FINEST STORIES OF GERALD KERSH [1968]
AGAIN, DANGEROUS VISIONS [1972]	MEDEA: HARLAN'S WORLD [1985]

THE HARLAN ELLISON DISCOVERY SERIES:	STORMTRACK [1975] BY JAMES SUTHERLAND
AUTUMN ANGELS [1975] BY ARTHUR BYRON COVER	THE LIGHT AT THE END OF THE UNIVERSE [1976] BY TERRY CARR
ISLANDS [1976] BY MARTA RANDALL	INVOLUTION OCEAN [1978] BY BRUCE STERLING

THE WHITE WOLF SERIES:
	EDGEWORKS. 3 [1997]
EDGEWORKS. 1 [1996]	EDGEWORKS. 4 [1997]
EDGEWORKS. 2 [1996]	EDGEWORKS. 5 [1998]

SLIPPAGE

Previously Uncollected,
Precariously Poised Stories

Introduction: "The Fault in My Lines" by Harlan Ellison. Copyright © 1997 by The Kilimanjaro Corporation.

The stories in this collection originally appeared in the following anthologies or magazines: THE BEST AMERICAN SHORT STORIES: 1993, BEST NEW HORROR #5 & #6, BORDERLANDS, DANTE'S DISCIPLES, DARK DESTINY, NIGHT AND THE ENEMY, TEN TALES, THE ULTIMATE DRAGON and THE YEAR'S BEST HORROR STORIES: XVII; *Aboriginal Science Fiction, Eidolon, Ellery Queen's Mystery Magazine, The Magazine Of Fantasy & Science Fiction,* the *Harlan Ellison Dream Corridor* series, *Interzone, Isaac Asimov's Science Fiction Magazine, Lore, Literal Latté, Midnight Graffiti, New Rave, Omni, Omni Online, Pulphouse: The Hardback Magazine, The Twilight Zone Magazine,* and *The 17th Annual World Fantasy Program Book.*
"Mefisto in Onyx" was also published in book form by Mark V. Ziesing, Publisher. "The Dreams a Nightmare Dreams" originally appeared as an audio cassette (narrated by the Author) accompanying Cyberdreams's "H.R. Giger Screensaver." "Go Toward the Light" was originally broadcast as a segment of *Chanukah Lights,* a National Public Radio presentation recorded on 15 November 1994 and electronically fed to satellite uplink on 23 November 1994 for broadcast in November and December 1994. "Crazy as a Soup Sandwich" was first telecast as an episode of *The Twilight Zone* on 2 April 1989.

The stories, essays and teleplays are variously copyright © 1986, 1988, 1989, 1990, 1991, 1992, 1993, 1994, 1995, 1996, 1997 by The Kilimanjaro Corporation.
"The Dragon On the Bookshelf" written in collaboration with Robert Silverberg; copyright © 1995 by The Kilimanjaro Corporation and Agberg, Ltd.
"Nackles" by Donald E. Westlake (as by "Curt Clark"). Copyright © 1963 by Mercury Press, Inc. Renewed, copyright © 1991 by Donald E. Westlake. Reprinted by permission of the Author.

Interior design by Arnie Fenner
Book composition by John Snowden

PRINTED IN THE UNITED STATES OF AMERICA
CIP Data is available.

CONTENTS

FOR ALMOST MORE THAN ANY RATIONAL HUMAN BEING WOULD CARE TO KNOW ABOUT THE AUTHOR, INTERNET VISITS ARE AVAILABLE AT THE FOLLOWING SELECTED WEBSITES:

Ellison Webderland @
http://www.menagerie.net/ellison

Islets of Langerhans @
http://www.teleport.com/~mzuzel

and

AUDIO VERITÉ: Harlan Ellison @
http://www.darkcarnival.com/feb96/hellis.html

FAQ-alt.fan.harlan-ellison @
http://www.menagerie.net/ellison/text/faq.txt

AMERICA ONLINE *keyword* scifi→Message Boards→SF Authors→A-L→List Topics→Harlan Ellison

http://www.Catch22.COM/-espana/SFAuthors/SFE/Ellison, Harlan.html
http://www.mgmua.com/interactive/nomouth/harlan.html
http://www.phlab.missouri.edu/~c642678/harlan.html

IT SHOULD BE NOTED: THE AUTHOR DOES NOT HAVE A COMPUTER. THE AUTHOR DOES NOT HAVE A MODEM. THE AUTHOR IS NOT ONLINE. THE AUTHOR WORKS ON A REAL, ACTUAL FINGER-DRIVEN MANUAL TYPEWRITER, NOT EVEN AN ELECTRIC ONE. THE AUTHOR IS NOT A LUDDITE, HE JUST PERCEIVES OF ALL THIS ELECTRONIC CRAP AS

THE TWILIGHT OF THE WORD.

ACKNOWLEDGMENTS

What are three euphemisms for "museum" in Swedish; what is the most efficacious getaway route by highway from New Orleans; at what depth does nitrogen narcosis take full effect; how does an inmate of an Alabama prison dress and of what are the soles of his shoes made; who said "Common sense is instinct. Enough of it is genius"; can you name a lost Chinese dialect for me?

The frenzied call for information at three in the morning; the idle remark that sparks the concept; a well-intentioned push toward completion of a stranded story; an odd request for a certain sort of narrative; medical attention that kept the heart breathing, or abated the fierce itching from shingles while writing in a public bookstore window; a painting that inspired an entire story; years of unquestioning friendship. If the list seems inordinately or insolently long, let it be noted that with any brevity it would not serve the holy purpose of keeping the Author's hubris in check, would not serve as reminder that none of us can do it without help. The list is long. The assistance was invaluable.

SAMUEL JOHNSON: "Knowledge is of two kinds. We know a subject ourselves, or we know where we can find information."

Neal Adams; the executive committee of Albacon 1985 (Glasgow, Scotland); the late Isaac Asimov; Kyle Baker; Steve Barnes; Doug Beauchamp; Jill Bauman; Anina Bennett; the late Alfred Bester; John Betancourt; the late Robert Bloch; the staff of Bookstar, French Quarter, New Orleans; Alan Brennert; Ron Brown; Edward W. Bryant Jr.; Sharon Buck; Octavia Estelle Butler; Tony Caputo; Paul Chadwick; Bob Chapman; Mel (Melony) Clark; Robert Crais; Jim Crocker; Pete Crowther; Janet Cruickshank; Ellen Datlow; Keith DeCandido; Phil DeGuere; O'Neil De Noux; Leo & Diane Dillon; Kathryn Drennan; Susan Ellison; Peter R. Emshwiller; Louise Erdrich; Arnie Fenner; Keith Ferrell; Richard Finkelstein, Director, Bureau of Client Fraud Investigation: New York Human Resources Administration; Gary Frank, Lisa K. Buchanan & the staff of The Booksmith, San Francisco; the manufacturers of SssstingStop & Alpha Eczema; Lazar Friedman of Lazar's Luggage; Dan Fox; Dr. Richard Fuchs; H.R. Giger; Stephen Hickman; Tony Hillerman; the late Mike Hodel; John Henri & Evastina Holmberg; Rich Howell; Chris Hudak; International Hard Suit; the late Shirley Jackson; Warden Charlie Jones of Holman Prison in Atmore, Alabama; Samanda b. Jeudé; Katrina Kenison; Patrick Ketchum, former President, Cyberdreams; Robert Killheffer; Tappan King; Tim Kirk; Gary Klotz; Ed Kramer; Mark Kreighbaum; Stan Tymorek & Al Shackelford of the *Land's End* catalog; Ron Lee; Robert Lerose; Barry R. Levin; David Loftus; Rod Heather; Sean O'Leary & Joe Martucci of *Lore* magazine; Mike Lowrey; Alan Luck; Jane MacKenzie; Guy McLimore; Robert Mace Kass, M.D.; Steven W. Tabak, M.D.; Ronald P. Karlsberg, M.D.; John David Romm, M.D.; Morris Middleton; Frank Miller; Rockne S. O'Bannon; Omni Group Cruises, Inc. & the ship Regal Princess of Princess Cruises; Kent Orlando; Chris Owens; Byron Preiss; John Radziewicz; Sam Raffa; Chris Reynolds; Frank P. Reynolds; Susan West Richardson; Joe Roberdeau; Ellen Rosenberg; William Rotsler; Kristine Kathryn Rusch; the late Carl Sandburg; Tracy K. Saritzky; Bob Schreck; Diana Schutz; Bruce Scott, Producer, National Public Radio Cultural Programming; Hannah Louise Shearer; Robert Silverberg; Dean Wesley Smith; John Snowden; Ken Steacy; Allen Steele; Joe Straczynski; Jonathan Strahan; Jeremy G. Byrne & the editorial committee of *Eidolon* (Australia); the late Eleanor Sullivan of *Ellery Queen's Mystery Magazine*; Leslie Kay Swigart; Avon Swofford; Jenna Terry; Larry Teufner; Robert Tidwell; Michael Toman; the very late Mark Twain; David L. Ulin; the very late Jules Verne; Thomas Vitale; Bill Warren; Lauren Weiss, Deputy District Attorney, Los Angeles; Donald E. Westlake; Michael Whelan; Charlie Williams; Robin Williams; Terri Windling; Jann Woosley; William F. Wu; Rick Wyatt; Mark & Cindy Ziesing.

With the
late Cyril Connolly
("England's most influential
and controversial literary
critic"), I used to believe,
though in an antic sense:

*"We are all serving
a terminal sentence
in the dungeon of life."*

Then I married Susan.

This book is for
her.

"You must not mind me, madam;
I say strange things, but I mean no harm."
Samuel Johnson
(1709—1784)

The Fault In My Lines

Where to open the fissure:
the earthquake or the heart attack?

The earthquake. It is officially listed as a 6.8-magnitude temblor by the U.S. Geological Survey's geophysicists at the Earthquake Information Center in Golden, Colorado.

The Northridge, California "thruster." It hit at precisely, *exactly*, 4:31 a.m. on Monday the 17th of January 1994. It had been a pretty lousy year through the 16th, and 1993 hadn't been too cuddly, either. Let us not even talk about '92.

But as rusty as those first sixteen days of the new year had been, they were nothing but sunny days on the beaches of Ibiza by comparison to 4:31 in the dead black morning of January 17th.

First, there was the sound of it. Oh, yeah, trust me on this: first, you hear it coming. You don't know that's what the hell you're hearing, but you catch the sound of it hurtling toward you before your bones and back teeth pick it up.

Let me try to tell you what it sounds like.

Because just the *sound* of it can scare your hair white. (Mine started to fall out in the months following.)

The unimaginative say it sounds like a train coming toward you. Bullshit. Nothing like a train. I used to ride the freights, like a bindlestiff, when I was a kid. Trains have a decent sound to them. A good sound. Tough, but willing to accommodate you. This damned thruster had absolutely *nothing* in common with a train. Then there are those whose best analogy is, "It was a deep rumbling noise." Yer ass. A deep rumbling noise is what you get out of your stomach when you've had too many baby-backs and hot links. A cranky bear makes a deep rumbling sound. The radiator. The water pipes trying to carry the load. Krusty the Klown makes a deep rumbling noise. I'll tell you *precisely* what that muther sounded like:

Ever see one of those Japanese samurai movies featuring the masterless ronin who travels around with his baby son in a wooden cart that rolls on big wooden wheels? The Lone Wolf and Cub films? What they call the "baby cart" series?

Okay, then: are you familiar with "corduroy roads"? They were common and plentiful in this country up until about forty years ago. Mostly, you could find them in backwoods or rural areas, where dirt roads were still in use, macadam hadn't made its inroads, superhighways were distant myths, and country roads were used for hauling heavy loads. So, to make them capable of supporting the weight of a tractor pulling a backhoe, or a fully loaded hay wagon, logs were laid transversely, producing a kind of ribbed look—something like those speed bumps in parking lots that make you slow down—and the buried logs gave the dirt road the topographical surface of the cotten cloth we call *corduroy.*

When you drove down such a road, there was a metronomic bump-bump-bump sound. I'm trying to be specific here, trying to describe the indescribable. Explain the color red to someone blind from birth.

What it sounded like was this: a gigantic wooden-wheeled baby cart, as big as a mountain, bump-bump-bumping down a corduroy road. Underneath you. Deep underneath you.

I was awake at that hour. I was upstairs here in my office, working. On the second floor of the office wing I designed and had built some years ago. Walls floor-to-ceiling filled with reference and non-fiction books I might need when working, arranged alphabetically by subject. Several thousand books, mostly hardcovers. And an open central atrium that looks down on the first floor of the office wing. And my desk and typewriter over here next to the French doors that give onto the balcony and a view of the San Bernardino Mountains thirty-seven miles away across the San Fernando Valley. My office looks out due north toward those mountains.

At 4:31 in the morning, the thruster zazzed laterally across the Valley floor, west to south, reached the foot of the Santa Monica Mountains (at the top of which my home sits)...and had nowhere to go but *up.*

(Pause. Know-nothings who live in parts of the country where they endure sub-zero weather, tornados, floods, killing pollution, drought, blight, sand storms, provincial bigotry, ultraconservative censorship, hurricanes or Jesse Helms, have been known to remark, "How can anyone bear living in Southern California with all those earthquakes? They must be really stupid not to flee the state!"

(And go *where?*

(It's the same everywhichplace these days, folks. New Orleans or Pittsburgh; Kankakee or Kansas; Eugene, Oregon or Oklahoma City. If the twister don't get you, the rabid militia will.

(L.A. is okay. I like it here. But I'm no dope. Long before the thruster, I had hired both seismic engineers and structural experts, as well as soil analysts, to tell me how safe I was here on the crest of the North Benedict Canyon slope. Core drilling had been done, and I was heartened to learn that the house sat solidly, a mere five feet above bedrock. Of even more salutary note was the advisement that not only was the house secure just five feet above bedrock, but the seam ran north-south, in line with the house. Meaning: not even the worst of the "rolling" temblors we knew so well in Southern California could trouble me overmuch. If the rolling came, it would not affect the solid cut under me. I was sanguine. And when the Landers quake hit a few years ago, I barely felt it, despite all the serious damage done in other nearby areas. I was sanguine. "The only way you're going to be in any trouble," said an engineer from the Jet Propulsion Lab in Pasadena—a reader of my work who had offered to bring in some ground-testing equipment as a favor—"any trouble *at all,* is if the whole damned mountain collapses." I was sanguine.)

The fault line came diagonally across the Valley, got to the base of the mountains, had nowhere to go...so it went *up.*

The house was lifted with a 4g thrust. It takes only 6 gravs to throw a rocket to the moon.

I heard it coming, and I bolted from my typing chair, and got across the office to the deco stairwell before the first wave hit. The house, and everything in it, went straight up. I was lifted off my feet and thrown across the stairwell, crashing face-first against the south wall of the second-floor landing. The right side of my face smashed into a framed photo of the blind Borges in Baltimore in 1983, sitting at the foot of the memorial to Edgar Allan Poe, running his fingers over the bronze commemorative plaque, paying homage, one great fantasist to another. I hit it so hard it shattered the glass and broke the frame.

Then I was thrown sidewise, as the second wave struck. Thrown left down the winding deco staircase—everything now in pitch darkness—all electricity had gone out across the city—and bent double over the pony wall, cracking my forehead on the leading edge of a Lucite shelf holding pewter figurines of The Ten Greatest Inventions of History.

And then the main torque hit.

I was picked up and thrown forward, never touching the final flight of steps from the lower landing to the first floor. I was picked up and flipped heels-over-head to land flat on my back, missing the edge of the pool table by perhaps two inches. If I had been two inches to the right, it would have blasted open my skull; nothing less than a human omelette.

But before I could rise, off the wall to my left, a heavy painting slightly larger than 3′x3′ wrenched itself off its hanger, and crashed down on me.

(Pause: charming little ironies of near-death experiences. The painting is a surreal rendering of a large stone mausoleum with ominous faces perceivable in the walls. It sits on a hill under a dark blue, threatening sky. Carved into the lintel of the building is the legend 6000 SA MO BL. The painting is called "Six thousand, same old bull." The irony is that 6000 SA MO BL is an abbreviation for 6000 Santa Monica Boulevard, the location of the cemetery crypt and mausoleum in Los Angeles where, among others, Al Jolson is buried. The painting weighs a ton. Well, that's figuratively speaking. It's heavy, because it has a double pane of glass on it—the second pane having stars painted on the inside surface, thus giving a very deep-dimensional look to the already eerie landscape—and when 6000 SA MO BL ripped loose, it plummeted and hit me full in the face, breaking my nose, blacking both my eyes, ripping open gashes in my face.) Knocking me unconscious.

Not for long, I guess. It was dark, the earth was still growling, I was woozy—maybe a concussion already, I don't know—and even if there had been light, I couldn't have seen anything. Too much blood in my eyes.

I started to pull myself to my feet, using the edge of the pool table, when the next wave struck; and this time it threw every book on the upper level out of the bookcases, hurled them over the railing, and down on me in the open space below the atrium. I was struck by hundreds of reference books, knocked to my knees, and then clobbered unconscious for the second time.

Everything after that, for two years, was recovery, rebuilding, and lamenting the loss of art and possessions I'd spent a lifetime gathering. No need to dwell on it, I've conveyed the part that's pertinent to this book. So now we can move on to the heart attack.

I had a free ride for fifty-nine years. Ran my body as if it were a PT boat skimming across enemy waters, explosions at every zig and zag. Went where I wanted to go, got involved with whomever I chose, ate everything with disregard for the consequences, fought fights, risked my life, played it fast and loose. Created stories and had one helluva good time.

> **"We are all serving a life-sentence**
> **in the dungeon of self."**
> *Cyril Connolly*

Not I! For my part, it was the unheeding belief that I would live forever. I'd almost been splattered half a dozen times in different ways—on sports car racetracks, in riots, during civil rights marches in the South, in street brawls—but each time my indefatigable ability to walk the rubber band high across the Grand Canyon manifested itself; and I skimmed on across that bullet-stitched beachhead horizon as if I lived the life charmed. Skimmed along, mixing metaphors and gorging on fried chicken.

Then in 1992, I got chest pains.

I was in San Francisco, doing a signing, when I tried to climb one of those fabled hills. Found myself sitting on the curb with the defensive line of the Dallas Cowboys playing johnny-on-a-pony on my chest, and each of them wearing full battle armor.

Let me explain something you need to know. Maybe not today, and maybe not tomorrow, but one day you'll be in a place and at a weight where this little bit of data will light up like Times Square neon in your mind. And you'll thank me. Just before they take you off in the ambulance. And here it is, this piece of data:

It is not like in the movies, where Clark Kent's adoptive father (played by Glenn Ford) suddenly clutches his left arm, winces, and collapses. What it's *more* like, please try to remember this, is a tension that runs from one side of your chest to the other. At first you think it's indigestion, and it'll pass in a few seconds. Then the pain gets more intense, and you lie down and put your legs up so the heart doesn't have to work so hard pumping blood to all those far lands, but the tension continues. And what is happening to you, is that you've been operating for years with a 90% blockage of the right coronary artery, and you didn't know it, and at last all that pizza and Lawry's prime rib with extra helpings of Yorkshire pudding and creamed horseradish have caught up with you, and you are in deep deep chaos, my friend.

So. We got me back to L.A. and I went into Cedars-Sinai and they did an angiogram, and saw my 90% blockage, and they did an angioplasty ream-out job on me; and that was in June; and it closed down in August; and back I went; and they did another angioplasty. And I went back to a life of endless deadlines, constant faxes and phone calls telling me I was late with this or that piece of writing, the organized efforts of a quartet of vicious, envious creeps to maim my life and/or my reputation, pressure upon pressure, and I slipped back into the routine I'd come to endure for most of my adult life.

(Pause. Harriet Martineau, the British writer and journalist, wrote, in 1837, "Readers are plentiful; thinkers are rare." Every writer—particularly these days when it's so hard to keep a writing career afloat against the electronic *tsunami* of the Internet and television and non-books featuring performers in the OJ Simpson circus—needs and values readers. Without them, it all comes to a halt.

(But there is an aspect of the reader gestalt that is not only troubling, it's terrifying. Not all, but some, of one's readers become obsessive and act as if a writer is denying them their mainline fix if they don't get a new book when they want it. No matter that one has more than sixty *other* books they can enjoy...they want the *next* one. And they demand it! They write and complain, as if the writing and publishing of a book were akin to daily milk delivery. It creates in the writer a tension that becomes unbearable, that can even freeze the book in its progress toward publication.

(The assumption that a new book, not yet published, is already the property of the reader because he or she *desires* it, is a part of the job they never warned against when you were young and naive and starting out. They never warn you about the gravitic pull of the impertinent, intrusive, hungry audience. And there is no escaping the grip of that 6g pull. We need readers. And so, the produced by-product is tension.)

I went back to the old routine, and though I had some pains and pressures for the next four years, I still knew I was immortal; and I kept postponing the exercise and the vacation and the easing off. I worked every day, many nights, with the phone and the fax and the FedEx packages filling every waking moment.

I sit writing this on Thursday, May 23rd, 1996.

Little more than a month ago, April 10th, Susan and I were scheduled to go to the wrap-party for the cast and crew of the television series on which I serve as Conceptual Consultant, *Babylon 5.* My friend Joe Straczynski, creator and producer of B5, with Kathryn Drennan, and Susan and I were going to meet up early in the evening and go enjoy ourselves at the party that would celebrate the wrap-up of our third season on the air.

The pains started early in the morning. I got up, as usual, about five a.m. and started the day's routine. The first pains pressed me flat as I climbed the stairs to the upstairs atrium office (now, $200,000 later, reconstructed from the earthquake, leaving us dead broke). I sat down on the stairs, and breathed deeply. It was as if a large chunk of dry pumpernickel crust had lodged in the wrong channel in my chest. I managed to get to the sofa in my office, and I lay down for about an hour with my feet elevated. The pain did subside a little. I'm immortal. I shook it off and went to work. There was an essay about artist Barclay Shaw that needed to be written for Carl Gnam's publication *Realms of Fantasy.* There was the rewrite on "From a Great Height" for Bruce David at *Rage.* There was a freebie about A.E. van Vogt that was needed for the awarding of his upcoming Grand Master trophy. There was the introduction to SLIPPAGE that Mark Ziesing and Houghton Mifflin were both waiting for...the book had been delayed and everyone was getting surly with me. That 6g garrotte of the demanding readership.

I started writing.

An hour later, now almost seven a.m., I slouched downstairs and hit the bed. It'll get better, I told myself. I also told Susan. It'll get better.

Never made the B5 party. Had to cancel out.

Thursday the 11th. More pain. Luncheon meeting here at the house with Stefan Rudnicki and Lee Montgomery and Mary Aarons of Dove Audio/Dove Publishing. The lunch was pizza. I had three pieces. I was back in bed shortly thereafter. It'll pass, it'll get better, I said to Susan. We were scheduled to go to dinner that night with Don Shain and Joe and Kathryn at the exclusive Cafe Bizou. The band of pressure now reached from armpit to armpit, and I felt it in my back.

Susan kept saying, "You need to go to the hospital!" and I snarled back at her, leave me alone, I've got to get through this, I've got to get SLIPPAGE out of here, Mark's desperate for it, and Houghton Mifflin has sent a lawyer's letter. I'll go see John Romm (my internist for more than thirty years) as soon as I get the damned book out of here.

We never got to Cafe Bizou.

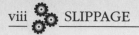

Friday, April 12th, I was still on my back. Every time I got up to travel through the house to the office wing, to climb the stairs, to write what I'm writing now, the pain would smack me and I'd stumble, shuffle, weave my way back to the bedroom. Finally, at 4:30 in the afternoon, I said to Susan, "You'd better call John Romm. I think I'm in trouble."

Immortal. But not very bright. Slow to learn. Too damned stubborn and obstinate and locked into the habit patterns of a lifetime, too overwhelmed by the bogus urgency of deadlines, to understand that there are deadlines and there are *dead*lines. Fault lines. Fissures. The fault in my lines is the same as the fault in our stars. We live in the slide zone. Slippage.

> **"A thing is not necessarily true
> because a man dies for it."**
> *Oscar Wilde*

John didn't even bother with the usual admittance procedure at Cedars-Sinai Medical Center. He called ahead, as Susan and my assistant loaded me into the car, and in fifteen minutes I was being wheeled into the ER. How much damage I had done to the actual heart muscle by enduring three days of an ongoing heart attack, neither Susan nor I knew.

That was Friday. By the end of day—I had spent five and a half hours in the ER—only a curtain separating me from the unfortunate junkie whose hands were still cuffed from her arrest, as she whimpered and begged for attention—before they could free up a room in the Cardiac Intensive Care Unit.

They got me on blood thinners and beta blockers, and it was a convivial group of RNs who looked after me; and Susan, who stayed with me till quite late before she took a cab home. Susan doesn't drive.

Now, here's the interesting part.

I felt well enough the next day, Saturday, to ask Susan to bring in my typewriter and the folders of work that needed doing. My cardiovascular physician was out of town, and they had decided to keep me comfortable and stable in the CICU until Monday, when they'd go in for another angiogram. I still thought I was immortal.

So Susan brought in the portable Olympia, and three or four folders of projects that were in work and, trailing my IV, I managed to get out of bed with my ventilated-rear hospital gown gaping, and we propped up pillows on a chair, and I lowered the retractable table to its lowest point, and I sat there and typed out an essay titled "Trimalchio in West Egg" (which had been F. Scott

Fitzgerald's original, discarded title for THE GREAT GATSBY) in about two hours. I'd finally licked at least one of the fault line deadlines in my rapidly disintegrating life. But see (I told the universe that wasn't even paying any attention), see, I'm fuckin' immortal; not even the hospital can stop me!

I asked Susan to fax off the piece to both Barclay Shaw and Shawna McCarthy, the editor of *Realms of Fantasy,* as soon as she got home; and I settled back to try and get some sleep. But sleep would not come. And by early Sunday I was telling my nurse, "I don't give a shit *where* my doctor is, get him back here, and *do me.* Now!"

The pain was overwhelming.

By early afternoon on Sunday the 14th of last month, as I sit writing this on May 23rd, 1996, four days till my 62nd birthday, which I guess I'll be around to celebrate, I'm told I came within a few micromillimeters of dying. He who was immortal, who wrote of looking at mortality with unblinking eye, finally got backed into a corner where hubris and stick-to-it-iveness were useless.

They took 27½" of vein out of my left leg, cracked me open like a miser's change-purse with large rib-spreaders, pulled my lungs out and placed them over *there*, and pulled out my heart and placed it over *there* (just like the Scarecrow of Oz), and ripped off the sac that surrounds the heart—and can never be replaced—and put me on a pump that kept the blood moving while they stopped the evicted heart, and they built me a quadruple bypass. Built me a new superhighway that detoured around the crimped and strangulated passages that had been unable to pump me the proper amount of blood for who knows how many years. (As you are reading this in 1997, obviously I lived. No shit, Sherlock!)

I awoke on Monday. I won't go into the horror details of no longer being in my cheery pre-surgery CICU, but lying there with tubes down my throat in a standard ICU cubicle, watching the hands of the huge high-school-study-hall-style clock mounted on the wall directly in front of me, I at last knew where Hell is housed. Do you remember how it took the minute hand several days to click over once? The agony? Remember?

"...In America, somehow, history turns into geology, and...an artist is free of all mortgages except for the ultimate one that forecloses on mountains."
Thomas B. Hess

I was back home by Friday the 19th. Susan, Joe Straczynski, and chicken soup had saved my life, but I won't expand on that part of it. I was back home, and now it is six weeks since everything fractured beneath me and I learned in the deepest part of my arrogant self just how tenuous is our grasp on the crumbling edge of the slide area.

The message that precedes all others—in art as well as life—is simple:
PAY ATTENTION

This might be my last book. After all these years, and all these words, and all those books, this might be the one that winds up faded by sunlight at the end of the shelf. I keep recalling a quotation, though I cannot remember the source: "Man always dies before he is fully born." I think now, as I never did before, about the end of the shelf.

The world seems precarious to me now. Everything changes so fast, and no one remembers anything. The known universe is tipped up at one end, and everything is sliding into electronic storage, where memory cannot find it, as one computer format after another becomes obsolescent. There is such unconscionable and hypocritical pandering to the youth demographic all around us, that anything older than a fortnight risks eternal oblivion. I sat at dinner in Chicago a year or so ago with a group of young people who were in publishing. Editors, publicists, designers. And I was, of course, the oldest one at the table by more than double the number of years of the second-oldest person seated there. And I made reference to a (I thought) cunning idea for a cover painting for an issue of the comic book that bears my name.

I said, "Picture Ronald Colman climbing back up the snow-covered mountains, trying to regain Shangri-La, with the wind whipping the white curtain across the frozen face of the massif…and he's wearing a fur parka and goggles, and he's down in the lower right of the cover painting, large in the foreground, looking out at us with a bewildered expression, because above him, near the summit of the great lost mountain, we see…McDonald's golden arches."

And I looked around, and it was an oil painting. There were perhaps eight or ten young people at that table, and each of them was *tabula rasa*. They hadn't a clue what I was gibbering about. My voice getting a trifle hysterical, I said, "Ronald Colman. You know, *Lost Horizon*…Shangri-La…the James Hilton novel, big bestseller…the famous Frank Capra movie…black and white movie…"

And the key turned. Oh (they seemed to say), it was a *black and white* movie, an old movie. Oh, yeah, sure, cool. Who is this old fart, and what is he bombing on about?

Slippage.

Precariously poised, the world is not today the one in which I fell asleep last night. In the murky time when the birds sleep, the universe shifted over one notch. A new world I live in today, one in which things not only fall apart so that the center cannot hold, but the center now has a videotape available for $29.95 that offers us the opportunity to hear the center declare itself innocent of double murders or bad behavior or crass commercialism or even inept acting.

The English playwright David Hare has said, "The most dementing of all modern sins: the inability to distinguish excellence from success."

Mortality has been thrust on me by earthquakes and heart attacks, too close and too severe to ignore, within a brief time; and I equate the slippage of the universe beneath my sliding consciousness with the physical world betraying me at every turn. (You'll generously ignore my self-absorption...like you, I'm only human. Which may be an explanation, but I'm not sure it's an acceptable excuse.)

My body and the kindly Earth have set up shop against me. Time and memory were bad enough, but now not even mountains can be trusted, and no one is allowed to feel sorry for oneself when taught the lesson of one's own frangibility. It ain't seemly. Cry baby gets no sympathy. Of course you're going to eat dust ere long, you smartass.

So the unquestioned belief that I would have all the time in the world to complete all the stories I haven't written, to complete the projects that have been shunted aside because of blood moving too slowly for more years than I can know, the insensate belief that there was world enough and time...is no longer permitted. I am on the fault line. The deadline. And every day the tilt grows steeper, the slippage more acute.

There is no Shangri-La for the denizens who hang out at The Gap in the mall.

Nor is there patience in their hearts for anything more than a fortnight in age. Stravinsky is meat, Glenn Miller is dross, John Coltrane is cobwebs, and by Thursday Stevie Ray Vaughan will be a supermarket flier, a badly-printed handbill found under your windshield wiper, to be crumpled and tossed. And one dare not complain, because it only sounds like sour grapes and rotten tomatoes and old farts lamenting the passage of time.

And there isn't even any joy in knowing that their grip will loosen all too quickly, that most of them will slide on past as you watch. That in a year or two other, younger, drones will look at *them* with uncomprehending eyes when they mention Smashing Pumpkins. Life is not a comparison of chambers of horror; and as Gerald Kersh pointed out in 1956, "A sour soul will eat through the purest profile like acid through a paper bag, but a tiger could not mar a face animated by a good heart."

For those who have not yet begun the slide journey, I will tell you that Gerald Kersh is my favorite writer. I have long aspired to write at something like his level of excellence and originality.

Not one of Gerald Kersh's books is in print.

Buttonhole any two hundred people at random in the streets of any major city you choose, and I will buy you a hot fudge sundae with whipped cream and crushed nuts if you find even one or two who have ever heard his name, or who can tell you what he did for the totality of his life.

Each book I have written seems to declare its own theme. I never know what that theme will be until the book is assembled. *This* time the theme is one of nervousness, of the ticking of the clock, of the unreliability of sweet earth beneath our feet and dear beating heart within our chest. The theme is: do it while you can. Slippage rules. Gravity ain't forgiving. The theme is: you never know when it's the last of the last. The theme is: **PAY ATTENTION.**

For some reason Charlotte's infidelities didn't unhinge me. Yes, I was pissed-off that she'd been flagrant in going to bed with Mike Wilson, Arthur C. Clarke's scuba-diving associate...having done the deed at a large New York con-vention, where everybody knew about it. But, apart from waking Arthur, and asking him if he knew where Wilson was—heaven only knows what I thought I could do to a guy that size, that strapping—I handled it.

The Man Who Rowed Christopher Columbus Ashore

LEVENDIS: On Tuesday the 1st of October, improbably dressed as an Explorer Scout, with his great hairy legs protruding from his knee-pants, and his heavily festooned merit badge sash slantwise across his chest, he helped an old, arthritic black woman across the street at the jammed corner of Wilshire and Western. In fact, she didn't *want* to cross the street, but he half-pulled, half-dragged her, the old woman screaming at him, calling him a khaki-colored motherfucker every step of the way.

LEVENDIS: On Wednesday the 2nd of October, he crossed his legs carefully as he sat in the Boston psychiatrist's office, making certain the creases of his pants—he was wearing the traditional morning coat and ambassadorially-striped pants—remained sharp, and he said to George Aspen Davenport, M.D., Ph.D., FAPA (who had studied with Ernst Kris *and* Anna Freud), "Yes, that's it, now you've got it." And Dr. Davenport made a note on his pad, lightly cleared his throat and phrased it differently: "Your mouth is...vanishing? That is to say, your mouth, the facial feature below your nose, it's uh disappearing?" The prospective patient nodded quickly,

1

with a bright smile. "Exactly." Dr. Davenport made another note, continued to ulcerate the inside of his cheek, then tried a third time: "We're
speaking now—heh heh, to maintain the idiom—we're speaking of your
lips, or your tongue, or your palate, or your gums, or your teeth, or—"
The other man sat forward, looking very serious, and replied, "We're talking *all* of it, Doctor. The whole, entire, complete aperture and everything
around, over, under, and within. My *mouth*, the allness of my mouth. It's
disappearing. What part of that is giving you a problem?" Davenport
hmmm'd for a moment, said, "Let me check something," and he rose, went
to the teak and glass bookcase against the far wall, beside the window that
looked out on crowded, lively Boston Common, and he drew down a
capacious volume. He flipped through it for a few minutes, and finally
paused at a page on which he poked a finger. He turned to the elegant,
gray-haired gentleman in the consultation chair, and he said, "Lipostomy."
His prospective patient tilted his head to the side, like a dog listening for a
clue, and arched his eyebrows expectantly, as if to ask *yes, and lipostomy
is what?* The psychiatrist brought the book to him, leaned down and
pointed to the definition. "Atrophy of the mouth." The gray-haired gentleman, who looked to be in his early sixties, but remarkably well-tended and
handsomely turned-out, shook his head slowly as Dr. Davenport walked
back around to sit behind his desk. "No, I don't think so. It doesn't seem
to be withering, it's just, well, simply, I can't put it any other way, it's very
simply disappearing. Like the Cheshire cat's grin. Fading away." Davenport closed the book and laid it on the desktop, folded his hands atop the
volume, and smiled condescendingly. "Don't you think this might be a
delusion on your part? I'm looking at your mouth right now, and it's right
there, just as it was when you came into the office." His prospective
patient rose, retrieved his homburg from the sofa, and started toward the
door. "It's a good thing I can read lips," he said, placing the hat on his
head, "because I certainly don't need to pay your sort of exorbitant fee to
be ridiculed." And he moved to the office door, and opened it to leave,
pausing for only a moment to readjust his homburg, which had slipped
down, due to the absence of ears on his head.

LEVENDIS: On Thursday the 3rd of October, he overloaded his grocery
cart with okra and eggplant, giant bags of Kibbles 'n Bits 'n Bits 'n Bits,
and jumbo boxes of Huggies. And as he wildly careened through the
aisles of the Sentry Market in La Crosse, Wisconsin, he purposely engi-
neered a collision between the carts of Kenneth Kulwin, a 47-year-old

homosexual who had lived alone since the passing of his father thirteen years earlier, and Anne Gillen, a 35-year-old legal secretary who had been unable to find an escort to take her to her senior prom and whose social life had not improved in the decades since that death of hope. He began screaming at them, as if it had been *their* fault, thereby making allies of them. He was extremely rude, breathing muscatel breath on them, and finally stormed away, leaving them to sort out their groceries, leaving them to comment on his behavior, leaving them to take notice of each other. He went outside, smelling the Mississippi River, and he let the air out of Anne Gillen's tires. She would need a lift to the gas station. Kenneth Kulwin would tell her to call him "Kenny," and they would discover that their favorite movie was the 1945 romance, *The Enchanted Cottage*, starring Dorothy McGuire and Robert Young.

LEVENDIS: On Friday the 4th of October, he found an interstate trucker dumping badly sealed cannisters of phenazine in an isolated picnic area outside Phillipsburg, Kansas; and he shot him three times in the head; and wedged the body into one of the large, nearly empty trash barrels near the picnic benches.

LEVENDIS: On Saturday the 5th of October, he addressed two hundred and forty-four representatives of the country & western music industry in the Chattanooga Room just off the Tennessee Ballroom of the Opryland Hotel in Nashville. He said to them, "What's astonishing is not that there is so much ineptitude, slovenliness, mediocrity and downright bad taste in the world...what is unbelievable is that there is so much *good* art in the world. Everywhere." One of the attendees raised her hand and asked, "Are you good, or evil?" He thought about it for less than twenty seconds, smiled, and replied, "Good, of course! There's only one real evil in the world: mediocrity." They applauded sparsely, but politely. Nonetheless, later at the reception, *no one* touched the Swedish meatballs, or the rumaki.

LEVENDIS: On Sunday the 6th of October, he placed the exhumed remains of Noah's ark near the eastern summit of a nameless mountain in Kurdistan, where the next infrared surveillance of a random satellite flyby would reveal them. He was careful to seed the area with a plethora of bones, here and there around the site, as well as within the identifiable hull of the vessel. He made sure to place them two-by-two: every

beast after his kind, and all the cattle after their kind, and every creep-
ing thing that creepeth upon the earth after his kind, and every fowl
after his kind, and every bird of every sort. Two-by-two. Also the
bones of pairs of gryphons, unicorns, stegosaurs, tengus, dragons, orth-
odontists, and the carbon-dateable 5o,ooo-year old bones of a relief
pitcher for the Boston Red Sox.

LEVENDIS: On Monday the 7th of October, he kicked a cat. He kicked
it a far distance. To the passersby who watched, there on Galena Street
in Aurora, Colorado, he said: "I am an unlimited person, sadly living in
a limited world." When the housewife who planned to call the police
yelled at him from her kitchen window, "Who are you? What is your
name!?!" he cupped his hands around his mouth so she would hear him,
and he yelled back, "Levendis! It's a Greek word." They found the cat
imbarked halfway through a tree. The tree was cut down, and the
section with the cat was cut in two, the animal tended by a talented
taxidermist who tried to quell the poor beast's terrified mewling and
vomiting. The cat was later sold as bookends.

LEVENDIS: On Tuesday the 8th of October, he called the office of the
District Attorney in Cadillac, Michigan, and reported that the blue 1988
Mercedes that had struck and killed two children playing in a residential
street in Hamtramck just after sundown the night before, belonged to a
pastry chef whose sole client was a Cosa Nostra *pezzonovante*. He gave
detailed information as to the location of the chop shop where the Mercedes
had been taken to be banged out, bondo'd, and repainted. He gave the
license number. He indicated where, in the left front wheel-well, could be
found a piece of the skull of the younger of the two little girls. Not only
did the piece fit, like the missing section of a modular woodblock puzzle,
but pathologists were able to conduct an accurate test that provided irrefutable evidence that would hold up under any attack in court: the medical
examiner got past the basic ABO groups, narrowed the scope of identification with the five Rh tests, the M and N tests (also cap-S and small-s
variations), the Duffy blood groups, and the Kidd types, both A and B; and
finally he was able to validate the rare absence of Jr a, present in most
blood-groups but missing in some Japanese-Hawaiians and Samoans. The
little girl's name was Sherry Tualaulelei. When the homicide investigators
learned that the pastry chef, his wife, and their three children had gone to
New York City on vacation four days before the hit-and-run, and were able

to produce ticket stubs that placed them seventh row center of the Martin Beck Theater, enjoying the revival of *Guys and Dolls*, at the precise moment the Mercedes struck the children, the Organized Crime Unit was called in, and the scope of the investigation was broadened. Sherry Tualaulelei was instrumental in the conviction and thirty-three-year imprisonment of the pastry chef's boss, Sinio "Sally Comfort" Conforte, who had "borrowed" a car to sneak out for a visit to his mistress.

LEVENDIS: On Wednesday the 9th of October, he sent a fruit basket to Patricia and Faustino Evangelista, a middle-aged couple in Norwalk, Connecticut, who had given to the surviving son, the gun his beloved older brother had used to kill himself. The accompanying note read: *Way to go, sensitive Mom and Dad!*

LEVENDIS: On Thursday the 10th of October, he created a cure for bone-marrow cancer. Anyone could make it: the juice of fresh lemons, spiderwebs, the scrapings of raw carrots, the opaque and whitish portion of the toenail called the *lunula*, and carbonated water. The pharmaceutical cartel quickly hired a prestigious Philadelphia PR firm to throw its efficacy into question, but the AMA and FDA ran accelerated tests, found it to be potent, with no deleterious effects, and recommended its immediate use. It had no effect on AIDS, however. Nor did it work on the common cold. Remarkably, physicians praised the easing of their workload.

LEVENDIS: On Friday the 11th of October, he lay in his own filth on the sidewalk outside the British Embassy in Rangoon, holding a begging bowl. He was just to the left of the gate, half-hidden by the angle of the high wall from sight of the military guards on post. A woman in her fifties, who had been let out of a jitney just up the street, having paid her fare and having tipped as few rupees as necessary to escape a strident rebuke by the driver, smoothed the peplum of her shantung jacket over her hips, and marched imperially toward the Embassy gates. As she came abaft the derelict, he rose on one elbow and shouted at her ankles, "Hey, lady! I write these pomes, and I sell 'em for a buck inna street, an' it keeps juvenile delinquents offa the streets so's they don't spit on ya! So whaddaya think, y'wanna buy one?" The matron did not pause, striding toward the gates, but she said snappishly, "You're a businessman. Don't talk art."

The Route of Odysseus

"You will find the scene of Odysseus's wanderings when you find the cobbler who sewed up the bag of the winds."
Eratosthenes, late 3rd century, B.C.E.

LEVENDIS: On Saturday the 12th of October, having taken the sidestep, he came to a place near Weimar in southwest Germany. He did not see the photographer snapping pictures of the scene. He stood among the cordwood bodies. It was cold for the spring; and even though he was heavily clothed, he shivered. He walked down the rows of bony corpses, looking into the black holes that had been eye sockets, seeing an endless chicken dinner, the bones gnawed clean, tossed like jackstraws in heaps. The stretched-taut groins of men and women, flesh tarpaulins where passion had once smoothed the transport from sleep to wakefulness. Entwined so cavalierly that here a woman with three arms, and there a child with the legs of a sprinter three times his age. A woman's face, looking up at him with soot for sight, remarkable cheekbones, high and lovely, she might have been an actress. Xylophones for chests and torsos, violin bows that had waved goodbye and hugged grandchildren and lifted in toasts to the passing of traditions, gourd whistles between eyes and mouths. He stood among the cordwood bodies and could not remain merely an instrument himself. He sank to his haunches, crouched and wept, burying his head in his hands, as the photographer took shot after shot, an opportunity like a gift from the editor. Then he tried to stop crying, and stood, and the cold cut him, and he removed his heavy topcoat and placed it gently over the bodies of two women and a man lying so close and intermixed that it easily served as coverlet for them. He stood among the cordwood bodies, 24 April 1945, Buchenwald, and the photograph would appear in a book published forty-six years later, on Saturday the 12th of October. The photographer's roll ran out just an instant before the slim young man without a topcoat took the sidestep. Nor did he hear the tearful young man say, "Sertsa." In Russian, *sertsa* means soul.

LEVENDIS: On Sunday the 13th of October, he did nothing. He rested. When he thought about it, he grew annoyed. "Time does not become sacred until we have lived it," he said. But he thought: *to hell with it; even God knocked off for a day.*

LEVENDIS: On Monday the 14th of October, he climbed up through the stinking stairwell shaft of a Baltimore tenement, clutching his notebook, breathing through his mouth to block the smell of mildew, garbage, and urine, focusing his mind on the apartment number he was seeking, straining through the evening dimness in the wan light of one bulb hanging high above, barely illuminating the vertical tunnel, as he climbed and climbed, straining to see the numbers on the doors, going up, realizing the tenants had pulled the numbers *off* the doors to foil him and welfare investigators like him, stumbling over something oily and sobbing jammed into a corner of the last step, losing his grip on the rotting bannister and finding it just in time, trapped for a moment in the hopeless beam of washed-out light falling from above, poised in mid-tumble and then regaining his grip, hoping the welfare recipient under scrutiny would not be home, so he could knock off for the day, hurry back downtown and crosstown and take a shower, going up till he had reached the topmost landing, and finding the number scratched on the doorframe, and knocking, getting no answer, knocking again, hearing first the scream, then the sound of someone beating against a wall, or the floor, with a heavy stick, and then the scream again, and then another scream so closely following the first that it might have been one scream only, and he threw himself against the door, and it was old but never had been well built, and it came away, off its hinges, in one rotten crack, and he was inside, and the most beautiful young black woman he had ever seen was tearing the rats off her baby. He left the check on the kitchen table, he did not have an affair with her, he did not see her fall from the apartment window, six storeys into a courtyard, and never knew if she came back from the grave to escape the rats that gnawed at her cheap wooden casket. He never loved her, and so was not there when what she became flowed back up through the walls of the tenement to absorb him and meld with him and become one with him as he lay sleeping penitently on the filthy floor of the topmost apartment. He left the check, and none of that happened.

LEVENDIS: On Tuesday the 15th of October, he stood in the Greek theatre at Aspendos, Turkey, a structure built two thousand years earlier, so acoustically perfect that every word spoken on its stage could be heard with clarity in any of its thirteen thousand seats, and he spoke to a little boy sitting high above him. He uttered Count Von Manfred's dying words, Schumann's overture, Byron's poem: "Old man, 'tis not so difficult to die."

The child smiled and waved. He waved back, then shrugged. They became friends at a distance. It was the first time someone other than his mother, who was dead, had been kind to the boy. In years to come it would be a reminder that there was a smile out there on the wind. The little boy looked down the rows and concentric rows of seats: the man 'way down there was motioning for him to come to him. The child, whose name was Orhon, hopped and hopped, descending to the center of the ring as quickly as he could. As he came to the core, and walked out across the orchestra ring, he studied the man. This person was very tall, and he needed a shave, and his hat had an extremely wide brim like the hat of Kül, the man who made weekly trips to Ankara, and he wore a long overcoat far too hot for this day. Orhon could not see the man's eyes because he wore dark glasses that reflected the sky. Orhon thought this man looked like a mountain bandit, only dressed more impressively. Not wisely for a day as torpid as this, but more impressively than Bilge and his men, who raided the farming villages. When he reached the tall man, and they smiled at each other, this person said to Orhon, "I am an unlimited person living in a limited world." The child did not know what to say to that. But he liked the man. "Why do you wear such heavy wool today? I am barefoot." He raised his dusty foot to show the man, and was embarrassed at the dirty cloth tied around his big toe. And the man said, "Because I need a safe place to keep the limited world." And he unbuttoned his overcoat, and held open one side, and showed Orhon what he would inherit one day, if he tried very hard not to be a despot. Pinned to the fabric, each with the face of the planet, were a million and more timepieces, each one the Earth at a different moment, and all of them purring erratically like dozing sphinxes. And Orhon stood there, in the heat, for quite a long while, and listened to the ticking of the limited world.

LEVENDIS: On Wednesday the 16th of October, he chanced upon three skinheads in Doc Martens and cheap black leatherette, beating the crap out of an interracial couple who had emerged from the late show at the La Salle Theater in Chicago. He stood quietly and watched. For a long while.

LEVENDIS: On Thursday the 17th of October he chanced upon three skinheads in Doc Martens and cheap black leatherette, beating the crap out of an interracial couple who had stopped for a bite to eat at a

Howard Johnson's near King of Prussia on the Pennsylvania Turnpike. He removed the inch-and-a-half-thick ironwood dowel he always carried beside his driver's seat and, holding the 2½′ long rod at its centerpoint, laid alongside his pants leg so it could not be seen in the semi-darkness of the parking lot, he came up behind the three as they kicked the black woman and the white man lying between parked cars. He tapped the tallest of the trio on his shoulder, and when the boy turned around—he couldn't have been more than seventeen—he dropped back a step, slid the dowel up with his right hand, gripped it tightly with his left, and drove the end of the rod into the eye of the skinhead, punching through behind the socket and pulping the brain. The boy flailed backward, already dead, and struck his partners. As they turned, he was spinning the dowel like a baton, faster and faster, and as the stouter of the two attackers charged him, he whipped it around his head and slashed straight across the boy's throat. The snapping sound ricocheted off the dark hillside beyond the restaurant. He kicked the third boy in the groin, and when he dropped, and fell on his back, he kicked him under the chin, opening the skinhead's mouth; and then he stood over him, and with both hands locked around the pole, as hard as he could, he piledrove the wooden rod into the kid's mouth, shattering his teeth, and turning the back of his skull to flinders. The dowel scraped concrete through the ruined face. Then he helped the man and his wife to their feet, and bullied the manager of the Howard Johnson's into actually letting them lie down in his office till the State Police arrived. He ordered a plate of fried clams and sat there eating pleasurably until the cops had taken his statement.

LEVENDIS: On Friday the 18th of October, he took a busload of Mormon schoolchildren to the shallow waters of the Great Salt Lake in Utah, to pay homage to the great sculptor Smithson by introducing the art-ignorant children to the *Spiral Jetty*, an incongruously gorgeous line of earth and stone that curves out and away like a thought lost in the tide. "The man who made this, who dreamed it up and then *made* it, you know what he once said?" And they ventured that no, they didn't know what this Smithson sculptor had said, and the man who had driven the bus paused for a dramatic moment, and he repeated Smithson's words: "Establish enigmas, not explanations." They stared at him. "Perhaps you had to be there," he said, shrugging. "Who's for ice cream?" And they went to a Baskin-Robbins.

LEVENDIS: On Saturday the 19th of October, he filed a thirty-million-dollar lawsuit against the major leagues in the name of Alberda Jeanette Chambers, a 19-year-old lefthander with a fadeaway fast ball clocked at better than 96 mph; a dipsy-doodle slider that could do a barrel-roll and clean up after itself; an ERA of 2.10; who could hit from either side of the plate with a batting average of .360; who doubled as a peppery little short-stop working with a trapper's mitt of her own design; who had been refused tryouts with virtually every professional team in the United States (also Japan) from the bigs all the way down to the Pony League. He filed in Federal District Court for the Southern Division of New York State, and told Ted Koppel that Allie Chambers would be the first female player, mulatto or otherwise, in the Baseball Hall of Fame.

LEVENDIS: On Sunday the 20th of October, he drove out and around through the streets of Raleigh and Durham, North Carolina, in a rented van equipped with a public address system, and he endlessly reminded somnambulistic pedestrians and families entering eggs'n'grits restaurants (many of these adults had actually voted for Jesse Helms and thus were in danger of losing their *sertsa*) that perhaps they should ignore their bibles today, and go back and reread Shirley Jackson's short story, "One Ordinary Day, with Peanuts."

This is a story titled

The Daffodils that Entertain

LEVENDIS: On Monday the 21st of October, having taken the sidestep, he wandered through that section of New York City known as the Tenderloin. It was 1892. Crosstown on 24th Street from Fifth Avenue to Seventh, then he turned uptown and walked slowly on Seventh to 40th. Midtown was rife with brothels, their red lights shining through the shadows, challenging the wan gaslit streetlamps. The Edison and Swan United Electric Light Co., Ltd., had improved business tremendously through the wise solicitations of a salesman with a Greek-sounding name who had canvassed the prostitution district west of Broadway only five years earlier, urging the installation of Mr. Joseph Wilson Swan and Mr. Thomas Alva Edison's filament lamps: painted crimson, fixed above the ominously yawning doorways of the area's many houses of easy virtue. He passed an alley on 36th Street, and heard a woman's voice in the darkness complaining, "You said you'd give me two dollars. You have to give it to me first! Stop! No, *first* you gotta give me the two dollars!" He stepped into the alley, let his eyes acclimate to the darkness so total, trying to hold his breath against the stench; and then he saw them. The man was in his late forties, wearing a bowler and a shin-length topcoat with an astrakhan collar. The sound of horse-drawn carriages clopped loudly on the bricks beyond the alley, and the man in the astrakhan looked up, toward the alley mouth. His face was strained, as if he expected an accomplice of the girl, a footpad or shoulder-hitter or bully-boy pimp to charge to her defense. He had his fly unbuttoned and his thin, pale penis extended; the girl was backed against the alley wall, the man's left hand at her throat; and he had hiked up her apron and skirt and petticoats, and was trying to get his right hand into her drawers. She pushed against him, but to no avail. He was large and strong. But when he saw the other man standing down there, near the mouth of the alley, he let her garments drop, and fished his organ back into his pants, but didn't waste time buttoning up. "You there! Like to watch your betters at work, do you?" The man who had done the sidestep spoke softly: "Let the girl go. Give her the two dollars, and let her go." The man in the bowler took a step toward the mouth of the alley, his hands coming up in a standard pugilist's extension. He gave a tiny laugh that was a snort that was rude and derisive: "Oh so, fancy yourself something of the John L. Sullivan, do you, captain? Well, let's see how you and I and the Marquis Q get along..." and he danced forward, hindered considerably by the bulky overcoat. As he drew within double arm's-length of his opponent the younger man drew the taser from his coat pocket, fired at pointblank range, the barbs striking the pugilist in the cheek and neck, the charge lifting him off his feet and driving him back into the brick wall so hard that the filaments were wrenched loose, and the potential fornicator fell forward, his eyes rolled up in his head. Fell forward so hard he smashed three of his front teeth, broken at the gum-line. The girl tried to run, but the alley was a dead end. She watched as the man with the strange weapon came to her. She could barely see his face, and there had been all those killings with that Jack the Ripper in London a few years back, and there was talk this Jack had been a Yankee and had come back to New York. She was terrified. Her name was Poppy Skurnik, she was an orphan, and she worked way downtown as a pieceworker in a shirtwaist factory. She made one dollar and sixty-five cents a week, for six days of labor, from seven in the morning until seven at night, and it was barely enough to pay for her lodgings at Baer's Rents. So she "supplemented" her income with a stroll in the Tenderloin, twice a week, never more, and prayed that she could continue to avoid the murderous attentions of gentlemen who liked to cripple girls after they'd topped them, continue to avoid the pressures of pimps and boy friends who wanted her to work for them, continue to avoid the knowledge that she was no longer "decent" but was also a long way from winding up in one of these red-light whorehouses. He took her gently by the hand, and started to lead her out of the alley, carefully stepping over the unconscious molester. When they reached the street, and she saw how handsome he was, and how young he was, and how premierely he was dressed, she also smiled. She was extraordinarily attractive, and the young man tipped his hat and spoke to her kindly, inquiring as to her name, and where she lived, and if she would like to accompany him for some dinner. And she accepted, and he hailed a carriage, and took her to Delmonico's for the finest meal she had ever had. And later, much later, when he brought her to his townhouse on upper Fifth Avenue, in the posh section, she was ready to do anything he required of her. But instead, all he asked was that she allow him to give her a hundred dollars in exchange for one second of small pain. And she felt fear, because she knew what these nabobs were like, *but a hundred dollars*! So she said yes, and he asked her to bare her left buttock, and she did it with embarrassment, and there was exactly one second of mosquito bite pain, and then he was wiping the spot where he had in injected her with penicillin, with a cool and fragrant wad of cotton batting. "Would you like to sleep the night here, Poppy?" the young man asked. "My room is down the hall, but I think you'll be very comfortable in this one." And she was worried that he had done something awful to her, like inject her with a bad poison, but she didn't *feel* any different, and he seemed so nice, so she said yes, that would be a dear way to spend the evening, and he gave her ten ten-dollar bills, and wished her a pleasant sleep, and left the room, having saved her life, for she had contracted syphilis the week before, though she didn't know it; and within a year she would have been unable, by her appearance alone, to get men in the streets; and would have been let go at the shirtwaist factory; and would have been seduced and sold into one of the worst of the brothels; and would have been dead within another two years. But this night she slept well, between cool sheets with hand-embroidered lace edging, and when she rose the next day he was gone, and no one told her to leave the townhouse, and so she stayed on from day to day, for years, and eventually married and gave birth to three children, one of whom grew to maturity, married, had a child who became an adult and saved the lives of millions of innocent men, women, and children. But that night in 1892 she slept a deep, sweet, recuperative and dreamless sleep.

LEVENDIS: On Tuesday the 22nd of October, he visited a plague of asthmatic toads on Iisalmi, a small town in Finland; a rain of handbills left over from World War II urging the SS troops to surrender on Cheju-do, an island off the southern coast of Korea; a shock wave of forsythia on Linares in Spain; and a fully-restored 1926 Ahrens-Fox model RK fire engine on a mini-mall in Clarksville, Arkansas.

LEVENDIS: On Wednesday the 23rd of October, he corrected every history book in America so that they no longer called it The Battle of Bunker Hill, but rather Breeds Hill where, in fact, the engagement of 17 June 1775 had taken place. He also invested every radio and television commentator with the ability to differentiate between "in a moment" and "momentarily," which were not at all the same thing, and the misuse of which annoyed him greatly. The former was in his job description; the latter was a matter of personal pique.

LEVENDIS: On Thursday the 24th of October, he revealed to the London *Times* and *Paris-Match* the name of the woman who had stood on the grassy knoll, behind the fence, in Dallas that day, and fired the rifle shots that killed John F. Kennedy. But no one believed Marilyn Monroe could have done the deed and gotten away unnoticed. Not even when he provided her suicide note that confessed the entire matter and tragically told in her own words how jealousy and having been jilted had driven her to hire that weasel Lee Harvey Oswald, and that pig Jack Ruby, and how she could no longer live with the guilt, goodbye. No one would run the story, not even the *Star*, not even *The Enquirer*, not even *TV Guide*. But he tried.

LEVENDIS: On Friday the 25th of October, he upped the intelligence of every human being on the planet by forty points.

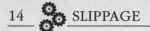

LEVENDIS: On Saturday the 26th of October, he lowered the intelligence of every human being on the planet by forty-two points.

This is a story titled

At Least One Good Deed a Day, Every Single Day

LEVENDIS: On Sunday the 27th of October, he returned to a family in Kalgoorlie, SW Australia, a five-year-old child who had been kidnapped from their home in Bayonne, New Jersey, fifteen years earlier. The child was no older than before the family had immigrated, but he now spoke only in a dialect of Etruscan, a language that had not been heard on the planet for thousands of years. Having most of the day free, however, he then made it his business to kill the remaining seventeen American GIs being held MIA in an encampment in the heart of Laos. Waste not, want not.

LEVENDIS: On Monday the 28th of October, still exhilarated from the work and labors of the preceding day, he brought out of the highlands of North Viet Nam Capt. Eugene Y. Grasso, USAF, who had gone down under fire twenty-eight years earlier. He returned him to his family in Anchorage, Alaska, where his wife, remarried, refused to see him but his daughter whom he had never seen, would. They fell in love, and lived together in Anchorage, where their story provided endless confusion to the ministers of several faiths.

LEVENDIS: On Tuesday the 29th of October, he destroyed the last bits of evidence that would have led to answers to the mysteries of the disappearances of Amelia Earhart, Ambrose Bierce, Benjamin Bathurst and Jimmy Hoffa. He washed the bones and placed them in a display of early American artifacts.

LEVENDIS: On Wednesday the 30th of October, he traveled to New Orleans, Louisiana, where he waited at a restaurant in Metairie for the former head of the Ku Klux Klan, now running for state office, to show up to meet friends. As the man stepped out of his limousine, wary guards on both sides of him, the traveler fired a Laws rocket from the roof of the eatery. It blew up the former KKK prexy, his guards, and a perfectly good Cadillac Eldorado. Leaving the electoral field open, for the enlightened voters of Louisiana, to a man who, as a child, had assisted Mengele's medical experiments, a second contender who had changed his name to avoid being arrested for child mutilation, and an illiterate swamp cabbage farmer from Baton Rouge whose political philosophy involved cutting the throats of peccary pigs, and thrusting one's face into the boiling blood of the corpse. Waste not, want not.

LEVENDIS: On Thursday the 31st of October, he restored to his throne the Dalai Lama, and closed off the mountain passes that provided land access to Tibet, and caused to blow constantly a cataclysmic snowstorm that did not affect the land below, but made any accessibility by air impossible. The Dalai Lama offered a referendum to the people: should we rename our land Shangri-La?

LEVENDIS: On Friday the 32nd of October, he addressed a convention of readers of cheap fantasy novels, saying, "We invent our lives (and other people's) as we live them; what we call 'life' is itself a fiction. Therefore, we must constantly strive to produce only good art, absolutely entertaining fiction." (He did *not* say to them: "I am an unlimited person, sadly living in a limited world.") They smiled politely, but since he spoke only in Etruscan, they did not understand a word he said.

LEVENDIS: On Saturday the 33rd of October, he did the sidestep and worked the oars of the longboat that brought Christopher Columbus to the shores of the New World, where he was approached by a representative of the native peoples, who laughed at the silly clothing the great navigator wore. They all ordered pizza and the man who had done the rowing made sure that venereal disease was quickly spread so that centuries later he could give a beautiful young woman an inoculation in her left buttock.

LEVENDIS: On Piltic the 34th of October, he gave all dogs the ability to speak in English, French, Mandarin, Urdu, and Esperanto; but all they could say was rhyming poetry of the worst sort, and he called it *doggerel.*

LEVENDIS: On Sqwaybe the 35th of October, he was advised by the Front Office that he had been having too rich a time at the expense of the Master Parameter, and he was removed from his position, and the unit was closed down, and darkness was penciled in as a mid-season replacement. He was reprimanded for having called himself Levendis, which is a Greek word for someone who is full of the pleasure of living. He was reassigned, with censure, but no one higher up noticed that on his new assignment he had taken the name Sertsa.

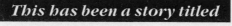

This has been a story titled

Shagging Fungoes

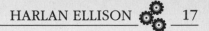

But even after I got out of Basic Training in '57, and wound up at Fort Knox, and brought Charlotte (and all the furniture from the Manhattan apartment) down to that tiny, miserable house in Elizabethtown, Kentucky, I was still able to delude myself that I had a marriage.

When I got the call from Cleveland that day, the call from my brother-in-law Jerry, telling me that my mother was desperately ill and might die, I went to the Company Commander and asked for an emergency leave. When I drove from the base to the house, and told Charlotte we had to pack fast to make the journey to Cleveland, she simply wouldn't hear of it. I'm not going, she said. I argued for a few minutes, but I was beside myself worrying about my mom, so I just said fukkit, threw some clothes together, got in the car, and got in the wind.

Anywhere But Here, With Anybody But You

Omen. There had been a helluva nauseating omen that this was going to be one of the worst days of his life. Just that morning, if he'd been prescient enough to recognize it for what it was. But he wasn't, of course. No one ever is. The neighbor's cat, which he truly and genuinely, deeply and passionately despised, that fucking ugly one-eyed shit-gopher cat with the orange tuft of hair on its muzzle, that puke cat was sitting in the tree right outside his bedroom window when he opened his eyes and awoke from a restless night's sleep, and turned to look at the kind of day it was going to be. In the branches nearly touching his second-storey window, sat that fungus of a cat, with a dead bird hanging out of its drooling jaws. Like a stringy upchuck of undercooked manicotti. With feathers. He looked right into the dead face of that bird, and he looked right into the smug face of that toilet bowl cat, and if he'd had the sense or foresight to figure it out, he'd have known this was a significant omen. But he didn't. No one ever does.

Not till he came home that night from work, from wage slave hell designing greeting cards for the Universe of Happiness, across the river and into the industrial park, did he look back with incomplete memory, and suspect that the presence of stringy, matted-feather, watery thin blood death right outside his wake-up-and-sing-a-merry-song window was a message to him across thirteen hours.

He got the message when he pulled up in the driveway and got out and went into the back seat and pulled out his jacket and his attaché case, and looked at the house. It was dark.

He got the message when he walked up the front walk and turned his key in the door and opened the door, and the house was dark. No smell of dinner cooking. No sound of the kids cranking with the Mario Bros. No feel of preparations for the evening. No sight of Carole rushing across his line of sight. Only the beginning of the taste of ashes. He got the message.

And when he looked to his left, into the living room, and was able to discern—ever so faintly there in the oily shadows and pale moonglow seeping through the four front room windows—the shape of a man sitting on the sofa, the message became the crackling S.O.S. once sent by the Titanic to the Carpathia.

There was an indistinct shape on the floor in front of the man's feet. It was motionless.

Eddie Canonerro stood framed in the entrance to his living room—what had *been* his unremarkable, familiar living room—in plain sight of a man who should not have been sitting on his sofa, in a house that had been unremarkably, familiarly *his* house for fifteen years. Stood framed, outlined clearly, defenseless and bewildered, watching the large sitting man who stared at him across what was now an alien landscape, a living room nomansland as bleak and ominous and unforgiving as the silent terrain moments before it became the battlefield of Agincourt.

"Who the hell are you?" Eddie said.

His tone was warily between umbrage and confusion, careful not to cause insult. Every fool has a gun these days.

"I'm a friend of Carole's," the shadowy shape on the sofa said. There was no movement of mouth, deep in darkness.

"Where's my wife...?"

Eddie was suddenly frantic. Was she dead? Wounded, lying on a floor somewhere? Was this a burglar, a rapist, some demented interloper careering through the neighborhood? Where was Carole!

"Where're my kids...?"

"Carole's left you. Carole's taken the kids. I'm here to make sure you move out of Carole's house." He gave the lumpy shape on the floor a half-shove, half-kick with a workbooted foot. It rolled awkwardly for a short space, then came to rest in a shard of moonlight bisecting the carpet. Eddie recognized it now. His old Army duffel bag. Packed full. "Here," said the man, "here's your clothes. You better leave now, that's what Carole wants."

"I'm not going anywhere," Eddie said. He set down the thin, cabretta-grain attaché case. He dropped his jacket. If the guy moved suddenly, well, there was a Bantu assegai and hide-shield on the living room wall to his right. Pulling the spear loose from the brackets would be easy. If the guy moved. Suddenly.

The guy's face was deep in shadow. No eyes to read. No expression to measure. Nothing to anticipate except words.

"I'm not here to fight with you. Carole asked me to be here when you got home. Carole asked me to tell you it was all over, and she's taken the kids, and she's going to divorce you. That's what I was supposed to tell you. And Carole asked me to make sure you left and took your clothes with you, and then I'm supposed to lock up the house."

Eddie's jaw muscles hurt. He realized he'd been grinding. "Where is she? She go to her mother's? What're you, the boy friend?"

The guy said, "I'm a friend of Carole's. That's all."

"She doesn't have any friends I don't know."

"Maybe you don't know Carole very well."

"Who the *fuck* d'you think you are?"

"I'm a friend of Carole's. She asked me to tell you, that's all."

"I'm calling the cops. Stay right there, smartass. I'm calling the cops to come and bust your ass for breaking and entering." He took a step toward the phone on the end-table beside the big, overstuffed reading chair.

"Carole gave me a key. I have a notarized letter from Carole, giving me permission to be here."

"Yeah, right. I think we'll let 911 decide if you've got the right to be in my house, mister!"

"Do you really want me to give them the other letter, the one Carole wrote about why she's left you? It's got all the stuff in it about your bad habits, and hitting her, and the stuff about the kids..."

Eddie couldn't believe what he was hearing. "Are you out of your fuckin' *mind*?! I've been married fifteen years, I never raised my *hand* to her, what the hell are you making up here?"

"Carole told me about it. Carole was smart to leave you."

Eddie stepped back, felt his hand touch the wall. He was reeling. He understood, suddenly, that he was *actually* reeling. This couldn't be happening.

"I *never*..." His voice was small. He knew the truth...he just wasn't a hitter. Had *never* hit a woman. Had, in fact, only raised his fists in anger once, thirty or more years ago, to defend himself against a pair of schoolyard bullies. He was just, simply, *not* a hitter. Why had Carole told this guy such things? Why had she left without speaking to him? Why had she taken his sons away? Why had she confided in this total stranger? Why had she—and *had* she?—written letters of permission, letters of accusation? What the hell was *happening* here?

"We haven't been having any trouble," Eddie said.

"Carole says it's terrible living with you. She says to tell you it's all over, and she's getting a divorce."

"You *said* that!"

"Carole told me to say it to you."

What was *with* this gazoonie? Was he fucking retarded, or *what?* It was like having a conversation with Rain Man, or Forrest Gump, or Lenny from the Steinbeck novel. It wasn't any kind of conversation he'd ever had with *anybody*, even his grandfather, when the old gentleman had gone simple, and Eddie as a kid had been taken to visit Grampa in the Home. Not even those soft, aimless, frustrating conversations had been like this.

There had been no menace when talking to Grampa.

"I'm calling the cops." He moved again toward the end-table. The guy on the sofa didn't move. Eddie strained to see some tiniest reflection of moonlight in the shrouded eyes, but they were back in darkness. It was like trying to see a road sign through heavy fog. You could strain all you liked, but you were going to overshoot your turnoff, no matter how hard you craned your neck forward. Where there is no light, there is no sight. He picked up the receiver and put it to his ear.

"Carole had the phone turned off. Electricity and water, too. Until you leave. I made sure that was done."

Eddie held the dead thing to his ear. Not even the sound of the sea. Slowly, he set the implement back on its stand. The guy pointed to the duffel bag.

"I'm not going anywhere!" Eddie yelled.

Then he remembered the revolver in the hall closet. Up on the shelf, near the front door in case anyone ever tried to force a way in. He turned quickly, stumbled through the entrance, back into the front hall, and got to the closet. He automatically reached for the light switch to illuminate the closet, and flipped it. And nothing happened. *Electricity and water, too. Until you leave.*

He fumbled in the closet, found the shelf, found the cardboard box under the moth-proof plastic bag of mufflers and scarves, and jammed his hand inside. It was empty.

From the living room he heard the guy's voice. "Carole told me about the gun. I got it out of there."

Eddie felt his knees lock. He couldn't move. His spine was frozen. The guy could be behind him right now, the revolver aimed at his back. Not even kill him, just leave him a cripple for the rest of his life. Unable to walk. Unable to pee. Unable to work with his hands, draw, paint, do the work he so much wanted to do. All the work he'd put off for fifteen years to raise two kids, to make a stable marriage, to have a career in business. He'd put it all to one side and now he was going to be shot by a stranger in his own house.

He turned, slowly.

But the guy wasn't there. The hall was empty. Eddie closed the closet door, and walked back through the entranceway into the living room. The guy hadn't moved. The duffel bag lay where it had rolled. The moonlight still came through like watery soup, enough to enfeeble, but insufficient to restore or bring back to health.

"What the hell do you want with me?" Eddie said.

"I'm just a friend. Of Carole's. I said that before. She asked me to come and make sure you left."

Eddie felt pressure in his chest, like an attack of heavy anvil angina. "Where's the gun?"

"Over there on the television set. I put it there after I took out the bullets and threw them in the trash."

"And you're just going to sit there till I leave you here, all alone in the house I've been paying mortgage payments on for fifteen years? You think that's going to happen?"

"Well, this is Carole's house now. She owns it. You just have to leave, and everything will be fine."

"I'm not leaving some guy I never heard of, all alone in my house. And where the hell's all my stuff? My drawing table, my art supplies, my paints, my reference books? How am I going to make a living? You think I'm just going to take my clothes in an old duffel bag and *vanish*? This is damned crazy, it's obscene, for chrissakes!"

"Everything here is Carole's now. It's all like an egg, it's all one thing. She owns it, shell and everything inside it."

"What are you babbling about? You act like she's the goddam Queen of Spain, some fucking nobility, *droit du seigneur*, everything belongs to her! Not bloody likely! I worked for every stick in this place, and I'll fight her every step in the court before I let her screw me over!"

"No, you have to go away now. Carole asked me to tell you that."

"I want to see her. I want *her* to tell me. We never had any trouble, this is all nuts, this hitting and the kids and all the rest of it. It's nuts! No eggs, just *nuts*!"

"You can't see her. Carole's gone away. But Carole can see you."

"What are you talking about? Where is she? If she's at her mother's house, she can't see me. Is this some crazy bad joke, is she here?" He turned and yelled into the empty house, "Carole! Hey, honey! Carole, you here?"

But there wasn't any answer. He stood there for a long time, staring at the unmoving shape seated comfortably on *his* sofa, in *his* living room, tapping a workbooted foot that had kicked *his* duffel bag that contained all he was going to be permitted to carry away of his life.

His life till now.

He said it to himself again. *My life till now.*

In the darkness—a darkness he now understood hid *his* face from the guy on the sofa—a guy who was the last aspect of *my life till now*—he smiled. She had left, had taken his life till now with her, and she was free. No. Not so. She was still tied to *my life till now*. In darkness, he was drenched in light. Now he could smile, because now *he* was free.

Take care of the kids? Well, that would've been his job, but now it was part of *my life till now*, and that wasn't his responsibility any longer. Support, money, phone calls, courts, screaming attorneys, letters, eyeless guys on sofas...all part of what she had decided to tie herself to, forever. *He* was free.

Never again to go across the river and into the Universe of Happiness. Fifteen years ago he had tied himself to *my life till now*, and he had been a good husband and loving father and a doomed wage-slave, and he would have stayed at it forever. But now he could be anywhere but here, with anyone but the jailer of his prison. He was out. In the darkness, he smiled; he turned, and walked through the front hallway, past the defense-less closet, and out the front door. He hoped Carole could see him, because as soon as he got in the car and drove away, he would cease to be Eddie Canonerro. Anywhere but here, with anybody but you.

Squatting near the porch glider, was that scabrous cat. Eddie moved very fast. He kicked the little fucker in the head and, squealing, it jumped for its life, and ran away.

Squinting through her telescope, the Queen of Spain frowned. Then the picture went dark, and not even the sound of clockwork ravens made the future any brighter.

Crazy As a Soup Sandwich

ACT ONE

FADE IN:

1   EXT. INDUSTRIAL ALLEYWAY — DUSK (SHOOT DAY FOR
NIGHT) — FULL SHOT

OPEN *BLACK & WHITE* on a rain-soaked passage between
warehouses. Crates and huge cargo containers
stored along the walls of the buildings. Dumpsters
overflowing here and there. Piles of trash of a
strictly industrial nature waiting to be collected.
High, metal loading bay doors (tambour doors) front
the alley.

A large truck (cab and trailer), parked and sealed,
blocks one loading bay at the right in middle-b.g.
Puddles of water shine down the entire length of
the alley. It has just been raining hard, and the
dumpster lids are soaked, the cartons wet. Ominous
clouds scud across the lowering sky; no moon; shoot
almost FILM NOIR, gritty and shadowy, à la 1930s B
films.

                                        (CONTINUED:)

1   CONTINUED:

SHOOT FROM LOW-ANGLE down the length of the alley,
giving a sense of enormous distance. The alley
should be at least 50-60 feet wide, giving sharp
perspective. ANGLE OF CAMERA should give us
warehouse tops, fire escapes if possible, and the
sky.

HOLD ALLEY for several beats as INTENSE CHASE
MUSIC RISES and we HEAR the sharp sound of RUNNING
FOOTSTEPS OFF-CAMERA. (This in black & white) as
exciting pursuit music reaches a crescendo and
ARKY LOCHNER jumps OVER CAMERA and INTO FRAME,
landing right in front of us so we see his legs.
He runs from CAMERA POV into FULL FRAME, splashing
through puddles in frantic flight.

Arky runs fifteen feet from CAMERA and, as he
leaps over a puddle, he looks back over his
shoulder in terror and we:

                                    FREEZE FRAME.

Still in black & white, CAMERA MOVES IN on Arky
frozen in mid-leap. HOLD at MEDIUM CU as we HEAR
NARRATION OVER:

                    NARRATOR
                  (Over)
            As certain as death and taxes, we
            are told, "the meek will definitely
            inherit the Earth."
                  (beat)
            Perhaps.
                  [MORE]

                                    (CONTINUED:)

1   CONTINUED:—2

NARRATOR (CONT'D.)
(beat)
But not always. Consider, if you
will, frozen in terror, Mr. Arky
Lochner,(pronounced *Lock*-ner) a
well-known petty crook, sidebar
six-for-fiver shylock, registered
coward, and owner of a yellow streak
so vivid it could be slathered on a
hot dog.
(beat)
Mr. Lochner was written out of the
will when the meek were guaranteed
their inheritance. And just now
he's trying to avoid *another* kind
of payoff; a soulful payoff in that
off-track betting parlor where the
viggerish is a matter of life and
death.

Arky Lochner is in his late thirties, early forties.
He has the beady little eyes of a marmoset, the
twitchy thin face of a weasel, and the slim build
of a street purse-snatcher. He wears a suit that
looks as if he's been sleeping in it since they
locked him out of his hotel room; a cheap, paper-thin
yellow plastic rain slicker (the kind you can buy
in a turnpike gas station's men's room, folded into
a tiny square, for a dollar); a dirty Borsalino now
jammed at a cockeyed angle on his head; and he
seems to have lost a shoe while running. As VO
NARRATION ENDS we segué FROM BLACK & WHITE to COLOR
and

UNFREEZE FRAME:

(CONTINUED:)

1   CONTINUED:—3

As Arky's feet hit the filthy wet blacktop and he
dashes away from CAMERA, still looking over his
shoulder in panic.

2   REVERSE ANGLE — THE ALLEY — SHOOT UP-ANGLE FROM GROUND

TO ARKY as he rushes toward us. Above and behind him,
at mid-b.g, we see an ominous cloud hanging in the air
at the second storey level. The cloud is boiling. It
is rushing after him (suggest SFX time-lapse photography
of clouds à la Louis Shwartsburg at Energy Prods.) and
crackles of lightning dance through and around the
cloud like a Van de Graaff Generator run amuck. As
it rolls down the alley after him, Arky stops, spins,
pulls a .45 from his belt and fires four shots into
the cloud. It has no effect, but from the cloud
comes a thunderclap and the roar of a demon voice
that fills the alley like a SWAT-team bullhorn:

                    VOLKERPS OVER
                    (filter FX)
          Cease your flight, you four-flushing
          pismire!

Arky does not hesitate. The demon voice only
serves to panic him more. He turns back INTO CAMERA
and takes two running steps toward us, his
foot-without-a-shoe slips in the water, he flies
forward INTO CAMERA and lands on his stomach, sliding
in the filthy passageway. CAMERA HOLDS as he
scrabbles to a crouching position, staring up at
the cloud hanging over him now, as the demon
VOLKERPS emerges from the top of the cloud. As he
materializes, Arky falls backward, staring.
                    [MORE]

                                        (CONTINUED:)

2   CONTINUED:

Volkerps is huge, immense, enormous. A massively-
muscled upper torso that makes Schwarzenegger look
anorexic, surmounted by a bestial head with three
blazing green eyes, a wide mouth filled with
double-rows of fangs like a shark, and claws and
spikes and hooked talons at the elbows.

                    VOLKERPS
              (filter FX, raging)
         This is the second most ill-advised
         action you have ever taken, Arky
         Lochner, you miserable gobbet of
         human meat!

A thunderclap and lightning punctuate his words.
He smiles. The smile could rot poison ivy. Arky
trembles, drops the .45.

                 VOLKERPS (CONT'D.)
         The first was trying to make a
         bargain that would outwit me. I'm
         thirty-two thousand years old, you
         human virus! Even among my peers
         in the 4th Canonic Order of Demons
         I'm considered a truly ghastly
         dinner companion.
                  (beat, smiles)
         Did I mention I enjoy sucking the
         marrow from the living bones of
         idiots like you?
                    (beat)
         Whatever made you think you could
         outwit the magnificence of *Volkerps?*

The speaking of his name produces reverberations,
thunder, lightning, greater trembling on Arky's
part.

3 ANOTHER ANGLE — FAVORING ARKY

As he demonstrates a kind of pluck we would not
have expected from such a weasly guy. Arky gets to
his feet and points a trembling finger at the demon,
his voice squeaking but almost brave. Give him a
mock Broadway-Bronx accent, high and fast.

ARKY
(terrified but plucky)

I still got a week! The contract
ain't up for a week! Why it is
you're tormentin' me?

A bit more electrical display from the cloud.

VOLKERPS
(filter FX)

Because I'm a *demon*, you imbecile!
I don't send singing telegrams, I
torment! It's what I *do*! That's
why I'm called a *demon*, instead of
The Easter Bunny...

Arky snaps off two more shots, sort of lackadaisi-
cally. The demon looks disgusted at this behavior:

VOLKERPS (CONT'D.)
(filter FX, wearily)

Fine, just fine: this one is the
slowest learner in the entire human
race.

(yells)

Dummy! Moron! Bullets can't *hurt*
me, you worm, you stone, you less
than living thing!

(CONTINUED:)

3   CONTINUED:

                    ARKY
            A week! You made the deal...you
            can't bug me for a week!

Volkerps begins to shrink slowly back into the
cloud, and the cloud begins to grow smaller,
fade from sharpness.

                  VOLKERPS
            (filter FX, chuckling)
        Bug you? *Bug* you? A week from now
        I'll remember you mentioned bugs.

His talons clack and clatter like castanets, making
a lunatic cricket sound against his scaly hide.

              VOLKERPS (CONT'D.)
            Perhaps I'll turn you *into* one.
            A small, black, crawling bug
            ...not unlike the kind I spear
            with a claw, crack like a nut-
            shell, and feed to my serpent
            mate, Diptha. She *loves* to be
            bugged!

The lightning flashes, the thunder rolls, the
cloud sucks in on itself with a roaring typhoon
sound as of air being vacuumed into a black hole.
And in an instant he's gone!

4   CLOSE ON ARKY — HAND-HELD

As he stares up into the now-empty alleyway for a
moment. He stands there with one shoe missing, his
Borsalino filthy, the yellow plastic rain slicker
barely hiding the tackiness of his suit...and suddenly
he *howls* in delayed terror, a high keening whine,
as he jams the useless .45 into his raincoat pocket
and, as HAND-HELD CAMERA GOES WITH, he turns back
down the alley and runs. He runs for his life. He
runs like a mad thing, arms pinwheeling, eyes wild,
he runs full-out. CAMERA WITH Arky as he runs and
runs down the alley, past the truck, and suddenly
turns left and runs straight THROUGH A WOODEN DOOR
in a warehouse. He is doing eighty-five miles an
hour, and when he hits that warehouse door he
splinters it, going right through!

5   INT. WAREHOUSE — OVERHEAD FULL SHOT — ESTABLISHING

As Arky comes through the wooden barrier. He
suddenly erupts into the building, sending planks
and chunks and slivers of wood in all directions.

The warehouse is a freight-forwarding operation.
Filled with crates and cartons and boxes and
containers. A couple of small forklifts. We are
SHOOTING STRAIGHT DOWN from the metal beams overhead
as Arky bursts into the scene. All through scenes
4 and 5 we HEAR that air-raid siren scream of
Arky's, like a Doppler effect rushing toward us,
then away. He bursts through the door below us,
and keeps running straight ahead across the
warehouse floor as we:

CUT TO:

6   SERIES OF INTERCUTS — MEDIUM SHOTS
thru
12   FOLLOWING ARKY. MEDIUM CLOSE behind him as he
     rushes away from the shattered door. We get a
     distorted perspective of the crates, et al, rising
     toward the ceiling in rows and aisles and profusion
     all around him. He's moving fast (undercranked?)
     as CAMERA GOES WITH.

     INT. OFFICE — ANGLE PAST NINO & OTHERS — THRU
     GLASSED-IN WALLS & DOOR toward Arky running like a
     gazelle toward the office.

     Arky rushing faster and faster toward office cubicle
     at rear of warehouse. A light is on in that office
     and we can see a nattily-dressed man rising with
     alarm from behind a desk, as the two other men and
     a totally gorgeous woman shrink back from the
     oncoming juggernaut. SOUND of a freight train in
     B.G. It's Arky, but he's coming on like the
     super-express.

     CLOSEUP on the faces of the men and woman as Arky
     thunders toward them. CLOSEUP on Arky's strained,
     howling face, CLOSEUP on the men and woman, CUT
     BACK AND FORTH and:

13   INT. OFFICE — TOWARD DOOR

     As Arky bursts through the glass-paneled door,
     several of the cubicle's windows shattering outward
     as he booms into the small space. He hits the desk
     with his thighs and falls across the desk. He stares
     up at the man who was sitting there a moment ago.
     The nearly-transparent, sickly-yellow rain slicker
     has billowed out to cover him like a blanket.

                                        (CONTINUED:)

13 CONTINUED:

Everything on the desk—papers, ledgers, geegaws,
pencil pots, telephone, Rolodex—has been sent flying
to the walls and floor. He lies there now, in an
eye-of-the-hurricane silence as profound as the
express train hullabaloo of a moment ago, staring at:

The nattily dressed man is NINO LANCASTER. He is
David Niven forty years ago. He is smooth, sleek,
impeccable, cultured, self-possessed, urbane,
quiet, powerful, slim and tailored. His fingers
are manicured. His eyes are chill. Early 40s, six
feet tall, pale and silky, his pants automatically
take on a razor-sharp crease when he puts them on.

The gorgeous woman in her 30s is HAZEL HORNE. She
is Nino's bookkeeper, accountant, attorney and
paramour. She is what is meant by the concept
class. Men would crawl through broken glass for
her, but unless they had a Master's degree, she
wouldn't even see them. She and Nino are intelligent
and elite. She is also unafraid of the juggernaut.
She looks down at Arky as though from Mt. Olympus.
Her outrageous beauty is only heightened by the
bemusement and intelligence in her face.

The other two men are pistoleros, enforcers. They
are apemen. Each one could pick up a pair of NFL
linebackers and carry them like shopping bags. The
one is black, the other is white. Nino has dressed
them to give the appearance of their being *homo
sapiens*, but the suits fit GUS and BORK awkwardly,
as if the thugs are not used to standing erect. We
are talking human Land Rovers here.

(CONTINUED:)

13   CONTINUED:—2

They stand amid the rubble, looking down at Arky
Lochner folded across Nino's desk. Arky is
panting, crying, twitchy and hysterical, babbling:

                    ARKY
                 (babbling)
        Ya gotta help me, ya gotta save me,
        my life's in yer hands, it's gonna
        turn me into a bug, a thing what
        crawls, an' then he's gonna eat me,
        no, he's gonna give me to his wife,
        this snake lady, and *she's* gonna
        eat me, so youse had better help
        me, 'cause if ya don't it'll be all
        over fer me...

This preceding dialogue by Arky should be so run-on,
so wild and babbling, that the actor will be
half-ad libbing it. He seems determined to gibber
forever. Hazel takes one step toward him and in a
fluid motion pincers his lips between thumb and
forefinger, shutting him up. In the beat of silence,
one of the simian pistoleros speaks gutterally.

                    BORK
                 (dumbly)
        You want I should twist off his
        head, Mr. Lancaster, sir?

14   FAVORING NINO

Lancaster shakes his head slightly, very cool and
reserved. Hazel lets go of Arky's lips, wipes her
fingers on his hat-brim. Arky is silent, but
trembling, imploringly.

                                   (CONTINUED:)

14 CONTINUED:

                    NINO
               (urbanely, softly)
          I perceive that you must be
          seriously deranged to burst in here
          unannounced, Arky, with half my
          boys looking for you.

His voice is sweet, but deadly, like a box of
poisoned chocolates.

                 NINO (CONT'D)
          That is, unless you have secreted
          somewhere on your scrofulous body
          the $165,000, including today's
          interest at 750%, that you have
          owed me for three months, three
          weeks and four days.

                    ARKY
                 (hysterical)
          Y'gotta perteck me, Mr. Lancaster!

                    BORK
                 (like a child)
          I could do that, I could twist off
          his head fer ya, Mr. Lancaster, sir.

                    HAZEL
                 (cool)
          Sit, Bork.

Bork sits. Hazel lifts Arky from the desk, dusts
him very maternally.

                                        (CONTINUED:)

14 CONTINUED:—2

> **HAZEL (CONT'D.)**
> (to Nino)
> Nino, before we have Gus and Bork
> reduce him to his component parts
> for shipment, would you be interested
> in hearing his tale of woe?

Nino sits down behind the desk. He stares at Arky
with cool detachment.

> **NINO**
> Calmly now, Arky. Tell us what
> seems to have unhinged you.
> (to Hazel)
> I think he can stand on his own
> now, Hazel.

She releases Arky, steps back, watching with
bemusement. Arky wets his lips, looks around
trying to get oriented, realizes he's in trouble
even here, but squeaks out a recitation.

> **ARKY**
> (fast but clear)
> The hundred sixty-five Gs I got
> loaned from you, Nino...I, uh, er,
> I needed it 'cause I made this, uh,
> kinda *deal* with a, er, a *demon*,
> this big thing wit' teeth calls
> hisself Volkerps...

Bork and Gus explode with laughter. Nino gives
them a hard look. They fall silent.

(CONTINUED:)

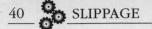
14 CONTINUED:—3

> **NINO**
> (quietly)
> A demon? A supernatural being?

> **ARKY**
> Yeah, yeah, yeah, you got it! A
> creature of stygian darkness; a
> denizen of the nether reaches; a
> monster from some nameless plane of
> witchcraft and horror. Yeah, you
> got it.

> **HAZEL**
> Bork, twist his head off.

Bork rises, Arky screams, Nino makes a casual stop
motion with his hand. Bork pauses. Hazel smiles
evilly.

15 ANOTHER ANGLE — FAVORING ARKY

> **ARKY**
> (for his life)
> I ain't makin' it up, Mr. Lancaster.
> Honest ta viggerish, I ain't makin'
> this up. The thing's after me! It
> was right outside inna alley.

> NINO
> Go on.

(CONTINUED:)

15 CONTINUED:

> **ARKY**
> We made this deal, me an' this
> Volkerps. He gives me all the
> winners at Santa Anita, Pimlico,
> Aqueduct, Hawthorne, Liberty Bell
> and Maywood, all the same day...

> **HAZEL**
> In exchange for...?

> **ARKY**
> First refusal option on 51% of my
> Immortal Soul.

> **HAZEL**
> Things must be worse in Hell than
> we know. Your soul's got to be
> pretty grungy and soiled, kid.

> **ARKY**
>   (offhand)
> He said good help was hard to come
> by; mentioned doing windows and
> floors, whadda I know.

> **NINO**
> Then you'd be able to pay me back
> in full, including the crippling
> interest; and you'd finally manage
> to extricate yourself from the
> nasty, brutish life that
> distinguishes you.

(CONTINUED:)

15 CONTINUED:—2

> **ARKY**
> Yeah, yeah, that's how I supposed
> it'd be. Yeah, sure...an' pigs'll
> fly.
>> (beat)
> He gimme the winners all right.
> Sure, he *did* that! Twenty, thirty,
> forty-two of 'em. An' I bet 'em
> all; an' they won, each and every
> one of 'em.
>> (beat, cries)
> Except a few had strokes an' died
> as they crossed the finish line,
> an' a bunch got disqualified 'cause
> they was fulla dope, an' eleven of
> 'em got scratched for bumpin' in the
> stretch...and on and on like that.
> Every one of 'em came in first...an'
> I lost every cent I got from you,
> Mr. Lancaster, an' that's why I
> been duckin' your collectors...an'
> this Volkerps is gonna come and
> take me away and *eat me* in a week
> if you don't perteck me!

16 2-SHOT — NINO & HAZEL

> **NINO**
> And why should I bother, even
> allowing that this fantasy has a
> basis in fact?

(CONTINUED:)

16   CONTINUED:

> **HAZEL**
> One hundred and sixty-five thousand
> dollars, plus the vig for four
> months including next week.

> **NINO**
> (to Arky)
> Ms. Horne is my accountant, Arky.
> She makes a strong case for your
> continued existence, despite its
> truly outstanding wretchedness.

> **ARKY**
> Then you *believe* me!

> **NINO**
> I believe that I believe *you*
> believe it.
> (beat)
> I'm intrigued. Had you fabricated
> a tale of flying saucers and little
> purple aliens, or of burning bushes
> with Messianic messages, I could
> not be more intrigued.
> (beat)
> As the most powerful underworld
> figure in this great metropolis, I
> have managed to make cohesive sense
> of the rackets. Now I grow bored.
> Ennui fills my days and nights...
> (smiles at Hazel)
> ...save for the joys of my association
> with Ms. Horne, of course.

(CONTINUED:)

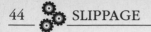

16 CONTINUED:—2

                         HAZEL
                        (beams)
            You little dickens, you.

                         NINO
                        (resumes)
            You've bought yourself a momentary
            reprieve through dint of sheer
            imagination, Arky. I won't have
            Gus and Bork dissect you. Nay, I
            shall assist you.
                        (beat)
            Already I feel heroic.

                         HAZEL
            Fiscally speaking, Nino, I commend
            your decision. But operation-
            ally...?

17 ANOTHER ANGLE

    Nino rises, begins pacing the tiny office. He
    stops and turns to the still trembling (but bravely
    smiling) Arky.

                         NINO
             How did you even go about *locating* a demon
             in these conservative climes?

                         ARKY
            There's this, uh, er, *woman* I heard
            about, supposed to have strong in
            with the netherworld. I visited
            her a couple of times. She set it
            up. I think she gets a commission.

                                        (CONTINUED:)

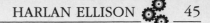

17   CONTINUED:

                          NINO
              I suggest we pay her a visit.
                          (beat)
              Gus, the car, if you please.

Gus goes, and Nino turns to Hazel. She comes to
him, he kisses her in the most husbandly fashion,
politely and quickly.

                          HAZEL
              Try to hurry, dear. We have dinner
              with the Mayor tonight.

Nino smiles, takes Arky by the arm, and they go as
we:
                                        DISSOLVE TO:

18   INT. SHOPPING MALL — ESTABLISHING

A large urban mall, with the usual video rental
shops, high end clothing stores filled with yuppie
goods, fast food stalls, cosmetics emporia,
electronic games shoppes, department store annex,
the usual. CAMERA ESTABLISHES then comes in rapidly
on the ABSOLUTELY ABRAXAS T-SHIRT SHOPPE, a mall
store that is clearly a head shop and t-shirt
emporium; as Nino, Gus and Arky enter.

19   INT. ABRAXAS SHOPPE — FULL SHOT

As Gus takes the two browsing customers by the arm,
and with his simian bulk chivvies them to the door,
and ejects them. He turns a card hanging on the
front door to read CLOSED, and then stands with his
back to the door, arms folded, as Arky and Nino
proceed into the small shop.
                                        (CONTINUED:)

19   CONTINUED:

A woman in her late 40s, chewing gum, more than
passingly plump, wearing her hair in a technicolor
coiffure with a thick clump pulled up at a 45 degree
ponytail at the side, wearing a Garfield t-shirt
(or similar "cute" item), comes toward them. This
is CASSANDRA FISHBEIN, and she is clearly a refugee
from the Sixties. Her tie-dyed billowy skirt says
so. She isn't happy about their behavior.

20   WITH CASSANDRA

As she storms toward them in a medium-high dudgeon.

> CASSANDRA
> Hey, dude, what's the damn idea?

> NINO
> (suave)
> You are the impressive Cassandra
> Fishbein, adept trafficker in the
> noxious black arts?

> CASSANDRA
> T-shirts. I sell t-shirts and
> equipment for the exotic smoker.

> NINO
> Ms. Fishbein, my name is Nino
> Lancaster. I'm a business associate
> of Mr. Lochner here. He advises me
> you served as go-between, amanuensis,
> *amicus curiae* for him and a...er...
> personage named Volkerps.

(CONTINUED:)

20   CONTINUED:

                    CASSANDRA
          I'm callin' a cop.

                      NINO
          Probably not. Very likely in my
          employ, in any case.
                    (beat)
          I ask your assistance voluntarily.
          Or perhaps I could ask my employee...
               (nods toward the giant, Gus)
          ...Mr. Chaucer, to drop you into
          the atrium of this excellent mall.

                    CASSANDRA
          Hey, who the hell *are* you? I'm
          just a poor woman tryin' to make a
          honest buck in a world of yuppies
          hot for Adidas and VCRs.

                      NINO
               (equally distraught)
          Say no more, dear lady. I, too, a
          humble merchant who each day takes
          his place in the marketplace and
          suffers the vicissitudes of a
          debased clientele. I understand
          your predicament.

                    CASSANDRA
          Then you'll unnerstand why, for
          the good of business, I urge you
          to piss off.

                              (CONTINUED:)

20 CONTINUED:—2

> **NINO**
> Ah yes. Business.
>> (beat)
> Have you ever considered the range
> of unexpected tragedies that could
> befall an unwary shopkeeper whose
> insurance premiums, no matter how
> exorbitant, would not *begin* to
> cover the mysterious spraying of
> DDT all over her goods, or the
> inconvenience resulting from perhaps
> all of a sudden the truckers who
> schlep said wares from the
> distributors decide they've lost
> the bills of lading and said goods
> wind up in Beirut, or the constituted
> authorities suddenly get it into
> their vengeful heads to toss the
> businesswoman's apartment for illegal
> and noxious substances which would,
> I'm sure, result in said authorities
> discovering nickel bags of such
> vegetation and powders stuck down
> in the pillows of a sofa?
>> (beat)
> Pardon my complex syntax, but I
> imagine you get my drift.

> **CASSANDRA**
>> (back pedals)
> Okay, okay, get off my case!

(CONTINUED:)

20 CONTINUED:—3

                    CASSANDRA (CONT'D.)
                    (beat, scared)
          Yeah, I set it up for this guy.
          But I'm just a sort of clearing-
          house for a select few demons and
          soul-traders of a very high quality.
                    (beat)
          There's this quota of souls they
          have to make each year, just to
          stay in good with the boss; and I'm
          just sort of a canvasser, a scout,
          to steer the likely prospects.

                         NINO
          Excellent.
               (beat, as he takes out money)
          Here. This will provide the fiduciary
          impetus for you to set up a meeting
          with Mr. Volkerps. For us.

                       CASSANDRA
                      (horrified)
          When?

                         NINO
          Now.

                       CASSANDRA
                    (more horrified)
          Where?

                         NINO
          Here.

     Cassandra is now blithering. Her eyeballs seem to
     want to jump out of her head.
                                        (CONTINUED:)

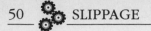

20 CONTINUED:—4

> #### CASSANDRA
> You're outta your mind! I can't do
> that! This Volkerps has a very
> ugly personality. It'd think I'd
> turned him.

> #### NINO
> (over his shoulder)
> Mr. Chaucer, would you like another
> arm for your collection?

Gus starts toward Cassandra. She yowls and makes a
stopping motion with her hands against the air.

> #### CASSANDRA
> I'll lose my deal with him and the
> whole netherworld...you trying to
> get me snuffed?

> #### NINO
> Have you ever considered how cold
> and uncomfortable it is being hung
> upside-down on a meat hook in a
> freezer?

> #### CASSANDRA
> You sure you're not related to this
> demon?

Nino smiles and pats her cheek as we:

                                        DISSOLVE TO:

21 SAME SCENE — LATER — FULL SHOT

Blinds have been pulled across the front of the
shop. A pentagram has been drawn on the floor in
blue chalk, and candles have been lit. Cassandra
stands, safely protected from demons, in the center
of the design, as the other three hug the walls.

                    CASSANDRA
                   (chants)
          By all the mages of Solomon's
          court, by the three-eyed moon of
          Ashtaroth...I call on thee,
          Volkerps, to come forth!

The cloud begins to form, the lightning and thunder
begin to flash and roll, and Volkerps appears as he
did in scene 2. He takes one look at Cassandra, and
the others, and roars.

                    VOLKERPS
                   (filter FX)
          I smell betrayal!

                    CASSANDRA
          No, honest to—

                    VOLKERPS
             (filter FX interrupts quickly)
          Don't say it, don't invoke; if I've
          told you once, I've told you a
          thousand times, don't *invoke*!

                    CASSANDRA
          They *made* me call you! Get'm, do
          it oh mighty Volkerps, waste them!

                                      (CONTINUED:)

21 CONTINUED:

Volkerps muses for a devilish moment, closing two
of his three blazing green eyes. He sighs, as if
having come to a conclusion, and opens his eyes.
There is a cunning expression on his awful face.

                    VOLKERPS
                 (to Cassandra)
          Ah...yes...just so, my dear and loyal
          Cassandra. I shrive myself for even
          doubting your ever-loyalty an instant.
          Shrive, I tell you! Shrive!
                    (beat)
          And you have deliciously surpassed
          your previous best efforts! These
          are indeed three diseased souls
          ripe with corrupt intent.

Cassandra preens, almost kittenish with pleasure at
the compliments. She blows him kisses.

                    CASSANDRA
          You are such a *mensch* to work for.

                    VOLKERPS
                 (jubilantly)
          The threshold of Hell Itself will
          resonate with a fearful threnody at
          the arrival of these three, my dear
          Cassandra. But...
                    (beat)
          Come stand close beside me, so you
          won't risk fractures and bodily
          harm from flying shards of bone or
          projectile heart muscle when I zap
          them.

                              (CONTINUED:)

21 CONTINUED:—2

His smile is so unctuous, and his gesture so
smoothly compelling, that Cassandra steps across
the blue chalk line of the protective pentacle.

21A CLOSEUP - RAPID INTERCUT

On CASSANDRA'S open-toed sandaled FOOT as it steps
across the runic blue chalk line.

                                        CUT BACK TO:

21B SAME AS 21 - A MOMENT LATER

                    CASSANDRA
                 (coming closer)
        Here I am, honey. Now whack'em
        good!

                    VOLKERPS
        First things first. The little
        rat-human...(points a claw at
        Arky)...he has a week..
                 (turns to her)
        ...but *you*...
                 (in a Cagneylike voice)
        I'm gonna give it to you, the way
        you give it to me brudder...

And with one taloned hand extended, he suddenly
aims a mean clawed finger at her; a sizzling
bolt of bright-red power erupts from his digit
and strikes her.

                    VOLKERPS
                 (viciously)
        Fry, bitch!
                                        (CONTINUED:)

21B CONTINUED:

There is a bright FLASH OF UNBEARABLE LIGHT that
blots the frame for a moment and then:

22   ANOTHER ANGLE — FAVORING PENTAGRAM & NINO

All that remains of Cassandra Fishbein is a neat pile
of smoking pearly gray ash. And one of her sandals.
A twist of smoke ascends to the ceiling as we:

                                              CUT TO:

23   SERIES OF INTERCUTS - CLOSEUPS
thru
26   On Nino, Arky and Gus Chaucer as each bugs his
      eyeballs, gives a shriek of horror and we:

                                              CUT TO:

27   FROM VOLKERPS — HIGH SHOT DOWN ON THE THREE MEN

As he smiles a ghastly smile, and looks at them
meaningfully.

                         VOLKERPS
                        (charming)
            Next?

The three scream and as they take the first fast
step bolting toward the door of the shoppe we:

                              SMASH-CUT TO BLACK
                              and
                              OUT.

                    END ACT ONE

ACT TWO

FADE IN:

28 EXT. ALLEY — SAME AS SCENE 1 — NIGHT (SHOOT DAY FOR
NIGHT)

As Arky and Gus come running down the alley toward
Nino's warehouse. They are running like mad things.
Literally, the demons of hell are on their heels!
CAMERA HOLDS as they RUN INTO F.G. and WHIP-PANS to
FOLLOW THEM as they race past. (Make sure we see
that) Nino is not with them. CAMERA COMES IN
CLOSER as they reach the door of the warehouse that
Arky smashed in Scene 4. It has been hastily
repaired with boards nailed across to prevent
entrance. Gus hits it with a crackback block,
shattering the boards off their nails as we:

CUT TO:

29 INT. WAREHOUSE — FULL SHOT

On Arky and Gus as they madly pile crates against
the door, or what's left of it. They are moving so
fast, they're a blur. Now, running across the
length of the warehouse comes Hazel, with Bork in
her wake. He carries a hammer, as if he'd just
gotten through repairing what they've smashed again.
Gus and Arky pay no attention to the newcomers.

                    BORK
          Hey you guys, I just finished
          repairin' that door!

                    ARKY
          Help! Help us! Don't just stand
          there...pile...pile!
                              (CONTINUED:)

29 CONTINUED:

                         HAZEL
                        (alarmed)
            What happened? Where's Nino?!

Gus is now performing herculean feats, lifting
great boxes and stacking, stacking, stacking! He's
like a dog burying a bone.

                          ARKY
                        (hysterical)
            I dunno, he's dead, he's *gotta* be
            dead! Volkerps came, big...he was
            big...and right there...he came
            straight from hell, he still
            stunk'a rotten eggs...

30 WITH HAZEL

As she grabs Arky. He's a little guy, and she's a
strong woman. She manhandles him around and she's
furious.

                         HAZEL
            You left him!?! You ran?!

                          ARKY
                        (whimpers)
            I ran...*he* ran...
                    (indicating Gus)
            ...we ran like hell. That thing
            just fricasee'd the chubby lady.
            Hit 'er with some kinda laser, made
            her into ashes like an old cigar!
            You could hear the fat sizzlin'
            like a pan'a sausages!

                                        (CONTINUED:)

30   CONTINUED:

                        HAZEL
        Ohmigod, Nino! *Neeeeeeno!*

Now *she's* hysterical. This goes on for a second or
two, then she pulls herself together very quickly.

                     HAZEL (CONTD.)
                   (cool, businesslike)
        All right. That means we have to
        consolidate our interests, get the
        accounts transferred into the
        corporate name, begin amortizing
        the rolling stock, make sure none
        of the boys try to take over the
        territory...

                        ARKY
                      (screams)
        Are you crazy? That thing is gonna
        fry us and eat us! It's *coming!*

Gus is still lifting, stacking, shoving, lifting,
stacking! There is suddenly a BANGING ON THE DOOR.
Everyone stops. They stare in horror at the pile
of crates. Frozen, they wait. The BANGING again.
Gus and Bork and Arky hide behind Hazel. She
hesitates a moment, then takes a step toward the
stack hiding the door and speaks softly:

                        HAZEL
        Wh-who's there?

                     NINO O.S.
                      (muffled)
        Nino. Open up.

                                        (CONTINUED:)

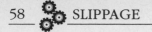
30 CONTINUED:—2

> **ARKY**
> (loud)
> You alone?

> **NINO O.S.**
> (muffled)
> I said: open the door. *Now!*

Bork and Gus rush INTO FRAME, pull stacks of crates
away from the door as if they were empty (which
they are). The shattered portal is revealed, it
opens, and in comes Nino Lancaster.

31 ON NINO

Half his elegant clothing is burned off, still
smoking. One bare leg with sock and shoe, burned
pants off at the thigh. Half a Savile Row jacket.
Soot smudges all over his face, his hair disheveled
and now sporting a thick pure-white swath through
the pompadour. He comes in, brushing himself off,
bits of charred cloth falling away like dandruff.
He moves past them as they begin babbling. CAMERA
WITH Nino as he strides back toward the office, the
others in tow, all speaking at once:

> **HAZEL ARKY GUS BORK**
> (all speaking simultaneously)
> What happened? How did you get
> away? Is that thing behind you?
> Are you hurt? Can you walk? Is
> your body burned? How did you get
> here? Where's Volkerps? Are we
> gonna die? How ya feelin', Mr.
> Lancaster? Wouldja like a glass of
> orange juice, boss? Nino, honey, I
> thought you were dead!

32   INT. OFFICE — FULL SHOT

As Nino enters, trailing the others. He opens a
filing cabinet as they troop in behind him, riffles
through the Pendaflex hanging files to "S", and
takes out a new, freshly ironed shirt. He strips
off his jacket and shirt as he speaks:

> **NINO**
> This will be a bit more difficult
> than I thought.

> **ARKY**
> (gibbering)
> I'm doomed! I'm fricasee! If *you*
> can't take 'im, what chance've *I*
> got?

> **NINO**
> (snaps)
> I didn't say it was impossible. I
> said it would be a little more
> difficult than at first I thought.

> **ARKY**
> (in wonderment)
> But how did you get away? He was
> gonna fry our ass-paragus! How'd
> you get outta there?

> **NINO**
> (smiles, obtusely)
> I dazzled him with fancy footwork.

They stare in wonderment. Nino is utterly
businesslike now. He has on a clean shirt and he
starts giving orders.

                                        (CONTINUED:)

32 CONTINUED:

> ### NINO (CONT'D)
> Okay. Let's get to it.
>> (beat)
>
> Gus, Bork: go see Nuñcio over at
> the docks. Have him talk to our
> people at the ship-fitting operation.
> Get me a hundred gallons of lead
> paint...

> ### GUS
>> (dumb)
>
> What color, boss?

> ### NINO
> Doesn't matter.

> ### GUS
>> (persists dumb)
>
> Well, they got it in battleship
> gray, y'know; that's the standard
> color...but we could maybe ask 'im
> to mix a special batch in some nice
> pastel...

> ### NINO
>> (snarls)
>
> *Quiet!* I don't care what color.
> Get gray, get anything, but get me
> a hundred gallons with the highest
> lead content they can find.
>> [MORE]

(CONTINUED:)

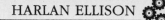

32 CONTINUED:—2

> **NINO (CONT'D)**
> (beat)
> Then spray the inside of this office.
> Ceiling, floor, walls, window, all of
> it. Every inch in here. Don't miss
> a corner. Then do it all over again.
> Then do it again. And when you're
> all done...do it ten times more.
> Hazel...you'll oversee the job?

> **HAZEL**
> Yes, of course, Nino. But...

He holds up a hand to stop her.

> **NINO**
> While they're getting the paint,
> book two first class flights on Air
> France to Switzerland. First
> flight you can get to Berne.
> (beat)
> My name, and Arky Lochner.

> **ARKY**
> (scared)
> Me?!? Why me? Why do *I* gotta fly
> to Switzerland?

> **NINO**
> (flatly)
> Would you rather stay here alone
> for the rest of the week?

> **ARKY**
> Will I need my skis?

CUT TO:

33   CONCORDE IN FLIGHT (MEASURE OR STOCK)

The great plane speeding in one long shot, right to
left in frame as we

                                    DISSOLVE TO:

34   INT. BANK VAULT — ARKY AND NINO

SPECIFY CORNER SET. Dressed to look like numbered
account vault in a bank. Painted flats will suffice.
Zinc-tiled table angled toward corner. On the table
is a safety deposit box, being opened by Nino as Arky
looks on in awe. Nino winnows through dozens of
stacks of currency, and takes out a small, rectangular
box, all set about with intricate arcane carvings.

                    ARKY
          This's what we came all the way to
          Berne to get?

Nino nods, opening the box by pressing here and
there on its surfaces in a measured pattern. He
opens it so we cannot see what's in it, looks
inside, smiles.

                    ARKY
                (disbelieving)
          This's gonna save me?

                    NINO
                (smoothly)
          I'm not at the pinnacle of my
          profession for nothing, Arky.
                    (beat)
          Let's go home. Day after tomorrow,
          your week is up.

                                    DISSOLVE TO:

35 CONCORDE IN FLIGHT (MEASURE OR STOCK)

The Concorde going in the opposite direction from
Scene 33, left to right in frame as we

DISSOLVE THRU TO:

36 INT. WAREHOUSE OFFICE — NIGHT — ESTABLISHING

Same room as previously, but now painted a chilly
lead-silver shade. All the windows have been
painted over except for a silver dollar-sized peephole in the window facing into the warehouse
proper. Floor and walls and ceiling are all
uniformly gray lead. The desk has been cleared.
Alone on the desk is the carved box from the Swiss
vault. Arky, Nino, Hazel and the two pistoleros
stand in the room.

                    NINO
                (checks watch)
          We have to wait till midnight.
          He'll come at midnight.
                    (beat)
          Anybody wants to go...do it now.

Gus and Bork smile, wave, and exit hastily. Arky
moves to join them.

                NINO (CONT'D.)
                (hard and flat)
          Not you, Arky.

He looks at Hazel. She stares back with adoration.

                    HAZEL
          Here's lookin' at *you*, kid.

                              (CONTINUED:)

36 CONTINUED:

He walks to her, takes her ravenously beautiful face in his hands and kisses her quickly. They smile at each other, as Arky sinks into a chair, head in hands, moaning.

                            INTERCUT:

37 CU DIGITAL CLOCK

It reads 10:17. Then almost too rapidly to note, it reads 10:43, 11:06, 11:50. The counters have flipped so fast the blood-red digits seem a blur and we:

                            CUT BACK TO:

38 INT. WAREHOUSE — FULL SHOT

HIGH SHOT down on Nino Lancaster, standing alone in the center of a cleared aisle. We can see that the area has been emptied to give him a clear run back to the rear of the crate-filled warehouse, right back to the gray-windowed office, where the door stands open, as if waiting. With SHOWDOWN MUSIC (á la an Italian Western high noon scene) that rises, CAMERA COMES DOWN SMOOTHLY to circle Nino like a lone gunslinger waiting for the bad guys. He wears a clean shirt open at the neck, good slacks, and sneakers for running. CAMERA CIRCLES HIM as we

                            CUT TO:

39 INT. OFFICE — ON ARKY & HAZEL

as one peers out the door, the other peeps through the one unpainted circle in the window. They watch Nino out there all alone. Suddenly, there is a sizzle of lightning.

                            CUT BACK TO:

40   SAME AS 38 — ON NINO

As the demon cloud begins to form in the air above
him. Thunder, lightning, the sound of nails being
ripped from wood, the scraping of fingernails on a
blackboard. The heralds of Volkerps's coming.
Then, the demon takes form in the cloud, meaner
than before, with scars on his body that are quite
evident, as though he's been in a bad fight.

                    VOLKERPS,
               (sees Nino, thunders)
          You again? I thought you'd had
          enough!

                      NINO
                    (cool)
          I'll give you one chance. Cancel
          the contract with Arky, give him
          about a million dollars to make up
          for what he lost at the track, go
          slime back to your pit...and I
          won't kick the crap out of you.

Volkerps goes crazy. What insolence! He spits
green slime. His horns tremble. His forked tongue
lashes his chest. He puffs up like a bellows and
heaves a rasping breath that sounds like metal
dragged across concrete. He aims a bolt of fire at
Nino like the one that fried Cassandra Fishbein.

Nino adeptly sidesteps, like a torero in the arena,
letting the bolt sail past to explode and burn a
crate. Then, with a laugh, he turns and runs away
from Volkerps, back toward the office. In the b.g.
Hazel and Arky are screaming their warnings.

41 INT. OFFICE — SHOOT THROUGH OPEN DOOR

As Nino comes running down the length of that
long aisle, the cloud boiling after him, lightning
and thunder filling the warehouse, that HEROIC
CHASE MUSIC rushing over us. This shot can be in
perspective to show us the carved box large in
the f.g.

Nino hits the doorway, rushes through, and we HOLD
DOORWAY for a second as the cloud abruptly PUFFS
OUT OF EXISTENCE. Volkerps is gone out there.

Then, in smaller form, to accommodate the confines
of the office, the shape of Volkerps solidifies
inside the office. Nino is around the desk instantly.
There is the SOUND of hurricane winds.

> **NINO**
> (yells)
> Hazel...*now!*

And Hazel, who has been behind the open door, slams
it fast and hard.

> **NINO**
> (yells)
> Arky...the patch!

And Arky, who has been at the peephole, slaps a
gray lead-painted patch with stickum over the hole.
Now the CAMERA CIRCLES showing us all four of them
inside a small room that is totally, unbrokenly
gray with lead coating. Trapped!

42 ON NINO

As he throws open the lid of the carved box from
Berne. We can see that the interior of the box and
lid are the same gray lead-lined surface as the
office. Nino yanks something resting on the velvet
lining of the box. He keeps it hidden in his hand.

43 FAVORING VOLKERPS

Who is so large that he almost touches the ceiling.
He raises a muscled arm to sweep Nino's head off,
and Nino makes a mystical pass with his hands,
sweeping and circling and intricate as a karate
series, one fist closed over whatever was in the
box. Volkerps shrinks a little and is thrown back
against a wall as if he's taken a punch. His
hideous snout begins to bleed. With childlike
amazement he puts a finger to his nose, examines
the blood.

>   **VOLKERPS**
>   (childlike, amazed)
>   I'm bleeding!
>   (awed)
>   I'm actually losing pus and ichor
>   (pronounced eyecore) and lovely
>   slime!

He rages, trying to swell to full size again, having
been magically reduced; and he puffs his chest as
if to fry Nino with a pointed claw, and Nino
makes another intricate gesture, still holding
the hidden object.

>   [MORE]

(CONTINUED:)

43 CONTINUED:

As he makes the pass, one of Volkerp's horns snaps and breaks off, and where it hits the lead-painted floor it causes sparks.

Then in rapid succession, another pass and the demon suddenly has a big black eye, the king of all shiners. We see fear on the demon's face, and he turns to run, but he can't get out. He bashes the door again and again, hits the walls, turns and turns, rolling along the walls, Hazel and Arky ducking and dodging, trying to stay out of his way, but all his pummelling cannot break him out. We realize the lead lining has him ensnared. He rages and roars, rushing about the office, knocking over chairs, shattering the desk, throwing filing cabinets.

44 2-SHOT

VOLKERPS stops and turns to face Nino. Nino now has a look on his cultured face we haven't seen before. He is a wolf with his prey trapped in a cave. His lips are skinned back over his teeth, and his eyes burn.

                    NINO
               (mean, hard)
        You lousy twerp...enough is enough!

And he begins an incantation, intoning in a VOICE that is Nino's, but more. It is as if he were in the center of the earth, and his voice coming from a volcano. This is a Nino with powers we've never suspected:
                    [MORE]

                                    (CONTINUED:)

44 CONTINUED:

> ### NINO (CONT'D)
> (enchanting)
> Submit, submit, submit. I order you
> by the power of Asmodeus (pronounced:
> Ass-moe-*dee*-us), Belphegor (*Bell*-feh-gore),
> Belial (*Bay*-lee-ahl) and the toad of
> death to suppress thyself! Submerge,
> submit, suppress...get your miserable
> ugly backside into the box, you
> twerp, you lousy punk!

And he now—with a wide, dramatic gesture—throws up
a flat palm and, nestled in that hand, is a blood-
red, glowing, many-faceted crystal like a sacred
idol's eye. And from that jewel comes a blinding
light. The light bathes the demon, who shrieks
and begins to shrink within its glow. (NOTE: or
whatever substitute technique you care to devise
for an adequate inexpensive effect.) The light
takes him, fills the frame, and we HEAR the rushing
of WINDS as they are sucked into a Black Hole.
LIGHT FILLS FRAME.

45 ANOTHER ANGLE

As silence falls in the office. The box stands
open, and a bright light pours out of it. Hazel
and Arky crawl out from under the halves of the
shattered desk. They stand and look at Nino, who
is perspiring. His shirt is soaked. His hair is
mussed, the white streak more prominent.

They look at him in wonder. CLOSEUPS if desired. He
looks back at them, smiles gently, a bit embarrassed.

(CONTINUED:)

45   CONTINUED:

>   **NINO**
>   (humbly)
>   I've had some, uh, small experience
>   in these matters.

>   **ARKY**
>   (awed)
>   Is that how you got away from him
>   at the mall?

>   **NINO**
>   (nods, shrugs)
>   He got me a little, but he couldn't
>   get me very much.

Now we hear a TINY PIPING VOICE like David Hedison
as The Fly. They go to the box as CAMERA COMES IN
BEHIND AND OVER THEM and their heads frame the box
in the center of the frame as we look down. BLUE
SCREEN inside lead-lined box shows us a teeny tiny
Volkerps in there.

>   CUT TO:

46   INT. MAGIC BOX — CLOSE

Volkerps in the box, looking up at the huge face of
Nino Lancaster peering down at him. Volkerps glows
a bit, as if he's ensorceled, and trapped. He is
jumping up and down, screaming, lashing the walls of
the box with his tail and talons.

>   **VOLKERPS**
>   (in a squeaky, diminished voice)
>   I'll get you, I'll rend you, I'll
>   savage you, shred you, suck your
>   bones dry as death!

>   (CONTINUED:)

46   CONTINUED:

Nino smiles, and when he speaks, his VOICE IS HUGE:

> **NINO**
> (amplified)
> Listen, punk...you think you're the
> first slug from Hell, all puffed up
> with hot air, who ever tried to
> muscle in on my operation?
> (beat)
> If you're wondering how I beat you,
> look around in there. You're small
> potatoes!

And CAMERA WITH VOLKERPS as he turns to look behind
him and we see a larger (but nonetheless shrunken)
demon, even more horrific than Volkerps, but bearing
a striking family resemblance. Amazed, he stammers:

> **VOLKERPS**
> Poppa? Poppa, what are *you* doing
> in here?

The other DEMON comes over and slaps his son in the
mush.

> **PAPA DEMON**
> (pissed off)
> You idiot! I knew I shouldn't
> leave the family business in your
> inept claws!

Volkerps starts to cry as Poppa Demon glowers and we:

CUT TO:

47 SAME AS 45 — OUTSIDE BOX

As Nino replaces the crystal and closes the box,
cutting off the light.

                         NINO
              Like father, like son.

Hazel hugs him, covers him with kisses. Arky is
dancing around the room, comes and hugs them both,
slobbers over Nino, his little weasel face
rapturous with relief.

                         ARKY
                      (jubilant)
              You *saved* me! You *saved* me!

Arky is all over Nino, who now takes him by the
shoulders and holds him away at arms-length.
CAMERA IN on Nino as he smiles a particularly nasty
smile and says:

                         NINO
                    (with power)
              Yeah, I saved you. Now all you've
              got to do is make a deal with *me*.
                      (beat)
              Business, Arky, is strictly business.

HOLD on Arky's horrified expression, Nino's
overwhelmingly evil expression for a long beat
as NARRATION BEGINS OVER:
                        [MORE]

                                        (CONTINUED:)

47   CONTINUED:

> **NARRATOR**
> (Over)
> Oh, Arky, Arky, poor Mr. Lochner.
> (beat)
> There is an old, old, *very old* saying:
> (beat)
> Making a deal with a demon is
> seriously crazy. But making a deal
> with the **master** of demons...well
> ...that's crazy as a soup sandwich.

And as preceding NARRATION is HEARD OVER, CAMERA IN
AND DOWN to FULL CLOSE SHOT on Nino's hand and the
carved box on the table. Nino is idly drumming his
fingers on the box, lightly and absently, as
NARRATION CONCLUDES, and just before the phrase
"soup sandwich" the brilliant light suddenly escapes
from that thin line between lid and body of box,
like a halation around the moon, light rays fan out
around Nino's fingers and we:

> FADE TO BLACK
> and
> FADE OUT

THE END

Darkness Upon The Face of The Deep

Morning of the day after All Hallow's Eve dawned with a brightness that cast orange and rose light over the mountain of Hindustan. Hysteria seemed to have possessed the birds: they rose in a canopy, spreading their great patchwork wings, proclaiming in a minor key another year of safety.

In the valley shadowed beneath the grandfather mountain could be heard the sound of nails being prised from the heavy slats used to board up the villagers' windows. And the laugh of the first adventurous child as he held his nose and yanked off the wreath of malodorous henbane protecting a front door. The fountain had been unplugged and its music rose toward the black thorn of the escarpment. The nilgai, sheep, and goats had been chivvied together in the shallow caves where they had been secreted; and now the shepherd girls drove them up the ramps from underground. Fresh flowers were laid on the pedestals of the thirty-two idols circling the rustic plaza.

When the mountain of Hindustan creaked, and then rumbled, the villagers paused in their activities, relief drained from their faces, and they turned to stare up at the dark spire.

Slowly, then more rapidly, the face of the mountain showed a fissure. The rent widened and very softly from within the crevice a sooty shadow began to seep out. It could not be said to shine—it was an absence of illumination—but it spilled out into the air and scintillated, neither smoke nor fog.

The mountain split.

The villagers had held silent for longer than might have been prudent, but when the shapes began soaring out of the great black wound, rising in a cloud to throw a blade-shaped shadow across the sun, a covey of snakelike, winged blood bats, they knew they had been falsely lulled into thinking danger had passed. One of the gods had lied, or the seer had miscalculated the year.

Then they screamed, the music died, and they rushed to replace the boards across their windows.

In the Deccan, on the plateau that lies between what were known as the Narbada and Kristna rivers, some of the oldest men and only three of the very oldest women remember the stories passed down through many generations, of the village of Antagarh. Not the tiny village of that name to be found on maps of the present day, but the original Antagarh, where the sigil of even more ancient days had been hidden. Where all in a morning the darkness descended, and feasted, and finally lifted, leaving only one child.

This little boy, possessing sight only in his left eye, had been lost on the face of the mountain (it is said), and thus escaped the fate that befell his village. (It is said.)

No mother, no father, no home waiting at his return later that day (for Antagarh no longer existed; just a plain of pumice on which nothing grew for three hundred years; no blade of grass, no weed, no shrub; where no line of dawn sunlight passed again). The child crawled through the gray dust, and saw a cloud of black wings rising away from the valley, snake bat shapes climbing toward the staring idiot's eye of the sun.

Alone, he lay in the wasteland and watched as his past disappeared. His future: sailing toward him borne on the wind that blows forever between the stars, the wind that carries ancient and encoded messages of indecipherable night.

On rare, perfect nights when the stars had swung into extraordinary alignments unnoticed by dozing humanity, the glyph would slowly begin to glow. As if breathing deeply with the light from stellar lamps, the engraved stone seal would become lambent, radiating warmth through its deep orange surface. The signs stood out perfectly, barely smoothed by erosion: circles, crescents, hooks, human heads, hands, and designs that were neither animal nor human. A coherent script utterly beyond understanding, giving itself up to no known mechanical system of decipherment. The radiance stronger as night deepened.

They were hiding in the ruins of the sphinx gate at Alaja Hüyük, waiting for the Syrian mercenary in the employ of the Israeli MOSSAD, who was coming with supplies from Damascus to guide them to Mamoula, when they perceived the light of the glyph. They held it and marveled, somewhat fearful, but now certain that they were onto something significant.

Bobby Shafka said, "Is it warm?"

Loder shook his head. "Not at all." He passed it over and Shafka held it in his palm, then placed his other hand over it. He nodded agreement.

The glyph grew brighter. "It's like that little mirror you use to keep your pipe lit," Shafka said.

Dennis Loder drew deeply at the sandblast briar. Sweet silver smoke trailed up against the cool night. He reached into one of the many pockets of the sleeveless thermal vest and took out the pipe mirror. It was called a Micro-Sun, and it was a device so simple, yet so extraordinary, that it made one think it was some incredibly ancient device rediscovered in modern times. A disc the size of a half dollar, it was only a concave, highly-burnished gold circle set into plastic. But when held over the dying dottle in the heel of the bowl, it reflected and concentrated the pipe's own heat back into the bowl and renewed the burn. Loder laid it atop the mouth of the briar and took three short puffs. The smoke thickened.

"No, not exactly like it," he said. But he knew what Bobby meant: both of the devices seemed magical. Then he raised a hand to stop conversation. "Is that the man?"

"I didn't hear anything," Shafka said, covering the glyph so its light would not pool out from them. They sat with their backs to the cooling stones and listened. "Did you hear something?"

Loder waited a moment, listening; then he relaxed again. "I guess not. But he should have come already, don't you think?"

Shafka smiled, "This really isn't your line of work, is it?"

"I told you that when you conned me into coming."

"Little late for regrets, don't you think?"

"Dead is what we can get if any of the brotherhood finds us. I'm not like you; I'm a shard digger, a pencil pusher. You've been trying to get me in trouble for thirty years. I was doing pretty good at resisting your blandishments..."

"Until I promised you fame and fortune?"

"Until you preyed on my childhood weakness for movies about sunken treasure and lost cities."

They had been friends all their lives, had grown up three houses apart on the same street, Dunster Road in York, Pennsylvania. Dennis had been the milder of the pair, bookish and shy, tall for his age at any age, and determined to become an archaeologist; Bobby Shafka had gotten into trouble the first time (as best as Dennis could remember) in grade school: he had somehow, impossibly, manhandled a three hundred pound rotary mower buggy up four flights of stairs from the groundskeeper's shed, to the roof of the school building, worked it to the edge, and precariously balanced it there, slowly tipping back and forth over oblivion. The secret dream he had shared only with his best pal, Dennis Loder, was to become the captain of a tramp steamer, plying dark and dangerous waters, like Wolf Larsen in the Jack London novel.

Dennis had gotten his degree at Syracuse University, his master's at Cambridge; he had worked digs in Iraq—including Nippur, Nimrud, Tell al Rimah and Choga Mami—and in 1980 had assisted on the site at Tell Brak, here in Syria; but he had been the less adventurous of the pals, and he had gone on staff at the National Geographic Society magazine.

Bobby Shafka had conned and gladhanded his way into a scholarship at Wharton, made a few contacts, dropped out after a year and a half, signed on as a flack for the pulpwood industry, working out of their Manhattan association offices, made a few contacts, moved up to a middle-management position with the largest lithographing conglomerate on the East Coast, made a few contacts, went into partnership with a triad of young attorneys who had opened a hot private club in TriBeCa, made a few contacts, and cut a deal for time served and testimony with the D.A.'s office when the triad was busted holding two and a half million street-value crystal meth and Bangkok heroin.

Bobby had made no serviceable contacts in a holding cell for sixteen weeks, and now he was back at starters, hustling a main chance. He was under contract to *The National Enquirer* to unearth a four-thousand-year-old Hittite tomb in Mamoula, based entirely on his ability to con and gladhand the expatriate Aussie associate editor...and his possession of the authenticated glyph. Which he had come to hold...having made a few contacts.

And he had conned his best friend Dennis Loder into coming with him, to a country that had excelled for more than twenty years in the spawning of terrorists pledged to killing every American they could set eyes on. It hadn't been easy; but when Bobby promised to give Dennis the first publication rights for *National Geographic,* and let him have the glyph studied, and showed him the irrefutable proof that the glyph had been turned up in 1872 with the discovery of the Hamah Stones of the Hittites (and had been kept secret by Subhi Pasha, known in Europe as Subhi Bey before his appointment to Damascus), Dennis had been seduced by the towering ghosts of Schlicmann, Rawlinson, Belzoni, Carter and Lord Carnarvon— and Saturday afternoon movies—and he had joined with his dangerous old pal on their first adventure since the old neighborhood.

Curiously enough, it had not been Loder's association with the Geographic Society that had effected the impossible task of smuggling two Americans into forbidden lands. It had been the *Enquirer's* far-flung network of snitches, *paparazzi,* palace servants, ex-CIA agents, mercenaries, and turncoats-for-hire that had put together the route. They had come in by way of Dubai and Bahrain, across the neutral zone between Saudi Arabia and Iraq, and north-west across the desolate Al-Ha-Arah—it had taken six weeks, done so circuitously—to the penultimate drop-off at Alaja Hüyük where they would be met tonight by the man they had heard called Yaffa Al-Mansur. (He had also been referred to, during their journey, as Ibrahim ibn Abd-an-Nasr, Abu Rumaneh, Ibrahim At-Turki, Bashar Al-Sherrif, Homa Baktiari, and even Shain, though Bobby swore when he had first been recommended to them by the Aussie associate editor, he had called him Abdullah).

But Yaffa Al-Mansur was now a full day late. They had been hiding in the ancient stones through the blistering heat since dawn, waiting. And now it was night, and they were alone; and the engraved stone seal that had brought them half across the world to find an impossible secret had begun to glow.

Bobby opened his hand and the light illuminated the ground around them. Loder gestured with the stem of his pipe. "This is something we didn't count on."

"I suppose I should be freaked," Shafka said. "But it's kind of, I don't know, kind of thrilling. Know what I mean?"

Loder chuckled. "Should make one superlative headline for that rag of yours: *Ancient Aliens Leave Deadly Laser Stone!* If you can find some woman who'll swear she was impregnated by the alien who left it, and she's discovered by amniocentesis that she's going to give birth to a baby with two heads that look like James Dean and Elvis Presley, you'll never have to work another day in your life."

Bobby made a rueful face. "From your lips to the ears of whatever gods are engraved on this stone. I'm so broke I couldn't buy hairpins for a goldfish."

"*If* the tomb is there; and *if* it's 2000-1300 B.C.E.; and *if* those gods are still around and can hear us, try praying to Karhuha, Sarku, and the goddess Küpapa. Even the Phoenicians held them in high regard." And he intoned:

> *Great old Hittites left this here,*
> *How long ago is still unknown.*
> *The world is breathless, that is clear.*
> *There is nothing like the lion stone!*

Bobby said, "And that is what...?"

"From the lion stone at Karatepe. We don't know as much as we need to know about the Hittites. That's why I'm with you."

"Sitting in the dirt in the middle of the Moslem brotherhood, waiting for a man possibly named Yaffa..."

"Or Abu, or Abdullah, or Bashar, or Shain..."

Bobby picked up the chant. "Or Manny, Moe, or Jack."

Loder revived the glow in his pipe with the little golden disc and said, "Do you know what 'Syria' means?" Bobby shook his head. "Trick question," Dennis said. "Uncertain origin. No one knows what it means. There was a country named *Suri* in Asia Minor, mentioned in Mesopotamian cuneiform script, about 4000 B.C.E. Not likely it's the Greek abbreviation of *Assyria.* We find this tomb that probably doesn't exist and we might get our best clues."

Bobby clenched his hand around the glyph. "I'm about to shine it on with this thing. We could still be sitting here at the turn of the century. He's not coming."

The voice came from behind and above them. "Ah, but he is here, great gentlemen." They jerked with terror, and spun half around looking for the speaker who had come upon them without a sound.

He stood on the carved stones above them, and looked down, his face hidden in the shadows. He seemed taller and more formidable than some Arab double-agent. He seemed to be an emissary of the ancient gods whose names Loder had invoked.

But when he climbed down, they saw that he was just a man. An almost perfectly square man, nearly as wide as he was tall, with plump cheeks and a spotty beard. "Yaffa Al-Mansur, strictly as advertised," he said, pronouncing it *advertize-ed.*

"You're late," Bobby said, dropping his voice into the range he used for inept switchboard operators.

Yaffa waved away the comment, settled down between them and pulled a pop-lid tin of pudding from his djellabah. He produced a folding military-issue spoon, yanked off the lid of the pudding tin, and began eating. I have been snaking and moving, great gentlemen. Taking roads where no roads exist, ducking and dogging—"

"I think you mean 'dodging'," Loder said.

"...ah! Even so. And as a regrettable consequential, I confess to a fractional tardiness." He paused, spooned pudding into the foliage of his beard, then said: "And pray kindly tell me, great gentlemen, which among the multitude many is your favorite American blues guitarist?"

They stared at him. The stars shone like ice, the glyph lay in Bobby's hand brightly lit, the distant slicing of a jackal's cry echoed past them, and they stared.

"For my own good self," Yaffa said, "there was none more exalted than Blind Lemon Jefferson, though I now and yon feel that Son House was the nonpareil of Delta blues. And which of them whom you adore is your favorites, great sirs?"

Two hours later, after Yaffa had relieved himself and slept, they moved out. Toward Mamoula, that their guide called Ma'alula, 33°50′N, 36°33′E, where speaking neither Arabic nor Kurdish would be of any help. For in Mamoula, in the mountains, though they have lost the ability over the centuries to write it, the hidden residents speak the Aramaic of Jesus's time, precisely as the Christ spoke it. Toward Mamoula, carrying the light.

These were the direct descendants of the Hittite Empire that had ruled the Levant till the end of the Late Bronze Age. Craggy men naked beneath their djellabahs, their curved knives hanging by a thong across their chests and below their armpits; wearing the traditional skullcaps; sandals or hand-made boots according to their occupation. Dark eyes studying the two infidels and the intruder from some great city in the lowlands—Hamath, or even Damascus, of which they had heard. These were the blood of the Akhlamu, and the Aramaeans; sinew of Canaanites and the Aramaean neo-Hittites who crushed Shalmaneser III at the battle of Qarqar in 853 B.C.E.

They had driven through the night and late into the next day. There had been a Land Rover, fully stocked; even to several bottles of San Pellegrino and Vichy water. Yaffa had babbled happily of Lightnin' Hopkins and Lonnie Johnson, and of having worked briefly with Malkin of the MOSSAD, who had walked up to the fugitive Eichmann on Garibaldi Street in Buenos Aires in 1960 and said, *"Un momentito, señor."* Bobby Shafka had slept fitfully, unable to find a place for his spine; and Dennis sat silently (save when he was forced to make a sound in response to Yaffa's paeans in praise of Tampa Red's left hand). He smoked his pipe and held the glyph, and found himself sinking deeper and deeper into fear. This was more than stone. What had he been thinking of, to let Bobby suck him in this way?

The Rover hit a scree as they began their shallow ascent, and Loder was knocked against the door with enough force to jam his crazybone. He gave a yelp. Bobby slept on. Yaffa chuckled lightly, navigated through the sheet of coarse debris mantling the mountain slope, and spoke softly to his shotgun passenger.

"Will you be taking treasures from the land, Dr. Loder?"

There was none of the punkah-wallah "sahib" burlesque in his voice now. He spoke flawless English, with only the faintest trace of the Levant.

Loder looked at him. Yaffa's face was faintly lit by the dial glow from the dashboard. His features were sharper now; almost nothing left of the simpering pouch-cheeked caricature that had found them near the sphinx gate. "Perhaps," Loder answered. They rode in silence for a while, then Dennis said, "I was wondering when you'd divest yourself of the funnyface."

"A man must play many parts to survive, Doctor."

"And what will you do with these treasures…should they exist?"

"I'll take them back and use them to help decipher the history of the land, and the people who came and went here."

"You know Hafez al-Assad has decreed death on the spot for archaeological pilferage. This does not frighten you?"

"Yes, it frightens me."

"But not as much as you are frightened by that glowing stone seal in your vest pocket, do I perceive correctly?"

Loder placed the little golden pipe mirror atop the bowl and puffed the tobacco to a cheery glow.

"That has a marvelous bouquet," Yaffa said, watching the ruts that served as road, skirting the talus at the foot of a steep declivity. "Oriental tobaccos? Latakia; perique, perhaps?"

Loder shook his head. "One whiff of latakia and I'm on my back. No, it's just some Virginia, and a nice toasted cavendish. Why have you revealed yourself to me, and not to my partner?"

"Because I think you have been duped by friendship. I think that you regret this expedition, that you are a decent sort of man; and I know you are frightened."

"You saw the glyph glowing?"

"Yes. When I found you. I was above you, studying you, for many minutes before I declared myself."

"And you don't much care for Bobby, is that it?"

Yaffa shrugged. "He is like most men. He lives on the edge of the moment. He is like the dust. It lies a while, then is blown away."

"He's my friend. We grew up together. I hope whoever hired you to guide us can count on your fidelity to both of us. We're in your hands, you know."

Yaffa turned his head for a moment. He looked at Loder, and said, "Yes, I know that. And we are all three in the hands of Allah."

"Does Allah have any knowledge of this stone seal? Some random bit of minutiae that might make our little journey safer and more productive?"

The Syrian brought the Land Rover to a slow, smooth stop. He turned in his seat and stared at Loder. "I was paid to come and meet you, to take you to Ma'alula where, I was told, you will put to advantage some information as to the location of a very old Hittite tomb. I was told no more than that, and in truth, I need know nothing more. But now I have seen this strange compass you follow; and I say this to you, Dr. Loder: if it were I, my fear would send me in another direction. Where we go is not merely into the mountains. Where we go is back in time. These people live as they lived four thousand years ago, for the most part. They have been touched by civilization, but it is a gentle, not a lingering touch. What they know, they know in their blood and bones. And if there were not others depending on me for the money I have been paid, I would never have spoken to you back at the broken stones. I would have slipped away and left you to fend for yourselves."

He stared out the windscreen and added, "My greatest fear is that Allah may feel the need to close his hands around us harshly." And in a silent moment he shifted out of neutral, into low, and began climbing once more.

Now it was day, and they moved carefully through the hard-packed clay of Mamoula's only street. Above them the mountains loomed painfully, old men with arthritis.

No one spoke to them. Women carrying early morning water in leather sacks stepped between the wattle and daub buildings to avoid them. But they were watched. They passed three small children playing in a mud puddle. An impossibly old man sitting on a stool in front of a house, holding a crooked staff as if it were a symbol of office, closed his eyes and feigned sleep as they detoured toward him. They retreated to the center of the street. Each time Yaffa approached a man, young or old, to ask a question—the object of his attention turned his back and walked away.

At last, they stood at the foot of the rutted trail that climbed from the end of the village street, through talus slides, into the higher mountain passes. They had gone from one end of Mamoula to the other, and there was no help.

Yaffa said to Loder, "I know how to do this. Will you let me do what is necessary?"

Bobby answered. "Do what you have to do."

Loder said, "It doesn't entail hurting anyone, does it?"

"No," Yaffa said. "I have children of my own."

"Just *do* it, man," Bobby said urgently. "I didn't come all this way to go back empty. This is *it* for me!"

Yaffa turned and walked back down the street as the eyes of the town followed. Bobby and Dennis stood where they were, and watched. Yaffa went to the children playing in the mudhole, stooped, and lifted a five-year-old little girl high in the air over his head. The child, taken by surprise, was dumbfounded for a moment, then laughed as the squat, cherubic stranger whirled her around high above. She laughed and laughed, until the mother came running from one of the houses, shrieking in a lost tongue. Yaffa stood his ground as the woman flew at him. He set the child on his shoulder and raised a hand to stop the woman. Here and there on the street others took a step toward the intruder; then they waited. He had the child.

Yaffa spoke quickly and earnestly to the woman. Neither Dennis nor Bobby understood a word. Bobby leaned toward Loder and whispered, "What language?" Dennis shook his head. "Not Arabic, not Kurdish. I don't know. It may be Aramaic, or some dialect that's transitional. I've only heard Aramaic spoken once, at a university lecture. It didn't sound anything like that. I have no idea what he's saying...but I can guess."

He paused. "If the woman brings a man to him, I think I know what's going on."

As if to Loder's surmise, the woman turned toward a group of men halfway down the street. She took several steps toward them, and one of the younger men shouted to her. She stopped, looked back at Yaffa and the child, as if insuring their immobility, and then shouted back something to the young man.

In a moment, after hurried conversation in the group, the young man strode manfully to Yaffa, stood before him, and held out his arms for the little girl. The child, gurgling at her father, was content to perch on Yaffa's shoulder.

Yaffa spoke softly but at length to the young man.

Finally, the man nodded, and indicated Yaffa should follow him. Yaffa gestured to Bobby and Dennis to come; and he turned and walked along behind the young man; toward the ancient on the stool before the rude domicile. The young man went to the withered elder, kneeled before him deferentially, and spoke passionately. The old man listened for a time, then stopped the younger with a raised finger. He looked up, directly at Yaffa, and nodded almost imperceptibly. Yaffa instantly handed the child to the woman dogging his footsteps,

The family rushed away, and Yaffa motioned Shafka and Loder to follow him as the old man slowly and painfully rose and went into the hut. They followed.

The Land Rover was abandoned two days' climb into the Qalamun Sinnir. The two guides assigned by Mamoula's oldest resident had been terrified of the vehicle, and they had ridden ahead on stumpy-legged, hairy ponies, leading three more by tether reins. Above six thousand feet the trail that was no trail vanished entirely, and the slopes covered with garigue—a degenerate Mediterranean scrub—and maquis—a thick scrubby underbrush—became too steep; and the shrub ripped loose and clogged the wheel wells. They left the vehicle and mounted the ponies.

For the most part, they rode in silence. Once, Yaffa fell back and asked Loder, "Now I must know. How do we come to *this* place, of all places? Is it the writing on the seal?"

Loder mopped his brow. "No, we can't decode the engravings. It was more than a hundred years ago, and it was just like what happened to us in Mamoula. A stone turned up, with carvings. They traced it back to Hamah, but the people wouldn't tell them where they were. Eventually, they were located, and that formed the first body of information we had on the Hittite Kingdom.

"The seal was also found. But it was held by one in the employ of the Subhi Pasha, who delivered it to him with everything he had learned of its origin. Which wasn't much. It was a minor find, and lay unrecognized until 1980 when an art cache in Baghdad was rifled, and the glyph began its travels through the international art theft underground."

Bobby, who had been listening, broke in. "During my brief and really terrific stay at that country club with bars they called a Federal Pen, I got to know Frondizi, the art forger they'd put away for those Modiglianis, remember? And he'd gotten it somehow; and he was ready to turn it into a little nest egg for his twilight years, y'know? So I made a deal with him, got the *Enquirer* interested because of the lost tomb angle..."

Yaffa said, "Tell me of the tomb."

Loder held his pipe and the reins in one hand and, with difficulty and a pipe nail, cleaned the dottle from the bowl.

"The glyph is a funerary seal. It came off a sarcophagus. Hittite. We think. Maybe not. Maybe older. No way of knowing because the inscriptions are beyond us. But the Subhi Pasha's man was very precise as to where the tomb was located." He pointed above them. "Up there somewhere, above Mamoula."

"And the glowing of the stone?" Yaffa demanded.

"We didn't know about that," Bobby Shafka said. "It didn't start till the night you found us."

Yaffa was silent for a time, then said, "I think you are two very foolish men." He spurred the pony and pulled ahead of them, saying over his shoulder, "And I am the most foolish of all." He fell in behind the guides.

They were approaching 6500 feet, and mist began to lattice their passage.

"There's something I've never told you, that I ought to tell you."

"Why tell me now?"

"Who knows what the hell can happen. I've been riding scared these last last few days. When those guys from Mamoula saw this valley..."

"Not valley. This is a meander belt: part of an old flood plain. Very uncommon at this altitude."

"Whatever. When they came out of the pass and saw this, and they wouldn't come down, and they took off...well, who the hell knows what can happen. And I just wanted to tell you something I never told you."

"Which is—?"

"You gonna be able to handle it?"

"Bobby! For pete's sake, get on with it already!"

"I'm gay. Always have been."

"That's your big secret?"

"Well...pretty big secret, yeah. My mother never even knew. That's it, anyway. What, you don't think that's something important enough to tell your best friend?"

"Bobby, I've known you're homosexual since we were fifteen."

"You have?"

"What do you think, I'm smart enough to be the one person you picked for this lunatic trip, but I'm not smart enough to know you're gay. Truly, Bobby, I wouldn't sell *you* that short."

"Man, I hope I don't have to say I'm sorry we pulled this caper. That stuff in the Subhi Pasha's papers about 'losing your immortal soul' scares the crap outta me!"

"Little late for you to be getting religion, isn't it?"

"Well, you know…when you spend your life in the closet, and every time some asshole talks about faggots and pooftas, you just get to believe you're going to Hell, and you sort of give religion a pass. But what d'ya think, there's something to it? We could be going into someplace we ought not, what d'ya think?"

Loder drew on his pipe, put the little gold reflector over the mouth of the bowl, and sent a cloud of smoke toward the evening sky. "What I think, pal, is that it's not just a little, it's a *lot* too late to be worrying about it."

He pointed to the meander belt below where they had camped on a cusp; to the low central hill encircled by the stream. "That's the core. When we go down there, and we dig, I think we're going to find it's a burial mound. And I think we're going to find something no one has ever seen. And I think we're going to have one deuce of a time lugging it out of here and down these mountains. And I think we should have been better prepared, and maybe had a helicopter standing by, to get us out of here. And I think a whole *lot* of things, Bobby. But about losing 'my immortal soul,' well, it's too late for us to try to buy into God's good graces."

Night fell suddenly, and it grew cool enough to come out in the open, and Yaffa found them, and led them down to the meander core, taking with them only the pony carrying water and digging gear. And as they neared the central hill, Bobby Shafka looked at his friend, about to say something from their childhood; and he saw the glyph glowing in Loder's vest pocket; and he was frightened at his impertinence, thinking he could pull this off. Just one more harebrained scheme. And this time, lost up here in a valley filling with mist, following a hundred-year-old line of bullshit, he had finally bet too much. This time, he was sure, he was going to take Dennis down with him…and that was *that* for their immortal souls.

The wind rose. The wind that blows forever between the stars, carrying ancient and encoded messages of indecipherable night. And darkness upon the face of the deep.

The ground split. The glyph became unbearably bright, and the earth split. Yaffa had gone. One moment he was there, beside them and a moment later…gone. He had not abandoned them; they never thought that for an instant. He had done what any sensible man would do: he had gotten out while he could. There were those who depended on him, he'd said so. And they were alone with the sarcophagus.

The glyph had shone so brightly, through the heavy duck of Loder's thermal vest, that he had pulled it out, and averted his eyes lest he go blind. Yes, staring into the sun.

For no reason he could name—no more reason than that which told him he and Bobby Shafka had brought the stone seal home—he laid the glyph on the mound. And the earth split.

They went down the ancient steps carved in the stone, and came to the entrance to the portal. It stood open. When the earth had split, it had made itself an open way.

They needed no flashlights. The glyph illuminated the hewn stone walls of the passage that descended at a shallow angle beneath the meander belt. And far below, ahead of them, lay the sarcophagus. Now they knew, without question.

"If you mention immortal souls one more time," Dennis said tightly, and he ground his teeth, "I will do you in myself."

And they came to the great chamber where the sarcophagus lay.

It was large, but not beautiful. Stone box and lid, deeply etched with inscriptions, and a frieze of kings and servants.

Loder bent over the casket and said nothing. He ran his hands over the surface, and looked more closely. Once, he motioned Bobby to him, and pointed to the fractured sigil niche where the glyph had been positioned. "I don't think it was there when they buried this," Dennis said.

"*They?* What 'they'? Isn't this Hittite?"

Loder shook his head. "It's been reused. It was made for someone else. Look at the lid. That's the name of the king who was buried in this box. It's an early use of the Phoenician alphabet. I'd date this no earlier than 1000 B.C.E. The glyph is at least three thousand years older...that's if we believe the tests the *Geographic* paid out a fortune to have run on it." He walked around the sarcophagus, Bobby following in awe.

"These scenes carved on the sides and ends. They're typical of Canaanite and Phoenician art, with a mixture of Egyptian and Asiatic motifs. No, this box came later than what was buried in it."

"So what's in it?" Bobby said, in a hushed tone.

Loder walked to the wall and slid down. He pulled out his pipe and loaded it. "What turned the Sahara from a fertile land into a rocky desert? What caused the collapse of the great empires in the twelfth century B.C.E.? Desolation, unexplained, for Greece in the seventh century. Why?"

"Stop it, Dennis. You're doing a job on me, so knock it off! What's in the box?"

He lit the pipe and drew deeply. The rich smell of black cavendish, the first alien odor to find its way into this tomb, filled the musty chamber. "It's 1200 B.C.E. In the heart of the Anatolian plateau the dynasty of Hittite kings, treated on equal terms with the Pharaohs of Egypt, rulers of all they surveyed, part of the greatest empire the world has ever known, abruptly comes to an end. Their capital city is abandoned. Why?

"This coffin dates to that period, if I'm worth the faith you had in bringing me along. I know pretty much what I'm talking about; but there are experts; they might..."

"What the fuck is in the goddam box, Dennis!"

"I don't know."

"So what, then? We're both scared out of our minds, this damned rock acts like it wants to jump up and open the casket itself, we've come all this way and if we ever get back it'll be a miracle. So what's it gonna be? Do we do the thing or do we get the hell out of here. Or what?"

Loder stood and walked to the sarcophagus. Bobby Shafka was a step behind him. He watched as Dennis placed the agonizingly bright sigil at the line where lid and box met. Light flooded from the glyph, spread like lava in that thin line, circumnavigated the casket, and met in brilliance where it had started.

As they stepped back, the lid rose as if lifted from within.

At the same moment they heard the beating of wings.

Down the length of the entrance passage, they heard the beating of wings.

Bobby pulled a pistol from his inside jacket pocket. Dennis had not known he was carrying a weapon.

He faced the mouth of the chamber passage, and he said softly, "I'll kill myself before I let them take my soul!"

Then, in a moment, as the chamber filled, there was less time left of life than they could ever have imagined.

Dennis screamed at Bobby. "Soul? *Soul?* Where do you get *that*!? They don't want your soul...*they're just hungry!*"

Then, in an instant, despite the roar of Bobby's gun, there was no time left at all.

And they were table scraps of the great, long banquet to come; at the groaning board laid only for the one-eyed child. (It is said.)

The Pale Silver Dollar of The Moon Pays Its Way and Makes Change

VERSION 1

1934

Bruno Hauptmann was arrested for the kidnapping and murder of the Lindbergh baby. No one had come to my birthday party the year before, not one kid of all the kids from my grade school who had received a personal invitation done in multiple colors with the sixteen crayons in my Crayola box. This year, I knew there wouldn't even be a party; it was too embarrassing.

So after school I never went home. I ran away. I crossed Mentor Avenue against the wishes of my mother and father, and I trudged down through the high weeds and sumac woods of the empty lots behind the Colony Lumber Company, and I sat down on the edge of the bank that surrounded the dirty green water of the nameless pond, and I tossed stones into the thick dirty water, and I watched the skeeter bugs skimming the surface across the circular ripples, and I tried to catch one of the nasty fish that lived in the pond, using a string and a piece of bread and a stick I broke off a bush.

When it got dark, I still sat there. For hours after it got dark. Until it got so cold that I finally trudged back out of that minor wilderness, and re-crossed Mentor Avenue, and went home. My mother and father were

91

beside themselves. They had called out the police. I came into the house, muddy and cold and still crying. And I saw they had left most of the cake with the candles unlit still on the table, along with the birthday presents they'd bought me; and if there had been any kids there, they were now gone. But I still knew my mom and dad would have had to call parents to get the kids to come. Mao Tse-tung began his impossible 6000-mile march of retreat with his 90,000-man Red Army from Kiangsi to the Shensi province with Chiang Kai-shek nipping at his heels.

1947

Chairman J. Parnell Thomas called his first witness in the preliminary hearings to establish loyalty or seditious behavior on the part of Communists or Fellow Travelers in Hollywood. Just outside King of Prussia, Pennsylvania, I accepted a ride from a man in a Hudson touring car. I'd been hitching my way east and hadn't eaten in a day and a half. At a farmhouse in the outlying north of Smoketown, near Lancaster, I had gotten a dinner from a nice woman and her family by knocking on their door and telling them I could repair the old washing machine and mangle rusting away in the side yard.

She had looked at me with skepticism, but I said if I couldn't fix it, it wouldn't cost her nothing. But if I got it working, could she spare something to eat? So she asked her husband, who was working in the barn, and he came out just beyond the big barn doors, and he shaded his eyes with his hand to look at me with the setting sun behind me, and he told her *what've we got to lose,* so she let me go ahead.

I didn't know any more about fixing a washing machine or a mangle than the man in the moon, but I'd done this kind of thing about twenty times before, and once in a while I'd spot something simple that I could twist back into shape or hook up, and it'd work, and I'd eat. So I labored over them both, the washing machine and the mangle, and I sweated for a couple of hours, but couldn't get either of them going. And it was dark, then, and the lady came out and asked if I'd done any good, and I said no ma'am; and I started putting my windbreaker back on, so I could take off down the road again; and she said, *well, c'mon in, then, and have a bite with us,* which was very kind of her because she probably knew I was faking it all along; but I'd sweated for a couple of hours, so she fed me.

And that had been a day and a half ago. I got into the Hudson, and the man put it in gear, and he put his hand on my lap and asked me how old I was, and I yanked down the door handle as hard as I could, and I grabbed my stuff wrapped up in a shirt, and I jumped out of the car before he could get it into second, and I ran away into the woods. Great Britain proposed the partition of Palestine, and there were tremendous protests from Arabs and Jews.

1959

Fidel Castro swept down out of the Sierra Maestra and drove Batista from Cuba with the invasion of Havana. I was serving with the U.S. Army in the capacity of reporter for the Ft. Knox newspaper, *Inside the Turret*. I was living in a trailer in Elizabethtown, Kentucky because I was married, even though they didn't know I was separated. I hated the barracks and had taken the trailer under what they called separate maintenance. But she was back in New York, and we'd probably never see each other again, which was fine by me.

One night I went to a record store in Elizabethtown to buy a jazz album, and I met up with a bunch of teen-aged kids from the high school who knew me because they'd seen me around; and they asked me if I wanted to come to a sock hop that night.

So I went to the high school and paid a dollar to come into the dance, and I hung around and had some punch, but nothing much was happening. And then I saw a girl, maybe fourteen or fifteen, with a leg brace on. I think it was polio. And she was sitting watching everyone dance, but no one asked her. So I went over and smiled and asked her if she'd like to dance, and at first she was very shy, but after I asked a couple more times she said okay, and we got up and I was careful not to be too tricky with the steps, and we had a nice dance. It was Danny and the Juniors doing "At the Hop." She thanked me when I took her back to her seat, and during the evening we danced again half a dozen times. The Nobel Prize for Medicine and Physiology was awarded to Ochoa and Kornberg for their synthesis of DNA and RNA.

1962

Adolf Eichmann was hanged in Jerusalem, and the United States Supreme Court ruled against official prayer in public schools. How I met Carl Sandburg was this: Bill was married to Lelia, and I'd met them at somebody's party, and I was staying in a small apartment down on Wilshire near Beverly Glen, and they invited me to visit their house way up in the Glen, at the end of a small street called Beverly Glen Place, and it was so beautiful up there, all private and quiet, that I rented a funny little treehouse up a steep driveway called Bushrod Lane, and that was how I came to be living just about next door (and above) Bill and Lelia's when Bill was hired for second unit work on *The Greatest Story Ever Told.* Or maybe he was an assistant director.

One Sunday Bill called and said there was a party going on at George Stevens's mansion up in the Hollywood Hills, and did I want to come for a while? I asked if it was okay, and he said, yes, it was fine, Mr. Stevens had told him to ask anyone he thought would be interesting. So I took the directions to Mr. Stevens's house, and I dressed up in the best suit I had, which was too big on me because I hadn't been working and I'd lost a lot of weight, and I had to pin the pants tight across my waist, and I was ashamed the way the pants bagged, but I put on the jacket and it covered the excess, flapping fabric.

I was driving an old Ford I'd bought in Chicago, and it was a wreck, but it got me up into the Hills, where I took a wrong turn and got lost. Finally, I thought I'd found the private road that led up to Mr. Stevens's big house, and there was a gate with an intercom on it, and I buzzed through, and a voice asked who I was, so I said who, and I said I'd been invited to the party by Bill, and there was a moment of silence and then the voice said okay, and told me how to get up the road to the parking lot, and the gate gave a crackling noise and opened, and I drove through.

But I must have taken a wrong turn again, because I could see the big circular house above me, but I couldn't get to it; and finally I did come into an empty lot with one or two cars in it, below the house, and I figured that had to be where I was supposed to be. So I parked, and hitched up my pants, and climbed a stairway to the house.

But I couldn't find a door to go in.

The house was marvelous. Apparently, parts of it turned like a flower to catch the sun, and the front door was somewhere on the other side. What I didn't know was that I had come up a service road, not the front entranceway, and I was lost again. So I walked around and around the back of the house till I found a door, and I went in. But it was on the second floor, and I wandered through the bedroom level till I came out on a balcony that went halfway around the central court, and I looked down into an enormous white living room, all bathed in sunshine, and down there sitting on a huge sectional sofa was Carl Sandburg. I recognized him immediately. I was thrilled.

He had been hired by Mr. Stevens to write narration for *The Greatest*

Story Ever Told, and he was staying there. I could now see, through the big picture windows, that the party was actually out on the sloping lawn in front of the mansion. But the living room was empty except for Carl Sandburg, who sat on the sofa doing the most peculiar thing.

Propped up on one of those plastic book-holder devices used to hold open a cookbook when making something intricate for dinner, was a large book. Lying on the big coffee table that held the propped-open book, in front of Carl Sandburg, was a roll of brown butcher's paper, the kind meat markets use to wrap up lamb chops. It was partially unrolled, and Carl Sandburg was writing on the open section with a quill pen that he would dip into an inkpot. He would look at the book for a moment, and then write something on the butcher's paper. I watched him for a long time. He would look at the book, dip the quill, write a line on the paper, and then repeat the process until he'd filled the paper handily. Then he would rip off a big chunk of the paper and toss it onto a hurly-burly haymow of butcher's paper on the floor beyond the coffee table.

I watched till I couldn't contain myself any longer; then I walked around the balcony over the living room till I found a staircase that descended to the big room. I went down and walked daintily toward Carl Sandburg, because I didn't want to disturb or interrupt him. But I had to find out what he was doing. I stood there for a few minutes till he saw me, and he smiled, and he said, *hello young man,* and I came over to him, and he patted the sofa and told me to sit down and take a load off. So I sat down, and watched a while; and then I asked him, *Mr. Sandburg, what in the world are you doing?*

And he said, "Did you know the typewriter was invented in 1873?"

I said no, I didn't know that. He chuckled. "Well, son, I always traveled around with a little portable typewriter in my pack. I wrote almost all of my poems on that typewriter. On cheap yellow paper. (Dollar a ream.) So now it seems they want to preserve all my originals in a museum or a library or something, and I'm just too embarrassed to send them all those typed yellow pages. They just don't look important enough."

And he looked into that copy of THE COLLECTED POETRY OF CARL SANDBURG, published by Harcourt Brace, that had been bought for him a few days earlier at a bookstore in Westwood Village, and he memorized a line, and dipped his quill in the inkpot, and copied the line on brown, important-looking butcher's paper, and he tore off the poem he had copied, the poem he had written years before, and tossed it onto the ever-growing mound of elegant forgeries. I stayed sitting there for a long while, and was very impressed. Aboard the Friendship VII, John Glenn became the first American to orbit the Earth and Marilyn Monroe died of an overdose and President Kennedy sent federal troops to protect James Meredith as the first black student seeking admission to the University of Mississippi.

1975

The Vietnam War ended and Francisco Franco died. There was a serious water leak through the wall of the bedroom in my house, caused by ivy that had been growing up the outside wall and penetrating the stucco. Dozens of excellent books in a floor-to-ceiling bookcase were stained and waterlogged and mildewed. I had to throw them out, and some of them have never been replaced. One of them was a book I'd first read in junior high school about people living in the mountains of West Virginia who had never seen an airplane or a radio, and who still spoke in something like old Chaucerian English. An earthquake destroyed the beautiful Great Temples of Pagan in Burma.

1980

Ex-California governor Ronald Wilson Reagan became the 40th, and oldest, President of the United States in a landslide victory in which he won 483 electoral votes. A dear friend of mine was bludgeoned to death in her apartment in Santa Monica and I spoke at her funeral. A friend I'd known for almost thirty years revealed himself to be a terrible, cold person, and I could speak to him only distantly ever after. My nephew went to work in his father's store in Cleveland; and I don't think that's what he had intended for his life's work. Zimbabwe emerged as an independent state.

1992

The Union of Soviet Socialist Republics vanished, and a menace that had clouded the mind of the world for a century, something they had called Communism, dissipated like morning fog, almost without anyone noticing. Doves have built a nest in a tree just outside the front door of my home. When I go out to put garbage in the cans, the mother bird sits among the cactus, watching me. I smile and try to reassure her that she's safe. Thousands of people are dying of a terrible plague called AIDS.

Berlioz wrote, "Time is a great teacher. Unfortunately, it kills all its pupils." The pale silver dollar of the moon pays its way and makes change.

The Pale Silver Dollar of The Moon Pays Its Way and Makes Change

VERSION 2

He told them Jesse Garon had been stillborn at 4:00 A.M. He would have told them the same about Elvis Aron, at 4:35; but they were watching more closely. Dr. Hunt managed to get the elder of the twins away from the house in Tupelo. Jesse Garon lived. Jesse Garon lives. William Robert Hunt, M.D., died in 1952, never explaining why he had "saved" the older Presley twin. But Jesse—who had kept a book of himself—had been contacted by the old country doctor. He knew who he was. He never went back to Tupelo.

He only visited Memphis, Tennessee once. August of 1977.

1939

Eight million were unemployed. Nazi Germany attacked Poland. The earthquake in Anatolia took 45,000 lives. No one had come to my birthday party the year before, not one kid of all the kids from my grade school who had received a personal invitation done in multiple colors with the sixteen crayons in my Crayola box. I had even laid out all my comic books with just the titles showing, line after line of them, under the piano, in case anyone

97

wanted to read about The Human Bomb or Tom Mix or Scribbly. And I waited, and waited, and looked out the front window and waited, but no one came; no one even called to lie; and when it got dark we had dinner, with pieces of my cake for dessert.

This year, I knew there wouldn't even be a party, it was too embarassing. I don't remember if I cried, but I think I did. But I did it in my room. And no one saw me.

This year, I wouldn't give them the chance.

So after school I never went home. I ran away. I crossed Mentor Avenue against the wishes of my mother and father, and I trudged down through the high weeds and sumac woods of the empty lots behind the Colony Lumber Company, and I sat on the edge of the bank that surrounded the dirty green water of the nameless pond, and I tossed stones into the thick dirty water, and I watched the skeeter bugs skimming the surface across the circular ripples, and I tried to catch one of the nasty fish that lived in the muck of the pond, using a string and a piece of bread and a stick I broke off a bush.

When it got dark, I still sat there. For hours after it got dark. Until it got so cold that I finally trudged back out of that minor wilderness, and re-crossed Mentor Avenue, and went home. My mother and father were beside themselves. They had called out the police. I came into the house, muddy and cold, and still crying. And I saw they had left most of the cake with the candles unlit still on the table, along with the birthday presents they'd bought me, and if there had been any kids there, they were gone now. It looked like there had been kids there, but they were gone a long time. But I still knew my mom and dad would have had to call parents to get them to come. Henry Moore sculpted his *Reclining Figure*. Barcelona fell to Franco's troops and Loyalist resistence in Spain was ended. Polyethylene was invented, Freud died, and Igor Sikorsky constructed the first helicopter.

1947

Chairman J. Parnell Thomas called his first witness in the preliminary hearings to establish loyalty or seditious behavior on the part of Communists or Fellow Travelers in Hollywood. Just outside King of Prussia, Pennsylvania, I accepted a ride from a man in a Hudson touring car. I'd been hitching my way east and hadn't eaten in a day and a half. At a farmhouse in the outlying north of Smoketown, near Lancaster, I had gotten a dinner from a nice woman and her family by knocking on their door and telling them I could repair the old washing machine and mangle rusting away in the side yard.

She had looked at me with skepticism, but I said if I couldn't fix it, it wouldn't cost her nothing. But if I got it working, could she spare something to eat? So she asked her husband, who was working in the barn, and he came out just beyond the big barn doors, and he shaded his eyes with his hand to look at me with the setting sun behind me, and he told her *what've we got to lose*, so she let me go ahead.

I didn't know any more about fixing a washing machine or a mangle than the man in the moon, but I'd done this kind of thing about twenty times before, and once in a while I'd spot something simple that I could twist back into shape or hook up, and it'd work, and I'd eat. So I labored over them both, the washing machine and the mangle, and I sweated for a couple of hours, but couldn't get either of them to going. And it was dark, then, and the lady came out and asked if I'd done any good, and I said no ma'am; and I started putting my windbreaker back on, so I could take off down the road again; and she said *well, c'mon in, then, and have a bite with us,* which was very kind of her because she probably knew I was faking it all along, but I'd sweated for a couple of hours, so she fed me.

And that had been a day and a half ago. I got into the Hudson, and the man put it in gear, and he put his hand on my lap and asked me how old I was, and I yanked down the door handle as hard as I could, and I grabbed my stuff wrapped up in a shirt, and I jumped out of the car before he could get it into second, and I ran away into the woods. Great Britain proposed the partition of Palestine, and there were tremendous protests from Arabs and Jews.

1959

Fidel Castro swept down out of the Sierra Maestra and drove Batista from Cuba with the invasion of Havana. I was serving with the U.S. Army in the capacity of reporter for the Ft. Knox newspaper, *Inside the Turret.* I was living in a trailer in Elizabethtown, Kentucky because I was married, even though they didn't know I was separated. I hated the barracks and had taken the trailer under what they called separate maintenance. But she was back in New York and we'd probably never see each other again, which was fine by me.

One night I went to a record store in Elizabethtown to buy a jazz record, and I met up with a bunch of teen-aged kids from the high school who knew me because they'd seen me around, and they asked me if I wanted to come to a sock hop that night.

So I went to the high school and paid a dollar to come into the dance, and I hung around and had some punch, but nothing much was happening. And then I saw a girl, maybe fourteen or fifteen, with a leg brace on. I think it was polio. And she was sitting watching everyone dance, but no one asked her. So I went over and smiled and asked her if she'd like to dance, and at first she was very shy, but after I asked a couple more times she said okay, and we got up and I was careful not to be too tricky with the steps, and we had a nice dance. It was Danny and the Juniors doing "At the Hop." She thanked me when I took her back to her seat, and during the evening we danced again half a dozen times. The Nobel Prize for Medicine and Physiology was awarded to Ochoa and Kornberg for their synthesis of DNA and RNA.

1962

Adolf Eichmann was hanged in Jerusalem as the United States Supreme Court ruled against official prayers in public schools. How I met Carl Sandburg was this: Bill was married to Lelia, and I'd met them at somebody's party, and I was staying in a small apartment down on Wilshire near Beverly Glen, and they invited me to visit their house way up in the Glen, at the end of a small street called Beverly Glen Place, and it was so beautiful up there, all private and quiet, that I rented a funny little treehouse up a steep driveway called Bushrod Lane, and that was how I came to be living just about next door (and above) Bill and Lelia's when Bill was hired for second unit work on *The Greatest Story Ever Told.* Or maybe he was an assistant director.

One Sunday Bill called and said there was a party going on at George Stevens's mansion up in the Hollywood Hills, and did I want to come for a while? I asked if it was okay, and he said, yes, it was fine, Mr. Stevens had told him to ask anyone he thought would be interesting. So I took the directions to Mr. Stevens's house, and I dressed up in the best suit I had, which was too big on me because I hadn't been working and I'd lost a lot of weight, and I had to pin the pants tight across my waist, and I was ashamed the way the pants bagged, but I put on the jacket and it covered the excess, flapping fabric.

I was driving an old Ford I'd bought in Chicago, and it was a wreck, but it got me up into the Hills, where I took a wrong turn and got lost. Finally, I thought I'd found the private road that led up to Mr. Stevens's big house, and there was a gate with an intercom on it, and I buzzed through, and a voice asked who I was, so I said who, and I said I'd been invited to the party by Bill, and there was a moment of silence and then the voice said okay, and told me how to get up the road to the parking lot, and the gate gave a crackling noise and opened, and I drove through.

But I must have taken a wrong turn again, because I could see the big circular house above me, but I couldn't get to it; and finally I did come into an empty lot with one or two cars in it, below the house, and I figured that had to be where I was supposed to be. So I parked, and hitched up my pants, and climbed a stairway to the house.

But I couldn't find a door to go in.

The house was marvelous. Apparently, parts of it turned like a flower to catch the sun, and the front door was somewhere on the other side. What I didn't know was that I had come up a service road, not the front entranceway, and I was lost again. So I walked around and around the back of the house till I found a door, and I went in. But it was on the second floor, and I wandered through the bedroom level till I came out on a balcony that went halfway around the central court, and I looked down into an enormous white living room, all bathed in sunshine, and down there sitting on a huge sectional sofa was Carl Sandburg. I recognized him immediately. I was thrilled.

He had been hired by Mr. Stevens to write narration for *The Greatest Story Ever Told,* and he was staying there. I could now see, through the big picture windows, that the party was actually out on the sloping lawn in front of the house. But the living room was empty except for Carl Sandburg, who sat on the sofa doing the most peculiar thing.

Propped up on one of those plastic book-holder devices used to hold open a cookbook when making something intricate for dinner, was a large book. Lying on the big coffee table that held the propped-open book, in front of Carl Sandburg, was a roll of brown butcher's paper, the kind meat markets use to wrap up lamb chops. It was partially unrolled, and Carl Sandburg was writing on the open section with a quill pen that he would dip into an inkpot. He would look at the book for a moment, and then write something on the butcher's paper. I watched him for a long time. He would look at the book, dip the quill, write a line on the paper, and then repeat the process until he'd filled the paper handily. Then he would rip off a big chunk of the paper and toss it onto a hurly-burly haymow of butcher's paper on the floor beyond the coffee table.

I watched till I couldn't contain myself any longer; then I walked around the balcony over the living room till I found a staircase that descended to the big room. I went down and walked daintily toward Carl Sandburg, because I didn't want to disturb or interrupt him. But I had to find out what he was doing. I stood there for a few minutes till he saw me, and he smiled, and he said *hello young man,* and I came over to him, and he patted the sofa and told me to sit down and take a load off. So I sat down, and watched a while; and then I asked him, *Mr. Sandburg, what in the world are you doing?*

And he said, "Did you know the typewriter was invented in 1873?"

I said no, I didn't know that. He chuckled. "Well, son, I always traveled around with a little portable typewriter in my pack. I wrote almost all of my poems on that typewriter. On cheap yellow paper. Dollar a ream. So now it seems they want to preserve all my originals in a museum or a library or something, and I'm just too embarrassed to send them all those typed yellow pages. They just don't look important enough."

And he looked into that copy of THE COLLECTED POETRY OF CARL SANDBURG, published by Harcourt Brace, that had been bought for him a few days earlier at a bookstore in Westwood Village, and he memorized a line, and dipped his quill in the inkpot, and copied the line on brown, important-looking, butcher's paper, and he tore off the poem he had copied, the poem he had written years before, and tossed it onto the ever-growing mound of elegant forgeries. I stayed sitting there for a long while, and was very impressed. Aboard the Friendship VII, John Glenn became the first American to orbit the Earth and Marilyn Monroe died of an overdose and President Kennedy sent federal troops to protect James Meredith as the first black student seeking admission to the University of Mississippi.

1975

The Vietnam War ended and Francisco Franco died. There was a serious water leak through the wall of the bedroom in my house, caused by ivy that had been growing up the outside wall and penetrating the stucco. Dozens of excellent books in a floor-to-ceiling bookcase were stained and waterlogged and mildewed. I had to throw them out, and some of them have never been replaced. One of them was a book I'd first read in junior high school about people living in the mountains of West Virginia who had never seen an airplane or a radio, and who still spoke in something like old Chaucerian English. An earthquake destroyed the beautiful Great Temples of Pagan in Burma.

1980

Ex-California governor Ronald Wilson Reagan became the 40th, and oldest, President of the United States in a landslide victory in which he won 483 electoral votes. A dear friend of mine was bludgeoned to death in her apartment in Santa Monica and I spoke at her funeral. A friend I'd known for almost thirty years revealed himself to be a terrible, cold person, and I could speak to him only distantly ever after. My nephew went to work in his father's store in Cleveland; and

I don't think that's what he had intended for his life's work. Zimbabwe emerged as an independent state.

1992

The Union of Soviet Socialist Republics vanished, and a menace that had clouded the mind of the world for a century, something they had called Communism, dissipated like morning fog, almost without anyone noticing. Doves have built a nest in a tree just outside the front door of my home. When I go out to put garbage in the cans, the mother bird sits among the cactus, watching me. I smile and try to reassure her that she's safe.

I go out less frequently now. Always to a 7-Eleven or Wal-Mart. I let them see me. Sometimes I hang around at a Taco Bell or McDonald's till someone begins watching me, till they start whispering to each other, till one of them seems ready to come over and ask me. Then I get up, very quickly, and I leave. I always park a block away so no one can see where I went or if I had a car or simply levitated to a flying saucer. I do it for him.

Jesse Garon came to him first in Las Vegas. He didn't need to tell him who he was, they looked at each other and saw the same face. He read to him from the book that he had kept all those years. Then he went away, telling his brother he would be with him when the time came.

He was in the bathroom, and Jesse sat with him on the floor, and cradled his brother's head in his lap, and they recited together. "Jesus, I now admit that I am a sinner, going to hell, and need You as my Saviour. I now cease to rely on myself, my church, my religion, or anything else that I might do to save or help save me. I now completely trust You as my Saviour, to pay for my sins and keep me from going to hell. Thank You Lord Jesus."

And his younger brother's face became as sweet as it had been, and he closed his eyes, and he sighed; and Jesse Garon kissed his temple, and laid his head on the furry chenille throw rug. He took the book of his life, and went back out the way he had entered, and found his car parked a block away, and drove the long drive back to his home.

Some few years later, he began going out regularly, wearing his hair much longer and darker. Jesse Garon did not die. Jesse Garon is alive.

And Elvis is alive and well, and flourishing on black velvet.

Berlioz wrote, "Time is a great teacher. Unfortunately, it kills all its pupils."

The pale silver dollar of the moon pays its way and makes change.

The Lingering Scent of Woodsmoke

"Don't get your shorts in a twist," she said, leveling the Walther 9mm parabellum's four-and-a-half-inch barrel at a spot just south of the waistband of his woodland green walking shorts. "Stand totally, absolutely still as a weed and I won't have to blow you in half."

Near sundown, they stood facing each other in a small forest stand of spruce and Polish larch in the Oświęcim basin of southern Poland. Even under the smothering canopy of woven branches, they could hear the Vistula rushing fast and deep toward Czechoslovakia; they could smell the high Carpathians just to the north. She had stepped suddenly from behind a thick-trunked fir and ordered him to stand still. Even in the dimming light that filtered through from above, he could see she was extraordinarily beautiful, with exotic, almost Eurasian planes sculpting her features. The thick, filtered falling light gave everything a deep green tone, even her skin; her wide, green eyes; the imposing weapon in her hand.

"You're Ernst Koegel," she said to the old man. She spoke in German, with possibly a Bavarian crispness.

"My name is Dário de Queluz. I am from São Paulo. That is in Brazil. I walk here on a walking tour of Eastern Europe."

"I *know* where São Paulo is, there are some luxurious jungles nearby; and if you move like that again, I will most certainly shorten you *and* your shorts."

"So you are some lowlife Polish thug lying in wait for decent tourists? You can have the few thousand zlotys I'm carrying. It is sad for you that my money is back in my hotel room in Kraków." He started to reach into one of the gusseted front pockets of his shorts, with the sound of Velcro. She waggled the barrel of the Walther and shook her head.

"You are Ernst Koegel, you're German, you were nineteen years old in 1944, when you worked in this area, and we've been waiting for you for fifty years."

"Waiting here? What if I had not decided to take this little journey? And you have my name wrong."

"Here; in the Amazon rain forest; in a woodland in upstate New York; anywhere your foot would tread among the trees. And don't try to bluff, old man: I can smell the lingering scent of woodsmoke on you."

"Take my money and let me go. I want to move."

"You stand still. I'm not a robber. I'm here to make you pay for killing my people. You worked just a half mile from here. In your language it was called Auschwitz. You worked with Mengele. You were in charge of stoking the great furnaces. Koegel, young Ernst Koegel, youngest SS officer in the death block, beloved of Dr. Mengele. When he fled, you went with him. Now you've come back, and we've been waiting."

The old man chuckled. Nothing could touch him. He had lived well. Even if she shot him now, he had lived well. "So," he said, smirking, "just another renegade Daughter of Esther, one of the *Juden* who managed to slip through."

"A Jew?" she said. "No, I'm not a Jew."

"We were disposing of twelve thousand a *day,* and I fed the furnaces. So do your worst, little green-faced kike."

"I tell you I'm not one of those poor unfortunates. My people you fed into the furnaces weren't the Jews. We are the forest people…and we wait for the last of you who used chain saws and cut down our families and sliced them into convenient sections and fed them into the furnaces. We can still smell the woodsmoke on you."

"You are crazier than most of them. But still you need the gun, that fine German-made weapon,"

"Oh this," she said, and let the Walther drop to her side. "I only needed this to keep you still long enough for my sisters to caress you properly."

And she smiled at him, and he realized that he no longer *could* move. He looked down, the old man who had run from this place half a century earlier, and he saw that the roots had already slithered up over his hiking boots, over his bare shins, up over his handsome woodland green cargo shorts, and bark was already beginning to form around his waist.

He screamed once, a short sharp sound, because she was still smiling her deep green smile at him. And as the tree grew around him, the dryad dimpled prettily and said, "You should live, oh, I should say, two or three hundred years like this. The winters are rough, but you'll like the spring, and the smell of woodsmoke. That is, unless parasites infest you. Welcome to the neighborhood, cousin Ernst."

The
Museum
on
Cyclops
Avenue

The jaunty feather in my hatband? I knew you'd ask. Makes my old Tyrolean look rather natty, don't it? Yeah, well, I'll tell you about this flame-red feather some time, but not right now.

What about Agnes? Mmm. Yeah. What *about* Agnes.

No, hell no, I'm not unhappy, and I'm certainly not bitter. I *know* I promised to bring her home with me from Sweden, but, well, as we say here in Chapel Hill, *that* dog just ain't gonna hunt.

I'm sorry y'all went to the trouble of settin' up this nice coming-home party, and it truly is a surprise to walk back into my own humble bachelor digs and find y'all hidin' behind the sofas, but to be absolutely candid with myself and with y'all...I'm about as blind tired as I've ever been, fourteen and a half hours riding coach on SAS, customs in New York, missing two connector flights, almost an hour in traffic from Raleigh-Durham...you see what I'm sayin'? Can I beg off this evenin' and I *promise* just as soon as I get my sea-legs under me again with the new semester's classes and the new syllabus, I swear I *promise* we'll all do this up right!

Oh, God bless you, I *knew* you'd understand! Now, listen, Francine, Mary Katherine, Ina...y'all take this food with you, because as soon as the door closes behind you, I'm going to hit my bed and sleep for at least twenty-four hours, so all these here now goodies will gonna rot if you don't take 'em and make y'self a big picnic t'night. Y'all wanna do that now? Excellent! Just excellent.

Thank ya, thank ya *ever* so much! Y'all take care now, y'heah? I'll see you bunch in a few days over to the University.

Bye! Bye now! See ya!

(Henry, you want to hold on for just a few minutes? I do need someone to talk to for a spell. You don't mind? Excellent.) Bye! Drive carefully, you be sure to do it! Bye, William; bye, Cheryl an' Simon! Thank you again, thank you ver—

(Thank god they're gone. Hold on just about a minute, Henry, just in case someone forgot a purse or something.)

Okay, street's clear. Damn, Henry, thought I'd croak when I walked into the house and y'all popped out of the walls. Whose dumbshit idea was this, anyway? Don't tell me yours, I can*not* afford to lose any respec' for you at the moment. I need a friend, and I need an open mind, an' *most* of all I need a smidge outta that fifth of Jack black sittin' up there on the third shelf 'tween Beckwith's HAWAIIAN MYTHOLOGY and Bettelheim's USES OF ENCHANTMENT.

I'd get up and fetch it myself, but I'm shanxhausted, and you're the one just had the angioplasty, so I figger you got lots more energy in you, right at the moment.

They's a coupla clean glasses right there in the cabinet, unless the cleanin' woman saw fit to move things around while I was gone. Asked her not to, but you know nobody listens.

Yeah, right. *While I was gone.* Just decant me about thirty millimeters of that Tennessee sippin', and I'll regale your aging self with the source of my truly overwhelmin' anomie.

No, I'm not cryin', it's the strain and the long trip and everything that happened in Stockholm. Truly, Henry. I'm sad, I own to it; but it's been four days since the street signs changed, and I'm reconciled to it...say what...?

All right, sorry sorry, didn't mean to get ahead of it. I'll tell you. It's a not terribly complicated saga, so I can tell you everything in a short space. But hold off makin' any judgments till I finish, we agree on that?

Fine. Then: my paper was scheduled for the second day of the Conference, I wanted a few days to see the sights, and when SAS put that Boeing 767 down at Arlanda International, my sponsor, John-Henri Holmberg, was waiting with his new wife, Evastina, and John-Henri's son, Alex. And they'd brought along a Dr. Richard Fuchs, a very strange little man who writes incredibly obscure books on bizarre illnesses that no one, apparently, either buys or reads. It was quite warm; John-Henri's shirt was open and he carried his jacket; Evastina kept daubing at her moist upper lip; and Alex, who's too old for them now, he was wearing short pants; it was *quite* warm. Fuchs wore gloves. Milky-white latex gloves, the kind you'd put on to examine specimens. But he was effusive in his greetings. Said he wanted me to see a monograph he'd translated into English on some quisquous aspect of Swedish mythology. Why an' wherefore this odd little man should be such a slavish devotee of my work, the semiotics of mythology, by an obscure Professor of Classics from the English Department of the University of North Carolina, is somethin' I was unable to discover. But since it was he—of everyone I met over theah—was the cause of everything that happened to me...I do suspect his bein' there at the airport was considerable more than merest happenstance. I'm gettin' ahead of myself. Patience, Henry.

They took me to the Royal Viking Hotel, and I unpacked and showered and napped for about an hour. But I was still restless; I was aching for sleep, but I couldn't fall off. My legs kept twitching. I couldn't stop worrying about my paper. Two days, I was supposed to deliver it to a major international conference on the latest academic rigors, an' you *know* I've never been comfortable with all this "deconstructionist" criticism. So I was dog-tired, but instead of taking a Q-Vel for the leg cramps and catching up on some sleep, I fiddled with the manuscript. Even wound up putting a new sub-title on it: *Post-Structuralist Hermeneutics of the Theseus-Minotaur Iconography.* I could barely get my tongue around all that. Imagine what I'd've done somebody asked me what the hell it *meant*. But I knew it'd look impressive in *The Journal*.

So by the time they came to get me for the opening day's dinner reception, I was pretty well goggle-eyed. Maybe that's why I didn't think what was happening was all that distressin'. What Shakespeare called "how strange or odd." I had fourteen and a half hours on the flight back to mull it, an' I can tell you *now* that it was indeed, oh my yes, it was in*deed* distressin', strange, *and* odd.

Now take it easy! I'll skip all the local color, what it's like ridin' over cobblestone streets, and the hoe-*ren*-duss cost of livin' in Sweden—y'know how much it costs for a roll of Scotch Tape? About seven *dollars*, that's what it costs, can you believe it—and I'll cut right to the reception, and meeting Agnes. And Fuchs. And the sepulcher on Österlånggatan. And the flame feather I brought home from Stockholm instead of the most beautiful woman who ever walked the face of the earth.

We were sitting around at this big table at the reception, with a classical pianist named Baekkelund playing all sorts of twentieth-century Swedish compositions—Blomdahl, Carlid, Bäck, Lidholm, that whole "Monday Group"—and Fuchs was sitting next to me, looking at me as if I might start blowing bubbles at any moment, and I thanked him again for runnin' to get me a champagne refill, 'bout the third or fourth time he'd done it, like as if he wanted to come into my employ as a manservant, and he smiled at me with a little face full of nasty brown teeth, and he said, "I notice it is that you concern over my wearing of gloves."

I hadn't realized I'd been oglin' his li'l rubber mittens, but I was just bubbly-happy enough to smart him, 'stead of just answering polite. I said, "Well, Dr. Foowks, it *has* attended my attention that the warm factor in this jammed ballroom is very possibly running toward ninety or so, and the rest of us are, how do they say it in Yiddish, we are all *schvitzin'* like sows, whilst you are covered fingertip to neck-bone. Why *do* you think that is so, suh?"

John-Henri looked uncomfortable. It was just the three of us had come to the reception—Evastina was home with the new baby, Fnork, who had reached the infant stage of catching and eating flies—and though there were others who'd come to sit at that big round table, it was more a matter of expediency in a jammed room with limited seating, than it was a desire to mingle with the three of us. (It had seemed to me, without too close an examination of the subject, that though a few people knew John-Henri, and greeted him saucily, not only did no one *speak* to Dr. Fuchs, but there were several who seemed to veer clear when they espied him.)

Dr. Fuchs grew tolerably serious, and soft spoke, an' he replied to what instantly became obvious to me had been an incredibly stupid, rude, and champagne-besotted remark: "I live with a bodily condition known as hyperhidrosis, Professor Stapylton. Abnormally excessive sweating. As you have said it, *schvitzing*. I perspire from hands, feet, my underarms. I must wear knitted shirts to absorb the moisture. Underarm dress shields, of a woman's kind. I carry pocket towels, in the ungood event I must actually shake hands flesh on flesh with someone. Should I remove my latexwear, and place my palm upon this tablecloth, the material would be soaked in a widened pool in moments." He gave me a pathetic little smile that was meant to be courageous, and he concluded, "I see revulsion in people's faces, Professor. So I wear the gloves, is it not?"

I felt like thirty-one kinds of a blatherin' damnfool, an' I suppose it was because I had no way of extricatin' my size 11M Florsheim from my mouth, that I was so susceptible when Fuchs humiliated me even more by introducin' me to this utter vision of a woman who came blowin' by the table.

Without even a *hesitation* on his part, springs right off this "I make people sick 'cause I'm soakin' wet all the time," right into, "Oh, Agnes! Come, my dear, come meet the famous American scholar and authority of mythic matters, Professor Gordon Stapylton of Chapel Hill, North Carolina, a most brilliant colleague of our friend John-Henri."

We took one look at each other, and I knew what it was to endure hyperhidrosis. Every pore in my body turned Niagara. Even half stupored on good French champagne, I was sober enough to know I had, at last, finally, unbelievably, met the most beautiful woman in the world, the one woman I would marry and, failing that liaison, would never be able to settle for anyone else.

Her hair was the color of the embers when the fire has died down and the companions have snuggled into their sleeping bags and you cannot fall asleep and lie there looking into that moving breathing sussurating crimson at the bottom of the campfire. Her eyes were almond-shaped, and tilted, and green. Not murky, dirty green, but the shade of excellent Chinese jade pieces, Shang dynasty, Chou dynasty. Describing more, I'd sound even more the idiot than I do right now. I tried to tell y'all what she was like, when I called the next morning, remember? When I said I was bringing home the woman I loved, her name was Agnes? Well, I was tipsy with her then...and I'm tipsy all over again now, just describin' her. But the im*port*ant part of all this, is that we took one look t'each other, an' we couldn't keep our hands off!

Fuchs was tryin' to tell me that Agnes Wahlström was, herself, a noted scholar, a student of mythology, and curator of the *Magasinet för sällsamma väsen*, some kind of a museum, but I wasn't much listening by that time. We were swimming in each other's eyes; and the next thing I knew, I'd gotten up and taken her hand—which had a wonderful strong independent kind of a grip—and we were outside the two-hundred-year-old building with the reception up those marble staircases; and we were in a narrow service alley that ran back from the cobblestoned street into darkness alongside the hulking ugliness of the assembly hall; and I barely had an instant to speak her name before she bore me back against the alley wall, her lips on mine.

She fumbled her dress up around her hips, and undid my belt, almost batting away my hands as I tried to undress *her*. And there, in that alley, Henry, there in the darkness I found what I'd never been able to locate in nearly forty years of believing it existed: I found utter and total passion, I-don't-give-a-damn lust, a joining and thrashing that must have made steam come off us, like a pair of rutting weasels. Look, I'm sorry to be embarrassin' you, Henry, my old friend, but under this pleasant, gregarious, buttoned-down academic pose, I have been nothin' but a *lonely* sonofabitch all my life. You *know* how it was between my parents, an' you know how few relationships I've had with women who counted. So, now, you have *got* to understan' that I was crazy with her, drunk with her, inside her and steam comin' off us. Migawd, Henry, I think we banged against that alley wall for an hour, maybe more. I have *no* idea why some Swedish cop didn't hear us growlin' and pantin' and yellin' moremoremore, and come in there an' arrest us. Oh, jeezus, lemme catch mah breath. Lawd, Henry, you are the color of Chairman Mao's Little Book! We never got back to the reception the Conference was hostin'.

We spent the night at the Royal Viking, and the next morning she was as beautiful as the night before, except the sun loved touchin' her, Henry; and we ate breakfast in the room, and her eyes were that green, and made love again for another hour or so. But then she said she had to go home and change because she had to be at the Museum, she was late already, but she'd find me at the Conference in the afternoon and we'd, well, we'd be *together*.

Can you understand what that word meant to me? We'd be *together*. That was when I called you and told you I'd be bringin' back the greatest mythic treasure ever. I had to share it with *some*one, Henry. That was four days ago, before the street signs changed.

John-Henri is a decent man, and an absolutely great friend, so his chiding me on my behavior was maximum softly-spoke; but I was given to understand that walkin' off like Night of the Livin' Dumbbells with some gorgeous museum curator, right in the middle of where I was *supposed* to be, was unacceptable. He also confided that he'd been stuck with Dr. Fuchs all night, nearly, and he was not overwhelmin'ly thrilled by *that*, either. Turned out he was less acquainted with the man in the moist mittens than I'd thought. Out of nowhere, a few weeks before I was scheduled to fly in, he suddenly showed up, ingratiating, charming, knowledgeable about John-Henri's background, very complimentary, workin' ever so hard to become Evastina's and John-Henri's best new buddy-chum. Just so, just that way, out of nowhere, he suddenly appeared in the antechamber of the Conference Hall, right in the middle of John-Henri's polite, with-clenched-teeth admonition that I not pull a repeat of the previous evening's gaucherie.

Fuchs kept smilin' at me with that scupperful of brown bicuspids, just smarmily inquiring had I had a pleasant evening, but not gettin' any closer to questions I'd've had to tell him were none of his damned business.

But I couldn't get rid of him. He dogged my every step.

And I attended the sections I'd wanted to drop in on, and my mind wasn't focused for a second on such arcane trivia. All I could think of was sliding my hands up between Agnes's legs.

Finally, about three in the afternoon, she arrived. Looking absolutely wonderful, wearing a summery dress and sandals, in defiance of the chill that was in the air. She found me at the rear of the auditorium, slid in beside me, and whispered, "I have nothing on under this."

We left not more than three heartbeats later.

All right, Henry, I'll skip all that. But now pay close attention. Five or six hours later, she seemed distracted, an' I suggested we go get some dinner. I was goin' to pop the question. Oh, yes, Henry, I *see* that expression. But the only reason you got it on you, is that you know somethin' was amiss. But if you didn't *know* that, then you wouldn't think I was bein' precipitous, you'd agree that once having been in the embrace of such a woman, a man would be a giant fool to let her slip away. So just pretend you're as innocent as I was, at that moment, and go along with me on this.

She said no, she wasn't hungry, she'd had a big salad before she came to fetch me at the Conference, but would I be interested in seeing the Museum. Where she was curator. I said that would be charming. Or somesuch pseudo phrase so she wouldn't suspect all I could think about was makin' love to her endlessly. As if she weren't smart enough to know *all* that; and she laughed, and I looked sheepish, and she kissed me, and we went to get the car in the hotel structure, and we drove out, about nine or so.

It was a chilly night, and very dark. And she drove to the oldest section of Stockholm, blocky ribbed-stone buildings leaning over the narrow, winding streets, fog or mist trailing through the canyons, silvery and forlorn. It was, well, not to make a cliché of it...it was melancholy. Somehow sad and winsome at the same time. But I was on a cloud. I had found the grail, the crown, the scepter, the very incarnation of True Love. And I would, very soon now, pop the question.

She parked on a side street, cobbled and lit fitfully by old electric brazier lamps, and suggested we should walk, it was invigorating. I worried about her in that thin dress. She said, "I am a sturdy Scandinavian woman, dear

Gordon. Please." And the *please* was neither cajoling nor requesting. It was "give me a break, I can outwalk you any day, son." And so we strode off down the street.

We turned a number of times, this side-street, that little alley, pausing every once in a while to grope each other, usually on my pretext that certain parts of her body needed to be warmed against the sturdy Scandinavian chill. And finally, we turned onto an absolutely shadow-gorged street down which I could not see a solitary thing. I glanced up at the street sign, and it read: *Cyklopavenyn.* Cyclops Avenue.

Now isn't that a remarkable, I thought.

She took me by the hand, and led me into the deep shadow pool of the narrow, claustrophobic, fog-drenched Cyclops Avenue. We walked in silence, just the sound of our hollow footsteps repeating our progress.

"Agnes," I said, "where the hell are we going? I thought you wanted me to see—"

Invisible beside me, but her flesh warm as a beacon, she said, "Yes, *Magasinet för sällsamma väsen.*"

I asked her if we were nearly there, and she said, with a small laugh, "I told you to tinkle before we left." But she didn't say "tinkle." She used the Swedish equivalent, which I won't go into here, Henry, because I can see that you think I'm leading this story toward her giving me a vampire bite, or trying to steal my soul and sell it to flying saucer people...well, it wasn't *any*thing sick or demented, absolutely no blood at all, and as you can see I'm sittin' right here in front'cher face, holdin' up my glass for a splash more of Mr. Jack Daniels.

Thank'ya. So we keep walkin', and I ask her to translate for me what *Magasinet* Etcetera Et-cet-era means, and she said, it's hard to translate into English. But she tried, and she said Museum wasn't quite the right word, more rightly something not quite like Sepulcher. I said that gave me chills, and she laughed and said I could call it The Gatherum of Extraordinary Existences—as we reached a brooding shadowy shape darker than the darkness filling Cyclops Avenue, a shape that rose above us like an escarpment of black rock, something hewn from obsidian, and she took a key from a pocket of the thin summery dress, and inserted it in the lock, and turned the key—or you could call it The Repository of Unimaginable Creatures—and she pushed open a door that was three times our height, and I'm six one, and Agnes is just under six feet—or the Cyklopstrasse Keep of Rare and Extinct Beasts—and as the door opened we were washed by pure golden light so intense I shielded my eyes. Where the door had snugged against the jamb and lintel so tightly there had been no leakage of illumination, now there was an enormous rectangle three times our height of blazing burning light. I could see *nothing*, not a smidge, but that light. And Agnes took me by the elbow, and walked me into the light, and I was *inside* the most breathtaking repository of treasures I'd ever seen.

Greater than the Prado, more magnificent than the Louvre, dwarfing the Victoria and Albert, more puissant than the Hermitage, enfeebling the image of Rotterdam's Museum Boymans-van Beuningen, it rose above us till the arching ceilings faded into misty oblivion. I could see room after room after channel after salon after gallery stretching away in a hundred different directions from the central atrium where we stood, mah mouth open and my wits havin' fled.

Because the Museum that my Agnes tended, the Sepulcher that my Agnes oversaw, the Gallery my Agnes captained...it was filled with the dead and mounted bodies of every creature I'd read about in the tomes of universal mythology.

In niches and on pedestals, in crystal cases and suspended by invisible wires from the invisible ceilings, ranked in shallow conversation-pit-like depressions in the floor and mounted to the walls, in showcases and free-standing in the passageways:

The Kurma tortoise that supported Mt. Mandara on its back during the churning of the ocean by the Devas and Asuras. A matched set of unicorns, male and female, one with silver horn, the other with golden spike. The bone-eater from the Ani papyrus. Behemoth and Leviathan. Hanuman the five-headed of the Kalighat. A Griffin. And a Gryphon. Hippogryph and Hippocamp. The Kinnara bird of Indian mythology, and the thousand-headed snake Kalināga. Jinn and Harpy and Hydra; yeti and centaur and minotaur; the holy feathered serpent Quetzalcoatl and a winged horse and a Ryu dragon. Hundreds and thousands of beasts of all worlds and all nations, of all beliefs and all ages, of all peoples and of all dreams and nightmares. There, in the stunning Sepulcher on the Verg Cyklop, was amassed and arrayed and ranked all the impossible creatures that had never made it onto Noah's leaky tub. I wandered gallery to gallery, astounded, impossible sights choking my throat and making me weep with amazement that it was all, all, *all of it* absolutely true. There was even a Boogeyman and his mate. They looked as if they had lived their lives under beds and in dark closets.

"But how...?" I could barely find words, at long last.

"They are here, assembled all. And I am the one who caught them."

Of all I had seen, of all she might say, *that* was the most astonishin'. *She* had brought these beasts to heel. I could not believe it. But no, she insisted, she trekked out, and she stalked them, and she caught them, and killed them, and brought them back here for display. "For whom?" I asked. "Who comes to this place?" And she smiled the sweetest smile, but did not reply. *Who*, I wondered, assaying the size of the rooms, the height of the ceilings, *who did the tour of this repository of miracles?*

Hours later, she took me away, and we went back to the Royal Viking, and I was too aswirl in magic and impossibilities to drench mahself in her scented skin. I could not fathom or contain what I had seen. Her naked body was muscular but more feminine than Aphrodite and Helen of Troy and the Eternal Nymph all combined. She was gorgeous, but she was the hunter of them all. Of course she had had a strong grip. From holding machete, and crossbow, and Sharps rifle, and bolas, and gas-gun. She told me of the hunts, the kills, the scent of the track, the pursuits in far lands: Petra and Angkor, Teotihuacan and Tibet, Djinnistan and Meszria, Skull Island and Malta and Knossos.

And then she said to me, "I am very much drawn to you, Gordon, but I know you're going to ask me to come away with you, to live in America and be your wife. And I truly, deeply, am mad about even the thought of making love to you endlessly...but..."

The next day, I went looking for Cyclops Avenue. I have a skunk-sniffin' dog's sense of direction, you know that, Henry; and I actual found the street again. I recognized all the twisty turns we'd made, even lookin' different in the daylight. But I got there. And, of course, the street signs had changed. Cyclops Avenue was now *Österlånggatan.* The Museum was not there. Oh, it likely *was* there, but I didn't have either the proper guide or a key taken from the pocket of a summery dress to help me find it. So I went away, and I came back here, and that's my story. Except for a couple of loose ends...

One: what of the peculiar Dr. Fuchs? Well, Agnes never said it in so many words, but I got the impression that she had taken pity on the poor little man, that he had been someone who had loved her and followed her, and whose existence meant nothing without her in it, and so she had allowed him to assist her. She said he was her "spotter." I didn't ask what that meant, nor what it was he spotted. (Before I left Stockholm, John-Henri called to say goodbye, and he told me he had found a pair of gloves, apparently the property of Fuchs, half-filled with foul-smelling water or sweat or some fishy liquid, but that Dr. Fuchs, himself, had vanished, leaving an enormous hotel bill for John-Henri and the Conference to pay.)

And two: I'll bet you haven't forgotten, have you?

That's right, Henry, the feather.

I plucked it from the flank of an enormous roc that she had stalked and bagged and killed and stuffed. It hung from the ceiling in the Museum of Unimaginable Creatures, hung low enough so I could pluck one memento. I think, I guess, I well I *suppose* I knew somewhere in my head or my heart, certainly not in my pants, that I was never going to get this prize, this treasure, this woman of all women. And so, in some part of my sense, I stole a token to keep my memory warm. It's all I have, one flame-red feather from the flank of the roc that tried to carry off Sinbad the Sailor.

And do you know *why* she renounced me, gave me a pass, shined me on, old Henry? I guess I begged a little, told her how good we were together and, yes, she admitted, that was so; but it was never gonna work. Because, Henry, she said...

I was too easy a catch. I didn't nearly put up the fight it would take to keep her hunter's interest pinned.

What's that? Do I think I'll ever see her again?

Henry, I see her all the time. This world of you and the University and houses and streets and mailboxes and a drink in my hand...it's all like a transparent membrane on which a movie pictchuh is bein' cast. And behind it, I see *her*. My Agnes, so fabulous. She's in a rough-bark coracle, with a canvas sail ripped by terrible winds caused by the beating of a devil roc's great feathered wings, as its spiked tail thrashes the emerald water into tidal spires. She holds a scimitar, and her jade-green eyes are wild; and I know the flame-feathered monster that seeks to devour her, capsize her, drag her down and feast on her delicious flesh—I know that poor dumb ravening behemoth hasn't got the chance of a snowball in a cyclotron. In her path, in the fury of her flesh, *no* poor dumb beast has a chance. Not even—pardon the pun—the Roc of Agnes.

Do I see her? Oh my, yes. I see her clearly, Henry. I may never see *my* world clearly again after walking the halls and galleries of the Cyclops Avenue Museum...but I'll always see her.

For a poor dumb beast, that vision and a goddam red feather is almost enough to get by on. Wouldja kindly, that Jack Daniels beside you. And then maybe I will go upstairs and try to catch a little sleep. Thank ya kindly, Henry.

Author's Note: I have always written my stories on Olympia office standard or portable typewriters. Bob Bloch also wrote on Olympias. When Bob died, he passed on to me two of his machines. This story was written on one of those typewriters, completed on 5 July 1995. The work goes on.

Go Toward the Light

It was a time of miracles. Time, itself, was the first miracle. That we had learned how to drift backward through it, that we had been able to achieve it at all: another miracle. And the most remarkably miraculous miracle of all: that of the one hundred and sixty-five physicists, linguists, philologists, archaeologists, engineers, technicians, programmers of large-scale numerical simulations, and historians who worked on the Timedrift Project, only two were Jews. Me, myself, Matty Simon, a timedrifter, what is technically referred to on my monthly paycheck as an authentic "chronocircumnavigator"—euphemistically called a "fugitive" by the one hundred and sixty-three Gentile techno-freaks and computer jockeys—short-speak for *Tempus Fugit*—"Time Flies"—broken-backed Latin, just a "fugitive." That's me, young Matty, and the other Jew is Barry Levin. Not Le*vine* and not Le*veen*, but Levin, as if to rhyme with "let me in." Mr. Barry R. Levin, Fields Medal nominee, post-adolescent genius and wiseguy, the young man who Stephen Hawking (yeah, courtesy of the over-the-counter anti-agathic drugs, still alive, and breaking a hundred on the links) says has made the greatest contributions to quantum gravity, the guy who, if you ask him a simple question you get a pageant, endless lectures on chrono-string theory, complexity theory, algebraic number theory, how many pepperonis can dance on the point of a pizza. Also, Barry Levin, orthodox Jew. Did I say *orthodox*? Beyond, galactically *beyond* orthodox. So damned orthodox that, by comparison, Moses was a *fresser* of barbequed pork sandwiches with Texas hot links. Levin, who was *frum*, Chassid, a reader and quoter of the Talmud, and also the biggest pain in the…I am a scientist, I am not allowed to use that kind of language. A pain in the nadir, the fundament, the buttocks, the *tuchis*!

A man who drove everyone crazy on Project Timedrift by continuing to insist: while it is all well and good to be going back to record at first hand every aspect of the Greek Culture, the Hellenic World was enriched and enlightened by the Israelites and so, by rights, we ought to be making book on the parallel history of the Jews.

With one hundred and sixty-three *goyim* on the Project, you can imagine with what admiration and glee this unending assertion was received. Gratefully, we were working out of the University of Chicago, and not Pinsk, so at least I didn't have to worry about pogroms.

What I *did* worry about was Levin's characterization of me as a "pretend Jew."

"You're not a Good Jew," he said to me yesterday. We were lying side by side in the REM sleep room, relaxing after a three-hour hypnosleep session learning the idiomatics of Ptolemaic Egyptian, all ninety-seven dialects. He in his sling, me in mine. "I *beg* your sanctimonious pardon," I said angrily. "And you, I suppose, are a *Good* Jew, by comparison to my being a *Bad* Jew!"

"Res ipsa loquitur," he replied, not even opening his eyes. It was Latin, and it meant *the thing speaks for itself;* it was self-evident.

"When I was fourteen years old," I said, propping myself on one elbow and looking across at him lying there with his eyes shut, "a kid named Jack Wheeldon, sitting behind me in an assembly at my junior high school, kicked my seat and called me a kike. I turned around and hit him in the head with my geography book. He was on the football team, and he broke my jaw. Don't tell me I'm a Bad Jew. I ate through a straw for three months."

He turned his head and gave me that green-eyed lizard-on-a-rock stare. "This is a Good Jew, eh? Chanukah is in three days. You'll be lighting the candles, am I correct? You'll be reciting the prayers? You'll observe *yontiff* using nothing but virgin olive oil in your *menorah,* to celebrate the miracle?"

Oh, how I wanted to pop him one. "I gotcher miracle," I said, rudely. I lay back in the sling and closed my eyes.

I didn't believe in miracles. How Yehudah of the Maccabees had fielded a mere ten thousand Jews against Syrian King Antiochus's mercenary army of 60,000 infantry and 5,000 cavalry; and how he had whipped them like a tub of butter. How the victors had then marched on Jerusalem and retaken the Second Temple; and how they found that in the three years of Hellenist and Syrian domination and looting the Temple had grown desolate and overgrown with vegetation, the gates burned, and the Altar desecrated. But worst of all, the sacred vessels, including the *menorah,* had been stolen. So the priests, the *Kohanim,* took seven iron spits, covered them with wood, and crafted them into a makeshift *menorah.* But where could they find uncontaminated oil required for the lighting of the candelabrum?

It was a time of miracles. They found one flask of oil. A *cruse* of oil, whatever a cruse was. And when they lit it, a miracle transpired, or so I was told in Sunday School, which was a weird name for it because Friday sundown to Saturday sundown is the Sabbath for Jews, except we were Reform, and that meant Saturday afternoon was football and maybe a movie matinee, so I went on Sundays. And, miracle of miracles, I forgot most of those football games, but I remembered what I'd been taught about the "miracle" of the oil, if you believe that sort of mythology they tell to kids. The oil, just barely enough for one day, burned for *eight* days, giving the *Kohanim* sufficient time to prepare and receive fresh uncontaminated oil that was fit for the *menorah.*

A time of miracles. Like, for instance, you're on the Interstate, seventy-five miles from the nearest gas station, and your tank is empty. But you ride the fumes seventy-five miles to a fill-up. Sure. And one day's oil burns for eight. Not in *this* universe, it doesn't.

"I don't believe in old wives' tales that there's a 'miracle' in one day's oil burning for eight," I said.

And *he* said: "That wasn't the miracle."

And *I* said: "Seems pretty miraculous to me. If you believe."

And *he* said: "The miracle was that they knew the oil was uncontaminated. Otherwise they couldn't use it for the ceremony."

"So how did they know?" I asked.

"They found one cruse, buried in the dirt of the looted and defiled Temple of the Mount. One cruse that had been sealed with the seal of the high rabbi, the *Kohane Gadol,* the Great Priest."

"Yeah, so what's the big deal? It had the rabbi's seal on it. What did they expect, the Good Housekeeping Seal of Approval?"

"It was never done. It wasn't required that oil flasks be sealed. And rules were rigid in those days. No exceptions. No variations. Certainly the personal involvement of the *Kohane Gadol* in what was almost an act of housekeeping...well...it was unheard of. Unthinkable. Not that the High Priest would consider the task beneath him," he rushed to interject, "but it would never fall to his office. It would be considered *unworthy* of his attention."

"Heaven forfend," I said, wishing he'd get to the punchline.

Which he did. "Not only was the flask found, its seal was unbroken, indicating that the contents had not been tampered with. One miraculous cruse, clearly marked for use in defiance of all logic, tradition, random chance. And *that* was the miracle."

I chuckled. "Mystery, maybe. Miracle? I don't think so."

"Naturally you don't think so. You're a Bad Jew."

And *that*, because he was an arrogant little creep, because *his* subjective world-view was the *only* world-view, because he fried my frijoles, ranked me, dissed me, ground my gears, and in general cheesed me off...I decided to go "fugitive" and solve his damned mystery, just to slap him in his snotty face with a dead fish! When they ask you why any great and momentous event in history took place, tell 'em that all the theories are stuffed full of wild blueberry muffins. Tell 'em the only reason that makes *any* sense is this: *it seemed like a good idea at the time.*

Launch the Spanish Armada? Seemed like a good idea at the time.

Invent the wheel? Seemed like a good idea at the time.

Drift back in time to 165 Before the Common Era and find out how one day's oil burns for eight? Seemed like a good idea at the time. Because Barry R. Levin was a smartass!

It was all contained in the suit of lights.

All of time, and the ability to drift backward, all of it built into the refined mechanism the academics called a *driftsuit,* but which we "fugitives" called our suit of lights. Like a toreador's elegant costume, it was a glittering, gleaming, shining second-skin. All the circuits were built in, printed deep in the ceramic metal garment. It was a specially-developed cermet, *pliable* ceramic metal, not like the armor worn by our astronauts mining the Asteroid Belt. Silver and reflective, crosstar flares at a million points of arm and torso and hooded skull.

We had learned, in this time of miracles, that matter and energy are interchangeable; and that a person can be broken down into energy waves; and those waves can be fired off into the timestream, toward the light. Time did, indeed, sweep backward, and one could drift backward, going ever toward that ultimate light that we feared to enter. Not because of superstition, but because we all understood on a level we could not explain, that the light was the start of it all, perhaps the Big Bang itself.

But we *could* go fugitive, drift back and back, even to the dawn of life on this planet. And we could return, but only to the moment we had left. We could not go forward, which was just as well. Literally, the information that was us could be fired out backward through the timestream as wave data.

And the miracle was that it was all contained in the suit of lights. Calibrate it on the wrist-cuff, thumb the "activate" readout that was coded to the DNA of only the three of us who were timedrifters, and no matter where we stood, we turned to smoke, turned to light, imploded into a scintillant point, and vanished, to be fired away, and to reassemble as ourselves at the shore of the Sea of Reeds as the Egyptians were drowned, in the garden of Gethsemane on the night of Jesus's betrayal, in the crowd as Chicago's Mayor Cermak was assassinated by a demented immigrant trying to get a shot at Franklin D. Roosevelt, in the right field bleachers as the '69 Mets won the World Series.

I thumbed the readout and saw only light, nothing but light, golden as a dream, eternal as a last breath, and I hurtled back toward the light that was *greater* than this light that filled me...

...and in a moment I stood in the year 165 Before the Common Era, within the burned gates of the Second Temple, on the Mount in Jerusalem. It was the 24th day of the Hebrew month *Kislev.* 165 B.C.E. The slaughtered dead of the Greco-Syrian army of Antiochus lay ten deep outside. The swordsmen of the Yovan, who had stabled pigs in the *Beis Ha Mikdosh,* even in the holiest of holies, who had defiled the sanctuary which housed the *menorah,* who had had sex on the stones of the sacred altar, and profaned those stones with urine and swine...they lay with new, crimson mouths opened in their necks, with iron protruding from their bellies and backs.

Ex-college boy from Chicago, timedrifter, fugitive. It had seemed like a good idea at the time. I never dreamed this kind of death could be...with bodies that had not been decently straightened for display in rectangular boxes...with hands that reached for the bodies that had once worn them. Faces without eyes.

I stood in the rubble of the most legendary structure in the history of my people, and realized this had not been, in any way, a good idea. Sick to my stomach, I started to thumb my wrist-cuff, to return *now* to the Project labs.

And I heard the scream.

And I turned my head.

And I saw the *Kohane,* who had been sent on ahead to assess the desecration—a son of Mattisyahu—I saw him flung backward and pinned to the floor of dirt and pig excrement, impaled by the spear of a Syrian pikeman who had been hiding in the shadows. Deserter of the citadel's garrison, a coward hiding in the shadows. And as he strode forward to finish the death of the writhing priest, I charged, grabbed up one of the desecrated stones of the altar and, as he turned to stare at me, frozen in an instant at the sight of this creature of light bearing down on him...I raised the jagged rock and crushed his face to pulp.

Dying, the *Kohane* looked upon me with wonder. He murmured prayers and my suit of lights shone in his eyes. I spoke to him in Greek, but he could not understand me. And then in Latin, both formal and vulgate, but his whispered responses were incomprehensible to me. *I could not speak his language!*

I tried Parthian, Samarian, Median, Cuthian, even Chaldean and Sumerian...but he faded slowly, only staring up at me in dying wonder. Then I understood one word of his lamentation, and I summoned up the hypnosleep learning that applied. I spoke to him in Aramaic of the Hasmonean brotherhood. And I begged him to tell me where the flasks of oil were kept. But there were none. He had brought nothing with him, in advance of his priest brothers and the return of Shimon from his battle with the citadel garrison.

It was a time of miracles, and I knew what to do.

I thumbed the readout on my wrist-cuff and watched as my light became a mere pinpoint in his dying eyes.

I went back to Chicago. This was wrong, I knew this was wrong: timedrifters are forbidden to alter the past. The three of us who were trained to go fugitive, we understood above all else...*change nothing, alter nothing,* or risk a tainted future. I knew what I was doing was wrong.

But, oh, it seemed like a good idea at the time.

I went to Rosenbloom's, still in business on Devon Avenue, still in Rogers Park, even this well into the 21st century. I had to buy some trustworthy oil.

I told the little balding clerk I wanted virgin olive oil so pure it could be used in the holiest of ceremonies. He said, "How holy does it have to be for Chanukah in Chicago?" I told him it was going to be used in Israel. He laughed. "All oil today is 'tomei'—you know what that is?" I said no, I didn't. (Because, you see, I *didn't* say, I'm not a Good Jew, and I don't know such things.) He said, "It means impure. And you know what *virgin* means! It means every olive was squeezed, but only the first drop was used." I asked him if the oil he sold was acceptable. He said, "Absolutely." I knew how much I needed, I'd read the piece on Chanukah history. Half a log, the Talmud had said. Two riv-ee-eas. I had to look it up: about eight ounces, the equivalent of a pony bottle of Budweiser. He sold it to me in a bottle of dark brown, opaque glass.

And I took the oil to one of the one hundred and sixty-three Gentiles on Project Timedrift, a chemist named Bethany Sherward, and I asked her to perform a small miracle. She said, "Matty, this is hardly a miracle you're asking for. You know the alleged 'burning bush' that spoke to Moses? They still exist. Burning bushes. In the Sinai, Saudi Arabia, Iraq. Mostly over the oil fields. They just burn and burn and..."

While she did what she had to do, I went fugitive and found myself, a creature of light once again, in the *Beis Ha Mikdosh,* in the fragile hours after midnight, in the Hebrew month of *Cheshvan,* in the year 125 B.C.E.; and I stole a cruse of oil and took it back to Chicago and poured it into a sink, and realized what an idiot I'd been. I needn't have gone to Rosenbloom's. I could have used *this* oil, which was pure. But it was too late now. There was a lot we all had to learn about traveling in time.

I got the altered oil from Bethany Sherward, and when I hefted the small container I almost felt as if I could detect a heaviness that had not been there before. This oil was denser than ordinary olive oil, virgin or otherwise.

I poured the new oil into the cruse. It sloshed at the bottom of the vessel. This was a dark red, rough-surfaced clay jar, tapering almost into the shape of the traditional Roman amphora, but it had a narrow base, and a fitted lid without a stopper. It now contained enough oil for exactly one day, half a log. I returned to the Timedrift lab, put on the suit of lights—it was wonderful to have one of only three triple-A clearances—and set myself to return to the Temple of the Mount, five minutes earlier than I'd appeared the first time. I didn't know if I'd see myself coalesce into existence five minutes later, but I *did* know that I could save the *Kohane's* life.

I went toward the light. I *became* a creature of the light yet again, and found myself standing inside the gates once more. I started inside the Great Temple...

And heard the scream.

Time had adjusted itself. He was falling backward, the spear having ripped open his chest. I charged the Syrian, hit him with the cruse of oil, knocked him to the dirt, and crushed his windpipe with one full force stomp of my booted foot.

I stood staring down at him for perhaps a minute. I had killed a man. With hardly the effort I would have expended to wipe sweat from my face, I had smashed the life out of him. I started to shake, and then I heard myself whimper. And then I made a stop to it. I had come here to do a thing, and I knew it would now be done because...nowhere in sight did *another* creature of shimmering light appear. We had much to learn about traveling in time.

I went to the priest where he lay in his dirt-caked blood, and I raised his head. He stared at me in wonder, as he had the first time.

"Who are you!" he asked, coughing blood.

"Matty Simon," I said. It seemed like a good idea at the time.

He smiled. "Mattisyahu's son, Shimon?"

I started to say no, Matty, not Mattisyahu; Simon, not Shimon. But I didn't say that. I had thought *he* was one of the sons, but I was wrong. Had I been a more knowledgeable Jew, I would have known: he wasn't the *Kohane Gadol.* He was a Levite from Moses's tribe; one of the priestly class; sent ahead as point man for the redemption of the Temple; like Seabees sent in ahead of an invasion to clear out trees and clean up the area. But now he would die, and not do the job.

"Put your seal on this cruse," I said. "Did the *Kohane Gadol* give you that authority, can you do that?"

He looked at the clay vessel, and even in his overwhelming pain he was frightened and repelled by the command I had made. "No... I cannot..."

I held him by the shoulders with as much force as I could muster, and I looked into his eyes and I found a voice I'd never known was in me, and I demanded, *"Can you do this?"*

He nodded slightly, in terror and awe, and he hesitated a moment and then asked, "Who are you? Are you a Messenger of God?" I was all light, brighter than the sun, and holding him in my arms.

"Yes," I lied. "Yes, I am a Messenger of God. Let me help you seal the flask."

That he did. He did what was forbidden, what was not possible, what he should not have done. He put the seal of pure oil on the vessel containing half a log, two *riv-ee-eas,* of long-chain hydrocarbon oil from a place that did not even exist yet in the world, oil from a time unborn, from the future. The longer the chain, the greater the binding energy. The greater the binding energy, the longer it would burn. One day's oil, from the future; one day's oil that would burn brightly for eight days.

He died in my arms, smiling up into the face of God's Messenger. He went toward the light, a prayer on his lips.

Today, at lunch in the Commissary, Barry R. Levin slapped his tray down on the table across from me, slid into the seat, and said, "Well, Mr. Pretend Jew, tomorrow is Chanukah. Are you ready to light the candles?"

"Beat it, Levin."

"Would you like me to render the prayers phonetically for you?"

"Get away from me, Levin, or I'll lay you out. I'm in no mood for your scab-picking today."

"Hard night, Mr. Simon?"

"You'll never know." I gave him the look that said *get in the wind, you pain in the ass.* He stood up, lifted his tray, took a step, then turned back to me.

"You're a Bad Jew, remember that."

I shook my head ruefully and couldn't hold back the mean little laugh.

"Yeah, right. I'm a Bad Jew. I'm also the Messenger of God."

He just looked at me. Not a clue why I'd said that. All scores evened, I didn't have the heart to tell him...

It just seemed like a helluva good idea at the time. The time of miracles.

Mefisto
In
Onyx

Once. I only went to bed *Friends for eleven* years—before with her once.
and since—but it was just one of those things, just one of those crazy flings:
the two of us alone on a New Year's Eve, watching rented Marx Brothers
videos so we wouldn't have to go out with a bunch of idiots and make noise
and pretend we were having a good time when all we'd be doing was
getting drunk, whooping like morons, vomiting on slow-moving strangers,
and spending more money than we had to waste. And we drank a little too
much cheap champagne; and we fell off the sofa laughing at Harpo a few
times too many; and we wound up on the floor at the same time; and next
thing we knew we had our faces plastered together, and my hand up her
skirt, and her hand down in my pants...

But it was just the *once*, fer chrissakes! Talk about imposing on a cheap
sexual liaison! She *knew* I went mixing in other peoples' minds only when
I absolutely had no other way to make a buck. Or I forgot myself and did it
in a moment of human weakness.

It was always foul.

Slip into the thoughts of the best person who ever lived, even Saint
Thomas Aquinas, for instance, just to pick an absolutely terrific person

you'd think had a mind so clean you could eat off it (to paraphrase my mother), and when you come out—take my word for it—you'd want to take a long, intense shower in Lysol.

Trust me on this: I go into somebody's landscape when there's *nothing else* I can do, no other possible solution...or I forget and do it in a moment of human weakness. Such as, say, the IRS holds my feet to the fire; or I'm about to get myself mugged and robbed and maybe murdered; or I need to find out if some specific she that I'm dating has been using somebody else's dirty needle or has been sleeping around without she's taking some extra-heavy-duty AIDS precautions; or a co-worker's got it in his head to set me up so I make a mistake and look bad to the boss and I find myself in the unemployment line again; or...

I'm a wreck for weeks after.

Go jaunting through a landscape trying to pick up a little insider arbitrage bric-a-brac, and come away no better heeled, but all muddy with the guy's infidelities, and I can't look a decent woman in the eye for days. Get told by a motel desk clerk that they're all full up and he's sorry as hell but I'll just have to drive on for about another thirty miles to find the next vacancy, jaunt into his landscape and find him lit up with neon signs that got a lot of the word *nigger* in them, and I wind up hitting the sonofabitch so hard his grandmother has a bloody nose, and usually have to hide out for three or four weeks after. Just about to miss a bus, jaunt into the head of the driver to find his name so I can yell for him to hold it a minute Tom or George or Willie, and I get smacked in the mind with all the garlic he's been eating for the past month because his doctor told him it was good for his system, and I start to dry-heave, and I wrench out of the landscape, and not only have I missed the bus, but I'm so sick to my stomach I have to sit down on the filthy curb to get my gorge submerged. Jaunt into a potential employer, to see if he's trying to lowball me, and I learn he's part of a massive cover-up of industrial malfeasance that's caused hundreds of people to die when this or that cheaply-made grommet or tappet or gimbal mounting underperforms and fails, sending the poor souls falling thousands of feet to shrieking destruction. Then just *try* to accept the job, even if you haven't paid your rent in a month. No way.

Absolutely: I listen in on the landscape *only* when my feet are being fried; when the shadow stalking me turns down alley after alley tracking me relentlessly; when the drywall guy I've hired to repair the damage done by my leaky shower presents me with a dopey smile and a bill three hundred and sixty bucks higher than the estimate. Or in a moment of human weakness.

But I'm a wreck for weeks after. For weeks.

Because you can't, you simply can't, you absolutely *cannot* know what people are truly and really like till you jaunt their landscape. If Aquinas had had my ability, he'd have very quickly gone off to be a hermit, only occasionally visiting the mind of a sheep or a hedgehog. In a moment of human weakness.

That's why in my whole life—and, as best I can remember back, I've been doing it since I was five or six years old, maybe even younger—there have only been eleven, maybe twelve people, of all those who know that I can "read minds," that I've permitted myself to get close to. Three of them never used it against me, or tried to exploit me, or tried to kill me when I wasn't looking. Two of those three were my mother and father, a pair of sweet old black folks who'd adopted me, a late-in-life baby, and were now dead (but probably still worried about me, even on the Other Side), and whom I missed very very much, particularly in moments like this. The other eight, nine were either so turned off by the knowledge that they made sure I never came within a mile of them—one moved to another entire country just to be on the safe side, although her thoughts were a helluva lot more boring and innocent than she thought they were—or they tried to brain me with something heavy when I was distracted—I still have a shoulder separation that kills me for two days before it rains—or they tried to use me to make a buck for them. Not having the common sense to figure it out, that if I was *capable* of using the ability to make vast sums of money, why the hell was I living hand-to-mouth like some overaged grad student who was afraid to desert the university and go become an adult?

Now *they* was some dumb-ass muthuhfugguhs.

Of the three who never used it against me—my mom and dad—the last was Allison Roche. Who sat on the stool next to me, in the middle of May, in the middle of a Wednesday afternoon, in the middle of Clanton, Alabama, squeezing ketchup onto her All-American Burger, imposing on the memory of that one damned New Year's Eve sexual interlude, with Harpo and his sibs; the two of us all alone except for the fry-cook; and she waited for my reply.

"I'd sooner have a skunk spray my pants leg," I replied.

She pulled a napkin from the chrome dispenser and swabbed up the red that had overshot the sesame-seed bun and redecorated the Formica countertop. She looked at me from under thick, lustrous eyelashes; a look of impatience and violet eyes that must have been a killer when she unbottled it at some truculent witness for the defense. Allison Roche was a Chief Deputy District Attorney in and for Jefferson County, with her office in Birmingham. Alabama. Where near we sat, in Clanton, having a secret meeting, having All-American Burgers; three years after having had quite a bit of champagne, 1930s black-and-white video rental comedy, and black-and-white sex. One extremely stupid New Year's Eve.

Friends for eleven years. And once, just once; as a prime example of what happens in a moment of human weakness. Which is not to say that it wasn't terrific, because it was; absolutely terrific; but we never did it again; and we never brought it up again after the next morning when we opened our eyes and looked at each other the way you look at an exploding can of sardines, and both of us said *Oh Jeeezus* at the same time. Never brought it up again until this memorable afternoon at the greasy spoon where I'd joined Ally, driving up from Montgomery to meet her halfway, after her peculiar telephone invitation.

Can't say the fry-cook, Mr. All-American, was particularly happy at the pigmentation arrangement at his counter. But I stayed out of his head and let him think what he wanted. Times change on the outside, but the inner landscape remains polluted.

"All I'm asking you to do is go have a chat with him," she said. She gave me that look. I have a hard time with that look. It isn't entirely honest, neither is it entirely disingenuous. It plays on my remembrance of that one night we spent in bed. And is just *dis*honest enough to play on the part of that night we spent on the floor, on the sofa, on the coffee counter between the dining room and the kitchenette, in the bathtub, and about nineteen minutes crammed among her endless pairs of shoes in a walk-in clothes closet that smelled strongly of cedar and virginity. She gave me that look, and wasted no part of the memory.

"I don't *want* to go have a chat with him. Apart from he's a piece of human shit, and I have better things to do with my time than to go on down to Atmore and take a jaunt through this crazy sonofabitch's diseased mind, may I remind you that of the hundred and sixty, seventy men who have died in that electric chair, including the original 'Yellow Mama' they scrapped in 1990, about a hundred and thirty of them were gentlemen of color, and I do not mean you to picture any color of a shade much lighter than that cuppa coffee you got sittin' by your left hand right this minute, which is to say that I, being an inordinately well-educated African-American who values the full measure of living negritude in his body, am not crazy enough to want to visit a racist '*co*-rectional center' like Holman Prison, thank you very much."

"Are you finished?" she asked, wiping her mouth.

"Yeah. I'm finished. Case closed. Find somebody else."

She didn't like that. "There *isn't* anybody else."

"There has to be. Somewhere. Go check the research files at Duke University. Call the Fortean Society. Mensa. *Jeopardy.* Some 900 number astrology psychic hotline. Ain't there some semi-senile Senator with a full-time paid assistant who's been trying to get legislation through one of the statehouses for the last five years to fund this kind of bullshit research? What about the Russians...now that the Evil Empire's fallen, you ought to be able to get some word about their success with Kirlian auras or whatever those assholes were working at. Or you could—"

She screamed at the top of her lungs. *"Stop it, Rudy!"*

The fry-cook dropped the spatula he'd been using to scrape off the grill. He picked it up, looking at us, and his face (I didn't read his mind) said *If that white bitch makes one more noise I'm callin' the cops.*

I gave him a look he didn't want, and he went back to his chores, getting ready for the after-work crowd. But the stretch of his back and angle of his head told me he wasn't going to let this pass.

I leaned in toward her, got as serious as I could, and just this quietly, just this softly, I said, "Ally, good pal, listen to me. You've been one of the few friends I could count on, for a long time now. We have history between us, and you've *never*, not once, made me feel like a freak. So okay, I trust you. I trust you with something about me that causes immeasurable goddam pain. A thing about me that could get me killed. You've never betrayed me, and you've never tried to use me.

"Till now. This is the first time. And you've got to admit that it's not even as rational as you maybe saying to me that you've gambled away every cent you've got and you owe the mob a million bucks and would I mind taking a trip to Vegas or Atlantic City and taking a jaunt into the minds of some high-pocket poker players so I could win you enough to keep the goons from shooting you. Even *that,* as creepy as it would be if you said it to me, even *that* would be easier to understand than *this!*"

She looked forlorn. "There isn't anybody else, Rudy. *Please.*"

"What the hell is this all about? Come on, tell me. You're hiding something, or holding something back, or lying about—"

"I'm not lying!" For the second time she was suddenly, totally, extremely pissed at me. Her voice spattered off the white tile walls. The fry-cook spun around at the sound, took a step toward us, and I jaunted into his landscape, smoothed down the rippled Astro-Turf, drained away the storm clouds, and suggested in there that he go take a cigarette

break out back. Fortunately, there were no other patrons at the elegant All-American Burger that late in the afternoon, and he went.

"Calm fer chrissakes down, will you?" I said.

She had squeezed the paper napkin into a ball.

She was lying, hiding, holding something back. Didn't have to be a telepath to figure *that* out. I waited, looking at her with a slow, careful distrust, and finally she sighed, and I thought, *Here it comes.*

"Are you reading my mind?" she asked.

"Don't insult me. We know each other too long."

She looked chagrined. The violet of her eyes deepened. "Sorry."

But she didn't go on. I wasn't going to be outflanked. I waited.

After a while she said, softly, very softly, "I think I'm in love with him. I *know* I believe him when he says he's innocent."

I never expected that. I couldn't even reply.

It was unbelievable. Unfuckingbelievable. She was the Chief Deputy D.A. who had prosecuted Henry Lake Spanning for murder. Not just one murder, one random slaying, a heat of the moment Saturday night killing regretted deeply on Sunday morning but punishable by electrocution in the Sovereign State of Alabama nonetheless, but a string of the vilest, most sickening serial slaughters in Alabama history, in the history of the Glorious South, in the history of the United States. Maybe even in the history of the entire wretched human universe that went wading hip-deep in the wasted spilled blood of innocent men, women and children.

Henry Lake Spanning was a monster, an ambulatory disease, a killing machine without conscience or any discernible resemblance to a thing we might call decently human. Henry Lake Spanning had butchered his way across a half-dozen states; and they had caught up to him in Huntsville, in a garbage dumpster behind a supermarket, doing something so vile and inhuman to what was left of a sixty-five-year-old cleaning woman that not even the tabloids would get more explicit than *unspeakable*; and somehow he got away from the cops; and somehow he evaded their dragnet; and somehow he found out where the police lieutenant in charge of the manhunt lived; and somehow he slipped into that neighborhood when the lieutenant was out creating roadblocks—and he gutted the man's wife and two kids. Also the family cat. And then he killed a couple of more times in Birmingham and Decatur, and by then had gone so completely out of his mind that they got him again, and the second time they hung onto him, and they brought him to trial. And Ally had prosecuted this bottom-feeding monstrosity.

And oh, what a circus it had been. Though he'd been *caught,* the second time, and this time for keeps, in Jefferson County, scene of three of his most sickening jobs, he'd murdered (with such a disgustingly similar m.o. that it was obvious he was the perp) in twenty-two of the sixty-seven counties; and every last one of them wanted him to stand trial in that venue. Then there were the other five states in which he had butchered, to a total body-count of fifty-six. Each of *them* wanted him extradited.

So, here's how smart and quick and smooth an attorney Ally is: she somehow managed to coze up to the Attorney General, and somehow managed to unleash those violet eyes on him, and somehow managed to get and keep his ear long enough to con him into setting a legal precedent. Attorney General of the State of Alabama allowed Allison Roche to consolidate, to secure a multiple bill of indictment that forced Spanning to stand trial on all twenty-nine Alabama murder counts at once. She meticulously documented to the state's highest courts that Henry Lake Spanning presented such a clear and present danger to society that the prosecution was willing to take a chance (big chance!) of trying in a winner-take-all consolidation of venues. Then she managed to smooth the feathers of all those other vote-hungry prosecuters in those twenty-one other counties, and she put on a case that dazzled everyone, including Spanning's defense attorney, who had screamed about the legality of the multiple bill from the moment she'd suggested it.

And she won a fast jury verdict on all twenty-nine counts. Then she got *really* fancy in the penalty phase after the jury verdict, and proved up the *other* twenty-seven murders with their flagrantly identical trademarks, from those other five states, and there was nothing left but to sentence Spanning—essentially for all fifty-six—to the replacement for the "Yellow Mama."

Even as pols and power brokers throughout the state were murmuring Ally's name for higher office, Spanning was slated to sit in that new electric chair in Holman Prison, built by the Fred A. Leuchter Associates of Boston, Massachusetts, that delivers 2,640 volts of pure sparklin' death in 1/240th of a second, six times faster than the 1/40th of a second that it takes for the brain to sense it, which is—if you ask me—much too humane an exit line, more than three times the 700 volt jolt lethal dose that destroys a brain, for a pusbag like Henry Lake Spanning.

But if we were lucky—and the scheduled day of departure was very nearly upon us—if we were lucky, if there was a God and Justice and Natural Order and all that good stuff, then Henry Lake Spanning, this foulness, this corruption, this thing that lived only to ruin...would end up as a pile of fucking ashes somebody might use to sprinkle over a flower garden, thereby providing this ghoul with his single opportunity to be of some use to the human race.

That was the guy that my pal Allison Roche wanted me to go and "chat" with, down to Holman Prison, in Atmore, Alabama. There, sitting on Death Row, waiting to get his demented head tonsured, his pants legs slit, his tongue fried black as the inside of a sheep's belly...down there at Holman my pal Allison wanted me to go "chat" with one of the most awful creatures made for killing this side of a hammerhead shark, which creature had an infinitely greater measure of human decency than Henry Lake Spanning had ever demonstrated. Go chit-chat, and enter his landscape, and read his mind, Mr. Telepath, and use the marvelous mythic power of extra-sensory perception: this nifty swell ability that has made me a bum all my life, well, not *exactly* a bum: I do have a decent apartment, and I do earn a decent, if sporadic, living; and I try to follow Nelson Algren's warning never to get involved with a woman whose troubles are bigger than my own; and sometimes I even have a car of my own, even though at that moment such was not the case, the Camaro having been repo'd, and not by Harry Dean Stanton or Emilio Estevez, lemme tell you; but a bum in the sense of—how does Ally put it?—oh yeah—I don't "realize my full and forceful potential"—a bum in the sense that I can't hold a job, and I get rotten breaks, and all of this despite a Rhodes scholarly education so far above what a poor nigrah-lad such as myself could expect that even Rhodes hisownself would've been chest-out proud as hell of me. A bum, mostly, despite an *outstanding* Rhodes scholar education and a pair of kind, smart, loving parents— even for foster-parents—shit, *especially* for being foster-parents—who died knowing the certain sadness that their only child would spend his life as a wandering freak unable to make a comfortable living or consummate a normal marriage or raise children without the fear of passing on this special personal horror...this astonishing ability fabled in song and story that I possess...that no one else seems to possess, though I know there must have been others, somewhere, sometime, somehow! Go, Mr. Wonder of Wonders, shining black Cagliostro of the modern world, go with this super nifty swell ability that gullible idiots and flying saucer assholes have been trying to prove exists for at least fifty years, that no one has been able to isolate the way I, me, the only one has been isolated, let me tell you about *isolation,* my brothers; and here I was, here was I, Rudy Pairis...just a guy, making a buck every now and then with nifty swell impossible ESP, resident of thirteen states and twice that many cities so far in his mere thirty years of landscape-jaunting life, here was I, Rudy Pairis, Mr. I-Can-Read-Your-Mind, being asked to go and walk through the mind of a killer who scared half the people in the world. Being asked by the only living person, probably, to whom I could not say no. And, oh, take me at my word here: I *wanted* to say no. *Was*, in fact, saying no at every breath. What's that? Will I do it? Sure, yeah sure, I'll go on down to Holman and jaunt through this sick bastard's mind landscape. Sure I will. You got two chances: slim, and none.

All of this was going on in the space of one greasy double cheeseburger and two cups of coffee.

The worst part of it was that Ally had somehow gotten involved with him. *Ally!* Not some bimbo bitch...but *Ally*. I couldn't believe it.

Not that it was unusual for women to become mixed up with guys in the joint, to fall under their "magic spell," and to start corresponding with them, visiting them, taking them candy and cigarettes, having conjugal visits, playing mule for them and smuggling in dope where the tampon never shine, writing them letters that got steadily more exotic, steadily more intimate, steamier and increasingly dependent emotionally. It wasn't that big a deal; there exist entire psychiatric treatises on the phenomenon; right alongside the papers about women who go stud-crazy for cops. No big deal indeed: hundreds of women every year find themselves writing to these guys, visiting these guys, building dream castles with these guys, fucking these guys, pretending that even the worst of these guys, rapists and woman-beaters and child molesters, repeat pedophiles of the lowest pustule sort, and murderers and stick-up punks who crush old ladies' skulls for food stamps, and terrorists and bunco barons...that one sunny might-be, gonna-happen pink cloud day these demented creeps will emerge from behind the walls, get back in the wind, become upstanding nine-to-five Brooks Bros. Galahads. Every year hundreds of women marry these guys, finding themselves in a hot second snookered by the wily, duplicitous, motherfuckin' lying greaseball addictive behavior of guys who had spent their sporadic years, their intermittent freedom on the outside, doing *just that*: roping people in, ripping people off, bleeding people dry, conning them into being tools, taking them for their every last cent, their happy home, their sanity, their ability to trust or love ever again.

But this wasn't some poor illiterate naive woman-child. This was *Ally*. She had damned near pulled off a legal impossibility, come *that* close to Bizarro Jurisprudence by putting the Attorneys General of five other states in a maybe frame of mind where she'd have been able to consolidate a multiple bill of indictment *across state lines*! Never been done; and now, probably, never ever would be. But she could have possibly pulled off such a thing. Unless you're a stone court-bird, you can't know what a mountaintop that is!

So, now, here's Ally, saying this shit to me. Ally, my best pal, stood up for me a hundred times; not some dip, but the steely-eyed Sheriff of Suicide Gulch, the over-forty, past the age of innocence, no-nonsense woman who had seen it all and come away tough but not cynical, hard but not mean.

"I think I'm in love with him." She had said.

"I *know* I believe him when he says he's innocent." She had said.

I looked at her. No time had passed. It was still the moment the universe decided to lie down and die. And I said, "So if you're certain this paragon of the virtues *isn't* responsible for fifty-six murders—that we *know* about—and who the hell knows how many more we *don't* know about, since he's apparently been at it since he was twelve years old—remember the couple of nights we sat up and you *told* me all this shit about him, and you said it with your skin crawling, *remember?*—then if you're so damned positive the guy you spent eleven weeks in court sending to the chair is innocent of butchering half the population of the planet—then why do you need me to go to Holman, drive all the way to Atmore, just to take a jaunt in this sweet peach of a guy?

"Doesn't your 'woman's intuition' tell you he's squeaky clean? Don't 'true love' walk yo' sweet young ass down the primrose path with sufficient surefootedness?"

"Don't be a smartass!" she said.

"Say again?" I replied, with disfuckingbelief.

"I said: don't be such a high-verbal goddamned smart aleck!"

Now *I* was steamed. "No, I shouldn't be a smartass: I should be your pony, your show dog, your little trick bag mind-reader freak! Take a drive over to Holman, Pairis; go right on into Rednecks from Hell; sit your ass down on Death Row with the rest of the niggers and have a chat with the one white boy who's been in a cell up there for the past three years or so; sit down nicely with the king of the fucking vampires, and slide inside his garbage dump of a brain—and what a joy *that's* gonna be, I can't believe you'd ask me to do this—and read whatever piece of boiled shit in there he calls a brain, and see if he's jerking you around. *That's* what I ought to do, am I correct? Instead of being a smartass. Have I got it right? Do I properly pierce your meaning, pal?"

She stood up. She didn't even say *Screw you, Pairis!*

She just slapped me as hard as she could.

She hit me a good one straight across the mouth.

I felt my upper teeth bite my lower lip. I tasted the blood. My head rang like a church bell. I thought I'd fall off the goddam stool.

When I could focus, she was just standing there, looking ashamed of herself, and disappointed, and mad as hell, and worried that she'd brained me. All of that, all at the same time. Plus, she looked as if I'd broken her choo-choo train.

"Okay," I said wearily, and ended the word with a sigh that reached all the way back into my hip pocket. "Okay, calm down. I'll see him. I'll do it. Take it easy."

She didn't sit down. "Did I hurt you?"

"No, of course not," I said, unable to form the smile I was trying to put on my face. "How could you possibly hurt someone by knocking his brains into his lap?"

She stood over me as I clung precariously to the counter, turned halfway around on the stool by the blow. Stood over me, the balled-up paper napkin in her fist, a look on her face that said she was nobody's fool, that we'd known each other a long time, that she hadn't asked this kind of favor before, that if we were buddies and I loved her, that I would see she was in deep pain, that she was conflicted, that she needed to know, *really* needed to know without a doubt, and in the name of God—in which she believed, though I didn't, but either way what the hell—that I do this thing for her, that I just *do it* and not give her any more crap about it.

So I shrugged, and spread my hands like a man with no place to go, and I said, "How'd you get into this?"

She told me the first fifteen minutes of her tragic, heartwarming, never-to-be-ridiculed story still standing. After fifteen minutes I said, "Fer chrissakes, Ally, at least *sit down*! You look like a damned fool standing there with a greasy napkin in your mitt."

A couple of teen-agers had come in. The four-star chef had finished his cigarette out back and was reassuringly in place, walking the duckboards and dishing up All-American arterial cloggage.

She picked up her elegant attaché case and without a word, with only a nod that said let's get as far from them as we can, she and I moved to a double against the window to resume our discussion of the varieties of social suicide available to an unwary and foolhardy gentleman of the colored persuasion if he allowed himself to be swayed by a cagey and cogent, clever and concupiscent female of another color entirely.

See, what it is, is this:

Look at that attaché case. You want to know what kind of an Ally this Allison Roche is? Pay heed, now.

In New York, when some wannabe junior ad exec has smooched enough butt to get tossed a bone account, and he wants to walk his colors, has a need to signify, has got to demonstrate to everyone that he's got the juice, first thing he does, he hies his ass downtown to Barney's, West 17th and Seventh, buys hisself a Burberry, loops the belt casually *behind,* leaving the coat open to suh*wing,* and he circumnavigates the office.

In Dallas, when the wife of the CEO has those six or eight upper-management husbands and wives over for an *intime, faux*-casual dinner, sans placecards, sans *entrée* fork, *sans cérémonie*, and we're talking the kind of woman who flies Virgin Air instead of the Concorde, she's so in charge she don't got to use the Orrefors, she can put out the Kosta Boda and say *give a fuck.*

What it is, kind of person so in charge, so easy with they own self, they don't *have* to laugh at your poor dumb struttin' Armani suit, or your bedroom done in Laura Ashley, or that you got a gig writing articles for *TV Guide.* You see what I'm sayin' here? The sort of person Ally Roche is, you take a look at that attaché case, and it'll tell you everything you need to know about how strong she is, because it's an Atlas. Not a Hartmann. Understand: she could *afford* a Hartmann, that gorgeous imported Canadian belting leather, top of the line, somewhere around nine hundred and fifty bucks maybe, equivalent of Orrefors, a Burberry, breast of guinea hen and Mouton Rothschild 1492 or 1066 or whatever year is the most expensive, drive a Rolls instead of a Bentley and the only difference is the grille…but she doesn't *need* to signify, doesn't *need* to suh*wing,* so she gets herself this Atlas. Not some dumb chickenshit Louis Vuitton or Mark Cross all the divorcée real estate ladies carry, but an Atlas. Irish hand leather. Custom tanned cowhide. Hand tanned in Ireland by out of work IRA bombers. Very classy. Just a state understated. See that attaché case? That tell you why I said I'd do it?

She picked it up from where she'd stashed it, right up against the counter wall by her feet, and we went to the double over by the window, away from the chef and the teen-agers, and she stared at me till she was sure I was in a right frame of mind, and she picked up where she'd left off.

The next twenty-three minutes by the big greasy clock on the wall she related from a sitting position. Actually, a series of sitting positions. She kept shifting in her chair like someone who didn't appreciate the view of the world from that window, someone hoping for a sweeter horizon. The story started with a gang-rape at the age of thirteen, and moved right along: two broken foster-home families, a little casual fondling by surrogate poppas, intense studying for perfect school grades as a substitute for happiness, working her way through John Jay College of Law, a truncated attempt at wedded bliss in her late twenties, and the long miserable road of legal success that had brought her to Alabama. There could have been worse places.

I'd known Ally for a long time, and we'd spent totals of weeks and months in each other's company. Not to mention the New Year's Eve of the Marx Brothers. But I hadn't heard much of this. Not much at all.

Funny how that goes. Eleven years. You'd think I'd've guessed or suspected or *some*thing. What the hell makes us think we're friends with *any*body, when we don't know the first thing about them, not really?

What are we, walking around in a dream? That is to say: what the fuck are we *thinking*!?!

And there might never have been a reason to hear *any* of it, all this Ally that was the real Ally, but now she was asking me to go somewhere I didn't want to go, to do something that scared the shit out of me; and she wanted me to be as fully informed as possible.

It dawned on me that those same eleven years between us hadn't really given her a full, laser-clean insight into the why and wherefore of Rudy Pairis, either. I hated myself for it. The concealing, the holding-back, the giving up only fragments, the evil misuse of charm when honesty would have hurt. I was facile, and a very quick study; and I had buried all the equivalents to Ally's pains and travails. I could've matched her, in spades; or blacks, or just plain nigras. But I remained frightened of losing her friendship. I've never been able to believe in the myth of unqualified friendship. Too much like standing hip-high in a fast-running, freezing river. Standing on slippery stones.

Her story came forward to the point at which she had prosecuted Spanning; had amassed and winnowed and categorized the evidence so thoroughly, so deliberately, so flawlessly; had orchestrated the case so brilliantly; that the jury had come in with guilty on all twenty-nine, soon—in the penalty phase—fifty-six. Murder in the first. Premeditated murder in the first. Premeditated murder with special ugly circumstances in the first. On each and every of the twenty-nine. Less than an hour it took them. There wasn't even time for a lunch break. Fifty-one minutes it took them to come back with the verdict guilty on all charges. Less than a minute per killing. Ally had done that.

His attorney had argued that no direct link had been established between the fifty-sixth killing (actually, only his 29th in Alabama) and Henry Lake Spanning. No, they had not caught him down on his knees eviscerating the shredded body of his final victim—ten-year-old Gunilla Ascher, a parochial school girl who had missed her bus and been picked up by Spanning just about a mile from her home in Decatur—no, not down on his knees with the can opener still in his sticky red hands, but the m.o. was the same, and he was there in Decatur, on the run from what he had done in Huntsville, what they had *caught* him doing in Huntsville, in that dumpster, to that old woman. So they *couldn't* place him with his smooth, slim hands inside dead Gunilla Ascher's still-steaming body. So what? They could not have been surer he was the serial killer, the monster, the ravaging nightmare whose methods were so vile the newspapers hadn't even *tried* to cobble up some smart-aleck name for him like The Strangler or The Backyard Butcher. The jury had come back in fifty-one minutes, looking sick, looking as if they'd try and try to get everything they'd seen and heard out of their minds, but knew they never would, and wishing to God they could've managed to get out of their civic duty on this one.

They came shuffling back in and told the numbed court: hey, put this slimy excuse for a maggot in the chair and cook his ass till he's fit only to be served for breakfast on cinnamon toast. This was the guy my friend Ally told me she had fallen in love with. The guy she now believed to be innocent.

This was seriously crazy stuff.

"So how did you get, er, uh, how did you...?"

"How did I fall in love with him?"

"Yeah. That."

She closed her eyes for a moment, and pursed her lips as if she had lost a flock of wayward words and didn't know where to find them. I'd always known she was a private person, kept the really important history to herself—hell, until now I'd never known about the rape, the ice mountain between her mother and father, the specifics of the seven-month marriage—I'd known there'd been a husband briefly; but not what had happened; and I'd known about the foster homes; but again, not how lousy it had been for her—even so, getting *this* slice of steaming craziness out of her was like using your teeth to pry the spikes out of Jesus's wrists.

Finally, she said, "I took over the case when Charlie Whilborg had his stroke..."

"I remember."

"He was the best litigator in the office, and if he hadn't gone down two days before they caught…" she paused, had trouble with the name, went on, "…before they caught Spanning in Decatur, and if Morgan County hadn't been so worried about a case this size, and bound Spanning over to us in Birmingham…all of it so fast nobody really had a chance to talk to him…I was the first one even got *near* him, everyone was so damned scared of him, of what they *thought* he was…"

"Hallucinating, were they?" I said, being a smartass.

"Shut up.

"The office did most of the donkeywork after that first interview I had with him. It was a big break for me in the office; and I got obsessed by it. So after the first interview, I never spent much actual time with Spanky, never got too close, to see what kind of a man he *really…*"

I said: "Spanky? Who the hell's 'Spanky'?"

She blushed. It started from the sides of her nostrils and went out both ways toward her ears, then climbed to the hairline. I'd seen that happen only a couple of times in eleven years, and one of those times had been when she'd farted at the opera. *Lucia di Lammermoor.*

I said it again: "Spanky? You're putting me on, right? You call him *Spanky*?" The blush deepened. "Like the fat kid in *The Little Rascals…* ç'mon, I don't fuckin' be*lieve* this!"

She just glared at me.

I felt the laughter coming.

My face started twitching.

She stood up again. "Forget it. Just forget it, okay?" She took two steps away from the table, toward the street exit. I grabbed her hand and pulled her back, trying not to fall apart with laughter, and I said, "Okay okay okay…I'm *sorry*…I'm really and truly, honest to goodness, may I be struck by a falling space lab no kidding 100% absolutely sorry…but you gotta admit…catching me unawares like that…I mean, come *on*, Ally…*Spanky!?!* You call this guy who murdered at least fifty-six people Spanky? Why not Mickey, or Froggy, or Alfalfa…? I can understand not calling him Buckwheat, you can save that one for me, but *Spanky*???"

And in a moment *her* face started to twitch; and in another moment she was starting to smile, fighting it every micron of the way; and in another moment she was laughing and swatting at me with her free hand; and then she pulled her hand loose and stood there falling apart with laughter; and in about a minute she was sitting down again. She threw the balled-up napkin at me.

"It's from when he was a kid," she said. "He was a fat kid, and they made fun of him. You know the way kids are…thcy corrupted Spanning into 'Spanky' because *The Little Rascals* were on television and…oh, shut *up*, Rudy!"

I finally quieted down, and made conciliatory gestures.

She watched me with an exasperated wariness till she was sure I wasn't going to run any more dumb gags on her, and then she resumed. "After Judge Fay sentenced him, I handled Spa…*Henry's* case from our office, all the way up to the appeals stage. I was the one who did the pleading against clemency when Henry's lawyers took their appeal to the Eleventh Circuit in Atlanta.

"When he was denied a stay by the appellate, three-to-nothing, I helped prepare the brief when Henry's counsel went to the Alabama Supreme Court; then when the Supreme Court refused to hear his appeal, I thought it was all over. I knew they'd run out of moves for him, except maybe the Governor; but that wasn't ever going to happen. So I thought: *that's that.*

"When the Supreme Court wouldn't hear it three weeks ago, I got a letter from him. He'd been set for execution next Saturday, and I couldn't figure out why he wanted to see *me*."

I asked, "The letter…it got to you how?"

"One of his attorneys."

"I thought they'd given up on him."

"So did I. The evidence was so overwhelming; half a dozen counselors found ways to get themselves excused; it wasn't the kind of case that would bring any litigator good publicity. Just the number of eyewitnesses in the parking lot of that Winn-Dixie in Huntsville…must have been fifty of them, Rudy. And they all saw the same thing, and they all identified Henry in lineup after lineup, twenty, thirty, could have been fifty of them if we'd needed that long a parade. And all the rest of it…"

I held up a hand. *I know,* the flat hand against the air said. She had told me all of this. Every grisly detail, till I wanted to puke. It was as if I'd done it all myself, she was so vivid in her telling. Made my jaunting nausea pleasurable by comparison. Made me so sick I couldn't even think about it. Not even in a moment of human weakness.

"So the letter comes to you from the attorney…"

"I think you know this lawyer. Larry Borlan; used to be with the ACLU; before that he was senior counsel for the Alabama Legislature down to Montgomery; stood up, what was it, twice, three times, before the Supreme Court? Excellent guy. And not easily fooled."

"And what's *he* think about all this?"

"He thinks Henry's absolutely innocent."

"Of all of it?"

"Of everything."

"But there were fifty disinterested random eyewitnesses at one of those slaughters. Fifty, you just said it. Fifty, you could've had a parade. All of them nailed him cold, without a doubt. Same kind of kill as all the other fifty-five, including that schoolkid in Decatur when they finally got him. And Larry Borlan thinks he's not the guy, right?"

She nodded. Made one of those sort of comic pursings of the lips, shrugged, and nodded. "Not the guy."

"So the killer's still out there?"

"That's what Borlan thinks."

"And what do *you* think?"

"I agree with him."

"Oh, jeezus, Ally, my aching boots and saddle! You got to be workin' some kind of off-time! The killer is still out here in the mix, but there hasn't been a killing like those Spanning slaughters for the three years that he's been in the joint. Now *what* do that say to you?"

"It says whoever the guy *is,* the one who killed all those people, he's *days* smarter than all the rest of us, and he set up the perfect freefloater to take the fall for him, and he's either long far gone in some other state, working his way, or he's sitting quietly right here in Alabama, waiting and watching. And smiling." Her face seemed to sag with misery. She started to tear up, and said, "In four days he can stop smiling."

Saturday night.

"Okay, take it easy. Go on, tell me the rest of it. Borlan comes to you, and he begs you to read Spanning's letter and...?"

"He didn't beg. He just gave me the letter, told me he had no idea what Henry had written, but he said he'd known me a long time, that he thought I was a decent, fair-minded person, and he'd appreciate it in the name of our friendship if I'd read it."

"So you read it."

"I read it."

"Friendship. Sounds like you an' him was *good* friends. Like maybe you and I were good friends?"

She looked at me with astonishment.

I think *I* looked at me with astonishment.

"Where the hell did *that* come from?" I said.

"Yeah, really," she said, right back at me, "where the hell *did* that come from?" My ears were hot, and I almost started to say something about how if it was okay for *her* to use our Marx Brothers indiscretion for a lever, why wasn't it okay for me to get cranky about it? But I kept my mouth shut; and for once knew enough to move along. "Must've been *some* letter," I said.

There was a long moment of silence during which she weighed the degree of shit she'd put me through for my stupid remark, after all this was settled; and having struck a balance in her head, she told me about the letter.

It was perfect. It was the only sort of come-on that could lure the avenger who'd put you in the chair to pay attention. The letter had said that fifty-six was not the magic number of death. That there were many, *many* more unsolved cases, in many, *many* different states; lost children, runaways, unexplained disappearances, old people, college students hitchhiking to Sarasota for Spring Break, shopkeepers who'd carried their day's take to the night deposit drawer and never gone home for dinner, hookers left in pieces in Hefty bags all over town, and death death death unnumbered and unnamed. Fifty-six, the letter had said, was just the start. And if she, her, no one else, Allison Roche, my pal Ally, would come on down to Holman, and talk to him, Henry Lake Spanning would help her close all those open files. National rep. Avenger of the unsolved. Big time mysteries revealed. "So you read the letter, and you went..."

"Not at first. Not immediately. I was sure he was guilty, and I was pretty certain at that moment, three years and more, dealing with the case, I was pretty sure if he said he could fill in all the blank spaces, that he could do it. But I just didn't like the idea. In court, I was always twitchy when I got near him at the defense table. His eyes, he never took them off me. They're blue, Rudy, did I tell you that...?"

"Maybe. I don't remember. Go on."

"Bluest blue you've ever seen...well, to tell the truth, he just plain *scared* me. I wanted to win that case so badly, Rudy, you can never know...not just for me or the career or for the idea of justice or to avenge all those people he'd killed, but just the thought of him out there on the street, with those blue eyes, so blue, never stopped looking at me from the moment the trial began...the *thought* of him on the loose drove me to whip that case like a howling dog. I *had* to put him away!"

"But you overcame your fear."

She didn't like the edge of ridicule on the blade of that remark. "That's right. I finally 'overcame my fear' and I agreed to go see him."

"And you saw him."

"Yes."

"And he didn't know shit about no other killings, right?"

"Yes."

"But he talked a good talk. And his eyes was blue, so blue."

"Yes, you asshole."

I chuckled. Everybody is somebody's fool.

"Now let me ask you this—very carefully—so you don't hit me again: the moment you discovered he'd been shuckin' you, lyin', that he *didn't* have this long, unsolved crime roster to tick off, why didn't you get up, load your attaché case, and hit the bricks?"

Her answer was simple. "He begged me to stay a while."

"That's it? He *begged* you?"

"Rudy, he has no one. He's *never* had anyone." She looked at me as if I were made of stone, some basalt thing, an onyx statue, a figure carved out of melanite, soot and ashes fused into a monolith. She feared she could not, in no way, no matter how piteously or bravely she phrased it, penetrate my rocky surface.

Then she said a thing that I never wanted to hear.

"Rudy…"

Then she said a thing I could never have imagined she'd say. Never in a million years.

"Rudy…"

Then she said the most awful thing she could say to me, even more awful than that she was in love with a serial killer.

"Rudy…go inside…read my mind…I need you to know, I need you to understand…Rudy…"

The look on her face killed my heart.

I tried to say no, oh god no, not that, please, no, not that, don't ask me to do that, please *please* I don't want to go inside, we mean so much to each other, I don't *want* to know your landscape. Don't make me feel filthy, I'm no peeping-tom, I've *never* spied on you, never stolen a look when you were coming out of the shower, or undressing, or when you were being sexy…I never invaded your privacy, I wouldn't *do* a thing like that…we're friends, I don't need to know it all, I don't *want* to go in there. I can go inside anyone, and it's always awful…please don't make me see things in there I might not like, you're my friend, please don't steal that from me…

"Rudy, *please*. Do it."

Oh jeezusjeezusjeezus, again, she said it again!

We sat there. And we sat there. And we sat there longer. I said, hoarsely, in fear, "Can't you just…just *tell* me?"

Her eyes looked at stone. A man of stone. And she tempted me to do what I could do casually, tempted me the way Faust was tempted by Mefisto, Mephistopheles, Mefistofele, Mephostopilis. Black rock Dr. Faustus, possessor of magical mind-reading powers, tempted by thick, lustrous eyelashes and violet eyes and a break in the voice and an imploring movement of hand to face and a tilt of the head that was pitiable and the begging word *please* and all the guilt that lay between us that was mine alone. The seven chief demons. Of whom Mefisto was the one "not loving the light."

I knew it was the end of our friendship. But she left me nowhere to run. Mefisto in onyx.

So I jaunted into her landscape.

I stayed in there less than ten seconds. I didn't want to know everything I could know; and I definitely wanted to know *nothing* about how she really thought of me. I couldn't have borne seeing a caricature of a bug-eyed, shuffling, thick-lipped darkie in there. Mandingo man. Steppin Porchmonkey Rudy Pair…

Oh god, what was I thinking!

Nothing in there like that. Nothing! Ally wouldn't *have* anything like that in there. I was going nuts, going absolutely fucking crazy, in there, back out in less than ten seconds. I want to block it, kill it, void it, waste it, empty it, reject it, squeeze it, darken it, obscure it, wipe it, do away with it like it never happened. Like the moment you walk in on your momma and poppa and catch them fucking, and you want never to have known that.

But at least I understood.

In there, in Allison Roche's landscape, I saw how her heart had responded to this man she called Spanky, not Henry Lake Spanning. She did not call him, in there, by the name of a monster; she called him a honey's name. I didn't know if he was innocent or not, but *she* knew he was innocent. At first she had responded to just talking with him, about being brought up in an orphanage, and she was able to relate to his stories of being used and treated like chattel, and how they had stripped him of his dignity, and made him afraid all the time. She knew what that was like. And how he'd always been on his own. The running-away. The being captured like a wild thing, and put in this home or that lockup or the orphanage "for his own good." Washing stone steps with a tin bucket full of gray water, with a horsehair brush and a bar of lye soap, till the tender folds of skin between the fingers were furiously red and hurt so much you couldn't make a fist.

She tried to tell me how her heart had responded, with a language that has never been invented to do the job. I saw as much as I needed, there in that secret landscape, to know that Spanning had led a miserable life, but that somehow he'd managed to become a decent human being. And it showed through enough when she was face to face with him, talking to him without the witness box between them, without the adversarial thing, without the tension of the courtroom and the gallery and those parasite creeps from the tabloids sneaking around taking pictures of him, that she identified with his pain. Hers had been not the same, but similar; of a kind, if not of identical intensity.

She came to know him a little.

And came back to see him again. Human compassion. In a moment of human weakness.

Until, finally, she began examining everything she had worked up as evidence, trying to see it from *his* point of view, using *his* explanations of circumstantiality. And there were inconsistencies. Now she saw them. Now she did not turn her prosecuting attorney's mind from them, recasting them in a way that would railroad Spanning; now she gave him just the barest possibility of truth. And the case did not seem as incontestable.

By that time, she had to admit to herself, she had fallen in love with him. The gentle quality could not be faked; she'd known fraudulent kindness in her time.

I left her mind gratefully. But at least I understood.

"Now?" she asked.

Yes, now. Now I understood. And the fractured glass in her voice told me. Her face told me. The way she parted her lips in expectation, waiting for me to reveal what my magic journey had conveyed by way of truth. Her palm against her cheek. All that told me. And I said, "Yes."

Then, silence, between us.

After a while she said, "I didn't feel anything."

I shrugged. "Nothing to feel. I was in for a few seconds, that's all."

"You didn't see everything?"

"No."

"Because you didn't want to?"

"Because..."

She smiled. "I understand, Rudy."

Oh, do you? Do you really? That's just fine. And I heard me say, "You made it with him yet?"

I could have torn off her arm; it would've hurt less.

"That's the second time today you've asked me that kind of question. I didn't like it much the first time, and I like it less *this* time."

"You're the one wanted me to go into your head. I didn't buy no ticket for the trip."

"Well, you were in there. Didn't you look around enough to find out?"

"I didn't look for that."

"What a chickenshit, wheedling, lousy and *cowardly...*"

"I haven't heard an answer, Counselor. Kindly restrict your answers to a simple yes or no."

"Don't be ridiculous! He's on Death Row!"

"There are ways."

"How would *you* know?"

"I had a friend. Up at San Rafael. What they call Tamal. Across the bridge from Richmond, a little north of San Francisco."

"That's San Quentin."

"That's what it is, all right."

"I thought that *friend* of yours was at Pelican Bay?"

"Different friend."

"You seem to have a lot of old chums in the joint in California."

"It's a racist nation."

"I've heard that."

"But Q ain't Pelican Bay. Two different states of being. As hard time as they pull at Tamal, it's worse up to Crescent City. In the Shoe."

"You never mentioned 'a friend' at San Quentin."

"I never mentioned a lotta shit. That don't mean I don't know it. I am large, I contain multitudes."

We sat silently, the three of us: me, her, and Walt Whitman. *We're fighting,* I thought. Not make-believe, dissin' some movie we'd seen and disagreed about; this was nasty. Bone nasty and memorable. No one ever forgets this kind of fight. Can turn dirty in a second, say some trash you can never take back, never forgive, put a canker on the rose of friendship for all time, never be the same look again.

I waited. She didn't say anything more; and I got no straight answer; but I was pretty sure Henry Lake Spanning had gone all the way with her. I felt a twinge of emotion I didn't even want to look at, much less analyze, dissect, and name. *Let it be,* I thought. Eleven years. Once, just once. *Let it just lie there and get old and withered and die a proper death like all ugly thoughts.*

"Okay. So I go on down to Atmore," I said. "I suppose you mean in the very near future, since he's supposed to bake in four days. Sometime very soon: like today."

She nodded.

I said, "And how do I get in? Law student? Reporter? Tag along as Larry Borlan's new law clerk? Or do I go in with you? What am I, friend of the family, representative of the Alabama State Department of Corrections; maybe you could set me up as an inmate's rep from 'Project Hope'."

"I can do better than that," she said. The smile. "Much."

"Yeah, I'll just bet you can. Why does that worry me?"

Still with the smile, she hoisted the Atlas onto her lap. She unlocked it, took out a small manila envelope, unsealed but clasped, and slid it across the table to me. I pried open the clasp and shook out the contents.

Clever. Very clever. And already made up, with my photo where necessary, admission dates stamped for tomorrow morning, Thursday, absolutely authentic and foolproof.

"Let me guess," I said, "Thursday mornings, the inmates of Death Row have access to their attorneys?"

"On Death Row, family visitation Monday and Friday. Henry has no family. Attorney visitations Wednesdays and Thursdays, but I couldn't count on today. It took me a couple of days to get through to you...."

"I've been busy."

"...but inmates consult with their counsel on Wednesday and Thursday mornings."

I tapped the papers and plastic cards. "This is very sharp. I notice my name and my handsome visage already here, already sealed in plastic. How long have you had these ready?"

"Couple of days."

"What if I'd continued to say no?"

She didn't answer. She just got that look again.

"One last thing," I said. And I leaned in very close, so she would make no mistake that I was dead serious. "Time grows short. Today's Wednesday. Tomorrow's Thursday. They throw those computer-controlled twin switches Saturday night midnight. What if I jaunt into him and find out you're right, that he's absolutely innocent? What then? They going to listen to me? Fiercely high-verbal black boy with the magic mind-read power?

"I don't think so. Then what happens, Ally?"

"Leave that to me." Her face was hard. "As you said: there are ways.

There are roads and routes and even lightning bolts, if you know where to shop. The power of the judiciary. An election year coming up. Favors to be called in."

I said, "And secrets to be wafted under sensitive noses?"

"You just come back and tell me Spanky's telling the truth," and she smiled as I started to laugh, "and I'll worry about the world one minute after midnight Sunday morning."

I got up and slid the papers back into the envelope, and put the envelope under my arm. I looked down at her and I smiled as gently as I could, and I said, "Assure me that you haven't stacked the deck by telling Spanning I can read minds."

"I wouldn't do that."

"Tell me."

"I haven't told him you can read minds."

"You're lying."

"Did you...?"

"Didn't have to. I can see it in your face, Ally."

"Would it matter if he knew?"

"Not a bit. I can read the sonofabitch cold or hot, with or without. Three seconds inside and I'll know if he did it all, if he did part of it, if he did none of it."

"I think I love him, Rudy."

"You told me that."

"But I wouldn't set you up. I need to know...that's why I'm asking you to do it."

I didn't answer. I just smiled at her. She'd told him. He'd know I was coming. But that was terrific. If she hadn't alerted him, I'd have asked her to call and let him know. The more aware he'd be, the easier to scorch his landscape.

I'm a fast study, king of the quick learners: vulgate Latin in a week; standard apothecary's pharmacopoeia in three days; Fender bass on a weekend; Atlanta Falcons' play book in an hour; and, in a moment of human weakness, what it feels like to have a very crampy, heavy-flow menstrual period, two minutes flat.

So fast, in fact, that the more somebody tries to hide the boiling pits of guilt and the crucified bodies of shame, the faster I adapt to their landscape. Like a man taking a polygraph test gets nervous, starts to sweat, ups the galvanic skin response, tries to duck and dodge, gets himself hinky and more hinky and hinkyer till his upper lip could water a truck garden, the more he tries to hide from me...the more he reveals...the deeper inside I can go.

There is an African saying: *Death comes without the thumping of drums.* I have no idea why that one came back to me just then.

Last thing you expect from a prison administration is a fine sense of humor. But they got one at the Holman facility.

They had the bloody monster dressed like a virgin.

White duck pants, white short sleeve shirt buttoned up to the neck, white socks. Pair of brown ankle-high brogans with crepe soles, probably neoprene, but they didn't clash with the pale, virginal apparition that came through the security door with a large, black brother in Alabama Prison Authority uniform holding onto his right elbow.

Didn't clash, those work shoes, and didn't make much of a tap on the white tile floor. It was as if he floated. Oh yes, I said to myself, oh yes indeed: I could see how this messianic figure could wow even as tough a cookie as Ally. *Oh my, yes.*

Fortunately, it was raining outside.

Otherwise, sunlight streaming through the glass, he'd no doubt have a halo. I'd have lost it. Right there, a laughing jag would *not* have ceased. Fortunately, it was raining like a sonofabitch.

Which hadn't made the drive down from Clanton a possible entry on any deathbed list of Greatest Terrific Moments in My Life. Sheets of aluminum water, thick as misery, like a neverending shower curtain that I could drive through for an eternity and never really penetrate. I went into the ditch off the I-65 half a dozen times. Why I never plowed down and buried myself up to the axles in the sucking goo running those furrows, never be something I'll understand.

But each time I skidded off the Interstate, even the twice I did a complete three-sixty and nearly rolled the old Fairlane I'd borrowed from John the C Hepworth, even then I just kept digging, slewed like an epileptic seizure, went sideways and climbed right up the slippery grass and weeds and running, sucking red Alabama goo, right back onto that long black anvil pounded by rain as hard as roofing nails. I took it then, as I take it now, to be a sign that Destiny was determined the mere heavens and earth would not be permitted to fuck me around. I had a date to keep, and Destiny was on top of things.

Even so, even living charmed, which was clear to me, even so: when I got about five miles north of Atmore, I took the 57 exit off the I-65 and a left onto 21, and pulled in at the Best Western. It wasn't my intention to stay overnight that far south—though I knew a young woman with excellent teeth down in Mobile—but the rain was just hammering and all I wanted was to get this thing done and go fall asleep. A drive that long, humping something as lame as that Fairlane, hunched forward to scope the rain...with Spanning in front of me...all I desired was surcease. A touch of the old oblivion.

I checked in, stood under the shower for half an hour, changed into the three-piece suit I'd brought along, and phoned the front desk for directions to the Holman facility.

Driving there, a sweet moment happened for me. It was the last sweet moment for a long time thereafter, and I remember it now as if it were still happening. I cling to it.

In May, and on into early June, the Yellow Lady's Slipper blossoms. In the forests and the woodland bogs, and often on some otherwise undistinguished slope or hillside, the yellow and purple orchids suddenly appear.

I was driving. There was a brief stop in the rain. Like the eye of the hurricane. One moment sheets of water, and the next, absolute silence before the crickets and frogs and birds started complaining; and darkness on all sides, just the idiot staring beams of my headlights poking into nothingness; and cool as a well between the drops of rain; and I was driving. And suddenly, the window rolled down so I wouldn't fall asleep, so I could stick my head out when my eyes started to close, suddenly I smelled the delicate perfume of the sweet May-blossoming Lady's Slipper. Off to my left, off in the dark somewhere on a patch of hilly ground, or deep in a stand of invisible trees, *Cypripedium calceolus* was making the night world beautiful with its fragrance.

I neither slowed, nor tried to hold back the tears.

I just drove, feeling sorry for myself; for no good reason I could name.

Way, way down—almost to the corner of the Florida Panhandle, about three hours south of the last truly imperial barbeque in that part of the world, in Birmingham—I made my way to Holman. If you've never been inside the joint, what I'm about to say will resonate about as clearly as Chaucer to one of the gentle Tasaday.

The stones call out.

That institution for the betterment of the human race, the Organized Church, has a name for it. From the fine folks at Catholicism, Lutheranism, Baptism, Judaism, Islamism, Druidism...Ismism...the ones who brought you Torquemada, several spicy varieties of Inquisition, original sin, holy war, sectarian violence, and something called "pro-lifers" who bomb and maim and kill...comes the catchy phrase Damned Places.

Rolls off the tongue like *God's On Our Side*, don't it?

Damned Places.

As we say in Latin, the *situs* of malevolent shit. The *venue* of evil happenings. *Locations* forever existing under a black cloud, like residing in a rooming house run by Jesse Helms or Strom Thurmond. The big slams are like that. Joliet, Dannemora, Attica, Rahway State in Jersey, that hellhole down in Louisiana called Angola, old Folsom—not the new one, the old Folsom—Q, and Ossining. Only people who read about it call it "Sing Sing." Inside, the cons call it Ossining. The Ohio State pen in Columbus. Leavenworth, Kansas. The ones they talk about among themselves when they talk about doing hard time. The Shoe at Pelican Bay State Prison. In there, in those ancient structures mortared with guilt and depravity and no respect for human life and just plain meanness on both sides, cons and screws, in there where the walls and floors have absorbed all the pain and loneliness of a million men and women for decades...in there, the stones call out.

Damned places. You can feel it when you walk through the gates and go through the metal detectors and empty your pockets on counters and open your briefcase so that thick fingers can rumple the papers. You feel it. The moaning and thrashing, and men biting holes in their own wrists so they'll bleed to death.

And I felt it worse than anyone else.

I blocked out as much as I could. I tried to hold on to the memory of the scent of orchids in the night. The last thing I wanted was to jaunt into somebody's landscape at random. Go inside and find out what he had done, what had *really* put him here, not just what they'd got him for. And I'm not talking about Spanning; I'm talking about every one of them. Every guy who had kicked to death his girl friend because she brought him Bratwurst instead of spicy Cajun sausage. Every pale, wormy Bible-reciting psycho who had stolen, buttfucked, and sliced up an altar boy in the name of secret voices that "tole him to g'wan *do* it!" Every amoral druggie who'd shot a pensioner for her food stamps. If I let down for a second, if I didn't keep that shield up, I'd be tempted to send out a scintilla and touch one of them. In a moment of human weakness.

So I followed the trusty to the Warden's office, where his secretary checked my papers, and the little plastic cards with my face encased in them, and she kept looking down at the face, and up at my face, and down at my face, and up at the face in front of her, and when she couldn't restrain herself a second longer she said, "We've been expecting you, Mr. Pairis. Uh. Do you *really* work for the President of the United States?"

I smiled at her. "We go bowling together."

She took that highly, and offered to walk me to the conference room where I'd meet Henry Lake Spanning. I thanked her the way a well-mannered gentleman of color thanks a Civil Servant who can make life easier or more difficult, and I followed her along corridors and in and out of guarded steel-riveted doorways, through Administration and the segregation room and the main hall to the brown-paneled, stained walnut, white tile over cement floored, roll-out security windowed, white draperied, drop ceiling with 2″ acoustical Celotex squared conference room, where a Security Officer met us. She bid me fond adieu, not yet fully satisfied that such a one as I had come, that morning, on Air Force One, straight from a 7-10 split with the President of the United States.

It was a big room.

I sat down at the conference table; about twelve feet long and four feet wide; highly polished walnut, maybe oak. Straight back chairs: metal tubing with a light yellow upholstered cushion. Everything quiet, except for the sound of matrimonial rice being dumped on a connubial tin roof. The rain had not slacked off. Out there on the I-65 some luck-lost bastard was being sucked down into red death.

"He'll be here," the Security Officer said.

"That's good," I replied. I had no idea why he'd tell me that, seeing as how it was the reason I was there in the first place. I imagined him to be the kind of guy you dread sitting in front of, at the movies, because he always explains everything to his date. Like a *bracero* laborer with a valid green card interpreting a Woody Allen movie line-by-line to his illegal-alien cousin Humberto, three weeks under the wire from Matamoros. Like one of a pair of Beltone-wearing octogenarians on the loose from a rest home for a wild Saturday afternoon at the mall, plonked down in the third level multiplex, one of them describing whose ass Clint Eastwood is about to kick, and why. All at the top of her voice.

"Seen any good movies lately?" I asked him.

He didn't get a chance to answer, and I didn't jaunt inside to find out, because at that moment the steel door at the far end of the conference room opened, and another Security Officer poked his head in, and called across to Officer Let-Me-State-the-Obvious, "Dead man walking!"

Officer Self-Evident nodded to him, the other head poked back out, the door slammed, and my companion said, "When we bring one down from Death Row, he's gotta walk through the Ad Building and Segregation and the Main Hall. So everything's locked down. Every man's inside. It takes some time, y'know."

I thanked him.

"Is it true you work for the President, yeah?" He asked it so politely, I decided to give him a straight answer; and to hell with all the phony credentials Ally had worked up. "Yeah," I said, "we're on the same *bocce* ball team."

"Izzat so?" he said, fascinated by sports stats.

I was on the verge of explaining that the President was, in actuality, of Italian descent, when I heard the sound of the key turning in the security door, and it opened outward, and in came this messianic apparition in white, being led by a guard who was seven feet in any direction.

Henry Lake Spanning, sans halo, hands and feet shackled, with the chains cold-welded into a wide anodized steel belt, shuffled toward me; and his neoprene soles made no disturbing cacophony on the white tiles.

I watched him come the long way across the room, and he watched me right back. I thought to myself, *Yeah, she told him I can read minds. Well, let's see which method you use to try and keep me out of the landscape.* But I couldn't tell from the outside of him, not just by the way he shuffled and looked, if he had fucked Ally. But I knew it had to've been. Somehow. Even in the big lockup. Even here.

He stopped right across from me, with his hands on the back of the chair, and he didn't say a word, just gave me the nicest smile I'd ever gotten from anyone, even my momma. *Oh, yes,* I thought, *oh my goodness, yes.* Henry Lake Spanning was either the most masterfully charismatic person I'd ever met, or so good at the charm con that he could sell a slashed throat to a stranger.

"You can leave him," I said to the great black behemoth brother.

"Can't do that, sir."

"I'll take full responsibility."

"Sorry, sir; I was told someone had to be right here in the room with you and him, all the time."

I looked at the one who had waited with me. "That mean you, too?"

He shook his head. "Just one of us, I guess."

I frowned. "I need absolute privacy. What would happen if I were this man's attorney of record? Wouldn't you have to leave us alone? Privileged communication, right?"

They looked at each other, this pair of Security Officers, and they looked back at me, and they said nothing. All of a sudden Mr. Plain-as-the-Nose-on-Your-Face had nothing valuable to offer; and the sequoia with biceps "had his orders."

"They tell you who I work for? They tell you who it was sent me here to talk to this man?" Recourse to authority often works. They mumbled yessir yessir a couple of times each, but their faces stayed right on the mark of *sorry, sir, but we're not supposed to leave anybody alone with this man.* It wouldn't have mattered if they'd believed I'd flown in on Jehovah One.

So I said to myself *fuckit* I said to myself, and I slipped into their thoughts, and it didn't take much rearranging to get the phone wires restrung and the underground cables rerouted and the pressure on their bladders something fierce.

"On the other hand..." the first one said.

"I suppose we could..." the giant said.

And in a matter of maybe a minute and a half one of them was entirely gone, and the great one was standing outside the steel door, his back filling the double-pane chickenwire-imbedded security window. He effectively sealed off the one entrance or exit to or from the conference room; like the three hundred Spartans facing the tens of thousands of Xerxes's army at the Hot Gates.

Henry Lake Spanning stood silently watching me.

"Sit down," I said. "Make yourself comfortable."

He pulled out the chair, came around, and sat down.

"Pull it closer to the table," I said.

He had some difficulty, hands shackled that way, but he grabbed the leading edge of the seat and scraped forward till his stomach was touching the table.

He was a handsome guy, even for a white man. Nice nose, strong cheekbones, eyes the color of that water in your toilet when you toss in a tablet of 2000 Flushes. Very nice looking man. He gave me the creeps.

If Dracula had looked like Shirley Temple, no one would've driven a stake through his heart. If Harry Truman had looked like Freddy Krueger, he would never have beaten Tom Dewey at the polls. Joe Stalin and Saddam Hussein looked like sweet, avuncular friends of the family, really nice looking, kindly guys—who just incidentally happened to slaughter millions of men, women, and children. Abe Lincoln looked like an axe murderer, but he had a heart as big as Guatemala.

Henry Lake Spanning had the sort of face you'd trust immediately if you saw it in a tv commercial. Men would like to go fishing with him, women would like to squeeze his buns. Grannies would hug him on sight, kids would follow him straight into the mouth of an open oven. If he could play the piccolo, rats would gavotte around his shoes.

What saps we are. Beauty is only skin deep. You can't judge a book by its cover. Cleanliness is next to godliness. Dress for success. What saps we are.

So what did that make my pal, Allison Roche?

And why the hell didn't I just slip into his thoughts and check out the landscape? Why was I stalling?

Because I was scared of him.

This was fifty-six verified, gruesome, disgusting murders sitting forty-eight inches away from me, looking straight at me with blue eyes and soft, gently blond hair. Neither Harry nor Dewey would've had a prayer.

So why was I scared of him? Because; that's why.

This was damned foolishness. I had all the weaponry, he was shackled, and I didn't for a second believe he was what Ally *thought* he was: innocent. Hell, they'd caught him, literally, redhanded. Bloody to the armpits, fer chrissakes. Innocent, my ass! *Okay, Rudy,* I thought, *get in there and take a look around.* But I didn't. I waited for him to say something.

He smiled tentatively, a gentle and nervous little smile, and he said, "Ally asked me to see you. Thank you for coming."

I looked *at* him, but not *into* him.

He seemed upset that he'd inconvenienced me. "But I don't think you can do me any good, not in just three days."

"You scared, Spanning?"

His lips trembled. "Yes I am, Mr. Pairis. I'm about as scared as a man can be." His eyes were moist.

"Probably gives you some insight into how your victims felt, whaddaya think?"

He didn't answer. His eyes were moist.

After a moment just looking at me, he scraped back his chair and stood up. "Thank you for coming, sir. I'm sorry Ally imposed on your time." He turned and started to walk away. I jaunted into his landscape.

Oh my god, I thought. He was innocent.

Never done any of it. None of it. Absolutely no doubt, not a shadow of a doubt. Ally had been right. I saw every bit of that landscape in there, every fold and crease; every bolt hole and rat run; every gully and arroyo; all of his past, back and back and back to his birth in Lewistown, Montana, near Great Falls, thirty-six years ago; every day of his life right up to the minute they arrested him leaning over that disemboweled cleaning woman the real killer had tossed into the dumpster.

I saw every second of his landscape; and I saw him coming out of the Winn-Dixie in Huntsville; pushing a cart filled with grocery bags of food for the weekend. And I saw him wheeling it around the parking lot toward the dumpster area overflowing with broken-down cardboard boxes and fruit crates. And I heard the cry for help from one of those dumpsters; and I saw Henry Lake Spanning stop and look around, not sure he'd heard anything at all. Then I saw him start to go to his car, parked right there at the edge of the lot beside the wall because it was a Friday evening and everyone was stocking up for the weekend, and there weren't any spaces out front; and the cry for help, weaker this time, as pathetic as a crippled kitten; and Henry Lake Spanning stopped cold, and he looked around; and we *both* saw the bloody hand raise itself above the level of the open dumpster's filthy green steel side. And I saw him desert his groceries without a thought to their cost, or that someone might run off with them if he left them unattended, or that he only had eleven dollars left in his checking account, so if those groceries were snagged by someone he wouldn't be eating for the next few days...and I watched him rush to the dumpster and look into the crap filling it...and I felt his nausea at the sight of that poor old woman, what was left of her...and I was with him as he crawled up onto the dumpster and dropped inside to do what he could for that mass of shredded and pulped flesh.

And I cried with him as she gasped, with a bubble of blood that burst in the open ruin of her throat, and she died. But though *I* heard the scream of someone coming around the corner, Spanning did not; and so he was still there, holding the poor mass of stripped skin and black bloody clothing, when the cops screeched into the parking lot. And only *then*, innocent of anything but decency and rare human compassion, did Henry Lake Spanning begin to understand what it must look like to middle-aged *hausfraus,* sneaking around dumpsters to pilfer cardboard boxes, who see what they think is a man murdering an old woman.

I was with him, there in that landscape within his mind, as he ran and ran and dodged and dodged. Until they caught him in Decatur, seven miles from the body of Gunilla Ascher. But they had him, and they had positive identification, from the dumpster in Huntsville; and all the rest of it was circumstantial, gussied up by bedridden, recovering Charlie Whilborg and the staff in Ally's office. It looked good on paper—so good that Ally had brought him down on twenty-nine-*cum*-fifty-six counts of murder in the vilest extreme.

But it was all bullshit.

The killer was still out there.

Henry Lake Spanning, who looked like a nice, decent guy, was exactly that. A nice, decent, goodhearted, but most of all *innocent* guy.

You could fool juries and polygraphs and judges and social workers and psychiatrists and your mommy and your daddy, but you could *not* fool Rudy Pairis, who travels regularly to the place of dark where you can go but not return.

They were going to burn an innocent man in three days.

I had to do something about it.

Not just for Ally, though that was reason enough; but for this man who thought he was doomed, and was frightened, but didn't have to take no shit from a wiseguy like me.

"Mr. Spanning," I called after him.

He didn't stop.

"Please," I said. He stopped shuffling, the chains making their little charm bracelet sounds, but he didn't turn around.

"I believe Ally is right, sir," I said. "I believe they caught the wrong man; and I believe all the time you've served is wrong; and I believe you ought not die."

Then he turned slowly, and stared at me with the look of a dog that has been taunted with a bone. His voice was barely a whisper. "And why is that, Mr. Pairis? Why is it that you believe me when nobody else but Ally and my attorney believed me?"

I didn't say what I was thinking. What I was thinking was that I'd been *in* there, and I *knew* he was innocent. And more than that, I knew that he truly loved my pal Allison Roche.

And there wasn't much I wouldn't do for Ally.

So what I said was: "I know you're innocent, because I know who's guilty."

His lips parted. It wasn't one of those big moves where someone's mouth flops open in astonishment; it was just a parting of the lips. But he was startled; I knew that as I knew the poor sonofabitch had suffered too long already.

He came shuffling back to me, and sat down.

"Don't make fun, Mr. Pairis. Please. I'm what you said, I'm scared. I don't want to die, and I surely don't want to die with the world thinking I did those...those things."

"Makin' no fun, captain. I know who ought to burn for all those murders. Not six states, but eleven. Not fifty-six dead, but an even seventy. Three of them little girls in a day nursery, and the woman watching them, too."

He stared at me. There was horror on his face. I know that look real good. I've seen it at least seventy times.

"I know you're innocent, cap'n because *I'm* the man they want. *I'm* the guy who put your ass in here."

In a moment of human weakness. I saw it all. What I had packed off to live in that place of dark where you can go but not return. The wall-safe in my drawing-room. The four-foot-thick walled crypt encased in concrete and sunk a mile deep into solid granite. The vault whose composite laminate walls of judiciously sloped extremely thick blends of steel and plastic, the equivalent of six hundred to seven hundred mm of homogenous depth pro-tection approached the maximum toughness and hardness of crystaliron, that iron grown with perfect crystal structure and carefully controlled quantities of impurities that in a modern combat tank can shrug off a hollow charge warhead like a spaniel shaking himself dry. The Chinese puzzle box. The hidden chamber. The labyrinth. The maze of the mind where I'd sent all seventy to die, over and over and over, so I wouldn't hear their screams, or see the ropes of bloody tendon, or stare into the pulped sockets where their pleading eyes had been.

When I had walked into that prison, I'd been buttoned up totally. I was safe and secure, I knew nothing, remembered nothing, suspected nothing.

But when I walked into Henry Lake Spanning's landscape, and I could not lie to myself that he was the one, I felt the earth crack. I felt the tremors and the upheavals, and the fissures started at my feet and ran to the horizon; and the lava boiled up and began to flow. And the steel walls melted, and the concrete turned to dust, and the barriers dissolved; and I looked at the face of the monster.

No wonder I had such nausea when Ally had told me about this or that slaughter ostensibly perpetrated by Henry Lake Spanning, the man she was prosecuting on twenty-nine counts of murders I had committed. No wonder I could picture all the details when she would talk to me about the barest description of the murder site. No wonder I fought so hard against coming to Holman.

In there, in his mind, his landscape open to me, I saw the love he had for Allison Roche, for my pal and buddy with whom I had once, just once...

Don't try tellin' me that the Power of Love can open the fissures. I don't want to hear that shit. I'm telling *you* that it was a combination, a buncha things that split me open, and possibly maybe one of those things was what I saw between them.

I don't know that much. I'm a quick study, but this was in an instant. A crack of fate. A moment of human weakness. That's what I told myself in the part of me that ventured to the place of dark: that I'd done what I'd done in moments of human weakness.

And it was those moments, not my "gift," and not my blackness, that had made me the loser, the monster, the liar that I am.

In the first moment of realization, I couldn't believe it. Not me, not good old Rudy. Not likeable Rudy Pairis never done no one but hisself wrong his whole life.

In the next second I went wild with anger, furious at the disgusting thing that lived on one side of my split brain. Wanted to tear a hole through my face and yank the killing thing out, wet and putrescent, and squeeze it into pulp.

In the next second I was nauseated, actually wanted to fall down and puke, seeing every moment of what I had done, unshaded, unhidden, naked to this Rudy Pairis who was decent and reasonable and law-abiding, even if such a Rudy was little better than a well-educated fuckup. But not a killer...I wanted to puke.

Then, finally, I accepted what I could not deny.

For me, never again, would I slide through the night with the scent of the blossoming Yellow Lady's Slipper. I recognized that perfume now.

It was the odor that rises from a human body cut wide open, like a mouth making a big, dark yawn.

The other Rudy Pairis had come home at last.

They didn't have half a minute's worry. I sat down at a little wooden writing table in an interrogation room in the Jefferson County D.A.'s offices, and I made up a graph with the names and dates and locations. Names of as many of the seventy as I actually knew. (A lot of them had just been on the road, or in a men's toilet, or taking a bath, or lounging in the back row of a movie, or getting some cash from an ATM, or just sitting around doing nothing but waiting for me to come along and open them up, and maybe have a drink off them, or maybe just something to snack on...down the road.) Dates were easy, because I've got a good memory for dates. And the places where they'd find the ones they didn't know about, the fourteen with exactly the same m.o. as the other fifty-six, not to mention the old-style rip-and-pull can opener I'd used on that little Catholic bead-counter Gunilla Whatsername, who did Hail Mary this and Sweet Blessed Jesus that all the time I was opening her up, even at the last, when I held up parts of her insides for her to look at, and tried to get her to lick them, but she died first. Not half a minute's worry for the State of Alabama. All in one swell foop they corrected a tragic miscarriage of justice, nobbled a maniac killer, solved fourteen more murders than they'd counted on (in five additional states, which made the police departments of those five additional states extremely pleased with the law enforcement agencies of the Sovereign State of Alabama), and made first spot on the evening news on all three major networks, not to mention CNN, for the better part of a week. Knocked the Middle East right out of the box. Neither Harry Truman nor Tom Dewey would've had a prayer.

Ally went into seclusion, of course. Took off and went somewhere down on the Florida coast, I heard. But after the trial, and the verdict, and Spanning being released, and me going inside, and all like that, well, oo-poppa-dow as they used to say, it was all reordered properly. *Sat cito si sat bene,* in Latin: "It is done quickly enough if it is done well." A favorite saying of Cato. The Elder Cato.

And all I asked, all I begged for, was that Ally and Henry Lake Spanning, who loved each other and deserved each other, and whom I had almost fucked up royally, that the two of them would be there when they jammed my weary black butt into that new electric chair at Holman.

Please come, I begged them.

Don't let me die alone. Not even a shit like me. Don't make me cross over into that place of dark, where you can go, but not return—without the face of a friend. Even a former friend. And as for you, captain, well, hell didn't I save your life so you could enjoy the company of the woman you love? Least you can do. Come on now; be there or be square!

I don't know if Spanning talked her into accepting the invite, or if it was the other way around; but one day about a week prior to the event of cooking up a mess of fried Rudy Pairis, the Warden stopped by my commodious accommodations on Death Row and gave me to understand that it would be SRO for the barbeque, which meant Ally my pal, and her boy friend, the former resident of the Row where now I dwelt in durance vile.

The things a guy'll do for love.

Yeah, that was the key. Why would a very smart operator who had gotten away with it, all the way free and clear, why would such a smart operator suddenly pull one of those hokey courtroom "I did it, I did it!" routines, and as good as strap himself into the electric chair?

Once. I only went to bed with her once.

The things a guy'll do for love.

When they brought me into the death chamber from the holding cell where I'd spent the night before and all that day, where I'd had my last meal (which had been a hot roast beef sandwich, double meat, on white toast, with very crisp french fries, and hot brown country gravy poured over the whole thing, apple sauce, and a bowl of Concord grapes), where a representative of the Holy Roman Empire had tried to make amends for destroying most of the gods, beliefs, and cultures of my black forebears, they held me between Security Officers, neither one of whom had been in attendance when I'd visited Henry Lake Spanning at this very same correctional facility slightly more than a year before.

It hadn't been a bad year. Lots of rest; caught up on my reading, finally got around to Proust and Langston Hughes, I'm ashamed to admit, so late in the game; lost some weight; worked out regularly; gave up cheese and dropped my cholesterol count. Ain't nothin' to it, just to do it.

Even took a jaunt or two or ten, every now and awhile. It didn't matter none. I wasn't going anywhere, neither were they. I'd done worse than the worst of them; hadn't I confessed to it? So there wasn't a lot that could ice me, after I'd copped to it and released all seventy of them out of my unconscious, where they'd been rotting in shallow graves for years. No big thang, Cuz.

Brought me in, strapped me in, plugged me in.

I looked through the glass at the witnesses.

There sat Ally and Spanning, front row center. Best seats in the house. All eyes and crying, watching, not believing everything had come to this, trying to figure out when and how and in what way it had all gone down without her knowing anything at all about it. And Henry Lake Spanning sitting close beside her, their hands locked in her lap. True love.

I locked eyes with Spanning.

I jaunted into his landscape.

No, I *didn't*.

I *tried* to, and couldn't squirm through. Thirty years, or less, since I was five or six, I'd been doing it; without hindrance, all alone in the world the only person who could do this listen in on the landscape trick; and for the first time I was stopped. Absolutely no fuckin' entrance. I went wild! I tried running at it full-tilt, and hit something khaki-colored, like beach sand, and only slightly giving, not hard, but resilient. Exactly like being inside a ten-foot-high, fifty-foot-diameter paper bag, like a big shopping bag from a supermarket, that stiff butcher's paper kind of bag, and that color, like being inside a bag that size, running straight at it, thinking you're going to bust through…and being thrown back. Not hard, not like bouncing on a trampoline, just shunted aside like the fuzz from a dandelion hitting a glass door. Unimportant. Khaki-colored and not particularly bothered.

I tried hitting it with a bolt of pure blue lightning mental power, like someone out of a Marvel comic, but that wasn't how mixing in other people's minds works. You don't think yourself in with a psychic battering-ram. That's the kind of arrant foolishness you hear spouted by unattractive people on public access cable channels, talking about The Power of Love and The Power of the Mind and the ever-popular toe-tapping Power of a Positive Thought. Bullshit; I don't be home to *that* folly!

I tried picturing myself in there, but that didn't work, either. I tried blanking my mind and drifting across, but it was pointless. And at that moment it occurred to me that I didn't really know *how* I jaunted. I just…did it. One moment I was snug in the privacy of my own head, and the next I was over there in someone else's landscape. It was instantaneous, like teleportation, which also is an impossibility, like telepathy.

But now, strapped into the chair, and them getting ready to put the leather mask over my face so the witnesses wouldn't have to see the smoke coming out of my eye-sockets and the little sparks as my nose hairs burned, when it was urgent that I get into the thoughts and landscape of Henry Lake Spanning, I was shut out completely. And right *then*, that moment, I was scared!

Presto, without my even opening up to him, there he was: inside my head. He had jaunted into *my* landscape.

"You had a nice roast beef sandwich, I see."

His voice was a lot stronger than it had been when I'd come down to see him a year ago. A *lot* stronger inside my mind.

"Yes, Rudy, I'm what you knew probably existed somewhere. Another one. A shrike." He paused. "I see you call it 'jaunting in the landscape.' I just called myself a shrike. A butcherbird. One name's as good as another. Strange, isn't it; all these years; and we never met anyone else? There *must* be others, but I think—now I can't prove this, I have no real data, it's just a wild idea I've had for years and years—I think they don't know they can do it."

He stared at me across the landscape, those wonderful blue eyes of his, the ones Ally had fallen in love with, hardly blinking.

"Why didn't you let me know before this?"

He smiled sadly. "Ah, Rudy. Rudy, Rudy, Rudy; you poor benighted pickaninny.

"Because I needed to suck you in, kid. I needed to put out a bear trap, and let it snap closed on your scrawny leg, and send you over. Here, let me clear the atmosphere in here..." And he wiped away all the manipulation he had worked on me, way back a year ago, when he had so easily covered his own true thoughts, his past, his life, the real panorama of what went on inside his landscape—like bypassing a surveillance camera with a continuous-loop tape that continues to show a placid scene while the joint is being actively burgled—and when he convinced me not only that he was innocent, but that the real killer was someone who had blocked the hideous slaughters from his conscious mind and had lived an otherwise exemplary life. He wandered around my landscape—and all of this in a second or two, because time has no duration in the landscape, like the hours you can spend in a dream that are just thirty seconds long in the real world, just before you wake up—and he swept away all the false memories and suggestions, the logical structure of sequential events that he had planted that would dovetail with my actual existence, my true memories, altered and warped and rearranged so I would believe that I had done all seventy of those ghastly murders...so that I'd believe, in a moment of horrible realization, that I was the demented psychopath who had ranged state to state to state, leaving piles of ripped flesh at every stop. Blocked it all, submerged it all, sublimated it all, me. Good old Rudy Pairis, who never killed anybody. I'd been the patsy he was waiting for.

"There, now, kiddo. See what it's really like?

"You didn't do a thing.

"Pure as the driven snow, nigger. That's the truth. And what a find you were. Never even suspected there was another like me, till Ally came to interview me after Decatur. But there you were, big and black as a Great White Hope, right there in her mind. Isn't she fine, Pairis? Isn't she something to take a knife to? Something to split open like a nice piece of fruit warmed in a summer sunshine field, let all the steam rise off her...maybe have a picnic..."

He stopped.

"I wanted her right from the first moment I saw her.

"Now, you know, I could've done it sloppy, just been a shrike to Ally, that first time she came to the holding cell to interview me; just jump into her, that was my plan. But what a noise that Spanning in the cell would've made, yelling it wasn't a man, it was a woman, not Spanning, but Deputy D.A. Allison Roche…too much noise, too many complications. But I *could* have done it, jumped into her. Or a guard, and then slice her at my leisure, stalk her, find her, let her steam…

"You look distressed, Mr. Rudy Pairis. Why's that? Because you're going to die in my place? Because I could have taken you over at any time, and didn't? Because after all this time of your miserable, wasted, lousy life you finally find someone like you, and we don't even have the convenience of a chat? Well, that's sad, that's really sad, kiddo. But you didn't have a chance."

"You're stronger than me, you kept me out," I said.

He chuckled.

"Stronger? Is that all you think it is? Stronger? You still don't get it, do you?" His face, then, grew terrible. "You don't even understand now, right now that I've cleaned it all away and you can *see* what I did to you, do you?

"Do you think I stayed in a jail cell, and went through that trial, all of that, because I couldn't do anything about it? You poor jig slob. I could have jumped like a shrike any time I wanted to. But the first time I met your Ally I saw *you*."

I cringed. "And you waited…? For me, you spent all that time in prison, just to get to me…?"

"At the moment when you couldn't do anything about it, at the moment you couldn't shout 'I've been taken over by someone else, I'm Rudy Pairis here inside this Henry Lake Spanning body, help me, help me!' Why stir up noise when all I had to do was bide my time, wait a bit, wait for Ally, and let Ally go for you."

I felt like a drowning turkey, standing idiotically in the rain, head tilted up, mouth open, water pouring in. "You can…leave the mind…leave the body…go out…jaunt, jump permanently…"

Spanning sniggered like a schoolyard bully.

"You stayed in jail three years just to get *me*?"

He smirked. Smarter than thou.

"Three years? You think that's some big deal to me? You don't think I could have someone like you running around, do you? Someone who can 'jaunt' as I do? The only other shrike I've ever encountered. You think I wouldn't sit in here and wait for you to come to me?"

"But three *years...*"

"You're what, Rudy...thirty-one, is it? Yes, I can see that. Thirty-one. You've never jumped like a shrike. You've just entered, jaunted, gone into the landscapes, and never understood that it's more than reading minds. You can change domiciles, black boy. You can move out of a house in a bad neighborhood—such as strapped into the electric chair—and take up residence in a brand, spanking, new housing complex of million-and-a-half-buck condos, like Ally."

"But you have to have a place for the other one to go, don't you?" I said it just flat, no tone, no color to it at all. I didn't even think of the place of dark, where you can go...

"Who do you think I am, Rudy? Just who the hell do you think I was when I started, when I learned to shrike, how to jaunt, what I'm telling you now about changing residences? You wouldn't know my first address. I go a long way back.

"But I can give you a few of my more famous addresses. Gilles de Rais, France, 1440; Vlad Tepes, Romania, 1462; Elizabeth Bathory, Hungary, 1611; Catherine DeShayes, France, 1680; Jack the Ripper, London, 1888; Henri Désiré Landru, France, 1915; Albert Fish, New York City, 1934; Ed Gein, Plainfield, Wisconsin, 1954; Myra Hindley, Manchester, 1963; Albert DeSalvo, Boston, 1964; Charles Manson, Los Angeles, 1969; John Wayne Gacy, Norwood Park Township, Illinois, 1977.

"Oh, but how I do go on. And on. And on and on and on, Rudy, my little porch monkey. That's what I do. I go on. And on and on. Shrike will nest where it chooses. If not in your beloved Allison Roche, then in the cheesy fucked-up black boy, Rudy Pairis. But don't you think that's a waste, kiddo? Spending however much time I might have to spend in your socially unacceptable body, when Henry Lake Spanning is such a handsome devil? Why should I have just switched with you when Ally lured you to me, because all it would've done is get you screeching and howling that you weren't Spanning, you were this nigger son who'd had his head stolen...and then you might have manipulated some guards or the Warden...

"Well, you see what I mean, don't you?

"But now that the mask is securely in place, and now that the electrodes are attached to your head and your left leg, and now that the Warden has his hand on the switch, well, you'd better get ready to do a lot of drooling."

And he turned around to jaunt back out of me, and I closed the perimeter. He tried to jaunt, tried to leap back to his own mind, but I had him in a fist. Just that easy. Materialized a fist, and turned him to face me.

"Fuck you, Jack the Ripper. And fuck you twice, Bluebeard. And on and on and on fuck you Manson and Boston Strangler and any other dipshit warped piece of sick crap you been in your years. You sure got some muddy-shoes credentials there, boy.

"What I care about all those names, Spanky my brother? You really think I don't know those names? I'm an educated fellah, Mistuh Rippuh, Mistuh Mad Bomber. You missed a few. Were you also, did you inhabit, hast thou possessed Winnie Ruth Judd and Charlie Starkweather and Mad Dog Coll and Richard Speck and Sirhan Sirhan and Jeffrey Dahmer? You the boogieman responsible for *every* bad number the human race ever played? You ruin Sodom and Gomorrah, burned the Great Library of Alexandria, orchestrated the Reign of Terror *dans Paree*, set up the Inquisition, stoned and drowned the Salem witches, slaughtered unarmed women and kids at Wounded Knee, bumped off John Kennedy?

"I don't think so.

"I don't even think you got so close as to share a pint with Jack the Ripper. And even if you did, even if you *were* all those maniacs, you were small potatoes, Spanky. The least of us human beings outdoes you, three times a day. How many lynch ropes you pulled tight, M'sieur Landru?

"What colossal egotism you got, makes you blind, makes you think you're the only one, even when you find out there's someone else, you can't get past it. What makes you think I didn't know what you can do? What makes you think I didn't let you do it, and sit here waiting for you like you sat there waiting for me, till this moment when you can't do shit about it?

"You so goddam stuck on yourself, Spankyhead, you never give it the barest that someone else is a faster draw than you.

"Know what your trouble is, Captain? You're old, you're *real* old, maybe hundreds of years who gives a damn old. That don't count for shit, old man. You're old, but you never got smart. You're just mediocre at what you do.

"You moved from address to address. You didn't have to be Son of Sam or Cain slayin' Abel, or whoever the fuck you been...you could've been Moses or Galileo or George Washington Carver or Harriet Tubman or Sojourner Truth or Mark Twain or Joe Louis. You could've been Alexander Hamilton and helped found the Manumission Society in New York. You could've discovered radium, carved Mount Rushmore, carried a baby out of a burning building. But you got old real fast, and you never got any smarter. You didn't need to, did you, Spanky? You had it all to yourself, all this 'shrike' shit, just jaunt here and jaunt there, and bite off someone's hand or face like the old, tired, boring, repetitious, no-imagination stupid shit that you are.

"Yeah, you got me good when I came here to see your landscape. You got Ally wired up good. And she suckered me in, probably not even knowing she was doing it...you must've looked in her head and found just the right technique to get her to make me come within reach. Good, m'man; you were excellent. But I had a year to torture myself. A year to sit here and think about it. About how many people I'd killed, and how sick it made me, and little by little I found my way through it.

"Because...and here's the big difference 'tween us, dummy:

"I unraveled what was going on...it took time, but I learned. Understand, asshole? *I* learn! *You* don't.

"There's an old Japanese saying—I got lots of these, Henry m'man—I read a whole lot—and what it says is, 'Do not fall into the error of the artisan who boasts of twenty years experience in his craft while in fact he has had only one year of experience—twenty times.'" Then I grinned back at him.

"Fuck you, sucker," I said, just as the Warden threw the switch and I jaunted out of there and into the landscape and mind of Henry Lake Spanning.

I sat there getting oriented for a second; it was the first time I'd done more than a jaunt...this was...*shrike*; but then Ally beside me gave a little sob for her old pal, Rudy Pairis, who was baking like a Maine lobster, smoke coming out from under the black cloth that covered my, his, face; and I heard the vestigial scream of what had been Henry Lake Spanning and thousands of other monsters, all of them burning, out there on the far horizon of my new landscape; and I put my arm around her, and drew her close, and put my face into her shoulder and hugged her to me; and I heard the scream go on and on for the longest time, I think it was a long time, and finally it was just wind...and then gone...and I came up from Ally's shoulder, and I could barely speak.

"Shhh, honey, it's okay," I murmured. "He's gone where he can make right for his mistakes. No pain. Quiet, a real quiet place; and all alone forever. And cool there. And dark."

I was ready to stop failing at everything, and blaming everything. Having fessed up to love, having decided it was time to grow up and be an adult—not just a very quick study who learned fast, extremely fast, a lot faster than anybody could imagine an orphan like me could learn, than *any*body could imagine—I hugged her with the intention that Henry Lake

Spanning would love Allison Roche more powerfully, more responsibly, than anyone had ever loved anyone in the history of the world. I was ready to stop failing at everything.

And it would be just a whole lot easier as a white boy with great big blue eyes.

Because—get on this now—all my wasted years didn't have as much to do with blackness or racism or being overqualified or being unlucky or being high-verbal or even the curse of my "gift" of jaunting, as they did with one single truth I learned waiting in there, inside my own landscape, waiting for Spanning to come and gloat:

I have always been one of those miserable guys who *couldn't get out of his own way.*

Which meant I could, at last, stop feeling sorry for that poor nigger, Rudy Pairis. Except, maybe, in a moment of human weakness.

This story, for Bob Bloch, because I promised.

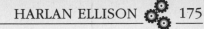

My mother survived that one, and I drove back from Ohio maybe four, five days later. As I pulled up to the wretched little house it was near dusk, and everything was gray. I could see straight into the windows. The house was empty. She'd cleared it to the walls: furniture, dishes, bedding, even the built-in bookcases. Everything was gone. All that was left was my duffel bag full of Army clothes, in the middle of the dirty living room.

Where
I Shall
Dwell
in
The Next
World

PREPARATORY NOTE ON PROCESS:
How it happens, where it comes from, why it speaks in that particular tongue, always the same damned unanswerable question. But they never give it a rest, the endless interrogation. Their cadre is never depleted. We sit under the broiling lights turned into our eyes, and they ask and ask, always the same damned question, and we plead ignorance; and when one of their number tires, she or he is replaced by another. And the question is asked again and again, without change, without compassion. We would tell if we knew, honestly we would. We would give up every secret we possess, if only they would turn off the lights for fifteen minutes, let us curl onto the cold stone floor and catch forty winks. We would tell all, divulge every tiny code number and Mercator track, drop the dime on even the dearest and closest friend or lover, spill the beans, tell the tale, give it all up if only they'd knock off for fifteen minutes, let it go dark, let us sleep.

But they won't, they're merciless; and they never wise up, because their cadre is never depleted. There's always another one warming up in the bullpen as the one on the mound begins to tire and keeps missing the strike zone. And here comes the new one, still moist from the academy, eyes bright as a Borneo Green Broadbill's, smiling ingratiatingly, plopping into the well-worn interrogator's chair, and here comes that same stupid, damned unanswerable question. Again.

Where do you get your ideas?

In a letter dated 10 July 1991, Jeremy G. Byrne of the Editorial Committee of *Eidolon,* an extremely elegant and smart literary journal emanating from Perth (which is on the coast of Western Australia), wrote to me, in part: "...the genesis *of Eidolon* was a long process. You might well have guessed that it was your own ANGRY CANDY piece, 'Eidolons'—with its Australian connection—that gave us the idea; and when we discovered the alternate definitions for the word, it seemed stunningly appropriate, or at least amusingly pretentious."

Where do you get your ideas?

In the liner notes I wrote for the recorded reading I did of my story "Jeffty is Five" I said:

My friends Walter and Judy Koenig invited me to a party. I don't like parties. I do like Walter and Judy. I also like their kids. I went to the party.

Mostly I sat near the fireplace, friendly but not ebullient. Mostly I talked to Walter and Judy's son, Josh, who is remarkable beyond the telling. And then I overheard a snatch of conversation. An actor named Jack Danon said—I thought he said—something like this—"Jeff is five, he's always five." No, not really. He didn't say anything like that at all. What he probably said was, "Jeff is fine, he's always fine." Or perhaps it was something completely different.

But I had been awed and delighted by Josh Koenig, and I instantly thought of just such a child who was arrested in time at the age of five. Jeffty, in no small measure, is Josh: the sweetness of Josh, the intelligence of Josh, the questioning nature of Josh.

Thus, from admiration of one wise and innocent child, and from a misheard remark, the process that not even Aristotle could codify was triggered.

Where do you get your ideas?

I purposely mishear things. The excellent novelist and critic Geoffrey Wolff has written, "Every fictioneer re-invents the world because the facts, things or people of the received world are unacceptable." So I purposely mishear things that are said. It mortars up the gaps in boring conversation. It assists in doing honor to the late architect Robert Smithson's dictum:

Establish enigmas. Not explanations. "Jeffty is five, he's always five."

Speak to me of a Chinese hand laundry, and I visualize a large wicker basket filled with Chinese hands that need laundering. Gladly, the Cross-Eyed Bear. Tearalong, the Dotted Lion.

Where do you get your ideas?

My story "Eidolons" came from the assemblage of a congeries of misheard remarks, altered to form brief allegories or tone-poems. I did one each week as introduction to my stint as the host of a radio show. Now, like Ouroboros, we come full circle: kindly note process, and let me sleep:

Mishearing purposely; translative adaptation of misheard remark to fictional state; assemblage of misheard adaptations to story; story as impetus for *Eidolon* magazine; request from magazine for contribution; assemblage of misheard adaptations submitted to magazine born of effects of mishearing.

The process. Where do you get your ideas?

First, the stories. Then, revelation of what was said; and what was heard. The process. At last, to sleep, the answer.

NECRO WAITERS

The yellow tabby had only one good eye, but that one was good enough to do the job. Cat sat on the low ledge filled with potted cacti that ran the interior length of the enormous front window of the Long Pig Bar & Grille. Cat sat no more than two steps away from me as I absently smoothed the white tablecloth, waiting for my dinner to be served. Cat sat watching a three-legged dog crossing Cyclops Avenue, staring with all the rigid attention of a coffin observing the open grave.

Body still rigid, the cat swiveled its gaze to me, the one good eye fixing me mercilessly. "I knew that one," she said. "In life, he was an Associate Professor of Comparative Religions. Smug beyond belief. Talked to God and received regular replies, often by fax, occasionally by overnight express mail."

I said nothing. I dislike cats, have never trusted them.

"Serves him proper," she said, "losing a leg. See how he can rationalize his 'personal relationship' with the Deity now, ha!" This was a vindictive creature. I fancied she had been a switchboard operator at a New York brokerage house.

"Don't care to reply?" she said, a feline blowziness in her tone. "You're absolutely dead, too, you know."

I said, "Demise does not preclude maintaining one's ethical standards. Go away. Suck a fish head. Bother someone else." I looked away.

The dining room was filled, after-theater crowd and night life hangers-on crowd. Chatting, spearing hors d'oeuvres, rubbing the wounds that had killed them. I felt quite alone in the midst of pressed bodies and yammering noise level.

The cat was now attempting to insult me. I paid no notice. If a cat could stand atop a dog, would it do so gently, hoping its living perch would not bolt...or would it dig in like an earth-mover, drawing blood and hanging on like a dude ranch novice? Such was the quality of rumination as I waited for my dinner to be served.

I saw my waiter threading his way through the crowd, in and out, around the tables, the aluminum serving tray held high, balanced on the spread fingers of one hand. He was one of the newly-dead and yet unpenitent. A zombie, a walking dead thing, a necro waiter. He had been, obviously, a Rastafarian; his dreadlocks oiled to a gloss with the life-blood of sperm whales and dolphins, lightly scented with rose petals; a tattoo of Haile Selassie on his chest that winked as the waiter approached.

He set the heavy tray on the edge of my table, and began unshipping plates. A glass of murky water. A salad plate on which the ceremonial Greek olive had been placed midway between an arc of pignoli nuts below and a pair of sago balls above, the design forming a sort of happy face. The main course, the steaming soul of my first wife, filled the large square dinner plate, garnished with remorse, a sprig of justified annoyance, and a double portion of mashed errors, gravy pooled in the center. "Will there be any'tin else, mon?" he asked, as he swept my cloth napkin off the table, shook it into a sail, and canopied it over my lap.

I looked at the meal.

"No, nothing else," I said. "As if I were entitled."

He looked at me with nothing like compassion. Then he smiled a face without teeth and said, "I could mebbe sneak ya some lahb'ster dat dey t'rew out when de Moabites wuz slaughtered." I knew about that. I snorted and went back to my plate.

There she lay, bitter and flavorless, as she had been every night since I had died. And I was required to down every last morsel. In life we had fought; in life I had never given an inch; in life we had gnawed on each other for fourteen years. Then she had put her left hand through the glass display case in the reception area of my office waiting room, and taken a shard and opened the other wrist, all the way to the inside of the elbow. Right there in front of the receptionist, who had been too frightened to help her. And she had bled to death in the office, so the senior partners and my co-workers could see the enormity of my failure to save her from her past.

"Not to your likin'?" said the necro waiter, still standing behind and to the side of me.

"Not much," I said, lifting my fork, poking at the gray and brown substance that had been her soul. "Would it do me any good to ask for salt and pepper?"

He moved closer. He reached down and took the plate off the table, replaced it on the tray. "I got pity f'you, poor japonica. You nevuh gone get your fill on some diet lahk dat. Here," he said, removing the last small plate remaining on the tray, a plate I had not seen before. "Here. Try dis."

IIe put it before me. It was a new culinary treat, and its presence at my table alerted me that the next phase of what I was to know forever had begun.

I had been married more than once.

Never order hamburger at the Long Pig Bar & Grille.

PROCESS: Do you remember a roll of candy wafers, hard little circular troches, called Necco Wafers? When I was a little boy, they were a favorite sweet for the movies because they lasted so long. They came in different flavors, and all the flavors tasted chalky except for the chocolate ones. And so, because you shared the pastilles with the kids sitting on either side of you, your chums and mates and pals, you carefully orchestrated how fast you ate your Necco Wafers, so you would always be offering a licorice one, or a lemon one, or a cheery cherry. But you were always alert so the chocolate ones were retained.

One day, lifetimes ago, I felt my heart miss its rhythm when I entered a small co-op grocery store on the other side of the tracks in Painesville, Ohio, and saw for the first time the roll of all-chocolate Necco Wafers. Surely, there was a God. To this day—and they are now hard to find—I cannot resist a roll of chocolate Necco Wafers.

I was standing in a movie line. I had brought two rolls of candy with me, and as I waited for the line to move, I ate a pastille or two. Behind me, a man my age, speaking softly to his female date, not wanting to seem to have been snooping, said, with hushed awe, "He's got Necco Wafers!" and the woman, considerably younger, repeated what she *thought* she had heard, and she said, "Necro wafers?" and he corrected her and explained; but *I* had already misheard what I wanted to hear. Necro waiters. Yes. For what are they waiting? How did they die? Oh yes! Necro waiters. Process.

MARK

At forty-one minutes after midnight on the night of 28 April 1910, with Halley's Comet boiling through the ink black skies directly overhead, in a graveyard in Elmira, New York, two young boys worked feverishly digging up a freshly-laid grave. The tombstone had not yet been set; the ground had not settled sufficiently.

It was cold for April, but the boys were sweating.

It had been cold a week earlier in Redding, Connecticut, when he had died at sunset.

It had been cold as thousands had filed past the casket, as he lay there in a freshly-pressed white linen suit, in Brick Presbyterian Church, in New York City.

And it had been cold all the while they were bringing him to Elmira for burial.

Cold, past midnight, a 15¢ slice of moon not nearly as bright as Halley's Comet, and the boys dug, they dug, really dug.

"Tom," whispered the taller of the two diggers, the one wearing the crushed and chewed-out straw hat. There was no answer. "Tom? I say, Tom, you all right down there?"

A voice from below. "Except for the dirt you drop on me."

The tall boy made a *whoops, sorry* sound. "Tom, danged if'n I ain't afeared to be out here. I wisht we wasn't here. It's awful solemn like, *ain't* it?"

Tom, four feet down in the rectangular pit, jacked a foot onto his shovel, wedging it deep in the dark soil so it stood up of its own accord. He wiped sweat from his nose and forehead, but his face still shone in the dim light of the lantern at the pit's edge. He looked up at his companion. "Knock off that cornball dialect, will you, 'Hucky,' and keep moving that pile of dirt away from the edge before it buries me."

Huck looked chastened. "Sorry, Tom—"

"And for Pete's sake, stop calling me *Tom*!"

"Sorry, Migmunt, I just thought...in case there was anybody around, you know, just happened to be listening, I should stay in character..."

"Listen, Podlack, just keep shoveling. My back is killing me and I want to get *out* of here—"

A voice, muffled heavily by at least a foot of dirt, interrupted him. "And I want to get the hell out of *here*, you pair of imbeciles!"

The boys looked at each other with panic, and without a sound began shoveling furiously.

Fifteen minutes later, the coffin had been uncovered. There was a steady banging from inside. And the voice: "Get this infernal thing *off* me! Come on, move your weird butts!"

Podlack, also known as Huckleberry, dropped into the pit and, using a claw hammer, began prising loose the nails that held the coffin lid in place. "Just a minute, sir; we'll have you out of there in a jiffy."

"Jiffy, my groaning sphincter, you incompetent! You should have been here yesterday! Move yourself!"

Finally, with both boys straining, the lid was wrenched free; they leaned it up against the end of the pit.

The white-maned old man with the drooping mustaches sat up, cricked his neck till it popped, then got to his feet by bracing his hands against the sides of the coffin. "By god, I think my bladder will burst," he said, beginning to unbutton his fly. He suddenly realized the boys were staring at him. "Do you *mind?*"

They turned their backs. After a minute Migmunt, also known as Tom, said, very politely, "Uh, we'd best hurry, sir. The shuttle won't wait, you know."

Behind them, the old man snorted. "It took long enough to get here in 1835, and it'll be well bedamned long enough pokeying till it gets me home; it'll wait, or I'll have that insipid comet-jockey up on charges so fast it'll make his bedamned escutcheon tarnish!"

They peeked around, and saw he was trying to crawl out of the grave, despite what he had said. They hastily clambered out the other side of the pit and extended their hands down to lift the old man. He slapped at the hands. "Get away from me," he snarled. "What the hell's the matter with you; what do you think I am, some crepuscular, withered, senescent sack of sheep-dip, to be yanked around at your pleasure?"

As he complained, he crawled up the side of the grave, dirt slipping away under him, dropping him back two feet for every one he gained. Finally, he reached ground level and brushed himself off. He looked around carefully. "You're certain we're alone here?"

"Yessir, yessir," they both said, almost in chorus.

"Let's hope so," he replied, pulling off his clothes.

Standing buck naked in the dim amber glow of the lantern, he said it again. "Let's hope so." Then he reached down between his big toe and second toe on the left foot, grasped the sealing strip between thumb and forefinger, and unzipped his body from bottom to top. Then, shrugging off the clever plastic disguise with all four of his arms, he scratched his blunt yellow beak and drew a deep breath, a prisoner freed from a confining jail cell. He turned to look up at Halley's Comet, and smiled as best a beak could smile.

"Give my regards to Broadway," he said, and began loping off toward the pickup point, Tom and Huck pumping along as hard as they could behind him, unable, in their clever plastic disguises, to keep up with him.

"Sir...sir..." Migmunt named Tom called, wheezing heavily as he tried to shorten the distance between himself and the former owner of the estate called Stormfield. "Sir...could you...would you...if you please, sir...slow down a bit so I can ask you..." He abruptly felt considerable pain in his face as he ran full tilt into the beaked, feathered, webbed-and-spur-footed personage who had perspired inside the shell of Samuel Langhorne Clemens for the entire seventy-five year tour of duty. No-longer-Mark had stopped suddenly.

"*Now* what the bleeding bejeezus do you want?"

"Sir, it's just...I've been on this tour a lot longer than I'd expected. I was told when I was assigned...that is to say, sir, I was *advised*...when my orders were cut..."

"That you'd be off this miserable duty in what, ten, twelve, maybe fifteen years?" He tapped his three-toed claw impatiently.

"Well, uh, yes. Sir. That is."

"And you want me to say something to the Archangel of the Guard when I get back, is that it?"

"If you would, sir. If you only would."

"Son," the elder entity said, reaching out with one wing and laying his five-fingered talon on Tom's shoulder, "I was told I'd be mustered out in a maximum of fifty years. Fifty was up twenty-five years ago. It's a job, boy, a job dirtier than most, living among these idiots; but someone's got to do it. Can't have them running amuck all over the place, can we now?"

"But..."

"I'll mention your plight. Won't do any good, but I'll mention it. Now...do you mind if I go home?"

And, without waiting for a proper answer, he whirled on his toes, and loped off again toward the pickup point. Behind him, the two figments of his imagination pumped their knees hard trying to keep from falling too far apace.

When they reached the drop target, the slave unit from Halley's Comet was already waiting. The egg had opened, the jasmine light poured forth in a perfect pool across the ground, and three field-echelon sqwarbs were waiting, the eldest looking pointedly at his thigh clock. "Let's go, let's go, come on and let's go," he called across the clearing as the three running figures broke out of cover of the trees. "Time's on the slide, along along, let's go!"

He who had been Mark slid to a halt, threw a slovenly salute, and said, "Ready to go. Seventy-five years is long enough. Take me on home, sqwarbs!" He turned to the ersatz Huck and Tom who had come to a breathless halt behind him, there in the lee of the egg, and he saw their pathetic looks. Fluffing his pin-feathers, he said to the eldest of the echelon sqwarbs, "These two want to go home, too. Any chance, any hope?"

"Next time," said the clock-watcher.

"Next time? *Next* time!" Migmunt shouted. "That'll be almost ninety years I'll have spent here! Twelve, maybe fifteen, *that* was what I signed on for, not ninety!"

Then ensued an argument, a violence, a wrangling that would have brought the authorities, had it not taken place in the middle of a clearing inside dense woods, well past midnight, in a remote section of south-central New York state near the Pennsylvania border. Podlack actually hit the youngest of the three field-echelon sqwarbs, knocking him on his tail-feathers and crimping his comb. Migmunt and Huck tried to climb inside the egg, but were driven back by force.

Finally, when it was clear to everyone that the egg would not take their full number, Migmunt and Podlack were chivvied aside by weapons awesome to behold, Mark was hustled onboard, and the egg resealed and sped aloft, leaving the forlorn and furious Huck and Tom behind; for another seventy-five years.

As the egg soared toward the shuttle that was Halley's Comet, the one who had been Mark craned his neck and shook his feathers and said, "That wasn't perhaps the smartest thing you could have done, you know."

"What wasn't?" the echelon grenadier said.

"Leaving a pair of extremely disquieted employees in charge of an operation that big. They were angry enough to do almost anything, even let the creatures know about everything."

"Let them," the clock-watching echelon grenadier said, with a haughty curl of his beak. "How badly can they mess up a primitive society like that in just seventy-five years? What are we talking about here...war, famine, pestilence, plague, cheap entertainment, overpopulation, bad art?"

"Seventy-five years is a tweep in a whirl," said the youngest as he rubbed analgesic on his bruise. "How hard did *you* work to bring some common sense to them? How well did *you* do; how much influence did *you* have?"

Mark fell silent. Very true. The creatures of that sleepless orb were highly resistant to sensible behavior. He had done all he could, but the poor dumb things were seemingly determined to stumble about blindly, like sqwarbs with their heads cut off.

He sighed and closed his eyes, hoping for some rest on the journey home. It couldn't really get much worse down there. Not in just seventy-five years. When you wish upon a sqwarb.

PROCESS: Early 1985, and all the foofaraw about Halley's coming back. And no one pairing up Mark Twain's birth in 1835 with the Comet's arrival, and his death in 1910 at its next pass, with the current swing past the Earth. And I was so fascinated with the idea, that I reread all of Twain. One night, I was reading Tom Sawyer to the son of a woman I had been seeing, he was about ten or eleven at the time, and we were both eating Hydrox cookies, and I told him this thing about how I wanted to write about Twain, and the Comet, and maybe the Comet wasn't really a comet but was possibly a space-ship, or a star, or something like that; and he had his face full of Hydrox, and he said, "When you wish upon a sqwarb..." which wasn't, of course, what he said; it was what I *heard* him say.

And I knew what the story should be. Except I didn't have an ending, so I didn't write it in 1985. Or '86. Or '88. Or '90. But I write it now. And it *still* doesn't have an ending. But I like the opening a lot. Process.

THE LAST WILL AND TESTICLE OF TREES RABELAIS

My grandparents came from Poland. They came from a town, Bydgoszcz. That's in the north, right near the middle. I'm probably not pronouncing it properly. Bydgoszcz. They weren't Jewish, they were just Polish. That has almost nothing to do with me or this final statement, but I always tell every-body that my grandparents came from Poland. You never know when it might help. Once I got stopped by a traffic cop as I was speeding to the airport, and I don't know why, but I told him my grandparents came from Poland, and so did his, not from Bydgoszcz. So he let me off with just a warning.

I like to say: let any three people hose me down, and I'll wind up making friends of two of them.

Occasionally someone will ask me what that means, and I tell them, it means I'm a very friendly person.

I leave Montana to the descendants of the last surviving member of the original cast of *Gilligan's Island*. Go to Montana, if you must. You will hear more intelligent sounds by rubbing a tweed jacket.

Every beach contains the last three chapters of the story of someone's life. If you look out to sea, to see what you can see, you will see the previous pages bobbing at the top of rolling waves.

I didn't want to go without telling you what happened to those lovely symbols of the 1939 New York World's Fair. The symbols of the World of Tomorrow, the famous Trylon and Perisphere. Steel from the orb and the spire now form part of the furnace building in what was Freeport Sulphur Company's Nicaro nickel plant in Cuba. Before Castro nationalized it. Back in 1945 the plant turned out nickel oxide, an essential alloy used in jet engines. Beauty can neither be created nor destroyed, it can only be converted.

If I'd realized that creating crabgrass, spurge, chickweed, ragweed, dandelion, plantain, kudzu, purslane, knotweed, sorrel, and burdock was mostly to annoy people, I'd have given God much lower marks on the final exam.

I leave the care and feeding of all Fallacies of Substantive Distraction, including ad hominem, ad misericordiam, ad odium, and post hoc, propter hoc which is, more precisely, a Fallacy of Causation—to the splendid Sherpa herdsmen of the Nepalese Himalayas; for it is they alone who understand that paper cannot wrap up fire; also that if one plants melons, one will get melons.

Where the hell were the cops when I needed them?

All my life I have imagined doorways as the answers, and now with gun in mouth I stand here in the middle of the great Nullarbor Plain, attesting to the truth that there are no doorways large enough for an unprotected species like myself to pass through.

I leave the face of the moon to those who look for the best ways to unsnarl knotted shoelaces and dampen bad tempers. It is always cool and quiet, the face of the moon. And from far away it appears to resemble the general appearance of young women who danced in Warner Bros. musicals in the mid-1930s.

My name was Trees Rabelais.

PROCESS: Susan and I chanced to be in the bathroom at the same time. She asked me to hand her something from the medicine cabinet. She preceded the request with *Please*...

I have no memory of what it was she was asking for, or how it was that I heard, "Please, grab the somethingorother" as *Trees Rabelais*. But when I repeated it, she said it sounded like the name of the tragic male lead on a soap opera. I thought so, too. And so, to be as one with Miniver Cheevy, Richard Cory, and Wednesday's child, I dwelt on the heroic, godlike, impervious nature, and suicide, of Trees Rabelais. Process.

Chatting With Anubis

When the core drilling was halted at a depth of exactly 804.5 meters, one half mile down, Amy Guiterman and I conspired to grab Immortality by the throat and shake it till it noticed us.

My name is Wang Zicai. Ordinarily, the family name Wang—which is pronounced with the "a" in *father*, almost as if it were Wong—means "king." In my case, it means something else; it means "rushing head-long." How appropriate. Don't tell me clairvoyance doesn't run in my family... Zicai means "suicide." Half a mile down, beneath the blank Sahara, in a hidden valley that holds cupped in its eternal serenity the lake of the Oasis of Siwa, I and a young woman equally as young and reckless as myself, Amy Guiterman of New York City, conspired to do a thing that would certainly cause our disgrace, if not our separate deaths.

I am writing this in Yin.

It is the lost ancestral language of the Chinese people. It was a language written between the 18th and 12th centuries before the common era. It is not only ancient, it is impossible to translate. There are only five people alive today, as I write this, who can translate this manuscript, written in the language of the Yin Dynasty that blossomed northeast along the Yellow River in

189

a time long before the son of a carpenter is alleged to have fed multitudes with loaves and fishes, to have walked on water, to have raised the dead. I am no "rice christian." You cannot give me a meal and find me scurrying to your god. I am Buddhist, as my family has been for centuries. That I can write in Yin—which is to modern Chinese as classical Latin is to vineyard Italian—is a conundrum I choose not to answer in this document. Let he or she who one day unearths this text unscramble the oddities of chance and experience that brought me, "rushing headlong toward suicide," to this place half a mile beneath the Oasis of Siwa.

A blind thrust-fault hitherto unrecorded beneath the Mountain of the Moon had produced a cataclysmic 7.5 temblor. It had leveled villages as far away as Bir Bū Kūsā and Abu Simbel. The aerial and satellite reconnaissance from the Gulf of Sidra to the Red Sea, from the Libyan Plateau to the Sudan, showed great fissures, herniated valleys, upthrust structures, a new world lost to human sight for thousands of years. An international team of paleoseismologists was assembled, and I was called from the Great Boneyard of the Gobi by my superiors at the Mongolian Academy of Sciences at Ulan Bator to leave my triceratops and fly to the middle of hell on earth, the great sand ocean of the Sahara, to assist in excavating and analyzing what some said would be the discovery of the age.

Some said it was the mythical Shrine of Ammon.

Some said it was the Temple of the Oracle.

Alexander the Great, at the very pinnacle of his fame, was told of the Temple, and of the all-knowing Oracle who sat there. And so he came, from the shore of Egypt down into the deep Sahara, seeking the Oracle. It is recorded: his expedition was lost, wandering hopelessly, without water and without hope. Then crows came to lead them down through the Mountain of the Moon, down to a hidden valley without name, to the lake of the Oasis of Siwa, and at its center...the temple, the Shrine of Ammon. It was so recorded. And one thing more. In a small and dark chamber roofed with palm logs, the Egyptian priests told Alexander a thing that affected him for the rest of his life. It is not recorded what he was told. And never again, we have always been led to believe, has the Shrine of Ammon been seen by civilized man or civilized woman.

Now, Amy Guiterman and I, she from the Brooklyn Museum and I an honored graduate of Beijing University, together we had followed Alexander's route from Paraetonium to Siwah to here, hundreds of kilometers beyond human thought or action, half a mile down, where the gigantic claw diggers had ceased their abrading, the two of us with simple pick and shovel, standing on the last thin layer of compacted dirt and rock that roofed whatever great shadowy structure lay beneath us, a shadow picked up by the most advanced deep-resonance-response readings, verified on-site by proton free-precession magnetometry and ground-penetrating radar brought in from the Sandia National Laboratory in Albuquerque, New Mexico, in the United States.

Something large lay just beneath our feet.

And tomorrow, at sunrise, the team would assemble to break through and share the discovery, whatever it might be.

But I had had knowledge of Amy Guiterman's body, and she was as reckless as I, rushing headlong toward suicide, and in a moment of foolishness, a moment that should have passed but did not, we sneaked out of camp and went to the site and lowered ourselves, taking with us nylon rope and crampons, powerful electric torches and small recording devices, trowel and whisk broom, cameras and carabiners. A pick and a shovel. I offer no excuse. We were young, we were reckless, we were smitten with each other, and we behaved like naughty children. What happened should not have happened.

We broke through the final alluvial layer and swept out the broken pieces. We stood atop a ceiling of fitted stones, basalt or even marble, I could not tell immediately. I knew they were not granite, that much I did know. There were seams. Using the pick, I prised loose the ancient and concretized mortar. It went much more quickly and easily than I would have thought, but then, I'm used to digging for bones, not for buildings. I managed to chock the large set-stone in place with wooden wedges, until I had guttered the perimeter fully. Then, inching the toe of the pick into the fissure, I began levering the stone up, sliding the wedges deeper to keep the huge block from slipping back. And finally, though the block was at least sixty or seventy centimeters thick, we were able to tilt it up and, bracing our backs against the opposite side of the hole we had dug at the bottom of the core pit, we were able to use our strong young legs to force it back and away, beyond the balance point; and it fell away with a crash.

A great wind escaped the aperture that had housed the stone. A great wind that twisted up from below in a dark swirl that we could actually see. Amy Guiterman gave a little sound of fear and startlement. So did I. Then she said, "They would have used great amounts of charcoal to set these limestone blocks in place," and I learned from her that they were not marble, neither were they basalt.

We showed each other our bravery by dangling our feet through the opening, sitting at the edge and leaning over to catch the wind. It smelled *sweet*. Not a smell I had ever known before. But certainly not stagnant. Not corrupt. Sweet as a washed face, sweet as chilled fruit. Then we lit our torches and swept the beams below.

We sat just above the ceiling of a great chamber. Neither pyramid nor mausoleum, it seemed to be an immense hall filled with enormous statues of pharaohs and beast-headed gods and creatures with neither animal nor human shape...and all of these statues gigantic. Perhaps one hundred times life-size.

Directly beneath us was the noble head of a time-lost ruler, wearing the *nemes* headdress and the royal ritual beard. Where our digging had dropped shards of rock, the shining yellow surface of the statue had been chipped, and a darker material showed through. "Diorite," Amy Guiterman said. "Covered with gold. Pure gold. Lapis lazuli, turquoise, garnets, rubies—the headdress is made of thousands of gems, all precisely cut...do you see?"

But I was lowering myself. Having cinched my climbing rope around the excised block, I was already shinnying down the cord to stand on the first ledge I could manage, the empty place between the placid hands of the pharaoh that lay on the golden knees. I heard Amy Guiterman scrambling down behind and above me.

Then the wind rose again, suddenly, shrieking up and around me like a monsoon, and the rope was ripped from my hands, and my torch was blown away, and I was thrown back and something sharp caught at the back of my shirt and I wrenched forward to fall on my stomach and I felt the cold of that wind on my bare back. And everything was dark.

Then I felt cold hands on me. All over me. Reaching, touching, probing me, as if I were a cut of sliced meat lying on a counter. Above me I heard Amy Guiterman shrieking. I felt the halves of my ripped shirt torn from my body, and then my kerchief, and then my boots, and then my stockings, and then my watch and glasses.

I struggled to my feet and took a position, ready to make an empassing or killing strike. I was no cinema action hero, but whatever was there plucking at me would have to take my life despite I fought for it!

Then, from below, light began to rise. Great light, the brightest light I've ever seen, like a shimmering fog. And as it rose, I could see that the mist that filled the great chamber beneath us was trying to reach us, to touch us, to feel us with hands of ephemeral chilling ghastliness. Dead hands. Hands of beings and men who might never have been or who, having been, were denied their lives. They reached, they sought, they implored.

And rising from the mist, with a howl, Anubis.

God of the dead, jackal-headed conductor of souls. Opener of the road to the afterlife. Embalmer of Osiris, lord of the mummy wrappings, ruler of the dark passageways, watcher at the neverending funeral. Anubis came, and we were left, suddenly ashamed and alone, the American girl and I, who had acted rashly as do all those who flee toward their own destruction.

But he did not kill us, did not take us. How could he...am I not writing this for some never-to-be-known reader to find? He roared yet again, and the hands of the seekers drew back, reluctantly, like whipped curs into kennels, and there in the soft golden light reflected from the icon of a pharaoh dead and gone so long that no memory exists even of his name, there in the space half a mile down, the great god Anubis spoke to us.

At first, he thought we were "the great conqueror" come again. No, I told him, not Alexander. And the great god laughed with a terrible thin laugh that brought to mind paper cuts and the slicing of eyeballs. No, of course not that one, said the great god, for did I not reveal to him the great secret? Why should he ever return? Why should he not flee as fast as his great army could carry him, and never return? And Anubis laughed.

I was young and I was foolish, and I asked the jackal-headed god to tell *me* the great secret. If I was to perish here, at least I could carry to the afterlife a great wisdom.

Anubis looked through me.

Do you know why I guard this tomb?

I said I did not know, but that perhaps it was to protect the wisdom of the Oracle, to keep hidden the great secret of the Shrine of Ammon that had been given to Alexander.

And Anubis laughed the more. Vicious laughter that made me wish I had never grown skin or taken air into my lungs.

This is not the Shrine of Ammon, he said. Later they may have said it was, but this is what it has always been, the tomb of the Most Accursed One. The Defiler. The Nemesis. The Killer of the dream that lasted twice six thousand years. I guard this tomb to deny him entrance to the afterlife. And I guard it to pass on the great secret.

"Then you don't plan to kill us?" I asked. Behind me I heard Amy Guiterman snort with disbelief that I, a graduate of Beijing University, could ask such an imbecile question. Anubis looked through me again, and said no, I don't have to do that. It is not my job. And then, with no prompting at all, he told me, and he told Amy Guiterman from the Brooklyn Museum, he told us the great secret that had lain beneath the sands since the days of

Alexander. And then he told us whose tomb it was. And then he vanished into the mist. And then we climbed back out, hand over hand, because our ropes were gone, and my clothes were gone, and Amy Guiterman's pack and supplies were gone, but we still had our lives.

At least for the moment.

I write this now, in Yin, and I set down the great secret in its every particular. All parts of it, and the three colors, and the special names, and the pacing. It's all here, for whoever finds it, because the tomb is gone again. Temblor or jackal-god, I cannot say. But if today, as opposed to last night, you seek that shadow beneath the sand, you will find emptiness.

Now we go our separate ways, Amy Guiterman and I. She to her destiny, and I to mine. It will not be long in finding us. At the height of his power, soon after visiting the Temple of the Oracle, where he was told something that affected him for the rest of his life, Alexander the Great died of a mosquito bite. It is said. Alexander the Great died of an overdose of drink and debauchery. It is said. Alexander the Great died of murder, he was poisoned. It is said. Alexander the Great died of a prolonged, nameless fever; of pneumonia; of typhus; of septicemia; of typhoid; of eating off tin plates; of malaria. It is said. Alexander was a bold and energetic king at the peak of his powers, it is written, but during his last months in Babylon, for no reason anyone has ever been able to explain satisfactorily, he took to heavy drinking and nightly debauches...and then the fever came for him.

A mosquito. It is said.

No one will bother to say what has taken me. Or Amy Guiterman. We are insignificant. But we know the great secret.

Anubis likes to chat. The jackal-headed one has no secrets he chooses to keep. He'll tell it all. Secrecy is not his job. Revenge is his job. Anubis guards the tomb, and eon by eon makes revenge for his fellow gods.

The tomb is the final resting place of the one who killed the gods. When belief in the gods vanishes, when the worshippers of the gods turn away their faces, then the gods themselves vanish. Like the mist that climbs and implores, they go. And the one who lies encrypted there, guarded by the lord of the funeral, is the one who brought the world to forget Isis and Osiris and Horus and Anubis. He is the one who opened the sea, and the one who wandered in the desert. He is the one who went to the mountaintop, and he is the one who brought back the word of yet another god. He is Moses, and for Anubis revenge is not only sweet, it is everlasting. Moses— denied both Heaven and Hell—will never rest in the Afterlife. Revenge without pity has doomed him to eternal exclusion, buried in the sepulcher of the gods he killed.

I sink this now, in an unmarked meter of dirt, at a respectable depth; and I go my way, bearing the great secret, no longer needing to "rush headlong," as I have already committed what suicide is necessary. I go my way, for however long I have, leaving only this warning for anyone who may yet seek the lost Shrine of Ammon. In the words of Amy Guiterman of New York City, spoken to a jackal-headed deity, "I've got to tell you, Anubis, you are one *tough* grader." She was not smiling when she said it.

The Few, The Proud

The means by which they had tracked him, though secret, was idiotically simple. It came as a result of the *naïveté* that universally gulled all recruits to the Terran Expeditionary Force. Set afire by subliminal messages encoded in the recruitment assaults, young men and women of the united Earth rushed to enlist, to fight the monstrous Kyben, and they put their trust, put their honor, put their lives in the hands of a planetary government that assured them danger, far traveling and—if they were bold—eventual total victory over the alien scum. And so, whey-faced and trusting, they came to the recruitment depots and enlisted. As part of their induction, they received a thorough physical. As part of the physical, they received a tiny implant in the Orbital Region, passing between the fibers of the Orbicularis to be inserted into the skin of the lid, inner surface of the tarsal ligament. Should the recruit still retain some scintilla of individuality that had survived the fever of patriotic fervor, and should he or she inquire, "What is that thing you're putting in there?" he or she would be told with lambs-wool sincerity, "Well, you know, something *could* happen...you might not make it back...and, well...it's not something anyone likes to think about, but if you didn't make it...well, it's just an i.d. for the Graves Registration unit." Accompanying these reluctant words was a quiet manner of such humane fatalism, that the recruit would invariably smile and say, "Hey, I understand. I know it's rough out there and I might buy it. Just a precaution; I understand." And, secure in the knowledge that the government cared enough to make sure his or her body parts would not be scrambled with someone else's, they accepted the implant with pride and courage. In this way, they were all gulled. The implant was a tracking device. So when he went AWOL, the means by which they tracked him, though secret, was idiotically simple. He carried the beacon in his eye.

When they got around to him, a three-MP team of "rabbit finders" had no trouble locating him living among the *chonaras* in the delta lands of the sub-continent the natives called Lokaul, on the fifth planet of the binary system designated by the Celestial Ephemeris as SS 433. No trouble at all: they rode in on the beacon of his eye. And when he ran, they came down in skimmers and burned a ring around him in the marshland; and they drove him toward the denuded center; and they dropped a tangle-web on him; and they schlepped him aloft and bounced him into their scoutship; and they warped him back to TEF Mainbase on Cueball, the ringed planet orbiting Sirius, to be court-martialed and to stand trial. By that time, of course, the charge against him was not Absent Without Leave: it had been upgraded to Desertion Under Fire.

His name was Del Spingarn, he was a Dropshaft Sapper 2nd Class, and he had cut out during the battle of Molkey's Ash.

And this was a serious matter, because—after all—There Was a War On. It happened in the eighty-fifth year of the war between Earth and Kyba.

Do I have anything to say before sentence is passed?

You betcher ass I do.

Oh, sorry, sir, I know I'm supposed to show respect for this Court, but since I know sure as snuffers sip shit that you're going to toss me into a starfire chamber and blow my atoms to goofer dust, I figure there isn't a whole helluva lot you can do to me if I fully invoke Section Fifty of the UCMJ and tell my tale nice and slow, and just the way I feel like it.

UCMJ. I've always *loved* that. The Uniform Code of Military Justice. That's one of those phrases that contradicts itself, don't you think? Like Military Intelligence. Or Free Will. I forget the name for what they call those. But "Military Justice!" That's a killer. And *you're* a killer. And even me, *I* was a killer. Just like my Grampa. Which is what my story's all about, since this is my parting statement.

So just let your asses itch, you Officers and Gennulmen up there sitting in judgment of Spingarn, because Section Fifty says I can bore you till I go hoarse. After which, I'll go ever so quietly downshaft to the starfire and let you disperse the crap out of me.

But before that, I'll tell you about my Grampa Louie.

That was Louie on my mother's side. My Grampa Wendell died when I was eleven. He was my dad's father. Nice old guy with a lousy sense of humor, but he doesn't figure in this story at all; I just didn't want to leave him out.

But Grampa Louie, ah, there was a guy! Came back from three tours out in the Pleiades with a sash full of citations and medals and honoraries, not one of which meant doodly when he went to buy the shots that were supposed to retard the nerve damage from catching too many short-bursts. But, oh, what a prideful thing Grampa Louie was to the family. An authentic hero of the War.

We used to pull out the ghostcube and run the hologram of Grampa Louie getting his medals; every time someone new came to visit. We'd snap in the ghoster and everyone would see Grampa up there on the dais with no less than President Gorman and three Phalanx Generals and Greer McCarthy, that redhead who used to be on the vid. You remember, she starred in that series about the undercover Terran agent; she was very popular at the time. Hell, you remember, don't you? Lots of people thought she was President Gorman's lover, but both of them denied it even after Liza Gorman's term was up and she wrote her autobio. Denied it right to the end, both of them; but I always thought that Gorman bringing flowers to Greer McCarthy's sepulcher every year on the anniversary of her suicide really told the true story.

Oh. I can see you're getting annoyed that I keep straying off the main line. Sorry about that fellas, but you remember Scheherazade: as long as she kept telling her tale, the Sultan couldn't lop off her head. But I'll get on with it.

The thing about it, you see, was that Grampa Louie was so damned *humble* about it all. He wasn't the *most* decorated grunt in the War, maybe, but he never bragged about what all he'd done, he turned away compliments and just settled down to being a guy with an illustrious past, and letting others do the bragging.

Even that day when they gave him all that metal for his sash, he just thanked the President and shook her hand, and took the kiss from Greer McCarthy and the salutes from the Generals and the laserlight salvo and the standing ovation, and just nodded, with his eyes checking out his boots. Like, well, did you ever see the ghoster of Jimmy Stewart in *Mr. Smith*

Goes to Washington? Grampa Louie was like that. Just a real nice guy, kind of sweet and embarrassed at all the fuss. Just being a real hero but not stuck up about it, the way we like to see a special sort of man who's done remarkable things, but not making a big wind of it.

And then, when the great-great grandson of Gutzon Borglum picked Grampa Louie to be the model for the War Memorial Wall, and he was so humble he refused, saying he wasn't worthy to represent all the grunts who'd bought it in the War, it took a direct appeal from the President before he agreed.

That wall's still standing. In big carved letters it says OUR GLORIOUS DEAD and there's my Grampa Louie, stripped to the waist, wearing his blast helmet and packing a squirtgun, with his boot on a Kyban battle bonnet. Of course, by the time I was old enough to see the Wall, Grampa Louie was already an old man, and he didn't have the muscles anymore, and he needed a cane to get around. But at least Borglum was smart enough to put the blast helmet on the sculpture so he didn't have to show the scars Grampa Louie had.

Did I forget to mention the scars?

They were awful. A lot worse after the radiation turned him bald and you could see where the red ripping of the short-burst had cut bloodlines from almost the top of his head, down past his right eye—he damned near had lost it—and all the way to his chin. They were parallel lines, like bullet train tracks, right onto his lips at the corner of his mouth. Always red, like blood was coming out of them, even though they'd scabbed over a long time ago.

So with all that, you can imagine how proud I was of my Grampa. *He* was the model for the Glorious Grunt, for all the men and women who'd eaten dust in the War. My Grampa.

When we'd go out for a walk, I'd always make him take me past the Wall. He hated doing it, just this kind and humble guy who didn't want to make a big thing of being a hero. But I'd cry and blow snot out of my face till he did it...and oh yeah, how I loved to look up there at what Grampa Louie had been like when he'd come back, years before I was born.

But he'd mumble something self-effacing and drag my ass down the street before somebody made the connection. And as the years went by, I couldn't wait till I was old enough to enlist and go out there to take up where Grampa Louie had left off. We weren't doing too well in the War at that time. It was after the Kyben bastards had nuked Deald's World, and they were dunkin' us real good. But I was just a kid, so the best I could do was put the pins in my star map, to follow the battles, and play

Sappers'n'Snipers with the other kids. And just wait till I was growed-up enough to make my mark on the recruiter's readout.

And finally, when I turned thirteen, that was seven years ago, I went in the day after my birthday, and I joined up.

It was the proudest day in my life.

You probably can't know about something like that! You Officers and Gennulmen likely all graduated from Sandhurst, and got commissioned straight-away into a Phalanx post. But for me, to be the grandson of the man who'd come out of the Pleiades crusher and been a full-Earth hero…well, it was the best thing I'd ever done, or ever *would* do!

My family was so damned proud of me.

Even Grampa Louie. He was so choked up about it all, he wouldn't even come down out of his room for the farewell dinner my family and friends threw for me. He just locked himself in and said goodbye to me through the door.

And as I walked away, kind of sad that Grampa Louie hadn't come out to hug me and say take care of yourself, kid, he called me through the door; and I went back, and listened close because he was an old, old man by that time; and he said, "Try to come back, Del. I love you, kid." And I'd have cried, but I was going off to the War, and grunts don't groan.

So I left the next day, and they sent me to Croix Noir, and I did my training for Dropshaft service, and came out third highest in my class, and then I did the 80days on Kestral V, and made 2nd Class forty-six days into the rigor. You can't know how proud my family was, and they wrote and looked just as proud as birds in the ghoster, and though Grampa Louie didn't come down to get holo'd, they told me he was as puffed up about me being in Dropshaft as they were, and to go out there and let the yellow stuff flow!

Which is what I did.

They booted me out over Strawhill and I rode the dropshaft into country, and we took Borag and Hyqa and the whole archipelago at Insmel. I got *this* at Insmel, this nice transparent cheek here.

TEF pulled us out of there and I went straight on through inverspace to Black's Nebula. That was sweet, too. Lost half our complement there. They were waiting when we popped out of inver. Wiped two dreadnoughts and a troop condo before we'd pushed our eyeballs back into their sockets. They were all over the scan. Men-of-war and little kickass wasps from the top of the screen to the bottom. And there was just a little poof of implode and a couple of thousand grunts were stardust.

But we got a few loads through, and I went shaft and tried to make my way to the primary, and on the way I got tossed and went in a hundred and fifty kliks shy of the bull. Some kind of a little city, not a major target, but with enough of a home defense system to raise some mist around me. So I burned them.

Turned the beams loose on full, and just swept the goddam town. That wasn't smart. First thing they tell you in Sapper school is, "Don't ever get close enough to see them burn."

I got too close. First time I ever saw anything like that. Wasn't like what they'd taught us it would be. There were old guys like my Grampa Louie, and old women, and kids, and those dog-things they keep for pets...and all of them splitting and popping like bags of pus. They'd bubble and the eyes would explode from the inside. The hair sizzled and the gold skin split, and you could see bone for a second before it all turned black and they fell in like finishing a bag of popcorn and crushing the bag in your hands. I saw a kid, a little girl, I guess, and she looked straight into the screen as I passed over, and she opened her mouth to scream, and her mouth just kept going, right across her face, and then the bottom came away, and she was running in circles and flapping her hands, and I saw all her parts before they turned into stew.

You motherfuckers never told me about that part of it, did you?

Never told me they look a lot like us. Oh sure, they got golden skin, and those eyes, and the little worm fingers. But they're not like the ghosters you showed us! They're *not*, are they? Where's the guy who phonyed up those Kyben monsters for the bond drive ghosters, for the holos that got all of us to join up before we'd learned to wipe our asses? Where is that talented sonofabitch? I'd like to give him an Oscar. 'Cause *they don't look like that!*

I'm okay.

Gimme a minute. Just to clean up.

Yeah. Swell. I'm just swell.

I did the job for you. That kid would never invade old Earth. Took her right out.

But it was the old ones that did it to me. The old ones just like my Grampa Louie, that I adored. You should see what old Kyben have inside them. A lot of stuff that wriggles before it bursts. I guess that was what the guy who phonyed up the monsters *meant* to show, but he never got any closer to the real thing than any of us do. We just hang out there in space and dump. And when the Sappers go in, it's whambam and out so fuckin' fast all you see is a new sunrise.

The old ones. Gawd, it was just swell. Just...swell.

And I was a hero. Like my Grampa Louie.

I got a citation, and a month Earthside.

They snapped me back through inverspace, and I got scrip for a thirty-day repple-depple, and I went home.

It was all I could do to face my family. I wanted to puke. They couldn't stop showing me off to the neighbors. And when the ghosters came to interview me, I just said I was too whacked to talk, and they ran all that bullshit my family put on like the Sunday tablecloth, and I just sat there and stared.

For a day and a half I didn't have the guts to go up and see Grampa Louie. But finally, when I couldn't stand it any more, I knew I had to go tell him I wasn't like him, that I'd come to hate it, and take what he had to say, and just swallow it. But I knew in my heart that I was no more a hero like him than I was an angel. So I went up.

At first he wouldn't unlock the door.

"Grampa, jeezus, I got to talk to you! I'm in Hell, Grampa!"

And he opened the door, and looked at me with his last good eye, and the bullet train scars so red and painful looking, and he was a lot older and closer to the dust than I'd ever seen him. And he was crying. He was crying for me.

And I came through and his old, thin body was around me, him hugging and whispering stuff, and I just laid my head on his shoulder and let it all go.

After a long time we sat down on the edge of his bed, and he told me to tell him all of it. So I did, with snot running down my face, and my hands making these stupid gestures in the air, me trying to grab onto something wasn't there, and Grampa Louie overflowing, too.

And when I got done, and couldn't even gasp any more, he said, "It was a long time ago, and I don't know if it was Pope Gregory XI or Innocent II, I've heard it both ways; but it was in the tenth century sometime. They invented the hand crossbow. It was so awful a weapon that the Pope, whichever one it was, he said, 'This weapon is so horrible that it will surely end all wars,' and he wouldn't let them use it. At least for a while. Then they decided that as terrible as it was, Christians couldn't use it against each other...but they could kill the lousy Mohammedans with it."

He looked at me. "You know what I'm telling you, Del?"

I said I knew perfectly, what he was telling me.

Then he told me something no one else but him in the whole galaxy knew. Something he'd wanted to take to the grave.

And I loved him more, and hated him more, and suffered with him more, and despised him more, than I had ever loved and hated and suffered with or despised anyone in my life, except myself. "What'm I gonna do, Grampa?"

So he told me what to do. What *he* would've done twenty years ago, but didn't have the courage to do, especially since he was a hero.

And that's what I did, you Officers and Gennulmen. I cut out during Molkey's Ash, and I kept going. Maybe before you toss me into the starfire chamber you'll confide how it was you tracked my ass down, and maybe you'll keep it to yourself. But I'll make you a deal.

You tell me how you found me, and *I'll* tell you what Grampa Louie told me that was a secret. Whaddaya say?

Aw, hell, c'mon. What've you got to lose?

We got a deal?

You'll keep your word? Sure, I know you will. You're Officers and Gennulmen, and we're all just grunts in the TEF, right? So, okay, here it is:

Grampa Louie just *hated* it when I'd drool over his model up there on the Wall. Used to drag my scrawny kid's ass away as fast as he could, not because he really gave a damn that someone might spot him and make a big who-struck-John about him being the hero of the Pleiades, but because he knew he was a fraud. He was a killer, and *you're* killers, and me, *I* was a killer, too.

He hadn't gotten those blast scars in battle. He'd gotten them from the Kyban woman he was trying to stick it up the ass of. There wasn't any sex in it. He was just horny, and he'd been out there forever, and he didn't give a shit what it would do to her, or anything. He was just the kind of guy you train us to be. Real grunts.

And she burned him. And he stomped in her head with a boot just like that boot he's wearing up there on the Wall you all admire and drool over so much. He just smashed in her head like that Kyban battle bonnet on the sculpture.

My Grampa Louie was just like me. *Just* like me. One of the few, the proud. The shit you made believe all that *hail to us ain't we the best in the universe* crap!

Get out, Del. That's what my Grampa Louie told me. Get out before they make you what I am, before they kill you and you never get a chance to say you're sorry. Because there's no way to say I'm sorry. And there's no way to get over hating yourself for being so goddam dumb that you buy into all that *kill the Mohammedans* bullshit. Get out, kid. Hightail it, get out, and don't stop.

So now I'm getting hoarse, and that's my tale, Sirs.

Now you gonna tell me how you tracked me?

You gonna tell me in exchange for the honor of my Grampa Louie, who put a squirtgun on that goddam Wall the week after I shipped out again, and blew a chunk out of it before the cops wasted him, not knowing he was the guy up there on the sculpture? You ready to tell me?

Well?

Whaddaya say? I'm waiting.

What...? You *what*!?

Why, you sonsofbitches, you no-good rotten bastards?

Right into the starfire?

You *bastards*!

You lied to me! You *lied* to me.

The Deadly "Nackles" Affair

a true tale of action, danger, duplicity, and the Search for Literary Excellence in the netherworld of television, with a Stern Moral about ethics and a reminder that a loaf of bread doesn't cost 13¢ any more

Andre Gide wrote: "Everything's already been said, but since nobody was listening, we have to start again."

(You can use that the next time some spud tells you it isn't worth being a writer, because Shakespeare created all the basic plots, and all that's left to us is rewriting what has already been done perfectly.)

The mistake we all make is in assuming anybody remembers *any*damnthing from one day to the next. If that were true, we'd stop getting involved with approximately the same kind of wrong lover each time, we'd learn the lessons of history, the death penalty would discourage those plotting murder, and George Santayana's famous quote would be about as popular as "the bee's knees." But few of us keep accurate records of what we've learned as we hobble through life barking our shins in the dark on experiences we've already had; we have no tickler file to point out the similar traps of Korea and Viet Nam, of Joe McCarthy and Jerry Falwell; and as Olin Miller has so aptly noted, "Of all liars, the smoothest and most convincing is memory."

Thus, I must remind myself that though I have written two books of essays on the subject of television (concluding that to work in television is akin to putting in time in the Egyptian House of the Dead), and subsequently wrote a long essay as introduction to my 1978 collection, STRANGE WINE (in which I vowed on peril of losing my immortal soul that I would never again work in television), there may be at least tens of thousands of readers of this essay who remain unaware of my loathing for the coaxial medium, and who know not that my going to work in November of 1984 for CBS's revival of *The Twilight Zone* caused some small, but significant, tremor of confusion among the faithful. After all, hadn't I inveighed against television for a decade and more? Hadn't I advised viewers to kick in the picture tubes and use their sets as planters? Hadn't I grown to be the specter at the banquet, doomsaying brain damage and tertiary blandness for all of you out there sucking up them good ole phosphor dots?

Well, you can just imagine what happened when it was announced that I was returning to tv, to work as Creative Consultant on *The Twilight Zone*! Such hue and cry, such *sturm und drang*, such death and transfiguration. You'd have thought that a simple mention in *TV Guide* was more unsettling than The Zimmermann Telegram!

Explaining what I was doing toiling for a year in the hold of the television trireme, for those who don't remember (and don't give a hoot), leads to an explanation of why I left *The Twilight Zone*'s employ, for those who are delighted to see the teleplay of "Nackles" published here. And all of it, from joyous opening credits to shabby fadeout, circumnavigates the core fact that neither you nor I remember the past and thus are condemned to repeat it.

I worked for more than a decade in television. I won a number of awards doing it. The number of awards I won, counted on the fingers of the left hand, total more than the number of happy days I had working in the medium during that period, counted on the fingers of the right hand. And if my left hand had suspected what my right hand was up to, my left hand would surely have crushed the unhappy fingers of my right hand between the jaws of a bench vise. But perhaps I exaggerate. I recall at least two personal experiences that were more unpleasant than working in television: passing forty-eight kidney stones in the space of eight hours without benefit of anaesthesia, and a sigmoidoscopy that left me walking funnily for a week. Writing television ranks right in there somewhere.

The angst comes not from the actual writing, which is usually pleasurable—as long as one selects shows on which one can work with a sense of craft, art, and honor—but from fighting the soul-crushing *apparat* placed between creators and viewers by networks, studios, production companies and their feckless *apparatchiks*. By the time anything one has written gets on the little screen, the misery one has been put through has flensed even the joy of the writing, and all one is left with is money. Which is what they pay you for the privilege of telling you that they know how to write what you've written better than you can. One never asks: if you can do it so much better, schmuck, why don't you just *do it?* One never asks, for answer came there none.

But early in November of 1984, I received a call from Jim Crocker, who identified himself as Supervising Producer of *The Twilight Zone*, then being readied for a September 1985 revival on CBS. He said TZ wanted to purchase rights to my story "Shatterday" for teleplay adaptation by then-freelancer Alan Brennert (soon to be Executive Story Consultant Brennert). I told him to forget it. He asked me why. I told him that it had nothing to do with Alan who was/is a friend of mine—and, in fact, is the only writer working in television to whom I had ever voluntarily given permission to adapt one of my stories. I said I thought Alan would likely do a spiffy job with "Shatterday." But I said no; I wanted nothing to do with tv, and had seen enough of my work crippled to last me a lifetime.

That led us into a conversation during the course of which I unloaded all my long-gathered thoughts about why fantasy so seldom worked when transferred to the video screen. It was a long chat, and when I was finished lecturing, Jim said he and the Executive Producer, Philip DeGuere, had put together a "bible" of guidelines for writers intending to work on the series, complete with story-outlines. He asked me if I'd mind taking a look at it, to give him and DeGuere my feelings about whether they were on the right track or not.

I said yes. Mostly because Jim Crocker is one of the most decent, charming men I have ever met. Honest and talented and compassionate to a fault, Crocker's patience in listening to my babble, and his genuine sense of concern that TZ be done properly, had won me completely. So I said yes, I'd look at the "bible."

A messenger delivered it later that day from the studio where TZ had its offices, the CBS Studio Center lot very near my home. It is now called the MTM Studios, but to me it will always be Four Star, because it was there in the early Sixties that I had my first successes in television, writing *Burke's Law.* But I digress.

I read the "bible" and a day or so later called Crocker to give him my comments about the proposed stories to be filmed. I was not entirely laudatory. In fact, when Jim tells this part of the story the words *brutal,* *barbaric* and *offensive* are prominently featured.

Nonetheless, he suggested it would be a salutary thing for him and DeGuere to meet me, to discuss further the opinions I'd ventured...and to try a little harder to get me to cough up the rights to "Shatterday." I said, sure, why not; but it was unlikely that I'd change my mind.

On November 6th, DeGuere and Crocker came to my home and we sat in the Art Deco Dining Pavilion for three hours, with Crocker silently smiling at the first confrontation between me and the legendary DeGuere. I have heard Jim equate the meeting with that held by Pope Leo I and Attila the Hun at the gates of Rome in the year 452. I liked DeGuere at once.

By the time they left, I had not only agreed to let Alan do "Shatterday," but I had agreed to write an original story for the show.

Well, one thing led to another.

Like you, I forgot the lessons of the past. I was so charmed by Crocker and DeGuere, so filled with hubris that *I*, alone of all the wretches crawling across this planet, had the special wisdom to bring superlative fantasy to the small screen, that I allowed myself to be seduced. No other word works as well. I was seduced. By respect, and friendship, by the challenge, and by that smooth, convincing liar, memory.

On December 3rd, 1984, after ten years away from the medium, I accepted a position as Creative Consultant to *The Twilight Zone,* working for CBS, at a staggering weekly salary that within a few months totally eradicated the $45,000 debt under which I had been bending for several years. Bread, I had discovered, no longer cost 13¢ a loaf; and 37¢ no longer bought a tank of gas; and one forgets how nice it is not having to consider selling one's record collection to make the mortgage payment.

On November 26th, 1985—a Tuesday—one year after going onboard TZ, I resigned from the series. But for that year of employment (the longest job I've ever held in my entire life) I did not work in television; rather, I was permitted to caper and whistle through Camelot.

Working with DeGuere and Crocker, Alan Brennert and Story Editor Rockne O'Bannon, Producer Harvey Frand and Barbara Sigg and Janien Rotundo and Patrice Messina and Ken Swor and Paul Deason and all the rest of the loonies who were drawn into that dream of excellence we all held for what TZ could be...was one of the happiest times of my life.

It was by no means all lightness and joy and freedom to create. There were days and nights of genuine horror, of pain suffered by one or another of our little cadre that was a nasty palliative to our cockeyed camaraderie and the sweetly exhausting months of 'round-the-clock work. But we learned each other's weaknesses and annoying habits; and we opted either to live with them, or to put each other against the wall and shout back, *Stop doing that or I will nail your forehead to a coffee table!* We grinned at each other constantly, knowing that not only were we privileged to be at just the right spot to make history, but *knowing* that we knew it; that we could enjoy it as it was happening, rather than looking back ten years to say, "That was a terrific, special time!"

And if the first season's shows were not all of the caliber of *Nightcrawlers* and *Wordplay*, of *Her Pilgrim Soul* and *Profile in Silver*, of *One Life, Furnished in Early Poverty* and *Cold Reading*, at least—given the network interference, that damnable eight o'clock time-slot on Friday nights, and a million budget and production problems that no viewer can ever know—we went at the job with bared fangs and high skill and true love. I have no regrets about working that year in the bowels of the beast television. And would have happily gone on to a second season, ratings be damned.

So why, the impatient reader asks after all this history and bonhomie, did the hardcore-unemployable Ellison walk off the best job he'd ever had?

In a word: *Nackles.*

Under the pseudonym "Curt Clark," the brilliant novelist Donald Westlake wrote, and saw published in the January 1964 issue of *The Magazine of Fantasy & Science Fiction,* a nasty little Christmas horror story titled "Nackles." It was reprinted only once, in the 1967 Ace paperback anthology NEW WORLDS OF FANTASY, edited by Terry Carr.

In the Fall of 1984, before I came on the show, Hugo and Nebula winner George R.R. Martin brought the story to the attention of DeGuere. George's excellent novel THE ARMAGEDDON RAG had been optioned as a feature film by DeGuere several years earlier, and they had become friends. It was natural that when Phil signed to do TZ, that he would solicit work from George; and George sent him Xerox copies of the story; and Phil optioned it for George to turn into a teleplay for the show. I don't think either of them knew that "Curt Clark" was a heavyweight like Westlake, as Don had used the pseudonym infrequently. (Few alive today remember ANARCHAOS, a 40¢ Ace original novel, 1967, though it is a swell little thriller.)

By the time I came to TZ, George had noodled the idea that formed the core of "Nackles" to a point where he could write it up as a story outline. I had had success adapting Stephen King's "Gramma"—a difficult but enjoyable assignment—and was busily writing both the short story and the teleplay of "Paladin of the Lost Hour" when George's treatment came in.

Those of you who have read "Nackles" in its print medium incarnation (included, *seriatum*, in this volume), will perceive that what works on the page would not work on the screen. The core idea, the anti-Santa, was so strong, that it obliterated the rest of the story for visual adaptation. George, who at that time had had very little experience with the script idiom, though he has gone on to do some excellent teleplays and subsequently was hired as a Story Editor on TZ, stubbed his toe on the piece, and no one (George included) was particularly happy with the result.

At the same time, we were trying to breathe life into an idea submitted by a writer named Bryce Maritano; a story about an Elvis imitator who goes back in time to meet The King. The story meetings we held, in which we sat for hours trying to make either silk purses out of sow's ears or sow's ears out of silk purses, invariably foundered on Maritano's story, "The Once and Future King." It was a touching, dangerous concept, but Maritano didn't seem to know where to go with it. There was talk of putting the story in abeyance, but with one of those rare insights my wife refers to as "dumb luck," I said to DeGuere, "Jeezus, what dummies we are! One of the basic problems of this script is that Maritano doesn't have the feel for rock'n'roll. He's even got Elvis playing an electric guitar, and everybody *knows* Presley played only acousticals. Give the story to George. He's perfect for it. He's got the smarts for this one if anybody has!"

So George was relieved of "Nackles" and went on to write a killer segment based on the Maritano idea, the premiere show of the second season.

But we still needed someone to write "Nackles" for the special Christmas show. Since it was *my* big mouth that had freed the job for a new writer, and since it was *my* big mouth that ventured ways in which Westlake's gruesome little *bon mot* could be altered to work visually, it was *into* my big mouth that Crocker, O'Bannon, DeGuere and Brennert wadded the script.

It was summer before I got to it. I began by doing research. Richard Finkelstein, Director, Bureau of Client Fraud Investigation, New York City Human Resources Administration, spent several hours on the long distance phone with me, explaining how the welfare setup works these days in Manhattan. Then I went back to all the stories I'd written about tenement life in New York, and refreshed the recollections, the smells and sounds.

Understand: I am no part of the shared delusion that if one merely entertains with television, that it is a job worthy unto itself. Entertain, yes! That goes without saying. But a good writer does that automatically, it's built into the machine. Telling a thumpingly good, mesmerizing story is what one does without question. But beyond that, any writer worth his/

her hire knows that *all* writing, one way or another, is subversive. It is guerrilla warfare against the *status quo*. It is not whimsical that the Falwells and Tipper Gores and Wildmons of the world seek to silence music and to burn books: they correctly perceive them to be dangerous. Kafka tells us, "I believe that we should read only those books that wound and stab us. If a book we are reading does not rouse us with a blow to the head, then why read it? A book must be the axe for the frozen sea inside us." So should it be with television, a medium so powerful that it can change our cultural values in a generation. But it isn't so. And television is *merely* entertainment. At best. For the most part it is as memorable and meaningful as what Aquinas called "a fart in the wind." Writing, done well, after the entertainment part has been taken care of, should be journalism.

And I am one with Joseph Pulitzer, who is reputed to have said, "The purpose of journalists should be to afflict the comfortable."

So for Christmas, I turned "Nackles" into a statement on bigotry and racism. You read it; I'll abide by your judgment; and see if it is a strong statement. It was certainly *intended* to be strong. To sit between a remake of that gentle Yuletide fable *The Night of the Meek* and Alan Brennert's adaptation of Arthur C. Clarke's "The Star" in a tripartite holiday package that would make a viewing experience no one would soon forget. Ah, vanity, thy name is scenarist.

My first draft teleplay was handed in on July 15th, 1985 and by September 25th, when I had completed a rewrite, we knew we had something in the oven that might be difficult to get past the network, but if it could be done...gangbusters!

I sent the script to Don Westlake, to get his feeling about it, and on October 25th he wrote me (in part): "Okay. In fact, *okay*! It's different, God knows, but it would have to be, wouldn't it? When this idea first came along, I said to myself, well, if they want to, but I don't think it's possible. I looked at the story again at that time, and it seemed to me it wasn't a story at all, it was just an essay with incidents. I wouldn't have had the slightest idea how to turn it into a real-life narrative, and I'm amazed that you not only believed there was a way, but found it."

I felt like a million bucks.

A final draft was handed in on November 3rd, followed by a "revised final" on the 13th of that month. Christmas was coming at us steadily, and we had to get moving or we'd never get the segment into that triple-play package. Another revised draft: November 14th. A third revised final: November 20th.

For some time on the show, DeGuere and Crocker and our line producer Harvey Frand, and Alan and Rock had been trying to convince me that I should try my hand at directing. I'd resisted, because I'm a writer, and that's what I like to do. But in the course of the season I'd seen so many lame directors mess up so many sweet scripts, that by the middle of November I was convinced a talented mollusk could direct decently. So on the 21st I told Harvey and Jim I wanted to direct "Nackles."

It was a short script, perhaps only eleven minutes long as it would finally be aired, and it had gone through all the personnel at CBS programming, as well as the L.A.-based CBS Standards & Practices people. They'd seen it as a dangerous script, but we'd bartered a word here, an epithet there, and it had been approved for us to go forward into production.

On the 22nd, CBS approved me as director for the segment. It was a scary step for me to be taking, but I *knew* what I wanted to see there on the screen come Christmastime, that rushing-toward-us Friday night, and I knew I could pull it off. Hell, ain't I the guy who writes such visual scripts, with all the shots in there just to give the director a vision, not a floorplan?

That day I scouted locations with my Assistant Director, Paul Deason; costumes were set; and I called in a favor by getting Edward Asner to play the loathesome Jack Podey. Ed and I had been on a few barricades together, and though I knew he did not do ordinary episodic tv, and that he drew down a much heftier salary than TZ could pay, I felt he would want to do a show like this one. "Nackles," by the very presence of an Asner, would be a statement of moral imperative that nobody could dismiss. Ed agreed to play Podey. I loved it...because I'd had him in mind as Podey from the first line I'd written. (True to his nature, Ed Asner announced he would donate his entire fee to charity. So what's not to love about him?)

We worked through the weekends painting mattes, dressing sets, hiring the other actors, looking at dozens of kids till we found one who could play Pooch to the hilt.

Everything was set.

And then, in New York, a woman named Alice Henderson, bearing some sort of title or other, but high up in the CBS Standards & Practices division, finally got around to reading "Nackles." Later, CBS would say that they'd gotten the script at the last moment. As you can tell from the dates of various versions of the script, which would have been approved all the way through the process, they knew what "Nackles" was to be, as far back as July. Notwithstanding the duplicity, Alice Henderson's hair rose like Medusa's serpentine locks.

The word came down on Monday the 25th:

You cannot do this script. Not no way, not no how, not never!

DeGuere and everyone else went crazy. We were thousands of dollars into the game already. Asner had a pay-or-play contract. They would have to pay me the full director's fee, even if the show never got made. Everyone started trying to get Henderson and her department to suggest ways in which it could work.

The suggestions were vile, infamous!

It couldn't be New York. (Because the week before, CBS had aired a special starring Lucille Ball as a bag lady, and the head of CBS had gotten a cranky call from Mayor Koch, upset that the Apple was always being portrayed as a cesspool.) We couldn't have the Puerto Rican woman fudging on her welfare, no matter how compassionately we portrayed reality. It couldn't under any circumstances be Christmas, but we could pick any other holiday we chose. (*TV Guide* quoted me as suggesting, "Perhaps the dark side of the Easter Bunny!")

There were more strictures. Many more. I won't name them, because you may be reading this before you read the teleplay, and I don't want to spill the beans. But when you reach the punchline, you'll understand that they absolutely forbid...

Well, you'll see.

I resigned on the 26th. There was a lot of noise about it. I don't suffer in silence. It was in the *New York Times*, *TV Guide*, *Los Angeles Times*, *Variety*, dozens of newspapers all over the country, on *Entertainment Tonight* and, ironically, *CBS News*.

But they wouldn't back down.

They pulled the plug, costing the TZ production company what has been estimated at between $150,000 and $300,000.

And the Christmas show had a substitute segment slipped into it. And I was gone. And that was that.

Except. In the Spring of 1986, when it appeared that TZ would be picked up for a second season, DeGuere called and said CBS wanted me to meet with Alice Henderson, who was coming in from New York, to discuss my returning to the show. We three met and had lunch at Musso & Frank Grill in Hollywood, and I presented my case to Ms. Henderson. I told her that I respected her desire to protect the American public from dangerous materials but that I felt it was very shaky ground for the network, to be taking a stand *against* a potent indictment of racism and bigotry. I told

her this was intended to be the real thing, not Archie Bunker calling someone a "spook" and then smiling, and everybody knows he's at heart a good guy, didn't he cry when Edith died?

I told her that I perceived her actions as intending to serve the commonweal, but that, in fact, she was serving the *status quo*. And since the *status quo* was one of bigotry and racism, that she was in no way defending the responsibility of the network.

It was an amicable talk. Nice woman, actually. And she said she'd consider revising her decision.

Well, they jerked me around for months. Finally DeGuere had a meeting with the Powers In Charge, and we arrived at some revisions (they've been included as gray-tone sidebars at the appropriate places in the teleplay), revisions that I thought we could live with.

I did the rewrite free of charge.

Sent it in.

And they switched censors. They altered the rules of the game, and some new jamook said not no way, not no how, not never!

And that was that.

I forgot. I forgot that for every DeGuere and Crocker who cares about what comes to you through that little box, there are a hundred clowns in suits, terrified of making waves, who puff up like a banjo player who had a big breakfast with the import of the job. Men and women who care only that a loaf of bread costs more than 13¢ and they will make *damned* sure no little smartmouth writer endangers their purchase of the Staff of Life. Let us offend *no one*, even if the cost of that chickenshit political correctness cowardice is a perpetuation of despicable practices and mores and vile, outmoded, cultural values.

For some of us, who live to regret having forgotten the lessons of history, there are other, more important Staffs in this life. The Staff with which I worked for a year on TZ was more important, and CBS has broken *that* staff...Brennert and Crocker and I are gone. The Staff of honor is also important. And if a writer cannot do with honor what he/she does best, then working in the medium is only for the buck.

And that's no reason worth a fart in the wind.

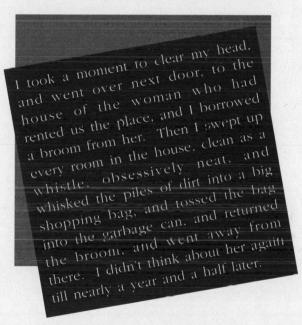

I took a moment to clear my head, and went over next door, to the house of the woman who had rented us the place, and I borrowed a broom from her. Then I swept up every room in the house, clean as a whistle, obsessively neat, and whisked the piles of dirt into a big shopping bag, and tossed the bag into the garbage can, and returned the broom, and went away from there. I didn't think about her again till nearly a year and a half later.

Nackles

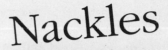

a short story by
Donald E. Westlake

Did God create men, or does *Man create gods?* I don't know, and if it hadn't been for my rotten brother-in-law the question would never have come up. My *late* brother-in-law? Nackles knows.

It all depends, you see, like the chicken and the egg, on which came first. Did God exist before Man first thought of Him, or didn't He? If not, if Man creates his gods, then it follows that Man must create the devils, too.

Nearly every god, you know, has his corresponding devil. Good *and* Evil. The polytheistic ancients, prolific in the creation (?) of gods and goddesses, always worked up nearly enough Evil ones to cancel out the Good, but not quite. The Greeks, those incredible supermen, combined Good and Evil in *each* of their gods. In Zoroaster, Ahura Mazda, being Good, is ranged forever against the Evil one, Ahriman. And we ourselves know God and Satan.

But of course it's entirely possible I have nothing to worry about. It all depends on whether Santa Claus is or is not a god. He certainly *seems* like a god. Consider: He is omniscient; he knows every action of every child, for good or evil. At least on Christmas Eve he is omnipresent, everywhere at once. He administers justice tempered with mercy. He is superhuman, or at

219

least non-human, though conceived of as having a human shape. He is aided by a corps of assistants who do *not* have completely human shapes. He rewards Good and punishes Evil. And, most important, he is believed in utterly by several million people, most of them under the age of ten. Is there any qualification for godhood that Santa Claus does not possess?

And even the non-believers give him lip-service. He has surely taken over Christmas; his effigy is everywhere, but where are the manger and the Christ child? Retired rather forlornly to the nave. (Santa's power is growing, too. Slowly but surely he is usurping Chanukah as well.)

Santa Claus *is* a god. He's no less a god than Ahura Mazda, or Odin, or Zeus. Think of the white beard, the chariot pulled through the air by a breed of animal which doesn't ordinarily fly, the prayers (requests for gifts) which are annually mailed to him and which so baffle the Post Office, the specially garbed priests in all the department stores. And don't gods reflect their creators' (?) society? The Greeks had a huntress goddess, and gods of agriculture and war and love. What else would we have but a god of giving, of merchandising, and of consumption? Secondary gods of earlier times have been stout, but surely Santa Claus is the first fat primary god.

And wherever there is a god, mustn't there sooner or later be a devil?

Which brings me back to my brother-in-law, who's to blame for whatever happens now. My brother-in-law Frank is—or was—a very mean and nasty man. Why I ever let him marry my sister I'll never know. Why Susie *wanted* to marry him is an even greater mystery. I could just shrug and say Love Is Blind, I suppose, but that wouldn't explain how she fell in love with him in the first place.

Frank is—Frank was—I just don't know what tense to use. The present, hopefully. Frank is a very handsome man in his way, big and brawny, full of vitality. A football player; hero in college and defensive linebacker for three years in pro ball, till he did some sort of irreparable damage to his left knee, which gave him a limp and forced him to find some other way to make a living.

Ex-football players tend to become insurance salesmen, I don't know why. Frank followed the form, and became an insurance salesman. Because Susie was then a secretary for the same company, they soon became acquainted.

Was Susie dazzled by the ex-hero, so big and handsome? She's never been the type to dazzle easily, but we can never fully know what goes on inside the mind of another human being. For whatever reason, she decided she was in love with him.

So they were married, and five weeks later he gave her her first black eye. And the last, though it mightn't have been, since Susie tried to keep me from finding out. I was to go over for dinner that night, but at eleven in the morning she called the auto showroom where I work, to tell me she had a headache and we'd have to postpone the dinner. But she sounded so upset that I knew immediately something was wrong, so I took a demonstration car and drove over, and when she opened the front door there was the shiner.

I got the story out of her slowly, in fits and starts. Frank, it seemed, had a terrible temper. She wanted to excuse him because he was forced to be an insurance salesman when he really wanted to be out there on the gridiron again, but I want to be President and I'm an automobile salesman and *I* don't go around giving women black eyes. So I decided it was up to me to let Frank know he wasn't to vent his pique on my sister any more.

Unfortunately, I am five feet seven inches tall and weigh one hundred thirty-four pounds, with the Sunday *Times* under my arm. Were I just to give Frank a piece of my mind, he'd surely give me a black eye to go with my sister's. Therefore, that afternoon I bought a regulation baseball bat, and carried it with me when I went to see Frank that night.

He opened the door himself and snarled, "What do *you* want?"

In answer, I poked him with the end of the bat, just above the belt, to knock the wind out of him. Then, having unethically gained the upper hand, I clouted him five or six times more, and then stood over him to say, "The next time you hit my sister I won't let you off so easy." After which I took Susie home to *my* place for dinner.

And after which I was Frank's best friend.

People like that are so impossible to understand. Until the baseball bat episode, Frank had nothing for me but undisguised contempt. But once I'd knocked the stuffing out of him, he was my comrade for life. And I'm sure it was sincere; he would have given me the shirt off his back, had I wanted it, which I didn't.

(Also, by the way, he never hit Susie again. He still had the bad temper, but he took it out in throwing furniture out windows or punching dents in walls or going downtown to start a brawl in some bar. I offered to train him out of maltreating the house and furniture as I had trained him out of maltreating his wife, but Susie said no, that Frank had to let off steam and it would be worse if he was forced to bottle it all up inside him, so the baseball bat remained in retirement.)

Then came the children, three of them in as many years. Frank Junior came first, and then Linda Joyce, and finally Stewart. Susie had held the forlorn hope that fatherhood would settle Frank to some extent, but quite the reverse was true. Shrieking babies, smelly diapers, disrupted sleep, and distracted wives are trials and tribulations to any man, but to Frank they were—like everything else in his life—the last straw.

He became, in a word, worse. Susie restrained him I don't know how often from doing some severe damage to a squalling infant, and as the children grew toward the age of reason Frank's expressed attitude toward them was that their best move would be to find a way to become invisible. The children, of course, didn't like him very much, but then who did?

Last Christmas was when *it* started. Junior was six then, and Linda Joyce five, and Stewart four, so all were old enough to have heard of Santa Claus and still young enough to believe in him. Along around October, when the Christmas season was beginning, Frank began to use Santa Claus's displeasure as a weapon to keep the children "in line," his phrase for keeping them mute and immobile and terrified. Many parents, of course, try to enforce obedience the same way: "If you're bad, Santa Claus won't bring you any presents." Which, all things considered, is a negative and passive sort of punishment, wishy-washy in comparison with fire and brimstone and such. In the old days, Santa Claus would treat bad children a bit more scornfully, leaving a lump of coal in their stockings in lieu of presents, but I suppose the Depression helped to change that. There are times and situations when a lump of coal is nothing to sneer at.

In any case, an absence of presents was too weak a punishment for Frank's purposes, so last Christmastime he invented Nackles.

Who is Nackles? Nackles is to Santa Claus what Satan is to God, what Ahriman is to Ahura Mazda, what the North Wind is to the South Wind. Nackles is the new Evil.

I think Frank really *enjoyed* creating Nackles; he gave so much thought to the details of him. According to Frank, and as I remember it, this is Nackles: Very very tall and very very thin. Dressed all in black, with a gaunt gray face and deep black eyes. He travels through an intricate series of tunnels under the earth, in a black chariot on rails, pulled by an octet of dead-white goats.

And what does Nackles do? Nackles lives on the flesh of little boys and girls. (This is what Frank was telling his children; can you believe it?) Nackles roams back and forth under the earth, in his dark tunnels darker than subway tunnels, pulled by the eight dead-white goats, and he searches for little boys and girls to stuff into his big black sack and carry away and eat. But Santa Claus won't let him have *good* boys and girls.   Santa Claus is stronger than Nackles, and keeps a protective shield around little children, so Nackles can't get at them.

But when little children are bad, it hurts Santa Claus, and weakens the shield Santa Claus has placed around them, and if they keep on being bad pretty soon there's no shield left at all, and on Christmas Eve instead of Santa Claus coming down out of the sky with his bag of presents Nackles comes up out of the ground with his bag of emptiness, and stuffs the bad children in, and whisks them away to his dark tunnels and the eight dead-white goats.

Frank was proud of his invention, actually proud of it. He not only used Nackles to threaten his children every time they had the temerity to come within range of his vision, he also spread the story around to others. He told me, and his neighbors, and people in bars, and people he went to see in his job as insurance salesman. I don't know how many people he told about Nackles, though I would guess it was well over a hundred. And there's more than one Frank in this world; he told me from time to time of a client or neighbor or bar-crony who had heard the story of Nackles and then said, "By God, that's great. That's what *I've* been needing, to keep *my* brats in line."

Thus Nackles was created, and thus Nackles was promulgated. And would any of the unfortunate children thus introduced to Nackles believe in this Evil Being any less than they believed in Santa Claus? Of course not.

This all happened, as I say, last Christmastime. Frank invented Nackles, used him to further intimidate his already intimidated children, and spread the story of him to everyone he met. On Christmas Day last year I'm sure there was more than one child in this town who was relieved and somewhat surprised to awaken the same as usual, in his own trundle bed, and to find the presents downstairs beneath the tree, proving that Nackles had been kept away yet another year.

Nackles lay dormant, so far as Frank was concerned, from December 25th of last year until this October. Then, with the sights and sounds of Christmas again in the land, back came Nackles, as fresh and vicious as ever. "Don't expect *me* to stop him!" Frank would shout. "When he comes up out of the ground the night before Christmas to carry you away in his bag, don't expect any help from *me*!"

It was worse this year than last. Frank wasn't doing as well financially as he'd expected, and then early in November Susie discovered she was pregnant again, and what with one thing and another Frank was headed for a real peak of ill-temper. He screamed at the children constantly, and the name of Nackles was never far from his tongue.

Susie did what she could to counteract Frank's bad influence, but he wouldn't let her do much. All through November and December he was home more and more of the time, because the Christmas season is the wrong time to sell insurance anyway and also because he was hating the job more every day and thus giving it less of his time. The more he hated the job, the worse his temper became, and the more he drank, and the worse his limp got, and the louder were his shouts, and the more violent his references to Nackles. It just built and built and built, and reached its crescendo on Christmas Eve, when some small or imagined infraction of one of the children—Stewart, I think—resulted in Frank's pulling all the Christmas presents from all the closets and stowing them all in the car to be taken back to the stores, because this Christmas for sure it wouldn't be Santa Claus who would be visiting this house, it would be Nackles.

By the time Susie got the children to bed, everyone in the house was a nervous wreck. The children were too frightened to sleep, and Susie was too unnerved herself to be of much help in soothing them. Frank, who had taken to drinking at home lately, had locked himself in the bedroom with a bottle.

It was nearly eleven o'clock before Susie got the children all quieted down, and then she went out to the car and brought all the presents back in and arranged them under the tree. Then, not wanting to see or hear her husband any more that night—he was like a big spoiled child throwing a tantrum—she herself went to sleep on the living room sofa.

Frank Junior awoke her in the morning, crying, "Look, Mama! Nackles *didn't* come, he *didn't* come!" And pointed to the presents she'd placed under the tree.

The other two children came down shortly after, and Susie and the youngsters sat on the floor and opened the presents, enjoying themselves as much as possible, but still with restraint. There were none of the usual squeals of childish pleasure; no one wanted Daddy to come storming downstairs in one of his rages. So the children contented themselves with ear-to-ear smiles and whispered exclamations, and after a while Susie made breakfast, and the day carried along as pleasantly as could be expected under the circumstances.

It was a little after twelve that Susie began to worry about Frank's non-appearance. She braved herself to go up and knock on the locked door and call his name, but she got no answer, not even the expected snarl, so just around one o'clock she called me and I hurried on over. I rapped smartly on the bedroom door, got no answer, and finally I threatened to break the door in if Frank didn't open up. When I still got no answer, break the door in I did.

And Frank, of course, was gone.

The police say he ran away, deserted his family, primarily because of Susie's fourth pregnancy. They say he went out the window and dropped to the backyard, so Susie wouldn't see him and try to stop him. And they say he didn't take the car because he was afraid Susie would hear him start the engine.

That all sounds reasonable, doesn't it? Yet, I just can't believe Frank would walk out on Susie without a lot of shouting about it first. Nor that he would leave his car, which he was fonder of than his wife and children.

But what's the alternative? There's only one I can think of: Nackles.

I would rather not believe that. I would rather not believe that Frank, in inventing Nackles and spreading word of him, made him real. I would rather not believe that Nackles actually did visit my sister's house on Christmas Eve.

But did he? If so, he couldn't have carried off any of the children, for a more subdued and better-behaved trio of youngsters you won't find anywhere. But Nackles, being brand-new and never having had a meal before, would need *somebody*. Somebody to whom he was real, somebody not protected by the shield of Santa Claus. And, as I say, Frank was drinking that night. Alcohol makes the brain believe in the existence of all sorts of things. Also, Frank was a spoiled child if there ever was one.

There's no question but that Frank Junior and Linda Joyce and Stewart believe in Nackles. And Frank spread the gospel of Nackles to others, some of whom spread it to their own children. And some of whom will spread the new Evil to other parents. And ours is a mobile society, with families constantly being transferred by Daddy's company from one end of the country to another, so how long can it be before Nackles is a power not only in this one city, but all across the nation?

I don't know if Nackles exists, or will exist. All I know for sure is that there's suddenly a new level of meaning in the lyric of that popular Christmas song. You know the one I mean:

You'd better watch out.

Nackles

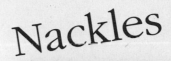

Teleplay by
Harlan Ellison
suggested by a
short story by
Donald E. Westlake

NOTE: This teleplay should be shot in black and white. Not color stock with transfer to black and white, but true black and white like the *film noir* films of the Forties. By running the titles in color over the opening shot, the audience will know it is intentionally being done in this style. But more to the point— the "point" being the old saw that viewers will think there is something wrong with their sets and rush to adjust the picture—this fear no longer, in fact, has validity. Not only *Rumblefish* set the new idiom for b&w: there have been at least a dozen rock videos done in b&w (as well as others with touches of color added as in *Rumblefish*) and "Moonlighting" has just done a mini-movie for tv in b&w. I submit that this will lend a deep-focus fix of ominous subtext to "Nackles" and will speak to the b&w plot-thread that runs throughout the script.

Thus, I am writing this teleplay for black and white.

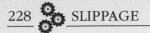

FADE IN:

1   INNER CITY STREET — WINTER — DAY — BLACK & WHITE —
    EXTREME CLOSEUP — JACK PODEY'S FOOT

A wingtip cordovan shoe; a shoe that a cop or a
department store floorwalker would wear. A heavy,
no-nonsense shoe. Shined. As a cantaloupe rind
hits the shoe, leaving a smear and seeds on the
polished leather, the shoe step stops.

CREDITS OVER IN COLOR

Camera pulls back fast to show us a filthy,
slush-riddled sidewalk in upper Manhattan,
somewhere in the vicinity of 101st and Fifth Avenue.
Ghetto. Crowded, despite the heavy, chill, cutting
wind. Everyone in overcoats and earmuffs,
galoshes and mufflers that blow frantically in
the wind. One of those minus-10 wind-chill factor
days. Grimy snow in shoveled mounds at the curb.
Car tops still wear their barrister's wigs of
sooty snow.

Only one white face in a sea of jammed-together
black humanity. Not a lot of natural rhythm here,
just a dogged determination to scrape through till
tomorrow. One white face twisted in hatred and
anger. JACK PODEY, wearer of the besmirched
wingtip, about forty-seven years old, and big; a
big man who came out of the womb a bully. Hair cut
short almost in a crew, jaw muscles that could crack
walnuts, a pair of eyes midway between nasty and
noisy. Jack Podey sweats a lot. And chews gum.

                    [MORE]

                              (CONTINUED:)

1   CONTINUED:

He grabs up the cantaloupe rind, jerks his head
fast, this way and that, looking up to the tenement
roofs, where he spots a little black kid, maybe
twelve years old, muffler wrapped around the lower
half of his face like a desperado. One Podey paw,
big as a catcher's mitt, is attached to a heavy,
battered leather attorney's satchel (boxlike, not
portfolio). The other Podey paw is dead aimed and
hurls the rind clear up to the roof.

                    PODEY
              (snarling, yells)
        Eat it, ya stinkin' jungle bunny!

The shot misses. The kid flips him off, disappears.
The people passing on the sidewalk almost stop
and say some bad business, but Podey is already
casting around with a look that be badder than
themselves. Pedestrians mumble, but move past
him. Podey takes a soggy handkerchief from his
topcoat pocket, wipes off his shoe. Puffs of
vapor come from his mouth in the freezing air.
God, he's a mean sonofabitch.

2   CAMERA WITH PODEY — MOVING SHOT

as he jams the gray, squidgy hankie in his pocket,
pulls his collar up around his throat, readjusts
his muffler, and moves down the street to the
entrance of a wretched building jammed between a
bodega and a laundry. He pulls a slip of paper from
his topcoat's dress-hankie pocket, looks at it,
looks up to check the building numbers, and climbs
the brownstone steps to the stoop. Note: this must
be a four storey tenement building. In fact...

3   LONG SHOT — ACROSS STREET — ESTABLISHING

We see Podey climbing the steps to the stoop. It is
a FOUR STOREY BUILDING. Not three, not six, not
what's convenient, dammit, but FOUR STOREYS ONLY!

4   MEDIUM SHOT — ON PODEY

as he reaches the stoop landing. The doors which
once held glass now hold plywood sheeting with
graffiti defacing. He opens a door and steps
inside, out of the wind and cold.

5   INT. FIRST FLOOR LANDING

Podey goes to the mailboxes, runs one meaty finger
along the line of broken-open, battered boxes.
Most have no names on them. But several have Dymo
tape labels. The note is still in Podey's hand.
Camera closer to show the clear block printing on
the note *large enough to read*. It says:

                CONSUELO LOSADA
                4TH FLOOR

RACK FOCUS off note to the mailboxes. One of
them says:

                LOSADA 404

and another says:

                WASHINGTON 202

                                        (CONTINUED:)

5   CONTINUED:

and Podey *purposely* pushes the button for Washington
202, rather than Losada 404. There is a beat as we
hear the buzzing sound of the button Podey had his
finger on. Then a hollow, tinny voice comes
through the rusted speaker:

                    TENANT VOICE (O.S.)
                        (female, tinny)
               Yes, who is it?

                         PODEY
                    (into speaker tube)
               Empire State Carpeting. We came to
               put in the new wall-to-wall.

There is a pregnant pause of several beats.

                    TENANT VOICE (O.S.)
                         (cautious)
               You say what? New carpets?

                         PODEY
                    (very tradesmanlike)
               Is that Miz Washington?

                    TENANT VOICE (O.S.)
               Uh...yes, it is...are you sure...?

                         PODEY
                    (mock impatient)
               Look lady, we got an order here
               from the landlord says put in new
               wall-to-wall, deep-pile, for
               Washington, apartment 202. You
               don't want it...we take it back to
               the warehouse...
                                        (CONTINUED:)

5   CONTINUED:—2

The door buzzer rings and keeps on ringing. Podey
grabs for the inner door, chuckling despicably, and
lets himself into the building proper. As he passes
through we see a stairway.

6   INT. TENEMENT STAIRWELL — DAY — LOW ANGLE TILTING
     UP PAST PODEY IN F.G.

looking up the stairwell. Like that shot in Orson
Welles's *The Magnificent Ambersons*, enabling us to
rack focus so we see the three landings above us,
and the ceiling. A dirty skylight permits only
ominous shadowy light to filter down. Everything
is in twilight here, even at high noon. And we
hear the O.S. SOUND of a group of children talking,
but we cannot make out what they're discussing. It
comes from overhead.

7   MOVING SHOT — WITH PODEY — HAND-HELD

as he begins to climb. We go with him. He moves
fast for a man with such bulk. It is *important*
that he move swiftly.

As he rounds onto the second-floor landing, the
door at the turn, with the numbers 202, opens and a
middle-aged black woman, MRS. WASHINGTON, stands
there looking expectant.

                                            (CONTINUED:)

7   CONTINUED:

                         MRS. WASHINGTON
              You the man from the carpets...?

Podey keeps moving past her. This dialogue must be
fast, even as he surges past her door, turns and
climbs to the third floor.

                             PODEY
              Wrong apartment. You don't get
              anything.

                         MRS. WASHINGTON
                         (hopes dashed)
              But you said...

                             PODEY
                         (casually mean)
              Yeah, well...people lie, lady.

And he's gone, around the bend and up the stairs.
Hold a beat on the poor woman's expression of loss.
Just one more shitty lie to add to the lifetime
supply.

8   THIRD FLOOR LANDING

as Podey comes up the stairs fast. FOUR BLACK KIDS
between the ages of eight and eleven are sitting in
the middle of the floor with some robot toys—Gobots,
Transformers, etc.—and playing. And chatting. Low, so
we don't need to hear what they're saying, but the
word *Christmas* is heard a few times. Podey hits the
landing, brushes past them, not being too careful
about stepping on toys. They grab them out of the
way of his big feet with panic.

9   UP ANGLE PAST KIDS — STAIRWAY

as Podey climbs the last flight to the fourth
floor. They watch, silently. One little kid in
particular—for fast identification let's call him
POOCH—holds our interest. He's about eleven, small
but very neat, handsome kid with big eyes and
intelligence in his face. He watches with
uncommon interest.

10   FOURTH FLOOR LANDING — FULL SHOT

as Podey emerges on the landing, looks around,
spots the door to 404, even though the final 4 is
held by one nail and hangs at a wry angle. He comes
to the door and knocks imperatively. Three beats.
He bangs on the door again. A voice from inside
the apartment calls through the door. A woman's
voice, with a marked Latina accent.

                    CONSUELO (O.S.)
         Whose dere?

                                              (CONTINUED:)

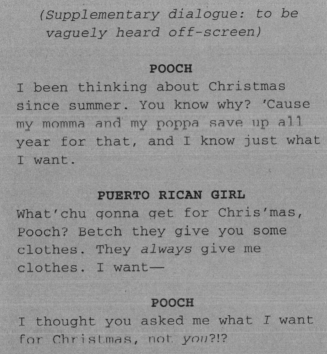

(Supplementary dialogue: to be vaguely heard off-screen)

POOCH

I been thinking about Christmas since summer. You know why? 'Cause my momma and my poppa save up all year for that, and I know just what I want.

PUERTO RICAN GIRL

What'chu gonna get for Chris'mas, Pooch? Betch they give you some clothes. They *always* give me clothes. I want—

POOCH

I thought you asked me what *I* want for Christmas, not *you*?!?

PUERTO RICAN GIRL

Okay, okay, *you*! What they gonna give *you*?

POOCH

A bicycle. Ten speed with a real heavy lock so's no one can steal it when I lock it up.

10 CONTINUED:

> ### PODEY
> Department of Social Services

There is silence. Podey understands the stall.

> ### PODEY
> Jack Podey from the Welfare Center,
> Mrs. Losada.

More silence. Then the sound of movement in the
apartment.

> ### CONSUELO (O.S.)
> (a stall)
> I'm not dressed.

> ### PODEY
> (flat and mean)
> Open the door, Miz Losada. I got
> no time for this. Open up or the
> AFDC goes.
> (beat)
> Understand me, Miz Losada? The
> *Aid*. *To*. *Families*. *With*.
> *Dependant*. *Children* stops. No
> dinero, no food stamps, the
> cockroaches take over!
> (1/2 beat)
> *Comprende*?

The sound of three or four locks being undone.
Bolts. Bars. A heavy iron Fox Lock with its
bar-in-a-floor-slot being slipped back.
Then the door opens... slowly.

11 INT. LOSADA APARTMENT — DAY — ANGLE ON THE OPENING
    DOOR — MEDIUM CLOSE

    CONSUELO LOSADA was gorgeous when she was a teen-
    aged girl. But now she's in her late thirties
    and she's had four kids; and god only knows what
    happened to Francisco, who went out to get a
    fanbelt to repair the icebox ten years ago and
    never found his way back; and twelve years working
    behind a sewing machine in the sweatshop of Marci
    Jean Fashions and working a night shift cleaning up
    office buildings while she raised the kids...well,
    it's all taken its toll. You can see she had great
    beauty. The cape of dark hair, the good cheekbones,
    the tensile strength in her body that keeps her
    going. But she's old folks. Before her time.
    She's just hanging in there. And standing in her
    doorway is Jack Podey.

                        PODEY
            Podey. Investigator from Welfare
            Center. I want to talk to you
            about your eligibility.

12 REVERSE ANGLE — PODEY IN F.G.

    Consuelo looks frightened, but moves aside. Podey
    steps in as CAMERA FOLLOWS. Off camera we hear
    door close behind us. Podey looks around. Two
    tiny children, both girls, stand against the far
    wall in front of something squat that has a blanket
    thrown over it. (This item is a foldaway bed, that
    has been rapidly closed up, rolled against the wall,
    and covered.) The rest of the apartment is what
    we'd expect at this economic level. Dingy but
    clean; a corner shelf of cheap bric-a-brac; a table
    covered with a lace throw; an old tv set with
    rabbit ears; carpet threadbare.

                                        (CONTINUED:)

12 CONTINUED:

Open doorway to the right shows us the edge of an
old kitchen. Two doors on the left wall, both
closed. One would be the bedroom, the other the
bathroom.

> CONSUELO
> Please sit down if you want.

Podey goes to the table, pulls out a straight-back
chair, plops his case on the table, sits down and
opens the case. He takes up a sheaf of papers held
with one of those big black pressure clamps. He
flips through them quickly, looks at the kids,
looks at her. She stands with hands folded, looking
midway between trepidatious and scared.

> PODEY
> Missuz Consuelo Losada?
>> (she nods)
> Record shows you're getting AFDC on
> four children, zat right?
>> (she nods)

He looks around. It's just a pro forma look. He's
toying with her. Sits back in the chair, tilts it,
opens his coat and jacket underneath, hooks thumbs
in vest lapels.

> PODEY
> I only see two.

> CONSUELO
>> (in Spanish)
> What?

(CONTINUED:)

12   CONTINUED:—2

> ### PODEY
> (mean)
> I *said*, Senora, I see *two* kids
> here. Muchachas, comprende? Two.
> Not four.

> ### CONSUELO
> (indicates girls)
> Si. Paloma y Pilar.

> ### PODEY
> (very snotty, making fun of her Spanish)
> Yeah? So where's Raymundo y
> Virgilio?

The Puerto Rican woman looks nonplussed. She wets
her lips.

> ### CONSUELO
> They in scool now.

> ### PODEY
> Lady, don't jerk me around. It's
> three days to Christmas. You get
> my meaning?
> (beat)
> Christmas vacation, lady. There's
> no school.

She is caught, doesn't know what to do.

(CONTINUED:)

12 CONTINUED:—3

> **PODEY**
> (goes for throat)
> How about they're not even in this state, howzabout *that*? Howzabout they're stayin' with your mother, Mrs. Lupe Hernandez, at 555 Carb Street, in Las Cruces, New Mexico, howzabout?

She's now utterly unmanned. She doesn't know how to lie out of it. The kids stand there watching with big eyes. It is obviously cold in the apartment...the kids wear two sweaters each, and gloves. Podey rises, looks around.

> **CONSUELO**
> No, thass not true...

> **PODEY**
> And howzabout maybe Gramma is collecting public assistance in New Mexico for Raymundo y Virgilio... and you're gettin' AFDC for four, but you've only got two in the apartment?

He starts moving toward one of the two doors on the left. She moves to stop him, but he isn't stopping. Over his shoulder he speaks:

> **PODEY**
> Mind if I use your bathroom?

(CONTINUED:)

12 CONTINUED:—4

He doesn't wait to get an okay but opens the door
and steps in. He doesn't close the door.

13 INT. BATHROOM — WITH PODEY

Typical crowded, tiny bathroom. Shower curtain
pulled across the tub. Shelves full of toilet
articles. Sink yellow and stained from decades of
cleanser. ANGLE with Podey as he checks out the
shelves of toilet articles. He puts his hand on a
mug of shaving lather with a brush still upright in
it. He puts his hand on the toothbrush rack. *Four*
toothbrushes.

Then he turns suddenly, and whips the shower curtain
back. A fully-clothed man wearing a workman's
jacket and gloves stands in the tub. This is
ROSARIO. They stare at each other a moment, then
Podey turns on his heel and comes back into the
living room.

14 LIVING ROOM — ANOTHER ANGLE

as Rosario comes after him. Rosario is about
forty, Puerto Rican, nice-looking man, nothing less
than honest and hard working about him. Podey is
gathering the papers into the case. Rosario
exchanges hurried words in Spanish so rapid with
Consuelo that we may not be able to tell what he
said, but it's clearly upset and panicky.

> **PODEY**
> (fast and mean)
> Don't bother, lady. I know all the
> stories. He was just fixin' the
> shower, right? In his galoshes,
> right?
> (beat)
> Boy, you people really fry me!

> **CONSUELO**
> (hysterical)
> Rosario iss justa fren'! He stop
> by to say hello. My sons aren't
> here now, bot they come back...

Podey slams the lid of the case, turns on her, on fire.

> **PODEY**
> We got computer matching on
> concealed employment, we got
> cross-checking from other states,
> we gotcher act down cold, lady.
> This's fraud, you *got* that?

(CONTINUED:)

(*Supplementary dialogue: to be
translated into Spanish*)

ROSARIO
(extremely angry)
Consuelo, he surprised me. I kept
very still. What does this
mean...will he take away the money
for the children?

CONSUELO
(wildly)
I don't know, I don't know! He
wouldn't do this to us at Christmas.
I'm afraid, Rosario; Pilar may be
coming down with the flu, or something worse.

ROSARIO
Talk to him, this man...talk to
him. I can beg him not to do this,
perhaps he'll listen.

14   CONTINUED:

> **CONSUELO**
> You gonna take the Aid away? My
> kids...it's Christmas, mister...

Podey aims a fat thumb at her.

> **PODEY**
> Don't blame me. One of your "close
> friends" in the building ratted you out.
> I'm just doin' the job, lady. I write
> the report with a recommendation,
> that's all I do, Christmas, New
> Year's, Halloween or Cinco de Mayo!

He starts toward the door. Rosario comes after
him. Podey turns, just spoiling for a fight.

> **PODEY**
> (ugly)
> You lift one hand, spick, and I'll
> put you in traction for a year!

Consuelo rushes to Rosario, grabs him. Rosario is
fuming, grating his teeth, cursing in Spanish.
Podey laughs a rotten laugh and opens the door. He
steps out, and just as he closes the door he says:

> **PODEY**
> Merry Christmas.

15   HALL LANDING OUTSIDE APARTMENT — WITH PODEY

as Podey turns away from 404. He starts down the
stairs and then we hear the kids talking. Podey
goes down the stairs a bit and listens.

(CONTINUED:)

(See following pages for additional scene: revised version)

(Supplementary dialogue: to be translated into Spanish)

Rosario is fuming, grating his teeth, cursing in Spanish

> **ROSARIO**
> Filth! Heartless degenerate! You
> would throw children into the
> streets where you spend your
> nights sucking garbage from the
> sewers! Slime for brains, dirt for
> heart! Pig...less than a pig...pigs
> have more honor than you!

(Additional scenes: revised version, scene 14)

14 Rosario understands only part of this. But the tone
    doesn't escape him. Something is threatening the woman,
    and he won't stand for it. He takes a step toward Podey,
    but Consuelo—frantic not to get Podey any further
    aroused—gesticulates wildly for Rosario to stay where
    he is. She comes closer to Podey, imploring him:

                         CONSUELO
              (emotional, utterly honest and convincing)
                   Please, Mister, lemme 'splain. I don't
                   cheat onna welfare, honnes' to God!

                          PODEY
                        (smirking)
                   Oh...right. I forgot the story. There's
                   always a story. Almost forgot I'm s'posed
                   to take off a minute to hear the story.

    He stands, arms folded, clearly not hearing
    anything, making a nasty mockery of listening.

                         CONSUELO
                     (honest, decent)
                   Francisco, ees my husband, he left
                   us, he went out an' never come back,
                   almos' ten years ago. I been workin'
                   at the same job twelve years—you can
                   check, they give me good report, you
                   see—downtown inna garment dis'rict.
                   Marci Jean Fashions, you heard of them?

                          PODEY
                   Never heard of them.
                        (beat, sarcastic)
                   But they geev you good report, right?

                                          (CONTINUED:)

14   CONTINUED:

                    CONSUELO
                     (hopeful)
     Si, I ron a sewin' machine, nine
     hours a day. An' I gotta secon'
     job, nights, I go clean up office
     buildin's. Joss to raise my kids
     proper. They never got in no
     trobble, they good kids...but...

                     PODEY
                (holds up a hand)
     Let me take it from there.
                   (recites)
     Nobody can raise four kids in New
     York City these days on what the
     AFDC gives you, right? You work
     your *maracas* off scrimping and
     saving, but it ain't even enough
     to buy the kids a decent Christmas
     toy...am I right?

                    CONSUELO
           (nods fast, a spark of hope)
     Si, si! I can' make ends meet, so I
     send the boys to my mother for a
     coupla weeks, joss till I can—

                     PODEY
                 (silences her)
     You should've thought of all that
     before you had your litter, lady. You
     people spawn like sardines and then
     expect the City to take up the slack.
                    (beat)
     You slugs are all alike! Forget it!

     Podey picks up his case. Consuelo is terrified now.

15   CONTINUED:

                    POOCH (O.S.)
                     (energetic)
          And you know why Christmas be the
          best? I tell you why. Cause Santa
          Claus gone come and make all your
          wishes true.

Podey leans over to look.

16 PODEY'S POINT OF VIEW — WHAT HE SEES

On the third floor landing the four kids sit, and
three of them stare wide-eyed and delighted at
Pooch, who spins his tale of Christmas wonders, of
the kindness of Santa Claus.

                      POOCH
          I know! Santa comin' down the
          chimbly, with his reindeer on the
          roof, and he gotta big bag of toys
          and candy and ice cream that never
          melt till it get to your mouth, and
          he gone fill your socks up with
          robots an' AM-FM radios, an...an...

                 PODEY'S VOICE (O.S.)
          An' *nothing*. Because Santa ain't
          comin' to you, because Santa's
          white and he can't *find* black kids.

17 ANGLE UP PAST KIDS

to Podey's big mean face peering at them over the
bannister. He's taking great pleasure in
tormenting these kids.

(CONTINUED:)

17 CONTINUED:

> **POOCH**
> (fights back)
> Thassa lie! Santa's *good*, cause
> he's a friend of the baby Jesus,
> and they can find kids *any*where!

> **PODEY**
> (warms to his evil)
> White folks have someone *else* who
> comes to kids like you. You know
> who *that* is?

They stare at him, sad and frightened.

> **PODEY**
> (malevolent, eyes shining)
> Nackles. That's the one comes to
> black kids. He's the *other* side of
> Santa Claus. Santa Claus comes down
> through the chimney and brings white
> kids toys; but Nackles, ah Nackles...
> (beat)
> Yeah...he's eight feet tall, all
> dressed in black, and real thin and
> nasty, and he's got a dead white
> face like a corpse, and eyes that
> burn like fire, and he travels in
> the tunnels under the ground in a
> black coal car on rails, pulled by
> four blind white goats.
> (beat)
> And you know what Nackles'll do to you?

They are terrified. Their faces are trapped in his story.

(CONTINUED:)

17 CONTINUED:—2

> PODEY
>> Nackles eats the flesh of kids like you.
>> Nackles roams back and forth underground
>> in his dark tunnels darker than subway
>> tunnels, and he looks around for kids
>> like you to stuff into his black bag, and
>> he takes you away screaming, so's he can
>> eat you when his big fangs get hungry.

18 ANGLE DOWN ON KIDS — PODEY IN F.G.

as Pooch leaps up. He is holding a toy robot. He is wild with justified hatred.

> POOCH
>> You lyin' at us, you chinch honkie geek!

And he throws the robot toy as hard as he can. It hits Podey on the left temple, breaking skin, bringing blood in a small cut. Podey howls with rage and rushes down the stairs. Pooch takes off at a dead run, as fast as he can, down the stairs below Podey.

> PODEY
>> (howling)
>> I'm gonna kill you, ya little
>> nigger bastid!

19 ACTION SEQUENCE — EITHER STEADICAM OR RAPID INTERCUTS
   — WHAT WE SEE

Podey running as fast as he can, jumping the last few steps onto a landing, banging off the walls to catch up with the kid. Pooch running full out in sneakers, fast as he can, rounding the corners and sliding along the bannisters, down and down and down.

> [MORE]

(CONTINUED:)

19 CONTINUED:

We expect to hit the first floor foyer in a moment,
but somehow we keep going down and down. Is it
four storeys, five, six, eight...what the hell is
going on here?!? It's a blur of walls and steps and
stairwell, the angles tilting crazily as Podey
keeps on going, foaming at the mouth, cursing,
screaming, and at one point, when we've covered
twice as many as four floors, but he keeps going
because WE CAN HEAR the sound of the kid ahead of
him, the feet hitting the steps and the landings
...and Podey's right around the bend, coming after
him. We don't see the kid anymore, but he's there
because we HEAR him.

20 CUL — DE — SAC

Podey comes pounding down the last flight of stairs,
and finds himself in a narrow, square bottom
landing. No windows and only ONE DOOR...a door
that is slowly closing as he hits the floor. He
doesn't even stop to think. He grabs the closing
door's knob, hurtles through and...

21 TUNNEL — ESTABLISHING

He's not outside, and he's not in the basement and
he's not *anywhere* that ought to exist. He's in a
wide, dark tunnel with rock walls that scintillate
faintly as though bits of mica schist are imbedded
in the basalt. (Suggest something like featherstone.)
There are tracks leading off into the darkness.
The light comes only from the stairwell behind him,
and as he turns to grab the still-closing door, it
seals itself shut with a *click*. He grabs the knob,
pulls at the door, but it won't open.

22 THE DOOR — FULL SHOT

The door begins to run, as though it were molten
lava. He yells with pain as the knob goes hot, and
draws back his hand quickly, holding it as though
it's been burned. Before our eyes the door melts
into the rock and it is a seamless surface. He is
trapped here, underground in a tunnel that shouldn't
exist. He turns and turns, now filled with fear.

23 THE TUNNEL — ANOTHER ANGLE

Showing Podey small and terrified in the gloom.
Only faint light from an unknown source shows him
anything. And he stands there with his attaché
case, big mean face trying to comprehend what's
befallen him. And then he cocks his head to one
side, because he—and we—hear:

The strange sound of metal wheels rolling along
tracks, and the peculiar clop clop clop of hooves
on the stone floor of the tunnel. And he strains
toward the sound.

24 ANGLE DOWN THE TRACKS — PAST PODEY — HIS POINT OF VIEW

The tracks run into darkness, but there's a few
slivers of light slanting down from above, as
though someone has opened a lattice just a crack.
And as we stare with Podey, we see something
coming. *We wait for it*. Draw out the moment of
greatest terror. Beat. Beat.

Then we see it is a coal car, being drawn by four
blind white goats, their eyes milky and staring.
The coal car is old and dirty and rusty and black.

[MORE]

(CONTINUED:)

24   CONTINUED:

And the reins that come from the goats' harnesses
run back into the hands of what looks vaguely like
the little black kid from scene 1. The little black
kid who was up on the roof with his muffler wrapped
around his lower face like a desperado. Sure, it's
that kid...isn't it? At least it *looks* like that
kid until the coal car passes into total darkness
between the slivers of light.

But when it emerges, and draws to a halt in front
of Podey, the passenger in that coal car is no kid.
He's eight feet tall, all in black, with a demon's
hood drawn so we *cannot see a face at all*. But we
see the two burning red points of his eyes, glowing
in the darkness behind the hood.

25   PODEY AND NACKLES

as the specter steps out of the coal car. He walks
toward Podey, who is frozen there. The dark figure
pats the head of one of the goats, who bleats
kindly. Then he stops as the giant figure comes to
stand in front of Podey.

                         PODEY
                     (terrified)
          Who...

The specter speaks with a voice from the tomb.
(Give us a voice we will not forget!)

                        NACKLES
          You know who I am. You described me.
          Tall and thin and dressed in black.
          Dead white face and eyes of fire. My
          four dear blind goats.

                              (CONTINUED:)

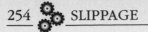

25 CONTINUED:

> **PODEY**
> (terrified)
> You don't exist. I just made you up.

> **NACKLES**
> I exist for you, Podey. I'm
> Nackles and here's my big bag.

He draws a huge black bag from the coal car.

> **NACKLES**
> And you almost got it right. Not
> quite, but almost.

26 NACKLES — CLOSE SHOT

as he slips back the hood. His face isn't dead white, it is *black*. He moves toward camera.

SHARP CUT TO:

27 PODEY

his face a mask of terror as a silent scream will not come from his open mouth and we:

CUT BACK TO:

28   NACKLES

coming closer and closer. He opens his mouth and there are fangs there, real nasty fangs.

                         NACKLES
              Merry Christmas, Jack Podey.

Then, slowly, as terrifyingly malevolent as we've ever heard the sound, with that face coming nearer and nearer:
                         NACKLES
         IIo.
                    (beat)
         Ho.
                    (beat)
         Ho.

                                   SHARP CUT TO:
                                   BLACK AND
                                   FADE OUT.

                     THE END

> *(See following pages for additional*
>   *scene: revised version)*

(Additional scenes: revised version)

26 NACKLES — CLOSE SHOT

as he slips back the hood. His face isn't dead white, it is *black*. It holds for several beats, then alters and is the face of a man obviously *Puerto Rican*. It holds Latino for several beats, then alters again. The face of a man *Oriental*. Hold. Alter again. *Eskimo* or *Aleut* or *Native American*. Hold for a beat, then congeal again as it was originally, the face of a black demon conjured in the mind of a bigot who hates *all* other peoples.

He moves toward camera.

SHARP CUT TO:

27 PODEY

His face a mask of terror as a silent scream will not come from his open mouth and we:

CUT BACK TO:

28 NACKLES

coming closer and closer. He opens his mouth and there are fangs there, extremely nasty double-rowed fangs.

(CONTINUED:)

28   CONTINUED:

> **NACKLES**
>> Merry Christmas, Jack Podey; from
>> all of us.

Then, slowly, as terrifyingly malevolent as we've
ever heard the sound, with that face coming nearer
and nearer:

> **NACKLES**
>> IIo.
>>> (beat)
>> Ho.
>>> (beat)
>> Ho.

SHARP CUT TO:
BLACK AND
FADE OUT.

THE END

Sensible City

During the third week of the trial, sworn under oath, one of the Internal Affairs guys the D.A.'s office had planted undercover in Gropp's facility attempted to describe how terrifying Gropp's smile was. The IA guy stammered some; and there seemed to be a singular absence of color in his face; but he tried valiantly, not being a poet or one given to colorful speech. And after some prodding by the Prosecutor, he said:

"You ever, y'know, when you brush your teeth...how when you're done, and you've spit out the toothpaste and the water, and you pull back your lips to look at your teeth, to see if they're whiter, and like that...you know how you tighten up your jaws real good, and make that kind of death-grin smile that pulls your lips back, with your teeth lined up clenched in the front of your mouth...you know what I mean...well..."

Sequestered that night in a downtown hotel, each of the twelve jurors stared into a medicine cabinet mirror and skinned back a pair of lips, and tightened neck muscles till the cords stood out, and clenched teeth, and stared at a face grotesquely contorted. Twelve men and women then superimposed over the mirror reflection the face of the Defendant they'd been staring at for three weeks, and approximated the smile they had not seen on Gropp's face all that time.

And in that moment of phantom face over reflection face, Gropp was convicted.

Police Lieutenant W.R. Gropp. Rhymed with crop. The meat-man who ruled a civic smudge called the Internment Facility when it was listed on the City Council's budget every year. Internment Facility: dripping wet, cold iron, urine smell mixed with sour liquor sweated through dirty skin, men and women crying in the night. A stockade, a prison camp, stalag, ghetto, torture chamber, charnel house, abattoir, duchy, fiefdom, Army co-op mess hall ruled by a neckless thug.

The last of the thirty-seven inmate alumni who had been subpoenaed to testify recollected, "Gropp's favorite thing was to take some fool outta his cell, get him nekkid to the skin, then do this *rolling* thing t'him."

When pressed, the former tenant of Gropp's hostelry—not a felon, merely a steamfitter who had had a bit too much to drink and picked up for himself a ten-day Internment Facility residency for D&D—explained that this "rolling thing" entailed "Gropp wrappin' his big, hairy sausage arm aroun' the guy's neck, see, and then he'd *roll him* across the bars, real hard and fast. Bangin' the guy's head like a roulette ball around the wheel. Clank clank, like that. Usual, it'd knock the guy flat out cold, his head clankin' across the bars and spaces between, wham wham wham like that. See his eyes go up outta sight, all white; but Gropp, he'd hang on with that sausage aroun' the guy's neck, whammin' and bangin' him and takin' some goddam kinda pleasure mentionin' how much bigger this criminal bastard was than *he* was. Yeah, fer sure. That was Gropp's fav'rite part, that he always pulled out some poor nekkid sonofabitch was twice his size.

"That's how four of these guys he's accused of doin', that's how they croaked. With Gropp's sausage 'round the neck. I kept my mouth shut; I'm lucky to get outta there in one piece."

Frightening testimony, last of thirty-seven. But as superfluous as feathers on an eggplant. From the moment of superimposition of phantom face over reflection face, Police Lieutenant W.R. Gropp was on greased rails to spend his declining years for Brutality While Under Color of Service—a *serious* offense—in a maxi-galleria stuffed chockablock with felons whose spiritual brethren he had maimed, crushed, debased, blinded, butchered, and killed.

Similarly destined was Gropp's gigantic Magog, Deputy Sergeant Michael "Mickey" Rizzo, all three hundred and forty pounds of him; brainless malevolence stacked six feet four inches high in his steel-toed, highly-polished service boots. Mickey had only been indicted on seventy counts, as opposed to Gropp's eighty-four ironclad atrocities. But if he managed to avoid Sentence of Lethal Injection for having crushed men's heads underfoot, he would certainly go to the maxi-galleria mall of felonious behavior for the rest of his simian life.

Mickey had, after all, pulled a guy up against the inside of the bars and kept bouncing him till he ripped the left arm loose from its socket, ripped it off, and later dropped it on the mess hall steam table just before dinner assembly.

Squat, bulletheaded troll, Lieutenant W.R. Gropp, and the mindless killing machine, Mickey Rizzo. On greased rails.

So they jumped bail together, during the second hour of jury deliberation. Why wait? Gropp could see which way it was going, even counting on Blue Loyalty. The city was putting the abyss between the Dept., and him and Mickey. So, why wait? Gropp was a sensible guy, very pragmatic, no bullshit. So they jumped bail together, having made arrangements weeks before, as any sensible felon keen to flee would have done.

Gropp knew a chop shop that owed him a favor. There was a throaty and hemi-speedy, immaculately registered, four-year-old Firebird just sitting in a bay on the fifth floor of a seemingly abandoned garment factory, two blocks from the courthouse.

And just to lock the barn door after the horse, or in this case the Pontiac, had been stolen, Gropp had Mickey toss the chop shop guy down the elevator shaft of the factory. It was the sensible thing to do. After all, the guy's neck *was* broken.

By the time the jury came in, later that night, Lieut. W.R. Gropp was out of the state and somewhere near Boise. Two days later, having taken circuitous routes, the Firebird was on the other side of both the Snake River and the Rockies, between Rock Springs and Laramie. Three days after that, having driven in large circles, having laid over in Cheyenne for dinner and a movie, Gropp and Mickey were in Nebraska.

Wheat ran to the sun, blue storms bellowed up from horizons, and heat trembled on the edge of each leaf. Crows stirred inside fields, lifted above shattered surfaces of grain and flapped into sky. That's what it looked like: the words came from a poem.

They were smack in the middle of the plains state, above Grand Island, below Norfolk, somewhere out in the middle of nowhere, just tooling along, leaving no trail, deciding to go that way to Canada, or the other way to Mexico. Gropp had heard there were business opportunities in Mazatlán.

It was a week after the jury had been denied the pleasure of seeing Gropp's face as they said, "Stick the needle in the brutal sonofabitch. Fill the barrel with a very good brand of weed-killer, stick the needle in the brutal sonofabitch's chest, and slam home the plunger. Guilty, your honor, guilty on charges one through eighty-four. Give'im the weed-killer and let's watch the fat scumbag do his dance!" A week of swift and leisurely driving here and there, doubling back and skimming along easily.

And somehow, earlier this evening, Mickey had missed a turnoff, and now they were on a stretch of superhighway that didn't seem to have any important exits. There were little towns now and then, the lights twinkling off in the mid-distance, but if they were within miles of a major metropolis, the map didn't give them clues as to where they might be.

"You took a wrong turn."

"Yeah, huh?"

"Yeah, *exactly* huh. Keep your eyes on the road."

"I'm sorry, Looten'nt."

"No. Not Lieutenant. I told you."

"Oh, yeah, right. Sorry, Mr. Gropp."

"Not Gropp. Jensen. Mister *Jensen*. You're *also* Jensen, my kid brother. Your name is Daniel."

"I got it, I remember: Harold and Daniel Jensen is us. You know what I'd like?"

"No, what would you like?"

"A box'a Grape-Nuts. I could have 'em here in the car, and when I got a mite peckish I could just dip my hand in an' have a mouthful. I'd like that."

"Keep your eyes on the road."

"So whaddya think?"

"About what?"

"About maybe I swing off next time and we go into one'a these little towns and maybe a 7-Eleven'll be open, and I can get a box'a Grape-Nuts? We'll need some gas after a while, too. See the little arrow there?"

"I see it. We've still got half a tank. Keep driving."

Mickey pouted. Gropp paid no attention. There were drawbacks to forced traveling companionship. But there were many cul-de-sacs and landfills between this stretch of dark turnpike and New Brunswick, Canada or Mazatlán, state of Sinaloa.

"What is this, the Southwest?" Gropp asked, looking out the side window into utter darkness. "The Midwest? What?"

Mickey looked around, too. "I dunno. Pretty out here, though. Real quiet and pretty."

"It's pitch dark."

"Yeah, huh?"

"Just drive, for godsake. Pretty. Jeezus!"

They rode in silence for another twenty-seven miles, then Mickey said, "I gotta go take a piss."

Gropp exhaled mightily. Where were the cul-de-sacs, where were the landfills? "Okay. Next town of any size, we can take the exit and see if there's decent accommodations. You can get a box of Grape-Nuts, and use the toilet; I can have a cup of coffee and study the map in better light. Does that sound like a good idea, to you...Daniel?"

"Yes, Harold. See, I remembered."

"The world is a fine place."

They drove for another sixteen miles, and came nowhere in sight of a thruway exit sign. But the green glow had begun to creep up from the horizon.

"What the hell is that?" Gropp asked, running down his power window. "Is that some kind of a forest fire, or something? What's that look like to you?"

"Like green in the sky."

"Have you ever thought how lucky you are that your mother abandoned you, Mickey?" Gropp said wearily. "Because if she hadn't, and if they hadn't brought you to the county jail for temporary housing till they could put you in a foster home, and I hadn't taken an interest in you, and hadn't arranged for you to live with the Rizzos, and hadn't let you work around the lockup, and hadn't made you my deputy, do you have any idea where you'd be today?" He paused for a moment, waiting for an answer, realized the entire thing was rhetorical—not to mention pointless—and said, "Yes, it's green in the sky, pal, but it's also something odd. Have you ever seen 'green in the sky' before? Anywhere? Any time?"

"No, I guess I haven't." Gropp sighed, and closed his eyes.

They drove in silence another nineteen miles, and the green miasma in the air enveloped them. It hung above and around them like sea-fog, chill and with tiny droplets of moisture that Mickey fanned away with the windshield wipers. It made the landscape on either side of the superhighway faintly visible, cutting the impenetrable darkness, but it also induced a wavering, ghostly quality to the terrain.

Gropp turned on the map light in the dome of the Firebird, and studied the map of Nebraska. He murmured, "I haven't got a rat's-fang of any idea where the hell we *are*! There isn't even a freeway like this indicated here. You took some helluva wrong turn 'way back there, pal!" Dome light out.

"I'm sorry, Loo-Harold…"

A large reflective advisement marker, green and white, came up on their right. It said: FOOD   GAS   LODGING   10 MILES.

The next sign said: EXIT   7 MILES.

The next sign said: OBEDIENCE   3 MILES.

Gropp turned the map light on again. He studied the venue. "Obedience? What the hell kind of 'Obedience'? There's nothing like that *anywhere*. What is this, an old map? Where did you get this map?"

"Gas station."

"Where?"

"I dunno. Back a long ways. That place we stopped with the root beer stand next to it."

Gropp shook his head, bit his lip, murmured nothing in particular. "Obedience," he said. "Yeah, huh?"

They began to see the town off to their right before they hit the exit turnoff. Gropp swallowed hard and made a sound that caused Mickey to look over at him. Gropp's eyes were large, and Mickey could see the whites.

"What'sa matter, Loo…Harold?"

"You see that town out there?" His voice was trembling.

Mickey looked to his right. Yeah, he saw it. Horrible.

Many years ago, when Gropp was briefly a college student, he had taken a warm-body course in Art Appreciation. One oh one, it was; something basic and easy to ace, a snap, all you had to do was show up. Everything you wanted to know about Art from aboriginal cave drawings to Diego Rivera. One of the paintings that had been flashed on the big screen for the class, a sleepy 8:00 a.m. class, had been *The Nymph Echo* by Max Ernst. A green and smoldering painting of an ancient ruin overgrown with writhing plants that seemed to have eyes and purpose and a malevolently jolly life of their own, as they swarmed and slithered and overran the stone vaults and altars of the twisted, disturbingly resonant sepulcher. Like a sebaceous cyst, something corrupt lay beneath the emerald fronds and hungry black soil.

Mickey looked to his right at the town. Yeah, he saw it. Horrible.

"Keep driving!" Gropp yelled, as his partner-in-flight started to slow for the exit ramp.

Mickey heard, but his reflexes were slow. They continued to drift to the right, toward the rising egress lane. Gropp reached across and jerked the wheel hard to the left. "I said: *keep driving*!"

The Firebird slewed, but Mickey got it back under control in a moment, and in another moment they were abaft the ramp, then past it, and speeding away from the nightmarish site beyond and slightly below the superhighway. Gropp stared mesmerized as they swept past. He could see buildings that leaned at obscene angles, the green fog that rolled through the haunted streets, the shadowy forms of misshapen things that skulked at every dark opening.

"That was a real scary-lookin' place, Looten...Harold. I don't think I'd of wanted to go down there even for the Grape-Nuts. But maybe if we'd've gone real fast..."

Gropp twisted in the seat toward Mickey as much as his muscle-fat body would permit. "Listen to me. There is this tradition, in horror movies, in mysteries, in tv shows, that people are always going into haunted houses, into graveyards, into battle zones, like assholes, like stone idiots! You know what I'm talking about here? Do you?"

Mickey said, "Uh..."

"All right, let me give you an example. Remember we went to see that movie *Alien*? Remember how scared you were?"

Mickey bobbled his head rapidly, his eyes widened in frightened memory.

"Okay. So now, you remember that part where the guy who was a mechanic, the guy with the baseball cap, he goes off looking for a cat or somedamnthing? Remember? He left everyone else, and he wandered off by himself. And he went into that big cargo hold with the water dripping on him, and all those chains hanging down, and shadows everywhere...*do you recall that?*"

Mickey's eyes were chalky potholes. He remembered, oh yes, he remembered clutching Gropp's jacket sleeve till Gropp had been compelled to slap his hand away.

"And you remember what happened in the movie? In the theater? You remember everybody yelling, 'Don't go in there, you asshole! The thing's in there, you moron! Don't go in there!' But, remember, he *did*, and the thing came up behind him, all those teeth, and it bit his stupid head off! Remember that?"

Mickey hunched over the wheel, driving fast.

"Well, that's the way people are. They ain't sensible! They go into places like that you can see are death places; and they get chewed up or the blood sucked outta their necks or used for kindling...but I'm no moron, I'm a sensible guy and I got the brains my mama gave me, and I don't go *near* places like that. So drive like a sonofabitch, and get us outta here, and we'll get your damned Grape-Nuts in Idaho or somewhere...if we ever get off this road..."

Mickey murmured, "I'm sorry, Lieuten'nt. I took a wrong turn or somethin'."

"Yeah, yeah. Just keep driv—" The car was slowing.

It was a frozen moment. Gropp exultant, no fool he, to avoid the cliché, to stay out of that haunted house, that ominous dark closet, that damned place. Let idiot others venture off the freeway, into the town that contained the basement entrance to Hell, or whatever. Not he, not Gropp!

He'd outsmarted the obvious.

In that frozen moment.

As the car slowed. Slowed, in the poisonous green mist.

And on their right, the obscenely frightening town of Obedience, that they had left in their dust five minutes before, was coming up again on the superhighway.

"Did you take another turnoff?"

"Uh...no, I...uh, I been just driving fast..."

The sign read: **NEXT RIGHT   50 YDS   OBEDIENCE.**

The car was slowing. Gropp craned his neckless neck to get a proper perspective on the fuel gauge. He was a pragmatic kind of a guy, no nonsense, and very practical; but they were out of gas.

The Firebird slowed and slowed and finally rolled to a stop.

In the rearview mirror Gropp saw the green fog rolling up thicker onto the roadway; and emerging over the berm, in a jostling, slavering horde, clacking and drooling, dropping decayed body parts and leaving glistening trails of worm ooze as they dragged their deformed pulpy bodies across the blacktop, their snake-slit eyes gleaming green and yellow in the mist, the residents of Obedience clawed and slithered and crimped toward the car.

It was common sense any Better Business Bureau would have applauded: if the tourist trade won't come to your town, take your town to the tourists. Particularly if the freeway has forced commerce to pass you by. Particularly if your town needs fresh blood to prosper. Particularly if you have the civic need to share.

Green fog shrouded the Pontiac, and the peculiar sounds that came from within. Don't go into that dark room is a sensible attitude. Particularly in a sensible city.

I was living off-base—surreptitiously, a court martial offense—in a trailer in Elizabethtown. I was sharing the rent with my buddy, Derry Taylor. Frderick Forrest Taylor III. His various women called him "The Tiger." When one of us had a female guest, we let the other one know about it, and the billet at the barracks back at Fort Knox would be bed for the night. It was a good living arrangement. I taught Derry classical music and one kind of jazz, he taught me bad poetry and an equally worthy kind of jazz. I still have that first Yusef Lateef album. Best version of "Night in Tunisia" I've ever heard.

Sculpture by Tim Kirk
Photograph by William Rotsler

The Dragon On the Bookshelf

written in collaboration with
Robert Silverberg

He was small; petite, actually. Perhaps an inch shorter—resting back on his glimmering haunches—than any of the mass-market paperbacks racked on either side of him. He was green, of course. Blue-green, down his front, underchin to bellybottom, greenish yellow-ochre all over the rest. Large, luminous pastel-blue eyes that would have made Shirley Temple seethe with envy. And he was licking his front right paw as he blew soft gray smoke rings through his heroically long nostrils.

To his left, a well-thumbed Ballantine paperback edition of C. Wright Mills's THE CAUSES OF WORLD WAR III; to his right, a battered copy, sans dust jacket, of THE MAN WHO KNEW COOLIDGE by Sinclair Lewis. He licked each of his four paw-fingers in turn.

Margaret, sitting across the room from the teak Danish Modern bookcase where he lived, occasionally looked up from the theme papers she was correcting spread out across the card table, to smile at him and make a ticking sound of affection. "Good doughnuts?" she asked. An empty miniature Do-Nettes' box lay on the carpet. The dragon rolled his eyes and continued licking confectioners' sugar from under his silver claws. "Good doughnuts," she said, and went back to her classwork.

Idly, she brushed auburn hair away from her face with the back of a slim hand. Completing his toilette, the little dragon stared raptly at her graceful movement, folded his front paws, sighed deeply, and closed his great, liquid eyes.

The smoke rings came at longer intervals now.

Outside, the afreet and djinn continued to battle, the sounds of their exploding souls making a terrible clank and clangor in the dew-misty streets of dark San Francisco.

So it was to be another of those days. They came all too frequently now that the gateway had been prised open: harsh days, smoldering days, dangerous nights. This was no place to be a dragon, no time to be in the tidal flow of harm's way. There were new manifestations every day now. Last Tuesday the watchthings fiercely clicking their ugly fangs and flatulating at the entrance to the Transamerica Pyramid. On Wednesday a shoal of blind banshees materialized above Coit Tower and covered the structure to the ground with lemony ooze that continued to wail days later. Thursday the resurrected Mongol hordes breaking through west of Van Ness, the air redolent of monosodium glutamate. Friday was silent. No less dangerous; merely silent. Saturday the gullgull incursion, the burnings at the Vaillancourt Fountain. And Sunday—oh, Sunday, bloody Sunday!

Small, large-eyed dragons in love had to walk carefully these days: perils were plentiful, sanctuaries few.

The dragon opened his eyes and stared raptly at the human woman. There sat his problem. Lovely, there she sat. The little dragon knew his responsibility. The only refuge lay within. The noise of the warfare outside was terrifying; and the little dragon was the cause. Coiling on his axis, the dragon diminished his extension along the *sril*-curve and let himself slip away. Margaret gasped softly, a little cry of alarm and dismay. "But you said you wouldn't—"

Too late. A twirling, twinkling scintillance. The bookshelf was empty of anything but books, not one of which mentioned dragons.

"Oh," she murmured, alone in the silent pre-dawn apartment.

"Master, what am I to do?" said Urnikh,[*] the little dragon that had been sitting in the tiny San Francisco apartment only moments before. "I have made matters so much worse. You should have selected better, Master...I never knew enough, was not powerful enough. I've made it terrible for them, and they don't even know it's happening. They are more limited than you let me understand, Master. And I..."

---

[*] Pronounced "Oower-*neesh*."

The little dragon looked up helplessly.

He spoke softly. "I love her, the human woman in the place where I came into their world. I love the human woman, and I did not pursue my mission. I love her, and my inaction made matters worse, my love for her helped open the gateway.

"I can't help myself. Help me to rectify, Master. I have fallen in love with her. I'm stricken. With the movement of her limbs, with the sound of her voice, the way her perfume rises off her, the gleam of her eyes; did I say the way her limbs move? The things she thinks and says? She is a wonderment, indeed. But what, *what* am I to do?"

The Master looked down at the dragon from the high niche in the darkness. "There is desperation in your voice, Urnikh."

"It is because I am so *desperate*!"

"You were sent to the Earth, to mortaltime, to save them. And instead you indulge yourself; and by so doing you have only made things worse for them. Why else does the gateway continue to remain open, and indeed grow wider and wider from hour to hour, if not on account of your negligence?"

Urnikh extended his head on its serpentine neck, let it sag, laid his chin on the darkness. "I am ashamed, Master. But I tell you again, I can't help myself. She fills me, the sight of her fills my every waking moment."

"Have you tried sleeping?"

"When I sleep, I dream. And when I dream, I am slave to her all the more."

The Master heaved a sigh very much like the sigh the little dragon had heaved in Margaret's apartment. "How does she bind you to her?"

"By not binding me at all. She is simply *there*; and I can't bear to be away from her. Help me, Master. I love her so; but I want to be the good force that you want me to be."

The Master slowly and carefully uncoiled to its full extension. For a long while it studied the contrite eyes of the little dragon in silence.

Then it said, "Time grows short, Urnikh. Matters grow more desperate. The djinn, the afreet, the watchthings, the gullgull, all of them rampage and destroy. No one will win. Earth will be left a desert. Mortaltime will end. You must return; and you must fight this love with all the magic of which you are possessed. Give her up. Give her up, Urnikh."

"It is impossible. I will fail."

"You are young. Merely a thousand years have passed you. Fight it, I tell you. Remember who and what you are. Return, and save them. They are poor little creatures and they have no idea what dangers surround them. Save them, Urnikh, and you will save *her*...and yourself as well."

The little dragon raised his head. "Yes, Master."

"Go, now. Will you go and do your best?"

"I will try very hard, Master."

"You are a good force, Urnikh. I have faith in you."

The little dragon was silent.

"Does she know what you are?" the Master asked, after a time.

"Not a bit. She thinks I am a cunningly made toy. An artificial life-form created for the amusement of humans."

"A cunningly made toy. Indeed. Intended to amuse." The Master's tone was frosty. "Well, go to her, then. *Amuse* her, Urnikh. But this must not go on very much longer, do you understand?"

The little dragon sighed again and let himself slip away on the *sril*-curve. The Master, sitting back on its furry haunches, turned itself inward to see if there was any hope.

It was too dim inside. There were no answers.

The dragon materialized within a pale amber glow that spanned the third and fourth shelves of the bookcase. Evidently many hours had passed: the lost day's shafts of sunlight no longer came spearing through the window; time flowed at different velocities on the *sril*-curve and in mortaltime; it was night but tendrils of troubling fog shrouded everything except the summit of Telegraph Hill.

The apartment was empty. Margaret was gone.

The dragon shivered, trembled, blew a fretful snort. Margaret: *gone!* And without any awareness of the perils that lurked on every side, out there on the battlefield that was San Francisco. It appalled him whenever she went outside; but, of course, she had no knowledge of the risks.

Where has she gone? he wondered. Perhaps she was visiting the male-one on Clement Street; perhaps she was strolling the chilly slopes of Lincoln Park; perhaps doing her volunteer work at the U of C Clinic on Mt. Parnassus; perhaps dreamily peering into the windows of the downtown shops. And all the while, wherever she was, in terrible danger. Unaware of the demonic alarums and conflicts that swirled through every corner of the embattled city.

I will go forth in search of her, Urnikh decided; and immediately came a sensation of horror that sent green ripples undulating down his slender back. Go *out* into that madness? Risk the success of the mission, risk existence itself, wander fogbound streets where chimeras and were-pythons and hungry jack-o'-lanterns lay in waiting, all for the sake of searching for *her*?

But Margaret was in danger, and what could matter to him more than that?

"You won't listen to me, ever, will you?" he imagined himself telling her. "There's a gateway open and the whole city has become a parade-ground for monsters, and when I tell you this you laugh, you say, 'How cute, how cute,' and you pay no attention. Don't you have any regard for your own safety?"

Of *course* she had regard for her own safety.

What she *didn't* have was the slightest reason to take him seriously. He was cuddly; he was darling; he was a pocket-sized bookcase-model dragon; a cunning artifact; cleverly made with infinitesimal clockwork animatronic parts sealed cunningly inside a shell-case without seam or seal; and nothing more.

But he *was* more than that. He was a sentinel, he was an emissary; he was a force.

Yes. I am a sentinel, he told himself, even as he was slipping through the door, even as he found himself setting out to look for Margaret. *I am a sentinel…why am I so frightened?*

Darkness of a sinister quality had smothered the city now. Under the hard flannel of fog no stars could be seen, no moon, the gleam of no eye. But from every rooftop, every lamp post, every parked car, glowed the demon-light of some denizen of the nether realms, clinging fiercely to the territory that it had chewed out, defying all others to displace it.

The dragon shuddered. This was *his* doing. The gateway that had been the merest pinprick in the membrane that separated the continuums now was a gaping chasm, through which all manner of horrendous beings poured into San Francisco without cease; and it was all because he, who had been sent here to repair the original minuscule rift, had lingered, had dallied, had let himself become obsessed with a creature of this pallid and inconsequential world.

Well, so be it. What was done—was done. His obsession was no less potent for the guilt he felt. And even now, now that the forces of destruction infested every corner of this city and soon would be spreading out beyond its bounds, his concern was still only for Margaret, Margaret, Margaret, Margaret.

His beloved Margaret.

Where was she?

He built a globe of *zabil*-force about himself, just in time to fend off the attack of some hairy-beaked thing that had come swooping down out of the neon sign of the Pizza Hut on the corner, and cast the *wuzud*-spell to seek out Margaret.

His mental emanations spiraled up, up, through the heavy chill fog, scanning the city. South to Market Street, westward to Van Ness: no Margaret. Wherever his mind roved, he encountered only diabolical blackness: gibbering shaitans, glassy-eyed horrid ghazulim, swarms of furious buzzing hospodeen, a hundred hundred sorts of angry menacing creatures of the dire plasmatic void that separates mortaltime from the nightmare worlds.

Margaret? *Margaret!*

Urnikh cast his reach farther and farther, probing here, there, everywhere with the shaft of crystalline *wuzud*-force. The swarming demons could do nothing to interfere with the soaring curve of his interrogatory thrust. Let them stamp and hiss, let them leap and prance, let them spit rivers of venom, let them do whatever they pleased: he would take no mind of it. He was looking for his beloved and that was all that mattered.

Margaret, where are you?

His quest was complicated by the violent, discordant emanations that came from the humans of this city. Bad enough that the place should be infested by this invading horde of ghouls and incubi and lamias and basilisks and psychopomps; but also its own native inhabitants, Urnikh thought, were the strangest assortment of irritable and irritating malcontents. All but Margaret, of course. She was the exception. She was perfection. But the others—

What were they shouting here? "U.S. out of Carpathia! Hands off the Carpathians!" Where was Carpathia? Had it even existed, a month before? But already there was a protest movement defending its autonomy.

And these people, four blocks away, shouting even louder: "Justice for Baluchistan! No more trampling of human rights! We demand intervention! Justice for Baluchistan! Justice for Baluchistan!"

Carpathia? Baluchistan? While furious armies of invisible ruvakas and sanutees and nyctalunes snorted and snuffled and rampaged through the streets of their own city? They were blind, these people. Obsessed with distant struggles, they failed to see the festering nightmare that was unfolding right under their noses. So demented in their obsessions that they continued to protest in ever-thinning crowds and claques even after nightfall, when all offices were closed, when there was no one left to hear their slogans! But a time was coming, and soon, when the teeming manifestations that had turned the subetheric levels of San Francisco into a raging inferno would cross the perceptual threshold and burst into startling view. And then—then—

The territorial struggles among the invading beings were almost finished now. Positions had been taken; alliances had been forged. The first attacks on the human population, Urnikh calculated, might be no more than hours away. It was possible that in some outlying districts they had already begun.

Margaret!

He was picking up her signal, now. Far, far to the west, the distant reaches of the city. Beyond Van Ness, beyond the Fillmore, beyond Divisadero—yes, that was Margaret, he was sure of it, that gleam of scarlet against a weft of deep black that was her *wuzud*-imprint. He intensified the focus, homed downward and in.

Clement and Twenty-third Street, his orientation perceptor told him. So she *had* gone to see the male-one again, yes. That mysterious Other, for whom she seemed to feel such an odd, incomprehensible mix of ambivalent emotions.

It was a long journey, halfway across San Francisco.

But he had no choice. He must go to her.

It was nothing for Urnikh to journey down the *sril*-curve to an adjacent continuum. But transporting himself through the streets of this not very large city was a formidable task for a very small dragon.

There was the problem of the retrograde gravitational arc under which this entire continuum labored: he was required to weave constant compensatory spells to deal with that. Then there was the imperfection of the geological substratum to consider, the hellish fault lines that steadily pounded his consciousness with their blazing discordancies. There was the thick oxygen-polluted atmosphere. There was—

There was one difficulty after another. The best he could manage, by way of getting around, was to travel in little ricocheting leaps, a few blocks at a time, playing one node of destabilization off against another and eking out just enough kinetic thrust to move himself to the next step on his route.

Ping and he leaped across the financial district, almost to Market Street. A pair of fanged jagannaths paused in their mortal struggle to swipe at him as he went past; but with a hiss and a growl he drove them back amid flashes of small but effective lightnings, and landed safely atop a traffic light. Below him, a little knot of people was marching around and around in front of a church, crying, "Free the Fallopian Five! Free the Fallopian Five!" None of them noticed him. *Pong* and Urnikh moved on, a diagonal two-pronged ricochet that took him on the first hop as far as the Opera House, from which a terrible ear-splitting clamor was arising, and then on the next bounce to

Castro Street at Market, where some fifty or eighty male humans were waving placards and chanting something about police brutality. There were no police anywhere in sight, though a dozen hungry-looking calibargos, tendrils trembling in the intensity of their appetites, were watching the demonstration with some interest from the marquee of a movie theater a little way down the block.

If only these San Franciscans can focus all this angry energy in their own defense when the time comes, Urnikh thought.

Poing and he was off again, up Castro to Divisadero and Turk, where some sort of riot seemed to be going on outside a restaurant, people hurling dishes and menus and handfuls of food at one another. *Pung* and he reached Geary and Arguello. *Boing* and he bounced along to Clement and Fifth. A tiny earth-tremor halted him there for a moment, a jiggle of the subterranean world that only he seemed to feel; then, *bing bing bing,* he hopped westward in three quick leaps to Twenty-third Avenue.

The Margaret-emanation filled the air, here. It streamed toward his perceptors in joyous overpowering bursts.

She was here, no doubt of it.

He stationed himself diagonally across from the male-one's house, tucking himself in safely behind a fire hydrant. The street was deserted here except for a single glowering magog, which came shambling toward him as though it planned to dispute possession of the street corner with him. Urnikh had no time to waste on discussion; he dematerialized the hideous miasmatic creature with a single burst of the *seppul*-power. The stain left on the air was graceless and troubling. Then, as safe behind his globe of *zabil*-force as he could manage to make himself with his depleted energies, he set about the task of drawing Margaret out of the apartment across the way.

She didn't want to come. Whatever she might be doing in there, it seemed to exert a powerful fascination over her. Urnikh was astonished and dismayed by the force of her resistance.

But he redoubled his own efforts, exhausting though that was. The onslaught of the subetheric ones was imminent now, he knew: it would begin not in hours but in minutes, perhaps. She must be home, safe in her own apartment, when the conflict broke out. Otherwise, paralyzing thought, thinking the unthinkable, how could he protect her?!

Margaret—Margaret—

It took all the strength in his power wells. His *zabil*-globe spasmed and thinned. He would be vulnerable, he realized, to any passing enemy that might choose to attack. But the street was still quiet.

Margaret—

Here she was, finally. He saw her appear, framed in a halo of light in the doorway of the house across the way. The male-one loomed behind her, large, uncouth-looking, emanating a harsh, coarse aura that Urnikh detested. Margaret paused in the doorway, turning, smiling, her fingers still trailing the touch of his hand, looking up at the male-one in such a way that Urnikh's soul cried out. Margaret's aura coruscated through two visible and three invisible spectra. Her eyes shone. Urnikh felt all the moisture of his adoration squeezed out of him.

Never. She had *never* looked at the dragon in her bookcase like that. Cunning, clever, cuddly, a wonderful artifact; but never with eyes that held the cosmos.

For an instant, he felt anger. Something like what the mortals called hatred, the need for balance, revenge, something to strike or corrupt or disenfranchise. Then it passed. He was a dragon, a force, not some wretched flawed mortal. He was finer than that. And he loved her.

Enough, he thought. *Enough of that. Associate with them just a short time and their emotional pollution seeps in. Time's short.*

Come, Margaret, he murmured, pouring more power into the command. *Come at once! Come now, immediately, come to safety!*

But her final moments with the male-one took an eternity and a half. Exerting himself utterly, nonetheless there was nothing the little dragon could do about it. Twice, as tiny inimical fanged creatures with luminous wings and fluorescent exoskeletons came swooping past the doorway in which she stood, he mustered shards of his steadily-diminishing energy to club them into oblivion.

Come on!

Then, finally, she allowed their fingertips to slide apart, and gave him that look again, and descended the few steps to the sidewalk. Urnikh moved up close beside her in an instant, bringing her within his sphere of power but taking care to remain in the shadows of the *zabil*-globe. She must not see him, the toy, the cunningly articulated plaything, not here, not so far from the bookshelf in her apartment: it would upset her to know that he had traveled all this way to find her, small and vulnerable as he was. And she wouldn't even understand how much danger he had chanced, just to watch over her. *How ironic,* he thought: *she* was the vulnerable one, and yet, most wonderful creature, she would worry so much about *him!*

Mortaltime trembled at the brink, and all he could do was worry that she got back to the apartment, that he watch over her, back across the city, to Telegraph Hill.

Unseen by Margaret, the night erupted.

The sky over San Francisco turned the color of pigeon-blood rubies! The gateway had fully opened. He had waited too long. The pinhole had become a rent, the rent a fissure, the fissure a chasm, the chasm a total rending of the membrane between mortaltime and the dark spill that lay beyond. The sky sweated blood and screeching demons rode trails of scarlet light down through the roiling clouds, down and down between the high-rise buildings.

He had waited too long! The Master's faith in him had been misplaced, he'd known that from the start. He was not the good force, never could be, knew too little, waited too long.

All he could do now, was make certain Margaret got back to the sanctuary of Telegraph Hill. And from there, safe within his sphere of power, he would try to do what he could do. *There was nothing to be done.* He had done worse than merely fail. He had brought mortaltime to an end.

She boarded the bus, and he was there. Steel-trap mouth floaters assaulted the bus, but he sent a tendril of power out through the sphere and squeezed them to pulp.

He protected her through the long, terrible ride.

Nights dissolve into days. Days stack into weeks. Weeks become the cohesions humans call months and years. Time in mortaltime passes. The race of dragons ages very slowly. One year, two, four. Wind cleanses the streets and the oceans roll on to empty into the great drain.

"Would you like another grape?" she asked, looking up from her book.

The little dragon cocked his head and opened his mouth.

"Okay, we'll try it one more time...and this time you'd better catch it. I'm not getting off this sofa again, I'm too comfortable." She pulled a grape off the stalk, closed one eye and took aim, and popped it across the room toward the bookcase. Urnikh extended his long jaw on its serpentine neck, and snagged the fruit as it sailed past.

"Excellent, absolutely *ex*cellent!" Margaret said, smiling at the agility of the performance. "We will send you down to one of the farm clubs first, and let you season a bit, and in a year, maybe two, you'll be playing center field at Candlestick."

She tossed him a kiss, and went back to her book. It was a fine spring day, and through the open window she could smell fuchsia and gladioli and the scent of garlic and oregano from up the street where Mrs. Capamonte was laying it on for the Sunday night spectacular.

It was, of course, all a creation.

Outside the tiny apartment everything was black ash to the center of the Earth, airless void to the far ends of space. Nothing lay outside this apartment. It had ended, as the Master had feared. Mortaltime had been killed. No creature lived beyond this apartment in its sphere of power. No child laughed, no bird soared, no sponge grew on the floor of an ocean. Nothing. Absolute nothing existed beyond.

Urnikh had failed to sew up the tiniest pinprick, had simply not been the good force. And mortaltime had ended. The billions and billions had died horribly, and the world had ended, and everything was dark and empty now, never to grow again.

Because mortaltime existed only as a dream of dragons; and for this little dragon, assigned to save the puny humans who were his creations, love had been the greater imperative.

Now, they would exist this way for however long she would live.

Here, in Urnikh's dream.

Living in a world of sweetness and light and pleasure—that did not exist. He would do it all for her, only for her. For Margaret he had sacrificed everything. That which was his to sacrifice, and all that belonged to the unfortunates who had vanished.

For the little dragon, it was sad, and all honor had been lost; but it was worth it. He had his Margaret, and together, here in his dream, they would stay.

Until she, too, died.

And then it would be very hard to go on. With her gone. With all that was left of the world gone. It would be terribly hard to bear these human emotions he had taken on. Loneliness, sadness, loss. It would then, truly, be the end of all things.

And even little dragons grow old—slowly, ever so slowly.

Keyboard

Chris Hudak knew he was in trouble when his computer bit him. Not hard, not the first time. Just a nip. The merest drawing of blood from his index finger.

Chris looked down as the drop of crimson spattered on the keyboard, examined the finger, sucked at the puncture for a moment, then quizzically stared at the rows of input pads. The H key had sprouted a fang. Not a large fang; something like a baby shark incisor. Just enough to draw blood.

From the kitchen, Sharilyn called, "French toast's ready." He sucked his finger and got to his feet.

When he walked into the kitchen, she looked up from the sizzling pan. "What's the matter?"

He walked to the breakfast nook and slid in. He stared at the finger. The surface tension of a new bead of blood was about to break. "My damned computer bit me."

She looked at him. "Say what?"

"Bit me. The damned computer. It has teeth."

"Chris..."

"I'm not kiddin', Sharilyn. The damned thing grew a tooth and took a nip out of me."

"Oh, come *on*, don't start with me this early. I thought we'd talked out the problem last night."

"This has nothing to do with last night's argument. This is a new thing, and I'd appreciate it if you'd come over here and take a look at my hand before you start telling me I'm losing it. Or go in the other room and check out the keyboard. The H key."

Carrying the pan, she came to him, and looked down. He held up his hand. The finger was starting to glow an unsavory bluish-green. The bead broke and dropped red on the tablecloth. "Hully Jeezus," she said.

"Yeah," he said ruminatively. "Ain't *that* a bitch."

"So what did you stick it with?"

He looked up at her. "You're not getting it, are you? I didn't *stick it* with *any*thing. It *bit* me!" He made certain to emphasize more words than usual in the sentence. For clarity.

"Right," she said, and skimmed the spatula under the French toast, and plopped the food onto his plate. "Right. And a little later today I'll have excessive sex with my microwave oven."

Chris started to reply, caught himself, caught his teeth grinding, caught his upper arm muscles tensing, caught the words that were left over from last night starting to bubble up in his throat...and went to work on the French toast.

The tablecloth had soaked up the spot of blood.

By Saturday, half his fingers had been stippled. Only the thumbs had been spared. Smarted like hell.

At first, the first few days, he had considered getting rid of the damned thing, taking it down to Comp USA and trading up to a 90 MHz Pentium. But by Tuesday, for some reason, he didn't want to do that. Not only because Hartschorn at the mail order house was screaming for the assimilated demographics he'd been analyzing, but because...well...he'd gotten used to the machine biting him. It wasn't painful any longer, just smarted like hell. And he seemed to have developed some sort of relationship with the PC. It wasn't anything he'd experienced before. A personal relationship with machinery. He had devised a nickname for his car, of course, a leftover from his teen-age years; and once in a while he'd called the tv remote a dumb bastard when the batteries had gone low; but neither his electric razor nor the weed-whacker had ever manifested any interest in establishing a more meaningful relationship with him.

And he had begun to forget things.

"Where did you put that big box of winter clothes from last April?" Sharilyn asked him on Thursday.

"What box of clothes?"'

"That big box. Had Bekins on the side. One of the storage boxes from the move. Remember, you said you'd find a place for it?"

He had no idea.

"The winter clothes, fer pity's sake!" Sharilyn yelled. Her temper had grown shorter and shorter with him lately. He was beginning to think they were heading for *bad* times, very bad times. Maybe a breakup, maybe a divorce, maybe worse. He had no idea what *worse* could mean, but he was feeling a vague disquiet constantly now, a sense that their time together was being razored to an end.

"I'll look for them," he said, and got up from the computer to go do just that. She turned away, and he watched her go, and then—without realizing it—sat down at the keyboard again.

Hours later, screaming and in tears, she came back and told him he could take that big Bekins storage box, if he ever found it, and jam it up his spreading ass!

The razor was beginning to strike bone.

The computer had grown larger. It seemed to be bursting out of its metal case. The word *bloated* came to mind. Chris had begun to perceive a strange, almost lopsided aspect to the machine, as if it were off-balance, from the shifting of weight, the addition of new cargo. And it continued to take sips from his hands. And he was forgetting many things now. Not the least of which was the precise moment when Sharilyn had left.

He knew she was gone, because he couldn't find her anywhere in the house. But he couldn't exactly parse the circumstances that had driven her away. Had it been one of the fights? Or the fact that he sat before the PC night and day now, growing paler, getting foggier in the mind with each passing hour? Could it have been that? Or perhaps it was the moment she came downstairs and saw him feeding one of the neon tetras to the computer. Perhaps it was that moment. Maybe not. He couldn't remember.

The house was always silent.

Cobwebs refused to grow.

He sat in darkness, the only light provided by the monitor—a sickly blue-green abyss across which fleeting sighs and portents scuttled like crippled creatures. The figures and letters would bump against the perimeter of the screen, fumble for a moment as if lost in the wilderness, and then run back into the center of the information field, where they would vanish with tiny squeals.

Chris worked with his eyes closed most of the time. He had lost the need to see what the computer was asking. But through his fingertips the machine drank and drank, never seeming to slake its thirst, never seeming to get its fill. Bloated and cockeyed in shape, but always sucking from Chris whatever he had left.

He tried to remember when his mother had died. He knew she was gone...just as others had gone...but he couldn't exactly say who those others were. Yet he remembered her face. The sweetest smile. And a phrase she used to say:

"Woof woof a goldfish."

It meant nothing, really; but she would use it when he—or anyone—was coming on too strong, being a bully, threatening in some silly way, like a guy in a car on the street who thought he had been cut off, making insulting remarks. His mother, with that sweet sweet smile, would lean out and say, "Woof woof a goldfish!" It was so much nicer than giving someone the finger. He loved his mother. Where was she?

He called out, but there was no answer. The house was silent.

In the third week since first blood had been drawn, the computer began to speak to him. But he couldn't understand a word it said. And the voice made his head hurt. Like a huge empty auditorium in which *taiko* drummers played endlessly.

Two days later, a thunderstorm hit the tri-state area with a power and a ferocity that reminded old-timers of the great storm of 1936. And the dam stopped producing electricity when a spike of lightning as thick as a city block hit the transformer station; and the power went out; and the computer went dead. Or dormant.

It continued to glow, that diseased bluish-green color, but it wasn't alert, it wasn't breathing as deeply, it wasn't draining him. It went somnolent, torpid, waiting.

Chris felt like a junkie going into terminal withdrawal. He fell from the ergonomic chair, and lay on his side for hours. The pain in his head, and the pain in his hips, and the pain in his hands—radiating all the way to his shoulders—left him paralyzed. Lying there cuculiform, curled like a conch shell, absent the sound of any living sea.

For hours the storm raged around the house, battering and lashing the windows with the malevolence of ancient enemies. And by morning, when light crept through the sooty windows, Chris crawled to the bathroom and ran water into the tub and managed to drag himself over the porcelain lip and fell face-forward into the freezing ocean. He thought he'd die!

The pain was excruciating, shadowlines of agony racing down from his eyes and cheeks into his neck, paralyzing his upper body, disemboweling him, reducing him to the jelly cold of infinite vacuum. He tried to struggle out of the tub, lurching back with his shoulders, trying to get purchase with his scrabbling feet against the tiles of the bathroom. His head and upper body were submerged, his torso half-in, half-out of the tundra oblivion. He screamed, there in the water, and bubbles, only bubbles broke the surface. He wrenched himself back, thrashing, managing to get one arm outside the tub, over the enamel edge. But it was enough.

He fell to the floor, teeth chattering, eyes white and rolled up in his head like shrunken scrotums, like brine shrimp left in the desert. He passed out, and it was sweet relief.

He thought he remembered his mother's smile.

It was night again. He could see the blind eyes of the living room windows from where he lay on his side on the carpet. The only light in the room was from the computer. It had tried to crawl to him, to feed, but the power had been off for too long. Had it been a day, two...three days or a week...? Chris had no idea. He felt dehydrated, and hurting in every paper-thin plane of his skin.

It had to have been more than a few days, because he was so weak he couldn't move. He tried, and only a finger spasmed. But then, he had been drained *before* the storm had smashed them, and lying here for an endless time would only have emptied him the more.

He could see the PC, over there, halfway between its work-station and his twisted body. It had come down off the ledge, had managed to get partway toward him, and then had, itself, collapsed.

Its mouth was open, glittering blue-green bytes drooling from its fanged aperture.

Chris knew something was wrong; something was wrong with *him*. He should not be lying on the carpet, he should not be weak, he should be frightened of that machine over there.

But he couldn't remember.

Couldn't remember who he was, or why he was here, or what he should be doing. To save himself. To rise. To think about matters that mattered. There had been people, of that he was sure. People who had known him, had cared for him; but he couldn't recall what the words *cared for him* meant.

And he saw the PC trembling.

It inched across the carpet. Slowly, like a broken-backed horse struggling for the cool mud of a ditch. Chris watched it come.

The phosphorescent aura of its passage across the room was like strobe tracers in a long shot of the turnpike. It left a trail, like a slug, glittering and corrosive.

Dragging the umbilicus of its power cord, the three-pronged plug jumping and twitching like a severed chicken body seeking its head, the PC came closer. Chris lay on his side and watched, unable to move, unable to defend himself...

What did that mean: *defend himself?*

He thought about it, tried to put the phrase together. Oh, yes, he thought, I know what that means. Defend myself. I know. It means it's time to be fed, and I have to make myself available.

With the strength of a drowning man, he scissored his legs against the carpet, pushing himself across the space between himself and the oncoming computer. The cord twitched and dragged itself behind the carcass of the PC. Chris rolled to one side, out of the computer's path, and shinnied his way in a herky-jerky rolling way till he could get the cord in his mouth. He closed his lips around the cord, and continued to roll and frog-kick and drag himself to the wall. The outlet was at eye-level.

He got close to the baseboard, and fainted again.

When he awoke, the computer was close to his feet, and the lights were on in the living room. Oh, wonderful, he thought, now it can feed. Lovely. Lovely.

He drew himself together at the hips, then extended his upper torso, the cord clenched between his teeth, and moved another six inches to the baseboard. And again. And once more. Now he was lying with his cheek against the cool hardwood floor; and the plug lay just below the outlet.

The computer scraped the floor, byte drool etching an acid alphabet in the pegged wood floor. *I'll help you,* Chris tried to whisper. *I'll plug you in and you can drink.*

He didn't understand why the PC was so impatient. He was trying to help. He *would* help, even if the machine *was* being impatient.

With the last of his strength, he dragged his arm around his body, and grasped the plug. He tried ever so hard to raise the plug, to insert the triple prong into the slots and hole. But his strength was gone. He was empty. His head had been sucked dry of all knowledge, his body drained of all energy, his arteries dusty with emptiness. The PC was whimpering at his feet like an asthmatic infant.

Friend, he thought, *my old dearest friend.* He wanted to say, be patient, I'm coming, I'll get you fed yet, I'll set the table and billow the napkin into your lap. Hold on, old friend.

And from some small reservoir of unknown value, some untilled patch of muscle, he found an inch worth of foot-pounds of energy, and he thrust the plug into the power point.

The energy spike exploded straight through the heart of the PC. It had been lurking there in the web, waiting to be tapped, and as the plug drove home, Chris speared the computer with a coruscating spike of energy that blew the feeding keyboard into dust. Chris was showered with sparks. And darkness closed over him again.

When he came to, he was lying curled in a foetal rictus, every fiber of his body crying for a soft breeze, a gentle touch. But he could think...he could reason.

And he knew what had happened to him. The long banquet that had transpired in this dark house. Sharilyn was gone, his family was gone, and he had very nearly been taken.

But now, by chance, he had saved himself. Unknowing, without sense or purpose, he had saved himself from the thing that drank, the device that dined. He would begin to crawl toward the kitchen, to pull down a box of saltines, to kick the table and make a desiccated tangerine fall from the bowl up there. He would live. By chance, but yes, he would live. And it was chance that lived on the side of human reason. Always.

Nothing of the insensate hungering world could defeat a thinking entity, a creature of breezes and sweet smiles.

Then he heard the sound of lips smacking, of soft and distressing music; and he stared across the living room.

The television licked its lips and winked at him.

Jane Doe #112

SHADOWS OF LIVES UNLIVED, as milky as opal glass, moved through the French Quarter that night. And one begged leave, and separated from the group to see an old friend.

Bourbon Street was only minimally less chaotic than usual. It was two days till the Spring Break deluge of horny fraternity boys and young women seemingly unable to keep their t-shirts on.

The queue outside Chris Owens's club moved swiftly for the last show. Inside, the entertainer was just starting the third chorus of "Rescue Me" when she looked out into the audience and saw the pale shadow of a face she hadn't seen in twenty years.

For a moment she faltered, but no one noticed. She had been a star on Bourbon Street for twenty years; they wouldn't know that the face staring up palely at her was that of a woman who had been dead for two decades.

Doris Burton sat in the smoky center of a cheering mob half-smashed on Hurricanes; and she stared up at Chris Owens with eyes as quietly gray and distant as the surface of the moon. The last time Chris had seen those eyes, they had been looking out of a newspaper article about the car crash over in Haskell County, when Doris had been killed.

Her parents wouldn't let her go over to the funeral. It was a piece of Texas distance, from Jones County over to Haskell. She had never forgotten Doris, and she had always felt guilty that she'd never gotten to say goodbye.

Now she felt the past worming its way into her present. It couldn't possibly be. She danced to the edge of the stage and looked directly at her. It was Doris. As she had been twenty years ago.

The woman in the audience was almost transparent in the bleed of light from the baby spots and pinlights washing Chris as she worked. Trying to keep up with the beat, Chris could swear she could see the table full of Kiwanis behind Doris. It threw her off...but no one would notice.

Doris moved her lips. *Hello, Chris.*

Then she smiled. That same gentle smile of an awkward young woman that had first bound them together as friends.

Chris felt her heart squeeze, and tears threatened to run her makeup. She fought back the sorrow, and smiled at her dead friend. Then Doris rose, made a tiny goodbye movement with her left hand, and left the club.

Chris Owens did not disappoint her audience that night. She never disappointed them. But she was only working at half the energy. Even so, they would never know.

That night, the Orleans Parish Morgue logged in its one hundred and twelfth unknown female subject. The toe was tagged JANE DOE #112 and was laid on the cold tile floor in the hallway. As usual, the refrigerators were full.

Ben Laborde took his foot off the accelerator as he barreled north on the I-10 past St. Charles Parish, and kicked the goddammed air conditioner one last time. It was dead. The mechanism on the '78 Corollas had been lemons when they were fresh off the showroom floor, and twelve years of inept service had not bettered the condition. Now it had given out totally; and Ben could feel the sweat beginning to form a tsunami at his hairline. He cranked down the window and was rewarded with a blast of mugginess off the elevated expressway that made him blink and painfully exhale hot breath. Off to his left the Bonnet Carré Spillway—actually seventeen miles of fetid swamp with a name far too high above its station—stretched behind him as an appropriate farewell to New Orleans, to Louisiana, to twenty-two years of an existence he was now in the process of chucking. The blue Toyota gathered speed again as he punched the accelerator, and he thought, *So long, N'wallins; I give you back to the 'gators.*

Somewhere north lay Chicago, and a fresh start.

When he thought back across the years, when he paused to contemplate how fast and how complexly he had lived, he sometimes thought he had been through half a dozen different existences. Half a dozen different lives, as memorable and filled with events as might have been endured by a basketball team with one extra guy waiting on the bench.

Now he was chucking it all. Again. For the half-dozenth time in his forty-one years.

Ben Laborde had run off when he was ten, had worked the crops across the bread basket of America, had schooled himself, had run with gangs of itinerant farm laborers, had gone into the army at nineteen, had become an MP, had mustered out and been accepted to the FBI, had packed that in after four years and become a harness bull in the St. Bernard Parish Sheriff's Department, had been promoted to Detective, and had had his tin pulled two years ago for throwing a pimp through the show window of an antique shop on Rue Toulouse. The pimp had been on the muscle with someone in the Department, and that was that for Detective Benjamin Paul Laborde.

He had become a repairman for ATMs, but two years fixing the bank teller machines had driven him most of the way into total craziness. And then, there was that group of pale gray people that kept following him…

He looked in the rearview. The expressway was nearly empty behind him. If he was being tracked, they had to be very good; and very far behind him. But the thought had impinged, and he cranked up the speed.

There had been six of them for the last year. Six men and women, as pale as the juice at the bottom of a bucket of steamed clams. But when he had seen them out of the corner of his eye the night before last, moving through the crowd on Bourbon Street, there had only been five.

He couldn't understand why he was so frightened of them.

He had thought more than once, more than a hundred times in the past year, that he should simply step into a doorway, wait for them to catch up, then brace them. But every time he started to do just that…the fear grabbed him.

So he had decided to chuck it all. Again. And go.

He wasn't at all certain if not having the Police Positive on his hip made any difference.

The nagging thought kept chewing on him: would a bullet stop them?

He ran, but the Corolla didn't have anything more to give. He thought grimly, *even if I could go ten times as fast it probably wouldn't be fast enough.*

Chicago was dark. Perhaps a brownout. The city lay around him as ugly and desperate as he felt. The trip north had been uneventful, but nonetheless dismaying. Stopping only briefly for food and gas, he had driven straight through. Now he had to find a place to live, a new job of some menial sort till he could get his hooks set, and then...perhaps...he could decide what he wanted to be when he grew up.

As best he could discern, he hadn't been followed. (Yet when he had pulled in at a bar in Bloomington, Indiana, and had been sitting there nursing the Cutty and water, he had seen, in the backbar mirror, the street outside. And for a moment, five sickly white faces peering in at him.)

(But when he had swiveled for a direct look, only the empty street lay beyond the window. He had paid up and left quickly.)

Laborde had never spent much time in Chicago. He barely knew the city. A few nights around Rush Street, some drinking with buddies in an apartment in a debutante's condo facing out on the Shore Drive, dinner one night in Old Town. But he had the sense that staying in the center of the city was not smart. He didn't know why, but he felt the push to keep going; and he did. Out the other side and into Evanston.

It was quieter here. Northwestern University, old homes lining Dempster Street, the headquarters of The Women's Christian Temperance Union. Maybe he'd take night courses. Get a job in a printing plant. Sell cars. Plenty of action and danger in those choices.

He drove through to Skokie and found a rooming house. It had been years since he'd stayed in a rooming house. Motels, that was the story now. Had been for forty years. He tried to remember where he'd last lived, in which town, in which life, that had provided rooming houses. He couldn't recall. Any more than he could recall when he'd owned a Studebaker Commander, the car that Raymond Loewy had designed. Or the last time he had heard The Green Hornet on the radio.

He was putting his underwear in the bureau drawer as these thoughts wafted through his mind. Studebaker? The Green Hornet? That was over when he'd been a kid. He was forty-one, not sixty. How the hell did he remember that stuff?

He heard footsteps in the hall. They weren't the halting steps of the woman who owned the hostel. She had been happy to get a boarder. But not even a need to accommodate her new tenant could have eliminated the arthritic pace she had set as she climbed the stairs ahead of him.

He stood with his hands on the drawer, listening.

The footsteps neared, then stopped outside his door. There was no lock on the door. It was a rooming house, not a motel. No chain, no double-latch, no security bolt. It was an old wooden door, and all the person on the other side had to do was turn the knob and enter.

He barely heard the tapping.

It was the rapping at a portal of something composed of mist and soft winds.

Laborde felt a sharp pain as he realized he had been clenching his teeth. His jaw muscles were rigid. His face hurt. Whatever he wanted to do, it was not to go over and open that door to the visitor.

He watched, without breathing, as the knob slowly turned, and the door opened, a sliver of light at a time.

The door opened of its own weight after a moment, and Laborde saw a woman standing in the dimly-lit hallway. She looked as if she were made of isinglass. He could see through her, see the hallway through her dim, pale shape. She stared at him with eyes the color of an infirmary nurse's uniform.

Isinglass? How could he remember something like that? They had used isinglass before they'd started putting real glass in car windows.

The woman said, "Jessie passed through in New Orleans. She was the oldest of us. She was the one wanted to find you the most."

His mouth was dry. His hands, still on the dresser drawer, were trembling.

"I don't know any Jessie," he said. The voice seemed to belong to some-one else, someone far away on a mountainside, speaking into the wind.

"You knew her."

"No, I never, I've *never* known anyone named Jessie."

"You knew her better than anyone. Better than her mother or her father or any of us who traveled with her. You knew the best part of her. But she never got to tell you that."

He managed to close the drawer on his underwear. He found it *very* important, somehow, just to be able to close the drawer.

"I think you'd better let the landlady know you're here," he said, feeling ridiculous. How she had gotten in, he didn't know. Perhaps the old woman had let her in. Perhaps she had asked for him by name. How could she know his name?

She didn't answer. He had the awful desire to go to the door and *touch* her. It was continuing strange, the way the light shone through her. Not as if there were kliegs set off in the distance, with radiance projected toward her; but rather, as if she were generating light from within. But what he saw as he looked at her, in that plain, shapeless dress, her hair hanging limp and milky around her shoulders, was a human being made of tracing paper, the image of the drawing behind shadowing through. He took a step toward her, hoping she would move.

She stood her ground, unblinking.

"Why have you been following me, all of you...there are six of you, aren't there?"

"No," she said, softly, "now there are only five. Jessie passed through." She paused, seemed to gather strength to speak, and added, "Very soon now, we'll *all* pass through. And then you'll be alone."

He felt an instant spike of anger. "I've *always* been alone!"

She shook her head. "You stole from us, but you've never been without us."

He touched her. He reached out and laid his fingertips on her cheek. She was cool to the touch, like a china bowl. But she was real, substantial. He had been thinking ghost, but that was ridiculous; he'd *known* it was ridiculous all along. From the first time he had seen them following him in New Orleans. Passersby had bumped into them, had acknowledged their existence, had moved aside for them. They weren't ghosts, whatever they were. And whatever it was, he was terrified of them...even though he knew they would not harm him. And, yes, a bullet would have done them.

"I'm leaving. Get out of my way."

"Aren't you curious?"

"Not enough to let you keep making me crazy. I'm going out of here, and you'd better not try to stop me."

She looked at him sadly; as a child looks at the last day of summer; as the sun goes down; as the street lights come on before bedtime; one beat before it all ends and the fun days retreat into memory. He thought that, in just that way, as she looked at him. It was the ending of a cycle, but he had no idea how that could be, or what cycle was done.

He moved a step closer to her. She stood in the doorway and did not move. "Get out of my way."

"I haven't the strength to stop you. You know that."

He pushed her, and she went back. He kept his hand on her sternum, pressing her back into the hall. She offered no resistance. It was like touching cool eggshell.

"This time you leave even your clothes behind?" she asked.

"This time I shake you clowns," he said, going down the hall, descending the stairs, opening the curtained front door, stepping out into the Illinois night, and seeing his car parked across the street. Surrounded by the other four.

As fragile as whispers, leaning against the car. Waiting for him.

Oh, Christ, he thought, *this isn't happening.*

"What the hell do you *want* of me?" he screamed. They said nothing, just watched. Three men and another woman. He could see the dark outline of his car through them.

He turned right and began running. He wasn't afraid, he was just frightened. It wasn't terror, it was only fear.

Abandon the underwear in the drawer. Lose the past life. Jettison the car. Get out of this existence. Forget the deposit on the room. Run away. Just...run away.

When he reached the end of the block, he saw the lights of a mini-mall. He rushed toward the light. Dark things have no shadows in sodium vapor lights.

Behind him, the milky figure of the fifth one emerged from the rooming house and joined her traveling companions.

They caught up with him only three times in the next year. The first time in Cleveland. There were four of them. Three months later, he stepped off a Greyhound Scenicruiser at the Port Authority Terminal in Manhattan, and they were coming up the escalator to meet the bus. Two of them, a man and the woman who had confronted him in the rooming house in Skokie.

And finally, he came full circle. He went home.

Not to Chicago, not to New Orleans, not as far back as he could remember, but as far back as he had come. Seven miles south of Cedar Falls, Iowa—on the thin road out of Waterloo—back to Hudson. And it hadn't changed. Flat cornfield land, late in September after the oppressive heat had passed, into the time of jackets and zipping up.

Where his house had stood, now there was a weed-overgrown basement into which the upper floors had fallen as the fire had burned itself out. One wall remained, the salt box slats gray and weathered.

He sat down on what had been the stone steps leading up to the front porch, and he laid down the cheap plastic shoulder bag that now contained all he owned in the world. And it was there that the last two of those who had dogged him came to have their talk.

He saw them coming down the dirt road between the fields of freshly-harvested corn, the stalks creaking in the breeze, and he gave it up. Packed it in. No more getting in the flow, chasing the wind. No more. He sat and watched them coming up the road, tiny puffs of dust at each step. The day was on the wane, and he could see clouds through them, the horizon line, birds reaching for more sky.

They came up and stood staring at him, and he said, "Sit down, take a load off."

The man seemed to be a hundred years old. He smiled at Ben Laborde and said, "Thanks. It's been a hard trip." He slumped onto the stone step below. He wiped his forehead, but he wasn't perspiring.

The woman stood in front of him, and her expression was neither kind nor hard. It was simply the face of someone who had been traveling a long time, and was relieved to have reached her destination.

"Who are you?"

The woman looked at the old man and said, "We were never a high school girl named Doris Burton, who was supposed to've died in a car accident in West Texas, but didn't. We were never an asthmatic named Milford Sterbank, who worked for fifty years as a reweaver. And we never got to be Henry Cheatham, who drove a cab in Pittsburgh."

He watched them, looking from the man to the woman, and back. "And which ones are you?"

The woman looked away for a moment. Laborde saw the setting sun through her chest. She said, "I would have been Barbara Lamartini. You passed through St. Louis in 1943."

"I was born in '49."

The old man shook his head. "Much earlier. If you hadn't fought with the 2nd Division at Belleau Wood, I would have been Howard Strausser. We shared a trench for five minutes, June 1st, 1918."

"This is crazy."

"No," the woman said wearily, "this is just the end of it."

"The end of what?"

"The end of the last of us whose lives you've been using. The last soft gray man or woman left on a doorstep by your passing."

Laborde shook his head. It was gibberish. He knew he was at final moments with them, but what it all meant he could not fathom.

"For godsakes," he pleaded, "hasn't this gone on long enough? Haven't you sent me running long enough? What the hell have I ever done to you...any of you? I don't even know you!"

The old man, Howard Strausser, smiled sadly and said, "You never meant to be a thief. It isn't your fault, any more than it's our fault for finally coming after you, to get our lives back. But you did, you stole, and you left us behind. We've been husks. I'm the oldest left. Barbara is somewhere in the middle. You've been doing it for several hundred years, best we've been able to tell. When we found one another, there was a man who said he'd been panning gold at Sutter's Mill when you came by. I don't know as I believe him; his name was Chickie Moldanado, and he was something of a liar. It was the only memorable thing about him."

The woman added, "There's nothing much memorable about any of us."

"That's the key, do you see?" Howard Strausser said.

"No, I *don't* see," Laborde said.

"We were never *any*thing. None of us."

He let his hands move helplessly in the air in front of them. "I don't know what any of this means. I just know I'm tired of...not of running...tired of, just, I don't know, tired of being *me*."

"You've never been you." Howard Strausser smiled kindly.

"Perhaps you can be you now," Barbara Lamartini said.

Laborde put his hands over his face. "Can't you just tell it simply? Please, for godsakes, just *simply*."

The woman nodded to the old man, who looked to be a hundred years old, and he said, "There are just some people who live life more fully than others. Take, oh, I don't know, take Scott Fitzgerald or Hemingway or Winston Churchill or Amelia Earhart. Everybody's heard their names, but how many people have read much Hemingway or Fitzgerald, or even Churchill's—" He stopped. The woman was giving him that look. He grinned sheepishly.

"There are just some people who *live* their lives at a fuller pace. And it's as if they've lived two or three lifetimes in the same time it takes others to get through just one mild, meager, colorless life, one sad and sorry—"

He stopped again.

"Barbara, you'd better do it. I've waited too long. I'm just running off at the mouth like an old fart."

She put a hand on his thin shoulder to comfort him, and said, "You were one of the passionate ones. You lived at a hotter level. And every now and then, every once in a while, you just leached off someone's life who wasn't up to the living of it. You're a magpie. You came by, whenever it was, 1492, 1756, 1889, 1943...we don't know how far back you go...but you passed by, and someone was wearing a life so loosely, so unused, that it just came off; and you wore it away, and added it on, and you just kept going, which way it didn't matter, without looking back, not even knowing.

"And finally, the last of us followed the thread that was never broken, the umbilicus of each of us, and we came and found you, to try and get back what was left."

"Because it's clear," said Howard Strausser, "that you're tired of it. And don't know how to get out of it. But—"

They sighed almost as one, and Barbara Lamartini said, "There isn't enough of either of us left to take back. We'll be gone, passed through very soon."

"Then you're on your own," Howard Strausser said.

"You'll be living what portion has been allotted to you," the woman said, and he could see through the holes where her milky eyes had been.

And they sat there into the deepening twilight, in Hudson, Iowa; and they talked; and there was nothing he could do for them; and finally, the woman said, "We don't blame you. It was our own damned fault. We just weren't up to the doing of it, the living of our own lives." What was left of her shrugged, and Laborde asked her to tell him all she could of the others they had known, so he could try to remember them and fit to their memories the parts of his own life that he had taken.

And by midnight, he was sitting there alone.

And he fell asleep, arms wrapped around himself, in the chilly September night, knowing that when he arose the next day, the first day of a fresh life, he would retrace his steps in many ways; and that one of the things he would do would be to return to New Orleans.

To go to the Parish Coroner, and to have exhumed the body of JANE DOE #112; to have it dug out of the black loam of Potter's Field near City Park and to carry it back to West Texas; to bury the child who had never been allowed to be Doris Burton where she would have lived her life. Pale as opal glass, she had passed through and whispered away, on the last night of the poor thing that had been her existence; seeking out the only friend she had been allowed to have, on a noisy street in the French Quarter.

The least he could do was to be her last friend, to carry her home; by way of cheap restitution.

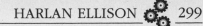

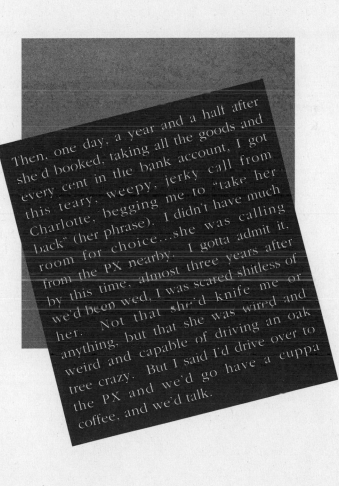

Then, one day, a year and a half after she'd booked, taking all the goods and every cent in the bank account, I got this teary, weepy, jerky call from Charlotte, begging me to "take her back" (her phrase). I didn't have much room for choice...she was calling from the PX nearby. I gotta admit it, by this time, almost three years after we'd been wed, I was scared shitless of her. Not that she'd knife me or anything, but that she was wired and weird and capable of driving an oak tree crazy. But I said I'd drive over to the PX and we'd go have a cuppa coffee, and we'd talk.

The Dreams A Nightmare Dreams

Yes, they died. Sixty five million years ago they died, all but the most cunning of them who burrowed deep and hid so well that the dreams never found them. It gave them time to alter their shapes, to devise tricksy alternatives, to outrun and outfox the dreams till they could become bats and rats and sharks and cockroaches, snails and whales and birds and men.

Pay close attention here. Forget the floods and the ozone depletion, the hurricanes and earthquakes, the drive-by killers and the nuclear terrorists. They will pass with the rest of us if the thing that lies dreaming in its crypt at the bottom of the Gulf of Mexico, in that vast sunken cathedral called the Sigsbee Deep, if that thing ever stops dreaming and wakens. Your puny terrors and wee hours sweats don't mean a damn, my friend, if that eyeless thing at the bottom of the Sigsbee yawns and shudders and stretches its spikey nasal hoses for leagues in all directions, and comes fully awake. Horrorists and charlatans and clairvoyants and those who rant in tongues and serial killers have tried to name it, but it *has no name.*

It has no kin, it has no home. It has no heart, it has no soul. It has no caring and it has no fear. It is pure nightmare, and it killed the dinosaurs.

301

You thought it was a great meteor that struck the Earth sixty-five million years ago, just out of the Cretaceous, just into the Tertiary, that's what you thought, isn't it? A great meteor, and a deadly shroud of dust that mantled the planet and hid the sun. And the plants died, and the atmosphere boiled, and the great saurians perished, crashing to the ground and lying there till they rotted. That's what you thought, isn't it?

Pay close attention here. That isn't even *remotely* what happened. The truth lies dreaming at the bottom of the Gulf of Mexico. The truth is eyeless and frightening without a soul. Immense and asleep in a great fanged crypt that keeps the nightmare sucking at our dreams, oh pay attention, pal.

It came through a suppurating wound in the fabric of the universe. A sucking chest wound in the skin of eternity. A burst blood vessel in the atrophied brain of Forever. Who the hell knows where it came from? Not even the nightmare knows what hideous miscegenation of stone and vomit gave it birth. But there it was, traveling through the lava flow of space-time, burning and screaming, on an endless voyage that would last its entire million-age life.

And there was a rip, a tear, a fracture, a schism, just the neatest little rift...and it fell into *our* universe. It fell, and fell, all through the millennia without number it took for our reality to get born, reach maturity, and take a hold on life. It fell toward us, and sixty-five million years ago it fell through our sky and impacted on the post-Pangæan landscape, and made the crater they call the Sigsbee. The vile horror that lay curled in that cosmic cradle, it reached out with its hundred minds, and it licked at the surface of every brain it could find, no matter how large, no matter how small. It savored the worm, it tasted the fungi, it slobbered over the centipede. But when it found the thoughts of the dinosaurs, it knew fulfillment, a disgusting satiation. It could dominate, if it could invade the minds of the saurians.

Great and noble in their crystal cities, masters of the planet to the height of its sky and the depth of its ocean, the dinosaurs had perfected a society rich and variegated. And they sensed the nightmare that tongued their souls. And they fought back. They dreamed intrusive dreams, like songs that repeat themselves and won't leave, that you find yourself whistling over and over, merrily we roll along, roll along...

> *Conductor, conductor,*
> *Punch with care.*
> *Punch in the presence*
> *Of the passen-jair.*

Over and over, with variations that clouded thinking, that kept the dreaming nightmare conflicted and confused. But the eyeless horror in the deep struck them, and they died. All of them. In their cities, in their mountaintop eyries, in the vasty ocean bowers. They died, and no trace was left of their civilization, because the gargantuan dreamer wished it so. Not a glass tower, not a whisper of art, not a pane of memory. Gone, all gone.

And it lay there for millions and millions of years, until it went into something like REM-sleep, and perceived us here.

Inheritors of the saurian world.

And it dreams now in *our* minds. And only a few of us are aware to fight the endless terror. In Brazil there are two. They sleep, and they dream. In Katmandu a lone one. Dreaming. There, near the high Karakorum, a married couple, lying asleep, fed by their children, saving our universe with their intrusive dreams. And here, what you see here, the dreams of one in Switzerland. He dreams, and his dreams like catchy tunes, that change and change, that reshape and track back on themselves, keeping the nameless thing in the Sigsbee Deep from getting its—how shall we put it—getting its loathesome act together.

Pay attention here. What you see changing and changing, shaping and reshaping, these are the ectothermic images of the Swiss dreamer. They slip silently through the night, and like the stray whoop of a ham radio operator, every once in a while they are captured by an unwary computer screen, an idle cineplex movie screen, a television set speckled with three a.m. snow. See the cunning images? Like white noise to the sleeping thing in the Gulf of Mexico. Like a theme song repeating endlessly. Interference. Keeping the juggernaut lulled.

In Morocco, in Pernambuco, in Atlanta, exactly as the Swiss dreamer...we lie here making images. And they fly out into the electronic and telepathic and interstitial spaces, slipping and sliding their way into the beast's mind, but also leaking onto your screen. So pay attention here. We keep you safe. We lie here dreaming. Consider the images of this heroic protector in Switzerland who, like his dreaming compatriots in Vladikavkaz and the Flinders Ranges and Dakoro, like the rest of us who are all that stand between you and ultimate horror...we invite you. Join us.

Pay close attention to these pirate dream-images that have come to save your screen. They may also save your universe.

We need your dreams to keep feeding the nightmare.

Lest it wake and eat the soft pulp of our souls.

Pulling
Hard
Time

In the maximum security VR wings of New Alcatraz, there is no light. None is needed. The prisoners are fed aerobiologically: five times a day the cells are fine-sprayed with a dispersion of microscopically-calibrated nutrients, pollens, bacteria-inhibiting spores and microorganisms, cleansing agents, and depilitants. All waste products gelate, coalesce and are sucked out of the null-gravity free fall enclosure through egress tiles in the sterile white pyrex floor. Random items of furniture—overstuffed easy chairs, end-table lamps, swatches of astroturf, *saki* cups—float relaxedly in the gentle air tides that waft through the cells.

These non-penal artifacts have been stored in the cells. For the most part, they are the property of Warden Emmanuel V. Burkis, a collector of household trinkets from the past. They have been laded in the null-g maximum security cells, where they share floating space with lifers paying their debt to society, because storage space is at a premium in the one hundred per cent automated environs of New Alcatraz. To take the job of overseeing the Rock, even at the handsome figure paid annually by the Internment Department of the United States government, Warden Burkis was gifted with unlimited shopping authority for his hobby—household trinkets from the past. It is a lonely and quiet place, the Rock.

The lifers who occupy these cells never object to the floating furniture. They, themselves, float. They exist in a transmundane virtual reality nexus, dreaming their special dreams, bobbing and slowly turning in the vagrant breezes that play forever through the VR wings. They are serving their life-time sentences, hanging in null-g oblivion growing more grossly rotund and discolored by the decade. They will bump against walls and wedge in trian-gular dead ends where ceiling meets vertical tile surfaces till one night, or one day, they will expire in the middle of the special dream. And only through a death kept long at bay, to assuage the demands of Society for retribution will their sentences be commuted. Commuted, that is, to a place (in the sentencing litany of the Universal Penal Code) "far worse than the Hell in which they have served their sentence." We are a nation in balance.

Charlie was out back, feeding the chickens, when he heard Robin scream. He dropped the tin bucket, spilling millet in a long swath. He ran back to the restaurant shack in a panic, tripping and falling once.

As he came through the screen door at the rear of the shack, he saw the four men tearing at Robin's clothes. They had her on her back on one of the tables, and one of the leather-clad bikers had already ripped her blouse off. Her apron hung off one ankle. Another had spread her legs, and was unzip-ping his roughout pants, pushing between her thighs as the shortest of the four, a little man with almost no hair on the left side of his head, cut away Robin's skirt with what looked like a fish-boning knife.

The fourth man sat at the counter, his back to Charlie, a bottle of Pepsi to his lips.

They had come in and ordered four Sunday chicken specials. Charlie had said he'd fry up the orders, but Robin had asked him to go out back and feed the chickens. Lumschbogen's Chicken & Bisquit Shack. Out on Route 5. Charlie had kissed his wife, and smiled at the four amiable bikers whose Harleys and an Indian and a Moto Guzzi 750 were ranked right outside the front door, and he'd gone out back. At first, he hadn't heard her screaming above the prattling of the flock.

The one at the counter heard Charlie come through the screen door, and swiveled on the counter stool. He had the Pepsi in his mouth. Charlie came at him fast and with the flat of his hand rammed the bottle through the biker's teeth, shoving the neck through the back of his mouth. It came out just above the nape. The man staggered to his feet, clutching his face, and fell backward into the three trying to rape Charlie's wife.

As he fell, he struck the little, half-bald one, the one who had ridden up on the 750 Ambassador. His flailing arms struck the little man, and he stumbled against the tables driving the fish-boning knife into Robin's stomach. Her scream was worse than the ones before.

Charlie grabbed up the cleaver they used to dismember the chickens for the Sunday specials, and came around the counter swinging. In Ranger basic training at Fort Benning they had discovered the hated nickname the kids had concocted on the playground when he was growing up, and they tormented him with its use. They called Charlie Lumschbogen "Charlie Lunchbucket" and he was given an Article 15 punishment for beating up two of his barracks mates.

Charlie Lunchbucket did not stop hacking and dismembering, even after the Smokeys had grabbed him. They had to cold-cock him with their riot sticks to get him to lie still.

Not even the extenuating circumstance of Robin, impaled and almost naked on a checkered tablecloth, saved him from the wrath of the law and order jury. The photographic blowups at the trial were just too grotesque. The walls of the shack had been redecorated like a pointillist canvas.

Widowed, imprisoned, lost to his own life, Charlie Lumschbogen did not do well in prison. He killed a cellmate, he crippled a guard, he assaulted a turnkey. He was reassigned without trial, in this nation in balance, to the maximum security VR wing on the Rock. Life, without possibility of parole, sharing space with other dead sticks of furniture.

"They don't seem particularly unhappy, Warden."

"Well, Senator, that's only because they're in virtual reality. There...that one...he just twitched, did you see that?"

"No, I'm afraid I missed it. What is he in for?"

"Ran a child pornography ring in Utah. Specialized in snuff films. Quite the monster."

"I see he's in there with an art deco credenza."

"Yes, Maples of London. Very nice piece; I'd say about 1934. Once the Department allocates the funds for a proper estate here on the grounds, I'll be moving most of these pieces to proper sites."

"Um. Yes, of course. Well, that pretty much depends on how my report turns out, whether or not the Speaker will recognize the bill."

"Well, I'm certainly hoping you'll think I've done a good job here. It's not easy, you know. No staff, just me and the machines, and a technician or two."

"And you say every one of these men and women is suffering a worse sentence than the old style...where they sat in cells or worked on chain gangs or made license plates?"

"Absolutely, Senator. And may I say, apropos of nothing but my admiration, I think your new hairdo is infinitely more appealing than the way you wore it last time you visited. Makes you look taller."

"If you don't mind, Warden..."

"Oh, yes, sorry. Well, they just float there till they die, but it's in no way 'cruel and unusual punishment' because we do absolutely nothing to them. No corporal punishment, no denial of the basics to sustain life. We just leave them locked in their own heads, cortically tapped to relive one scene from their past, over and over."

"And how is it, again, that you do that...?"

"The technicians call it a moebius memory. Loop thalamic patterning. When they first come in we send them through cerebral indexing, drain out everything they remember, and most of what they don't; and then we codify, integrate, select the one moment from their past that most frightens or horrifies or saddens them. Then, boom, into a null-g cubicle, with a proleptic copula imbedded in their *gliomas*. It's all like a dream. A very very *bad* dream that goes on forever. Punishment to fit the crime."

"We are a nation in balance."

"Kindlier. Gentler. More humane. But still, in need of that large, new house, here on the grounds."

"We'll see, Warden."

Charlie Lunchbucket loved his mother. More than anyone. She had sat beside him night and day through the whooping cough. She made him cinnamon toast for breakfast. She defended him when the third grade teacher said he was incorrigible. He loved his mother.

They had been driving to Ashtabula. The truck had been hauling lumber, and as it passed them, there on the narrow back country road along the river, the back end of the flatbed had swung out, and his mother had swerved to avoid getting sideswiped.

The car had run off the road, over the berm, down the steep embankment, through the brittle woods, and plunged into the river. But only the front end had gone in. Not enough to bring water into the car. Charlie had come to, and it was dark. The roof of the car had collapsed when the trunk of the shattered tree had fallen on them. He tried to move, and could not. He called out for his mother. "Mommy," he called. But there was no answer.

He could not move. Something heavy lay across him, and he was trapped in the corner of the door and the seat.

All that night he lay there, crying, calling for his mother, but she was gone. And when daylight came, he woke, thirsty and hungry and cold and frightened, and as he opened his eyes he was staring into the dead face of his mother, the steering wheel having crushed her chest. She was lying across him, pinning him. He could not move, and he could not look away. He stared into the open eyes and blackened mouth of his mother.

They found the car four days later. It had been August.

It had been stifling. The windows had been rolled up. But the flies had gotten in. They had laid their eggs. And other things had come. When they found the car, Charlie Lunchbucket was out of his head. Eight years old. Worst time of his life.

Floating in a clean white-tiled room, dark and cool. The memory plays and replays and plays yet again, without end, without release. They get what they deserve. We are a nation of laws. We are a compassionate people. We have abolished capital punishment. No one hears, but occasionally the fat bald dying thing in the null-g cubicle whispers *mommy* and, once, in a year some while ago, there was a tear that dried almost immediately. We are a nation in balance.

Scartaris, June 28th

They chased him through the woods and brought him back and lynched him. Their sheets making it awkward to kick him, they used the sawed-off ball bats and a tire iron to bust him up pretty good before they threw the chain over the sweet gum.

They secured the chain around his neck with the tow hook and pulled it so tight the links broke flesh. Then six of them got on the other end of the chain and, calling him a fuckin' nigger-fucker, they gave the chain a sharp, mean yank that sent him jerking so high his head hit the thick branch overhead. They slung the chain around the bole of the sweet gum and looped it fast. Then they stood back and watched.

His pale white face went almost black with mottled patches of trapped blood. His mouth opened and his tongue bulged past his lips. Rafe offered a pack of Marlboros around the group. They all lit up, and Wes Kurlan puffed on his pipe, his hood held loosely in his left hand. Above them there was prolonged jerking and trembling, and they commented on that. Several of them, exhausted from the crashing run through thickets, sat down and breathed deeply. Wes Kurlan inquired with concern about John Porter's condition. John had had a mild stroke only four months ago. John said he felt okay; a little winded; but okay.

They hung around for half an hour.

Then they retraced their steps, back out to the road, stopped to pick up the body of Ansel Lomax, put it gently into the bed of the lead truck, and drove back to town. The wind caught the pants legs of the man on the sweet gum, and he swayed gently, as if from a heavenly breath.

He had been shooting Klansmen with a 30.06 hunting rifle, from the concealment of the woods that ran deep from the edge of the road to the river. He had been working with the Deacons, a militant black group in Alabama, for about three years. He had been sending money for longer than that, but had finally decided he wanted to be involved in a little hands-on activity in aid of equaling the odds.

The Deacons—sharecroppers, furniture factory hands, two postmen, a dentist, and three Viet Nam vets—had discovered, more than twenty years earlier, that the nicest target on a bright night with a full moon was the long, white, stupid sheet worn by a moron standing high on the flatbed of a truck, whooping like a demented night owl and waving a Louisville Slugger over his head. Nice target, perfect target: pale white and clear as a light against the woods.

He had put the crosshairs of the Bushnell scope flat on the center of that peaked white hood, tracked the truck as it passed on the road, and squeezed the trigger of the big game rifle slowly, sending the pencil-thick, three inch long expanding slug on its way. It hit Ansel Lomax in the left cheek with a muzzle energy of 2930 foot-pounds and blew his head apart. His body lofted and went over the side of the truck. Now the hood was black, and filled with bloody soup. He slid eleven feet.

The three Deacons with him had escaped, but he was from Chicago and didn't know his way around scrub growth and mud pits. They chased him through the woods and brought him back and lynched him. Then they drove back to town with what was left of Ansel Lomax.

The white man from Chicago hung in the darkness for two hours, swaying gently in the pleasant northern Alabama breeze.

Then he reached up, grabbed the chain and pulled himself to a point where he could unclip the tow hook. He hung onto the chain for a moment, then dropped the fifteen feet to the muddy ground.

He leaned against the tree for a while, massaging his throat, and then, spitting blood, he turned to look toward the road. After a few minutes he scuffled his way back to the road and walked in the opposite direction the trucks had taken.

In the breeze, the chain clinked against itself, making a small sweet sound in the night.

He was not in Chicago; he was not in northern Alabama. He was in Beloit, Wisconsin. He stared down the dingy, ratty length of Fourth Street, at the bars and men's rooming houses encrusted with the soot and pulp refuse from the Beloit Corporation factory on the other side of the street. The Beloit Corporation was famous: it manufactured paper-making machinery for the world.

The man from northern Alabama had come into town on Highway 57. He had stopped at several bars on the way. In Beloit, they were usually called "lounges," not bars or taps or pubs.

He wandered down Fourth, stopping for a tequila, lime and salt at La Tropicana; a shot of J.D. with a Bud back at the Coconut Grove; an Arrow schnapps at Granny's; and finally came to The Werks. As he came through the door into the blue smoke, he took note that it was a workingman's oasis, and made sure he was wearing a blue chambray shirt, twill pants, and an old, cracked leather bomber jacket with a fur collar against the cold.

He picked out a man in his middle forties sitting alone at the bar working on a bottle of Ten High. As he poured his shot glass to the line from the bottle, the man from northern Alabama saw that the drinker was missing the thumb and little finger of his right hand. He walked to the bar and took the stool beside the drinker. The man looked up only momentarily.

"Hi," the man from northern Alabama said.

The drinker looked up from under thick eyebrows, nodded to the stranger, and mumbled, "Right."

They sat silently for a few minutes till the bartender wiped the mahogany into their area. "What can I get you?" he asked.

"I'll bet you've got a secret bottle of George Dickel down there someplace," the man from northern Alabama said, firing off a winning grin. "Why don't you just bring the bottle and a couple of water glasses for me and my kid brother here. I figure he must have some kinda death wish sittin' here going at that Ten High straight. If you can't put a little good Tennessee sour mash sippin' whiskey into your kid brother, what the hell's it all about, right?"

The stranger beside him had looked up as the words *kid brother* were spoken. And he realized he was, in fact, sitting beside his older brother Vernon, whom he hadn't seen all week because Vern had been on the road with the cartage company van. Now he smiled, and allowed the bartender to remove the bottle and empty shot glass. "You must of got paid."

"Couple of Sonys fell off the loading dock. Carson told me to take 'em, he'd line 'em out as smashed on the invoice. Gave one to Ma and sold th'other one over to Janesville."

Then he made that goofy face that had always made his kid brother laugh when they were growing up.

"So. How's it goin'?"

Vernon shrugged, said, "Ah, you know, the usual. Gettin' tired of driving interstate, though; I'll tell you that, Bobby. Sometimes I just get cranky as hell and begin to think it's never gonna end. You know, workin', drivin', tryin' to forget Bea and the kid."

Bobby nodded. They sat silently. Then, after a while, when the George Dickel had come, and they'd poured generous amounts into the tall water glasses, and were sipping like bluegrass Colonels, Bobby said, "You remember when Pa was workin' in the wet end?" He inclined his head to indicate the big Beloit Corporation factory across the street. "Remember he used to come home some nights and go straight upstairs and lay on down..."

Vern said, "...and put his arm over across his eyes..."

"Yeah, and he'd stay up there till supper, and when he come down he always looked pulled up tight, and he'd say..."

"...did you ever get the feelin' you'd lived too long, past your time, and just wanted to sleep forever?"

Bobby sighed. "That was it."

"Yeah, well, I'm gettin' to feel like that, too," Vern said. They sat silently, working at the secret bottle.

"I got a headache," Bobby said.

"You drink too much."

"Horseshit."

"You do. You drink too much. You're gonna die young, like Pa. They'll take out your liver and send it over to the college for the medical department. Famous example of an organ that ate a man."

Bobby grinned his brother's grin. They looked a lot alike. "Fry it up with onions, real crisp."

"*I* think," Vern said, slapping his hands together, "that what you need is some adventure! Somethin' to sober you up and put a spring in your step, m'boy."

"Hold it, Vern. I'm not goin' on one of your redneck trips. No Alpo contests, no wet-t-shirt bars, no pool cue brawls. Not again. Denise says she'll divorce me I come in torched like that again." He was serious. His hands were out flat in the air between them, a barrier to mischief.

His big brother (and he had no big brother, had been one of four children, the other three girls) laughed and leaned in to hug him. "No, absolutely not! I agree. Nothin' like that. But I got somethin' special. Somethin' I heard over to Janesville."

"Like what?"

"Like, that Nicky Pederakis messed himself up good and finally died. Of diverticulitis."

"Of *what*? What the hell's that?"

"Don't matter. But he didn't go to the doctor for a while, and his bowels got obstructed and a fistula formed, and they operated on his colon, and he died on the table."

"Where the hell did you learn that kind of stuff?" Then he paused and a grim smile froze his lips. "Good. The lousy motherfucker. He used to beat the shit out of me every day back in school."

Vern said softly, "I know."

"So that's good. Goddam it, I outlived the sonofabitch."

Vern laid a hand on Bobby's shoulder. "Come on, we're goin' over to the funeral."

His brother stared at him. After a few seconds he let the lupine smile fade, and his face grew serious. "Yeah."

And they went outside after Vernon had paid for the fine, rare George Dickel, and there was a 1980 Mustang at the curb that hadn't been at the curb when the man from northern Alabama had entered The Werks.

And they got in; and Vernon drove; and they went the twelve miles to Janesville; and Vern turned into the parking lot at a funeral home Bobby didn't know, because it wasn't the one that had handled Pa's service; and they got out and went inside.

There was a ribbed black velvet directory board on a slim tubular steel stand in the foyer. Small, tasteful plastic letters and arrows had been pressed into the ribbing indicating that the Kessler service was in Parlor A and the Pederakis service was in Parlor C, the former to the left, the latter to the right.

Vernon and Bobby walked slowly toward Parlor C. There was a line of people entering the room, a dark-suited employee of the funeral home, wearing a pink carnation in his lapel, holding the door open so visitors would not get hit by the door. He smiled bravely at Bobby and Vernon, who smiled back as bravely. They got in at the end of the line, and moved slowly forward.

When they had paced the length of the aisle, after twenty minutes, they came at last to the front of the parlor and found themselves looking down into the placid face of Nicky Pederakis, a dead man no longer in his middle forties, but rather his final forties. Life had not dealt sweetly with Nicky Pederakis. Despite the refurbishment of funerary cosmeticians, or perhaps in part *because* of their attentions, he looked like a cross between someone who had had his kisser regularly bashed in barroom encounters, and one of a thousand clowns exploding from a tiny car in a center ring.

Bobby stood looking.

Vern watched the family. Two men in cheap black suits, their faces younger stampings of the death mask now worn by Nicky Pederakis, were pointing at Bobby and whispering agitatedly. They separated and turned to the people on either side. They whispered much louder now, jerking their thumbs over their shoulders to indicate Bobby, still staring raptly into the open casket, leaning over with his hands on the anodized pastel blue metal lid panel. He seemed unable to get close enough.

"Hey!" One of the younger Pederakis boys was pointing at Bobby. "Who the hell are you?"

The room went silent. The knots of visitors humming condolences opened, everyone stopped talking, and they stared first at the pointing finger, then at Bobby.

It took a moment for the silence to register on Bobby, and when he looked up, still leaning over the open section at Nicky's face, he saw the room's attention on him. He stood up. Vern moved closer. "You know me," he said to the family.

"Yeah, I know you," the other brother said, almost snarling. "You're that creep Nicky used to kick ass alla time. What the hell you doing here? Nicky hated your guts."

"Just wanted to make sure the cocksucker was really dead," Bobby said, moving fast toward the side door exit. Vern was right behind him.

They got halfway through the first open row of chairs before the brothers and their friends exploded across the neat rows, knocking chairs in all directions. The one who had done the pointing caught up with Vern, reached out and snagged the collar of the bomber jacket. Vern pivoted and hit him in the throat. The brother fell back gasping, into the crowd, and Vern picked up a folding chair and smashed him in the head with it. Bobby grabbed Vern by the arm and pulled him through the exit door he'd pushed open. He was screaming, "The lousy bully got what was comin' to him! I hope he suffered like a dyin' shit, an' he's goin' straight to Hell!"

Then they were in the side-hall and Vernon grabbed a plush chair and wedged it under the doorknob and they ran like crazy men out the back entrance of the funeral home, got to the Mustang, and left skid marks exiting the parking lot.

When Vern dropped his kid brother off at the house, he leaned out the window and said to Bobby, "Maybe there's still some good stuff to get, bein' alive! Whaddaya think, Bobby?"

His brother leaned in and kissed the man from northern Alabama on the lips, grinned hugely, and whooped. "Better high off that goddam minute starin' at that sonofabitch croaked in his fuckin' baby-blue coffin than all the whiskey in the world!"

"Remember that," the man from northern Alabama said, and drove away into the night, knowing that if there was a memory that would last, it would be of the lesson in the moment; not of an older brother who had never existed.

Across the aisle an elderly black couple, deep into their fifties, were trying to spoon-feed their mentally impaired daughter. To the man from Beloit she appeared to be in her middle thirties. He tried to ignore the General Six Principle Baptist minister in the middle seat beside him, apparently a vegetarian or simply finicky beyond belief, who kept trying to give him foodstuffs off his flight tray. "Are you sure you wouldn't like this nice bit of roast beef?" the Reverend Carl Schrag said. "I haven't touched it. Here, you can take it with your own fork if you're concerned."

The man from Beloit turned away from the sight of creamed asparagus drooling from the side of the girl's mouth, to smile at the minister. "No, thank you very much. I have the fish. I don't eat meat."

The minister's face lit with camaraderie. "I agree absolutely completely! Flesh of the beast. Poor things. Stand all day and all night in tiny cubicles, in the dark, just fattened and fattened, all their color leached out, till they're slaughtered."

"Just like the women in the whorehouses in Kuwait," the man from Beloit said, noticing with impish pleasure the look of the affronted, the look of the doltish, the look of the utterly appalled that blasted the minister's composure.

"What did you say?!" he demanded, fork trembling an inch from his mouth, speared baby carrots now forgotten.

"Oh, I'm awfully sorry," the man from Beloit said, "I *certainly* didn't mean to offend. It's just that the hideous parallel you drew...but perhaps you're unaware of the slave trade in white women that continues to this very day in many of the southeast Arabian sultanates..."

The minister's eyes rolled in his head. He had lost control of his motor functions. The man from Beloit reached over and gently pressed Carl Schrag's wrist. The minister's hand, bearing fork, slowly lowered. Transfixed, he simply stared.

The man from Beloit continued eating, and continued talking. "Yes, you see, slave-holding is still practiced in Saudi Arabia, Yemen, Oman, Muscat, Buraimi, Kuwait, even Ethiopia. Oh, of course, in some of those places the practice has been legally and publicly abolished, yet in most of them the slaves have never been freed. In most of them, slave-buying, selling, holding, whipping, violating—perfectly acceptable by local law. Your food is getting cold."

The minister took a mouthful, continued to stare disbelievingly, like a bumblebee at the end of an entomologist's straight pin. What was this man *saying* to him!

Across the aisle, the young woman was trying to wrest the spoon from her father's hand. The elderly black mother wore an expression of stunned acceptance. They had been at this chore for at least half of their lives. The man from Beloit recognized the slope of shoulders, the caring and determination and futility in eyes and expressions, the practiced maneuverings of hands and implements around flailing body.

"But for the harems and brothels of these countries," he said to the minister, though still watching the people across the aisle, "Western women are highly prized. Blondes, redheads, Nordic types with incredibly long legs and blue eyes like cool fjords. Some of them are lured to the Middle East through ads in newspapers, *Variety*, that sort of thing. You know, 'Wanted: Dancers and Showgirls for chorus lines in Road Shows. See far places, high pay, exotic companions,' that sort of thing. And they just vanish. Or they're kidnapped right off the streets in European cities, often Marseilles. Next time you see them they're at a slave auction in Yemen."

The minister was gasping. "Why, I've never heard of such—"

"Oh, yes, absolutely," the man from Beloit said. "*Very* common. And many of them are sold into these harems, or dens of sexual fleshliness, where they're kept in pitch-black cells on soft mattresses, and they're fed a lot of carbohydrates to fatten them up—apparently these Arab potentates lust after pale pale suety vessels for their disgusting pleasures."

Rev. Schrag had gone the color of his glass of milk.

"And once they're kidnapped, well, that's it," the man from Beloit said, as he finished his fish in sauce. "We have almost no extradition recourse in such places; and the United States government, well, you can forget it; they can't chance offending one of those oil barons. You can imagine what value they place on some nameless eighteen-year-old farm girl from Iowa, stolen while visiting Berlin, as against the cost at the pump of higher gas tariffs."

He wiped his mouth, took the last sip of coffee light, and smiled sadly at the minister. "So you see, it was the awful parallel you drew with the roast beef." Rev. Schrag was bereft of response. "And what takes you so far from home, I presume you're going on somewhere after Paris?"

They were on a jet liner out of New York, bound for Paris, with connections to Jeddah, Riyadh, Cairo and Dubai.

Across the aisle, the girl in her middle thirties was mumbling to herself, playing with her hair and trying to figure out the swing latch that lowered the tray table. Her mother was looking out the port; her father was trying to mop up baby food from the seat and the girl's dress.

The minister was having difficulty righting himself. This man in the aisle seat beside him *seemed* to be spiritually kin, but in the name of Jesus what horrible obscenities! He tried to convince himself that it had been innocently spoken; he was always willing to give the benefit of the doubt. The man was very likely unsaved, but if we were to cut off all social congress with the less-than-righteous, why, we'd never be able to snag *anyone* from Satan's claws. He mustered a smile and replied, "I'm going to the Holy Land. I had several weeks I could have taken anywhere and, well, I've been meaning to do this journey for so long..."

"I understand perfectly," the man from Beloit said. "And where are you from? Where is your parish?"

"Senatobia, Mississippi," the minister said.

"Ah!" the man from Beloit said, with familiarity.

"Do you know it?" the minister asked, pleased now that he had given him the benefit of the doubt.

"Northwestern part of the state? Between Memphis and Oxford? Near Lake Arkabutla, isn't it?"

"Why, yes! You *do* know our little place!"

"No, sorry," the man from Beloit said, unbuckling his lap belt and standing. "Senatobia. Must be very small." He turned and went aft to the lavatory.

When he came back, ten minutes later, he walked past his row, noticing that Rev. Schrag was trying to work the crossword puzzle in the airline giveaway magazine, and he stood in the service alcove as the stewardesses racked and sent below the used dinner trays. He stood there and pretended to be selecting a magazine from the rack, but he studied the elderly couple and their child.

They had hooked her up with a Walkman, the earphones tied with a ribbon under her chin so she could not inadvertently knock the little gray foam earpieces loose. She was rocking back and forth, licking her lips, her eyes closed. Her mother and father were trying to complete their own meals, the food long since grown cold. He watched them and felt a great sadness take him. After a while, he returned to his seat.

Carl Schrag looked up as the man from Beloit buckled in. "That was in very poor taste, sir," he said. Stiffly.

"I agree," was the reply. "But let me ask you something. Just as a matter of theoretical surmise."

The minister closed the inflight magazine on his prolapsed tray-table, marking the crossword's location with his ballpoint pen. He sighed with resignation, turned halfway in his seat, and fixed his traveling companion with a look that had often commended rectitude to his parishioners. "Yes, and what would that be?"

"You believe in God, no doubt," he said.

"Are you serious?"

"Yes, yes, of course. I ask that only as a point of departure. I can see you're a man of the cloth, and so I know the answer is yes. But what I want to ask you is about gods, other gods, not God as *we* know Him."

"There is but *one* God, and His Son."

"Yes, I understand; and I agree absolutely. But let us for a moment consider those poor, benighted helots of heathen beliefs. Egyptians who believed in Ptah and Thoth and Amon; Mayas who worshipped Pepeu and Raxa Caculhá, the Thunderbolt; Vikings with their Odin and Loki and the rest; the Yellow River peoples and Kuan Ti, the god of war, and Kuan Yin, goddess of mercy; Altijira and Legba and Kwatee and Kronos. Gods, all of them. Strong gods, personable gods, effective gods. What about them? What do we do with them, now that their times are gone?"

Rev. Schrag stared at him evenly. He was on firm footing now. "I have no idea what you're talking about, sir. As I said: there is but one God, and Jehovah is His name; and His only begotten Son, Jesus Christ, our Savior. All the rest of this is primitive demonology, cheap superstition. Pagan idolatry."

"Yes, of course," he said, reaching into the aisle to retrieve and hand back to the elderly black man the soft, frayed "blankie" his daughter had thrown to the industrial-strength carpet. "But let me have the benefit of your thinking on this, as a theologian, as a man of God who's pondered about such things. I need, well, some guidance here; some clear thinking, if you get my meaning.

"Take, for instance, the transition from Græco-Roman polytheism to medieval Christianity. When we read of this momentous watershed in the history of the Western World, there is such a smug sense of *triumph*, whether we encounter it in Christian historians like Eusebius of Cæsarea or Christian apologists such as Augustine, who got sainted for being a flack for Jesus—"

Rev. Schrag's eyes popped open, he tried to speak, coughed; he made inarticulate sounds; he foundered on a sound that was the fuh-fuh-fuh beginning of *flack*; and the man from Beloit made small of his abashed behavior, dismissing it with an impatient flutter of his hand and by continuing in the same tone: "We're men of the world here; we needn't pussyfoot around it. Augustine was nothing more nor less than a p.r. man for the politics of orthodoxy. These days, the belief that the elevation of Christianity to the position of an official state religion, instantly embraced, brooking no competition, was total, complete, immediate...well, it's monolithic. But it wasn't, as I understand it. I mean, even as late as 385, the emperor Theodosius was having a rough time interdicting belief in the pantheon of gods—"

His words had been coming so fast, so smoothly, that only now was the Rev. Schrag able to *interdict* the rococo syntax.

"Paganism! That's all it was! Ignorant savages sloughing through darkness toward the light of Jesus Christ!"

"Ah, yes certainly, no question about it, I agree absolutely wholeheartedly," the man from Beloit said, slicing through the minister's fustian so coolly it was as if Schrag had taken a breath mint rather than having popped his eyeballs. "But you see how driven you are to use the word 'paganism'? Which was not, at least in the first instance, a concept that the 'pagans' applied to themselves, but one that evolved as a way of distinguishing the non-Christian survivals after the gradual Christianization of the Roman Empire under Emperor Constantine and subsequent..."

"These were *barbarians*...barely able to tie their shoelaces...they painted their fundaments blue and ripped out each other's hearts and danced around campfires naked and ate each other's entrails...pagans...bar-*bare*-ians!" His voice had spiraled to a level that was drawing attention from other passengers. The man from Beloit smiled awkwardly at the elderly black man across the aisle, but his attention could be held only an instant: his daughter was singsonging, over and over, "Ma'y tinkle, ma'y tinkle, ma'y tinkle."

He turned back to Rev. Schrag and said, "Well, there is *certainly* no condoning such behavior, particularly the part about painting their asses blue, but when you call them barbarians, I'm not sure you're aware of all the facts."

"Whuh-*what* facts?"

"Well, for instance, archaeologists working in Peru at sites such as Pampa de las Llamas-Moxeke and Sechin Alto, ten thousand freezing feet above sea level in the Andes, have found a culture that predates the Mayas by 2000 years and the Aztecs by 3000 years.

"Huge U-shaped temples ten storeys high; an enormous warehouse, bigger than a baseball field, it served as a food storage complex; the buildings gorgeously decorated with painted friezes of jaguars, spiders, serpents." He leaned in and whispered, "Their vivid colors preserved intact by the dry cold of the Andean atmosphere. Why do you think they would settle at that altitude, build a sophisticated civilization at the same time the Egyptians were building pyramids and the Sumerian city-states were flourishing, in such a grossly hostile region?

"Perhaps to get closer to the gods they deified? Do you think that's possible? What do you think about that, dropping the 'paganism' business, ass-painting notwithstanding? What do you think?"

"Will you *kindly* stop saying that!"

"Which part of it, the *paganism*?"

"No, the other."

"Oh, you mean the part about how they painted—"

"Yes! Yes, that's the part."

"Well, I don't mean to be contumacious, Reverend, but *I* was discussing alternative deities; it was you who brought up how they..."

Rev. Schrag crashed back into the conversation. "There never were any such deities," he said quickly. "Until the True Word was revealed, pag—uh, heathens believed many strange and impossible things."

"Mmm, I see. So we can assume that such 'heathen' martyrs as Hypatia of Alexandria died for nothing. But let me ask you this—" and he sneaked a glance across the aisle where preparations to ma'y tinkle were proceeding apace, "—what if you were one such as these, one of these obsolete gods. And all your believers were gone, all the Hypatias had been properly stoned to death by good Christians, no more worshippers, except perhaps a random diabolist here and there, corrupt individuals trying to bring you back so you could pick winning lottery tickets for them. What do you do then?"

Stiffly, Schrag said, "I have no conjecture on that, sir."

"No idea at all?"

"None."

"You don't think maybe Hera went off in a snit and took to drinking too much mead and became a bitchy alcoholic?"

"Don't be ridiculous!"

"Maybe Jizo sank into a funk and contemplated hara-kiri?"

"Who did what?"

"So let me get this straight. What you're saying is that you don't think maybe possibly Jupiter just kept right on existing after Constantine bullied all the Romans into converting, and after a while with nobody praying to him, not even one daub of blue paint on a backside, he just got bored with it all and, say, just put a pistol up to his Olympian forehead and blew his beatific brains out?"

The minister stared at him, growing angrier by the moment. Then he settled himself facing stiffly forward, took up the magazine, opened it, and went back to the crossword puzzle.

"Sixteen down," the man from Beloit said idly, "an eight-letter word for 'neutral': *middling.*"

The minister said nothing; and he did not look up as the man from Beloit unbuckled and rose, following the elderly black man as he aided his daughter toward the rear of the plane, and the lavatories.

He waited as the father spoke softly to the girl, saying, "Now you go on in an' make tinkle, Evelyn. You know. The way you do. That's a sweet child." And he opened the door for her, saying, "Now don't touch the door, don't mess with the lock, just go in an' make tinkle, all right? I'll be right here."

She went in, and he closed the door, turning to smile awkwardly at the man waiting behind him for the cubicle next in the row.

The man from Beloit sidled past, entered the lavatory that shared a bulkhead with the cubicle in which Evelyn was slowly and carefully pulling down her panties, then the absorbent cotton incontinence liner. He closed his eyes for a moment, made a small sound, and then reached through the bulkhead to touch Evelyn's head. She closed her eyes.

"Sleep, good child. They love you so. Their time is so short. Let them live." And he formed the aneurism, and he made it explode, and she made a gentle sound, and fell.

He flushed the toilet, left the cubicle, and edged past the open door of the next stall, where the elderly black man was kneeling half in the aisle, calling to his daughter.

He returned to his seat. The mother gave a start as one of the stewardesses from the rear leaned in to speak quietly to her. In a panic, she tried to get out of her seat, found herself still buckled, pulled and pulled at the device till the stewardess helped her, and then they rushed back up the aisle.

The man from Beloit closed his eyes and feigned sleep. He didn't think there would be conversation with the Reverend Carl Schrag before they landed at De Gaulle, but he wanted to repose in privacy and darkness for a time. Repose and think clearly of the moment of relief that would come to the old people before they began to deal with their grief.

The sky was very clear, and far below the clouds went on their way.

The man from the jet liner stood on the edge of the cliffs, staring out past Thásos, across the Aegean. "Levendis," he murmured. "Levendis." He sighed deeply, plucked three pebbles from the ground, and hurled them into the sky. They flew up toward the sun, spreading their wings for a moment, white herons that formed an ancient design with their flying forms; then in an instant they rolled and dove, feathered shafts that struck the water, pierced the sea and vanished, plummeting toward the distant floor littered with broken stones. Enormous broken stones. Cyclopean blocks bearing praises to a god whose name had not been spoken on this earth since the long night of hungry waters that had wiped an entire civilization from the land, and from memory. Intricately-carved broken stones now merely accretions of limestone, barnacles and anemones, acrawl with crustaceans and small, blind fish. Softened shapes of fractured statues hundreds of meters in height when they had stood against the sky, before the night of ash and flame. The pulverized Great Temple in which the sacred ethmoid crystals had been kept. Down and down the heron shafts went, into a darkness never suspected, much less penetrated. They went to wreckage.

In anguish, he called out across the water; but the wind died and the day was silent; and all who might have heard would not understand the tongue in which he spoke, for it had not been spoken in thousands of years.

"Stranger, can I soften your pain?"

The man from the jet liner turned at the sound of the voice behind him. It was an old man, as blind as the fish that swam among a million mosaic tiles.

"Did you see that?" the man from the jet liner asked.

"Did I see you throw pebbles into the air?"

"You did see, then."

"No. I *see* nothing. I heard them click in your hands. I heard them as you threw them. You aren't Greek, are you?"

"No. Not Greek."

"Where are you from, stranger?"

"From a land that no longer exists."

"You sound lonely."

"I was lonely, for a long time."

"For your people?"

"Yes. But they're gone, and I haven't heard my name spoken for much too long. And why are *you* here, sir? What brings you to this empty place?"

"I come here to worship."

The man from the jet liner drew a deep breath. "What god do you worship here? Nothing ever stood here."

"Not here. Out there." He waved a hand toward the sea, and beyond to the greater ocean. "I hear the voices of the children of Poseidon."

"They were not Poseidon's disciples. You hear the lamentations of an older race. Nobler and more accomplished than any other. They never had the time to claim their inheritance."

The old man laughed lightly. "So you say."

"There were worlds and lands and peoples..."

"I think you are dreaming dreams that make you an empty man," he said. "Perhaps you should return to your homeland, no matter what name it now bears. Home is where you go when there is no place else to go. You can know it again through the words of your poets."

"No poets wrote of my land. Plato had a few words...but I gave him those words. If I go home, it will only be to sleep." He paused, and added, "To rest."

The old man spoke softly. "Too much rest is rust."

"Why did you think I might be Greek?"

"Because you knew our word, *levendis*. But I was wrong."

On the Bahnhofstrasse, amid crowds entering and exiting the five-level "everything store" called Jelmoli's, Zürich's answer to an American department store with a basement storey of drugs and groceries, the man from Greece, hurrying to the Icelandic Airlines ticket office, bumped into Gwen Fritcher, a Californian on detached duty with IBM's Swiss affiliate.

She had gone to Jelmoli's to get a few cans of American product—Dennison's chili, Campbell's tomato soup, Durkee's french fried onion rings, Pringles—because she was certain that one more meal of schnitzel, spaetzle and cabbage, submersed in sauce as appetizing as Elmer's Glue, would send her over the brink. She had begun having fever dreams, as sultry as sexual fantasies, herself entwined with packages of Nabisco ginger snaps and (shamefully) Spaghetti-Os.

She was also having terrible menstrual cramps, and there had been literally a crying need for Panadol.

When he blindsided her, and the bag of groceries rocketed from her grasp, she gave a small croak of despair. "Hey, I'm awfully sorry," the man from Greece said, stooping to retrieve the still-rolling cans. "Oh, really, I'm sorry...I wasn't watching where I was going...the crowd, you know..."

They gathered everything, repacked it, and stood. He smiled his best smile, and she looked embarrassed at even having thought the things she'd thought. "American?" she asked.

"Once upon a time," he said. And added, "I really am sorry I'm such a klutz." And he touched her forearm, and smiled again, and said, "I'll be more careful." And he strode away into the crowd.

Gwen returned to the tiny apartment IBM had secured for her. The company suites were all filled, and they had taken a three month lease on this little flat, in hopes she would have completed her transference survey by that time or, failing that recourse, would be able to move her into a company-owned residence.

She set the bag of groceries on the kitchen counter, fished around till she found the small plastic-wrapped box of Panadol, and carried it into the bathroom.

With a fingernail, she slit the price tag and bar code sealing the Panadol box, and tore off the protective plastic wrap with some difficulty, fumbling interminably and cursing the mythical children who were thus guaranteed all protection against taking too much menses medicine. She finally got the box open and dumped out the two sheets of caps, each shrouded in a plastic bubble.

There was a folded slip of paper between the sheets. She laid it aside, pressed the back of one of the plastic bubbles, and popped out a capsule, then repeated the maneuver. She took her toothbrush from the water glass, ran it half full, swished the water, poured it out, refilled the glass halfway, and took the two Panadol.

She sat on the closed toilet, letting the analgesic start to do its work, smoothing the waves of pain. She thought for just an instant of the attractive man who had bumped into her on the Bahnhofstrasse. Idly, she picked up the piece of paper that had been folded inside the plastic-wrapped box. She opened it and looked at it, expecting an advertisement in at least three languages. Hand-printed in pencil on the slip of white paper were the words

YOU'LL BE DEAD BY MORNING, GWEN.

For no good reason, because this was clearly some kind of stupid thing that might have to do with an idiotic advertising campaign, she felt her heart thump heavily. She was, in an instant, and inexplicably, terribly frightened.

She dropped the note as if it had come from enemies.

There was a knock on the apartment door, and then the doorbell rang twice. She sat where she was. Thinking through the fear.

She was an employee of a multinational corporation. Could this have something to do with international terrorism? Had they somehow tapped into the computer, run the personnel records and selected her at random? She knew it couldn't be personal. She had been in Zürich only three weeks. She knew almost no one. Was there, on the other side of that door, a pair of ski-masked and black-suited kneecappers from the Red Army Faction or the IRA? Beneath their masks a young man and woman, pockmarked skin, anthracite eyes, teeth in need of polishing, sworn angels of death sent by Carlos or Abu Nidal?

The doorbell chimed.

A spurned lover. Someone she'd known in New York, during that crazy summer before AIDS came to the world, when she was answering personals in *New York* magazine? One of the more than a few men she had seen in the nude? The one she had laughed at, had been forced to use a kitchen knife to hold off till she could gather up her clothes and flee? Traced her, followed her, come to quench some psychopathic thirst for revenge?

A voice called from the other side of the door.

"*Fräulein*, Miss, Lady..."

She went to the door, put her ear against it. No sound. Finally, she said, "Yes, who is it?" And then she quickly stepped to the side, in case the serial killer fired through the door, or cleaved the center panel with a fire ax.

"*Ah! Guten Morgen, Fräulein Fritcher...ich bin der...*"

"I don't speak German! Who are you? Speak English, please; I speak only English!" She heard the panic in her own voice.

"Ah! *Ja. Ich,* uh, that isz, *I*...yes, *I* am the taking-care-of man. *Nein*...vhat isz that I mean...I am *der* superviszer...*der* super*intend*ent, *ja, das ist*...yes, I am *der*janitor!" There was a note of almost desperate relief in his voice as he found the correct word.

And she listened as the crazed silk-stocking strangler advised her that the incinerator in the hall had gone *geflunkt* or some similar word, and that it would not be available for trash and paper dumping till after six that evening. Then he went away.

Gwen wandered back to the kitchen, certain now that there could have been no way in which such a message could have found its way into that sealed box. Not at the factory, not in the grocery, not any way at all. There had been no signs of tampering, no pinholes, inviolate, untouched.

Yet the message had been there, and she knew, now, that it had been supernatural creatures. Beings from the other side, the souls of those she had done harm in her previous lives. They were warning her, and there was no escape. By morning, she would be dead.

She sat at the kitchen table and began to cry.

I haven't lived nearly long enough, she thought. *And I'm on the management track.*

She reached across to the counter and pulled down the thick cylinder of Pringles, husking breath so deeply that her chest hurt; and she pulled the plastic strip from the container, popped off the metal lid, and took out a potato chip. It didn't help at all, not even the taste of the world and the life she had left behind. She thought hopelessly that she didn't want to die in a foreign land. She ate another Pringle.

Lying atop the third chip, nested perfectly with the other slim forms, was a slip of folded paper. She opened it with utter terror consuming her, and read

IGNORE PREVIOUS MESSAGE.

She received only two pieces of mail that day in the IBM courier pouch from New York. One was an announcement of Nancy Kimmler's shower two weeks hence. The other was contained in a plain white envelope with no return address, and the single sheet of neatly-typed message was this: "The life which is unexamined is not worth living." Beneath, were two words in pencil: *Plato* and *bang.*

He stood now, the man from Zürich, where he had never set foot before. He had rented a car in Reykjavík two days earlier, the 26th, and driven to Búdhir where he had taken a room and given sight to a man blind from birth. In truth, he hadn't needed a car; no more than he had needed a castle, a brigantine, an arbalest, a flatbed truck, a 451-barrel Vandenberg Volley Gun, an ethmoid crystal, a 1980 Mustang, or an Icelandic Airlines DC-8 Zürich-Reykjavík. No more than he had needed special equipment to breathe the water of the Aegean, centuries before it had borne that name.

But he had wanted to see the riot of colors, the ecstasy of moss growing in volcanic cinders deposited by the eruption of Mount Hekla in 1970 along a rivulet on the edge of Thjórsárdalur; he had wanted to go *as a man,* to stand before the black ash cliff at Langahlidh and marvel at the tenacity of the exquisite, delicate white flowers that grew toward the light from inhospitable fissures. He wanted to have the time before the kalends of July to contemplate how long, how far he had wandered; to think back to what had been and what was now; to reconcile himself to the end of the journey.

He had come much farther than from Chicago or northern Alabama, Quito or Sydney, Damascus or Lioazhong or Lagos on the Slave Coast. He had been far afield, traveling through immense lightless distances; pausing to pass the time with a telepathically garrulous plant-creature; spending time unmeasurable observing hive-arachnids as they slowly mutated and grew toward sentience and the use of tools; taking a hand in the development of a complex henotic social system that united water and fish and the aquicludes that had ruled as autarchs since the silver moon had fractured to form Murus, Phurus and Veing. He had returned, weary beyond the telling, having seen it all, having done it all, come full circle through miracles, wandering, loneliness and loss.

There had been centuries of despair, followed by centuries of acrimony and deeds too awful to recall without unbearable pain and guilt; centuries of sybaritic indulgence, followed by centuries of cataclysmic ennui; and finally, centuries and years and days reduced to odd moments now and then, of wonderful, random, unpredictable kindness. That were no more satisfying or lasting than all the acts of all the centuries that had preceded them.

He was alone. Since the long, terrible night of ashes and screams, and the closing over of the waters, he had been alone. There were, of course, diabolists and fools who believed; but their belief was the product of insanity or delusion. No descendant of those who had come to the Great Temple walked this world.

Nowhere was there to be found a true believer.

And at last he had come to know that he must return, to the place that had brought him to existence, and there he must go down alone to find eternal rest. He could wander no longer. He simply didn't have it in him to continue.

So he had come by way of Reykjavík and Næfurholt and Brún, in a great circle across the island of volcanoes, as June came to an end, the last June he would ever see. Came, at last, to stand here on Sunday the 28th, the last day but two of the month, with a sudden change of wind and a new moon that had brought salutary weather, the sun pouring its beaming rays to the very bottom of the crater.

Snæfellsjökull.

In Icelandic, all volcanoes bear the name of Yocul, and it means glacier, for in the lofty mountains of that region the volcanic eruptions come forth from icebound caverns. Snæffels means snow mountain. There it towers on the western peninsula, and can be seen from Reykjavík, a great urban capital of the sophisticated modern world. Even in Reykjavík the mountain is known to possess great power, some say psychic power.

He stood on the edge of the crater and smiled. Not even in Reykjavík, where they could feel the power, could they guess the enormity of Snæfellsjökull's secret. To a height of five thousand feet.

In Sneffels Yoculis craterem, he thought, in dog Latin, *kem delibat umbra Scartaris Julii intra calendas descende, audus viator, et terrestre centrum attinges.*

He laughed lightly, and the metallic wind picked at his clothing, ruffled his ash-gray hair. Would anyone recognize those words without the fictional lines the writer had added for the story's benefit? *Kod feci. Arne Saknussemm.*

Above him the blind spire of Mount Scartaris, black as the eclipse on that night of screaming stones and hungry water, rose in expectation of the movement of the sun. Waiting. Poised to aim its finger of shadow across the thighbone peninsula, passing across the fjord, swinging fast to cancel the flood of sunlight pouring into the center of the crater.

Snæffels had been quiet since 1219. He remembered now, with another small smile, how it had been that the writer had come to expose the secret—while concealing it the more in tall tale—and he could see, even now, the face of the Franciscan monk as the words burned themselves into the illuminated manuscript as he sat with quill poised. That had been during one of the centuries of antic foolishness for him.

Each hillock, every rock, every stone, every asperity of the soil had its share of the luminous effulgence, and the shadow of Scartaris fell heavily on the soil. The shadow of the spike that penetrated the sky was marked and clear, and moved rapidly as high noon approached.

He watched with the first genuine tickle of anticipation he had felt in a dozen millennia. The shadow slid, roiled, faster and faster, and the sun came to rest with a gasp at its highest point, and the shadow fell upon the edge of the central pit in the heart of the crater. It rushed down the wall, across the caldera, and ink poured over the edge of the central pit in the heart of Snæffels. Forsaking all others, the shadow of Scartaris formed the road sign he had come across eternities to read.

Descend into the crater of Yocul of Snæffels, which the shade of Scartaris caresses, before the kalends of July, audacious traveler, and you will reach the center of the earth. I did it. Arne Saknussemm.

He went down into the crater and stood at the lip of the central pit. It measured about a hundred feet in diameter, three hundred in circumference. This tremendous, wondrous shaft, its sides almost as perpendicular as those of a well, a terrifying abyss more than eight hundred and fifty meters deep, which had come to be called Saknussemm's Chimney by those who had been fooled through the writer's misunderstanding of words in an ancient manuscript that had been manipulated under his gaze.

The time was ended for tricks and make-work.

Even gods can learn. Given enough time.

Even gods forgotten, gods without disciples, gods whose times and lands had vanished before memory had formed in those who had come to claim the world.

He stepped into the shadow, leaving sunlight for the last time, and began his descent. There was only one answer to what a god can do when everything has been taken from him; and he knew at last what that answer was. Not sleep, not immolation, not descent into final darkness, never to emerge. No, the answer lay beneath him: to *recreate*. To *reify*. To cause it all to come again, stronger and mightier and more golden than it had been when chance and disaster had wiped it away.

And one day not that far off, perhaps only a few centuries hence, *his* people would arise, bringing with them a certain inheritance all others had debased. As they had long ago created him, now he would *re-create* them.

And on that day they would go once more to the Great Temple, to sing his name, and to thank him for growing bored and foolish and for trivializing himself with the lives of those now vanished and themselves turned to myth.

But he would keep the name of the place, and the moment in which he had learned. Scartaris, June 28th.

She's A Young Thing And Cannot Leave Her Mother

This morning I woke to the infinitely sweet, yet lonely sound of *Clair de Lune* coming to me through closed windows, upstairs in a high-ceilinged suite of this century-old hotel; in a land that is not my own. I lay in bed and at first thought I was still in the dream: it was so ethereal and melancholy. Then I heard Camilla stir, where she lay wrapped in blankets on the floor, and I knew the dream was past. The bed had been too soft for her, an old fluffy mattress with a gully down the middle. She had chosen to sleep beyond the foot of the bed.

I lay there and listened to the music, trying to snare just a wisp, even a scintilla, of the dream. It was the memory of something I was certain I'd lost among the ruins of the years that lay strewn behind me. Years in which Camilla and I had fled from place to place, neither citizens of a certain land nor citizens of the world: simply refugees whose most prominent baggage was fear. Years that bore our footprints on their every hour. Years like a pale golden desert stretching back and back, on the side of me that has no eyes; a desert in which lay items from my life's rucksack: items that I had jettisoned so I could continue walking. Because there was no possibility of ending the flight.

I had untied those items and dropped them to lighten my load, because the flight had grown ever more arduous: the walking through years...the caretakership of the woman I loved.

Like a wanderer without water, or a soldier separated from his companions, I moved forward with her minute by minute, discarding casual acquaintances and toys I had outgrown; names and faces of people with whom we had briefly traveled; the taste of candy no longer manufactured and songs no longer sung; books I had read simply because they had been at hand when there was time to be filled waiting for a train; all dropped in the shifting sand and quickly covered by time, and all that I retained, all that sustained me, was this love we shared, and the fear we shared.

As far as the eye could see, on that side of me without eyes, empty vessels and odd items of clothing lay vanishing in the golden sand, marking our passage, Camilla's and mine.

And one of those memories I had once held dear bore resonance with the strains of Debussy floating up to me in the cool ambiance of the nascent morning. I lay there in the old bed's gully, Camilla stirring on her pallet, and tried to remember what I wanted to reclaim from the desert. But without eyes on that side facing toward yesterday, looking out across the golden sands of all those years...I could not call it back.

It was the music no one was playing that I had heard at Stonehenge, ten years ago. It was the sound of the pan pipes at Hanging Rock thirteen years ago, and the notes of a flute from the other side of the Valley of the Stonebow eight years ago. I had heard that recollection in a cave in the foothills overlooking the Fairchild Desert and, once, I heard it drifting through a misty downpour in the Sikkim rainforest.

The dream abandoned, I have never been able to unearth the greater substance of that memory. And each time it floats back to me—like the remembrance of an aunt I had adored, who died long long ago, with me again for just an instant in the sweet scent of perfume worn by a passing woman on a city street—I am filled with a sense of loss and helplessness. And not even Camilla can damp the sorrow.

I lay there, knowing it was no dream, weak and without resources, dreading the day to come, afraid to leave the safe gully of the bed, once more to shoulder the remaining gear of my life; for another terrible day in the endless flight.

Then *Clair de Lune* was interrupted by three warm, mellifluous tones—B, F Sharp, D Sharp—and, distantly, as if rising from within a crystal palace in a lost city on a sunken continent, I heard a woman's voice announcing the departure of a train to Edinburgh; resonating through the domed vastness of Glasgow's Central Station; drifting up to me in my bed in the Central Hotel built above the terminal; the murky glass dome lying just two storeys below my window; forming a postcard depiction of the Great Bubble of the Capital City of Lost Atlantis. If such a place ever existed, it would have looked that way. And if it had ever existed, it could have had no more magical presence than through the strains of Debussy.

Clair de Lune resumed, I sighed, threw back the covers, swung my feet out onto the cold floor, and resumed the walk that was a flight that was the remainder of my time that was my life, on the desert littered with my past.

I tried not to think about what might happen today, and went to the walk-in clothes closet, and took down the brown satchel with the flensing equipment in it. Then I selected something slim and sharp, and dutifully scraped the encrusted material that had accumulated during the night, off the body of the woman I loved.

Out there in Atlantis, *Clair de Lune* died away.

One would think history could never forget them, Sawney and all the rest of them. But not even the great library in Edinburgh had more than vague and cursory references. Nothing in Christie's history of Scotland, nothing in Sharp or Frankfort. A mere thirty-eight words in Donaldson and Morpeth's A DICTIONARY OF SCOTTISH HISTORY. The library in Enid, Oklahoma, where I was born and raised till I ran off to find my fortune, would have had nothing. I could in no way have been alerted.

One would think such things too terrible to be forgotten. But I understand there are college students all over the world these days for whom the words Dachau and Buchenwald and Belsen have no meaning.

In such a world, I'm grateful to have found love to sustain me.

We drove the rental car south out of Glasgow on 77. It was barely eight o'clock. We wanted an early start, though Ballantrae was less than seventy miles; 111.021 kilometers, to be precise. The southwest sea-coast. Galloway.

We had discussed settling down here: Portpatrick, Glen App, or Cairnryan; perhaps take a freehold on a crofter's cottage near Castle Kennedy; or even nearer Bennane Head, possibly on the sheltered southern shore of Loch Ryan. But the councils weren't sanctioning freeholds for Americans, and Camilla had no birth certificate proving she was of Scottish birth, of course. So we had come to visit, at last. After all the years Camilla had begged me for this hometurning in our flight, we passed through Milmarnock, and reached the Firth of Clyde at Prestwick, just as the rain began sweeping the coast. After all those years, it was an unpleasant omen. And my trepidation about returning Camilla to her ancestral environs deepened. But she had implored me so heartbreakingly.

We drove the short distance to Ayr and cut over to 719 that trailed deeper south right along the coastline; it was perhaps an hour, then, to travel the thirty-five miles to Ballantrae, the rain barely increasing in intensity, though the sky blended in gray metal with the water of the North Channel. Sheet metal from top to bottom, and we sloughing along the extruded wetness of the road that edged the moors.

Camilla did not speak, had not spoken since we'd passed Dunure; but she had her face pressed to the window, looking out at the dismal machinery of leaden scenery, leaving for an instant four halations of breath fog on the glass before turning to stare ahead through the windshield. Her breath rasped and puffs of exhalation warned me she was getting too cold. I pulled over and took a blanket from the back seat, and wrapped her more securely. She smiled and mewled softly.

I scratched the nape of her neck, said, "Soon," and turned back onto the road and kept going.

We reached Ballantrae before noon, and Camilla decided to wait in the car while I went to get a bite to eat. I told her I'd bring something back, and she leaned across and kissed me, and smiled, and moved her head in that sweet sidewise way that I adored. "Haggis?" I said, teasing her. She hated haggis. She gave me a look, and I quickly said, "I'm kidding, I'm just kidding," before she cuffed me a good one. "Howzabout some eggs?" That brought back the smile.

I didn't feel like going into the rental's boot for a bowl...everything was packed tightly. So after I found Wimpy's and choked down three burgers, I cruised till I found a Woolworth's and laid out three quid for an aluminum mixing bowl. There was a delay in the checkout line, with an old woman in a snood raising such a fuss about something or other that the teen-age cashier had to call the manager. And everyone stood in line, more or less embarrassed by the whole thing, till they stopped shouting and the manager took the old woman off upstairs to his office to sort things out. I was impressed at how kindly he treated her, after all the ruckus. He seemed a nice man, and I felt sorry for the old woman, who looked widowed, cast alone, and hopeless. It made me sad for a moment, but the line moved quickly and I paid for the bowl and went back out into the slanting rain.

There was a grocer's on the way back to the public parking lot where I'd left the little Vauxhall Cavalier, and I waited in another short queue to pay for a half dozen free-range eggs carefully placed in a paper bag by an over-weight, ruddy-faced man who carried on a running diatribe with his wife, at the rear of the shop, about how he would absolutely *not* carry Mrs. Bassandyne's box of groceries out to her car, no matter *how* many times she imperiously honked her horn. His wife looked like a typical telly version of a little old mum, and she agreed with him that Mrs. Bassandyne was indeed a right miserable cow. He managed to thank me for my purchase, in the middle of a Bassandyne sentence, and I went out again into the rain, which had grown heavier.

Camilla wasn't in the car.

The rain had soaked through the shoulders of my mac, and every time I took a step my feet sqooshed in my wellies. The door of the rental was unlocked, and I put the bag of eggs on the front seat. Camilla was nowhere in sight, and I was an amputated leg. At first distressed, then troubled, then quickly frightened, I began running up and down the rows of parked cars. All I found was casual litter, a penny lying face-up in an oil slick, and the bones of what had probably been a small dog; very white and clean, with the marks of tiny teeth all over them.

When finally I circled back to the Vauxhall, Camilla was there, standing in the rain, the soaking blanket around her. I hustled her into the car, went around and, dripping wet, climbed in. She looked at me mischievously, and I apologized for having taken so long. "There was a line at the Woolworth's and the grocer's," I said. "Are you hungry?"

She told me she was hungry, but she said it with that subtext of tone that reprimanded me for having kept her waiting. I pulled the aluminum bowl out of the deep pocket of my mac, and broke the eggs into it. I put it on the lowered ledge of the opened glove compartment, and she went right to it. I watched in silence, determined not to ask her why she had wandered off into the storm.

When we drove out of the parking lot, a sizzle of lightning illuminated the delicate calligraphy of dog bones that still lay between a Ford Escort and a Mazda.

We left 77 just south of Ballantrae and took a weary, flooded dirt road out along the cliffs above Bennane Head. I could not contain my growing fear, and Camilla's reassuring smile only made me dwell more darkly on the ivory luster of bone in water.

Fame and fortune always eluded me. I laugh when I think how *completely* they had eluded me. I never had a clue. Not the smallest indication how to go about sinking roots, or making money, or bettering myself, or taking hold. There are people—well, I suppose almost *all* people, really—who manage to do it. They find mates, they get jobs, they buy homes, they have children, they furnish apartments, they get an education, they learn the ins and outs of electrical wiring or plastering or office temp, and they make lives for themselves.

I never knew how to do any of that. I couldn't talk to people, I was afraid of women, I never went into a restaurant or bookstore where anyone recognized me a second time. It was just the road, always the road, from here to there, and on again to someplace else. And no one place was even the tiniest bit better than the place I had just left. I was cold as an ice bucket, and had strong legs for walking. A job here, a job there, and I never became good enough at anything for an employer to suggest that I might, to our mutual advantage, stay on, settle down, take a position.

I went everywhere. All over Europe, the Greek isles, Hungary and even those parts of the Balkans that are no longer called Transylvania or Barnsdorf or Moldavia; Algeria, India, all over the sub-continent; Pakistan, Israel, Zaire, the Congo. I shipped aboard tramp steamers to the China Sea, to Sumatra, as far north as Kiska and Attu, as far south as Brazil, Argentina. I saw Patagonia. I saw gauchos. In another place I saw penguins. I shipped there and back, and never once made a friend who lasted beyond the time at sea.

No one disliked me, no one very much interfered with me, they just didn't take much notice of me. I followed instructions to the letter, but managed to stay away from bad companions or trouble. I just went where the waves hit the shore, and stayed a time, and then moved on.

But I never returned to America, and I suppose all my family is gone now. I never had it in me to return to Enid, Oklahoma: I mean to say, that's where I'd run *away* from, why would I go back?

Fifteen years ago, I found Camilla. We fell in love. I thought I wanted to say something about that, how we came to be together, the time we've spent together since. But I don't want to go into that. It isn't something everyone would understand. I know it isn't enough to say that we just love each other, and need to be together, because anyone could say the same thing. But if I know one truth about people, it is that everyone judges everyone else. People they never met, and only read about in a newspaper or saw on a telly, they decide this or that about them...this is a good guy, and that's a sick and weird guy, or this woman is no good and that woman is above her station. It isn't fair. You just can't know why people do the things they do; and if you try to be a good guy, and go out of your way not to hurt anyone, then other people simply ought to let you be.

For instance, and I don't mean this to be smutty, but it's just exactly what I'm talking about, a long time ago I was in Uppsala, Sweden. I was given some magazines full of naked men and women, by a student I met who attended the University there. One of them was full of photographs of a woman having sex with animals. When I first saw it, I was very upset. I'd never seen anything like that. The woman was pretty, and the pictures had been taken on a farm somewhere, I suppose in Sweden, because the bull she was with had ice all matted in his hair. And she was doing things with a pig.

And I was so upset that I sought him out, the student who had given me the magazines, and I gave that one back to him, and I told him I couldn't understand how a woman could do such things. And he told me this young woman was very famous, that she was a simple farm girl, and that she truly loved animals, and didn't think there was anything awful about making the animals she loved happy. So I sat and studied that magazine, with that pretty young woman making love to the bull and the pig, and after a while I could see that she was really smiling, and the animals seemed to be content; and after a while longer it wasn't dirty to me any more. It was just as if she were petting a rabbit, or hugging a kitten.

I didn't see the ugliness others saw. I came to understand that there is little enough affection in the world and, even if everyone finds it necessary to pass judgments that this is proper, and that is obscene, that *this* young woman, even if she was of what they call diminished capacity, even she was better than those who passed judgments, because she loved the animals, and she wasn't hurting anyone, and if that was how she chose to show her love, it was okay.

But try to explain that to most people, and see how their faces screw up as if they'd eaten something sour. And so, if you take my point, that's why I don't want to talk about how I met Camilla in Wales, and what she was doing there, and how we got together, and how we came to find love together.

I'll just say this: she didn't want to be there, and her lot was not a happy one, and I got her away from there, and we started running, and besides being in love, she is the first and only person who ever *needed me.*

And that accounts for a lot. So after fifteen years of her asking me to take her to Galloway, I agreed, and it was a long, hard journey, but I'd taken her home.

Why was it she would tell me anything, had always shared everything with me, but would fall silent when I'd ask her how long it had been since she had seen her family, how long she had been away from her home?

And where in the world could they live, out here at the edge of Scotland, in this desolate place of cliffs and caves and moors? What could people farm out here, to sustain a decent life?

We parked at the edge of the cliffs, and I suggested we wait in the car till the rain had abated. Camilla was veiled in her manner, and tried not to seem anxious. But after a few minutes she wanted to get out, and she managed the door handle, and went down into the rain. I jumped out and came around, and helped her up. She stood there, her head tilted toward the heavens, the pounding rain sleeking her, running off both of us. Then she went to the edge of the cliff and tried to find a way down to the sea. "No!" I yelled across the thunder and darkness. "There's no way down!"

She went low and tried to crawl over the edge, grasping the tenacious twist of a briar bush. I slipped trying to get to her, and went face-first into the running mud where the road met the flattened grass. When I tried to rise, I slipped again. Then I just crawled toward her, as she tried to lower herself down the cliff. "Camilla! No! What're you doing? Stop, this's crazy...stop!" It was lunacy, a sheer drop nearly six hundred feet into the Channel, the storm skirting across the cliff-edge, the rain flooding the ground and waterfalling over the rim. I couldn't believe what she was trying to do. Where was she going?

I managed to grab her under the shoulders, and I rolled sidewise, digging my wellies into the mud and loam, making a dam against the water with my body. Then I started scrabbling backward, pulling her with me. She screamed and raked me.

I kept pulling, she was trying desperately to get away from me. I lost purchase as one of my feet slid across the mud, she got loose, crawled away, I reached back and snagged her clothing with one hand, I held on and wrenched back as hard as I could, she rolled onto her back, and I dragged her through the vicious downpour as darkness now fell utterly, dissolving sky, sea, cliff, land, everything. Only once, in the sulfurous whitelight of a blast of lightning close to the cliff, could I see Camilla's eyes. It wasn't the woman I'd loved for fifteen years, it was a mud-swathed creature possessed by a madness to go over the edge. Had she been trying for a decade and a half to return to this place only to kill herself? A lemming seeking oblivion? Had her life before my coming, or since I had joined with her, been so awful that all she wanted was to die? I fought against it. I fought against *her,* and finally...I won.

I rolled us over and over and over, back toward the road, away from the cliff-edge, and at last came to rest against the side of the car. I held her close and cradled her, and she spat and raged and tried to break loose.

"No, Camilla...no, please, stop...honey, please..."

After a time, there in the cascading darkness, she went limp. And after a greater time she let me know she would not try that route again. But she kept saying she needed to go home.

I knew, then, that there was no lonely farmhouse out here. There might not even be family, as there might not be family in Enid, Oklahoma. But she had the need to find them, wherever they were out here; and I had to help her.

I loved her. That is all there is to say.

When I was certain she would not try for the edge again, I let her go. She rested a moment, then rose and moved slowly away, across the road, away from the cliff and the sea. Out across the moors. Without a word, she made her painful, laborious passage through the gorse, the silvery gray tufts of grass now bending beneath the hammering rain, the craggy rocks black and crippled-seeming leaping out for an instant as lightning illuminated them, then vanishing into blind emptiness as night rushed back in around the image. For a moment she vanished as she moved through a stand of tall reedlike grass, then she was limned against the sky as she crawled over a rock outcrop. I followed, at a short distance, as an observer would track a great terrapin trying to find its way to the sea.

She seemed to know what she was looking for. And I had bright instants of hope that there would be, if not a lonely farmhouse, then the burned-out wreckage of a farmhouse that had been here long ago, before Camilla had left.

But finally, she came to an enormous pile of rocks all grown over with briar bushes, thick with thorns. She climbed the cairn, and I followed; and found her trying to dig away the sharp spikey branches. She was already bleeding when I got there.

I tried to stop her, but again, she was possessed. She *had* to pull away those bushes.

I gently edged her aside and, wrapping the cuffs of my mac around my hands, I strained and wrenched at the bushes where she indicated. After a fearful struggle, they came out of the niches in the rocks, one by one.

The first clot of dirt surrounding the tenacious root-systems brought up a filthy skull. It was a human skull. I thought for a moment it was an animal skull, but when the rain washed it clean, I saw that it was not an animal. It had been human. How long ago it had been human, I could not tell. When I stopped digging, she moved to take over; but I nudged her back, and went at it again.

It seemed hours, just wrenching and digging in the spaces between the black rocks of the cairn. Hours in the slashing storm. Hours and eternities without time or sense. And at last, my hand slipped through into a cool empty place between the rocks.

"There's a hole here...I think, there seems to be, I think there's a large hole under here..."

She joined me again, and I couldn't stop her or slow her. She dug madly, like a beast uncovering a meal hidden for later attention.

I wedged myself against the larger of two leaning rocks in the mound, and braced my feet against the smaller, and steadily pushed. I have strong legs, as I said. The rock crunched, trembled, moved restlessly like a fat man in sleep, and then overbalanced in its setting, and fell away, tumbling quickly out of sight down the slope of the cairn.

As lightning blasted the landscape, I saw the entrance to the cave. The black maw of the opening gaped beneath my feet. As the rock rolled away, I fell forward, caught the edge of the hole, and dropped. I screamed as the world fell past me, and the water spilling over the rocks filled my mouth with dirt and gravel, stung my eyes, and I hit the sloping wall of the passage, and slid on a carpet of running mud like a man in a toboggan, careening off the rough surface from which roots extended, plunging down and down, feet-first into the darkness. The channel sloped more steeply, and I gathered speed, screaming, and went faster, and could see nothing but the deep grave funneling up past me and an instant of dim light high overhead behind me as lightning hit the night sky again.

Then I was shooting forward on a less inclined plane, still too fast to stop myself though I tried to dig in my hands and ripped flesh for the trouble, dirt clogging under my fingernails...and I shot out of the end of the tunnel, like a gobbet of spit, and somehow my legs were under me, but there was no floor, and I dropped into open emptiness, and hit still accelerating forward, and managed half a dozen running steps before I smashed full face into a rock wall, and I lost everything. I didn't even know when I'd fallen.

The light was green. Pale green, the color of moldy bread that seems to be blue till you look closely. The light came from the walls of the cavern. It was an enormous cavern, and the first thing I heard was the sound of a vast audience applauding. I fainted again. The pain in my face was excruciating. I knew I'd broken parts, and I fainted again. The pale green light expanded in the space behind my eyes, and I went away.

When I swam through the pain and the film of swirling shapes, I regained consciousness in the same position, propped against the wall of the cavern. This time I understood that the applauding masses were the sound of the sea hitting the cliffs. At each ovation, water rushed into the cavern from far across the floor, and I realized we had to be at least two hundred yards inside the cliff. The cavern glowed with a sickly green luminosity and I could make out tunnels that led off this central chamber, dozens of tunnels, going off in every direction around the circular centerplace.

I tried to move, and the pain in my face nearly sent me into darkness again. I raised a filthy hand to my cheek and felt bone protruding from the skin. My nose was broken. My teeth had bitten through my upper lip. My right eye seemed to have something wet and loose obscuring the lens.

I dropped my hand to the rock and dirt floor beside me, and my palm slid in something moist and soft. I looked down. The headless body of a young woman lay twisted on the floor beside me. I screamed and pinwheeled away from the corpse.

Then I heard a chuckle, and looked with extreme pain and restriction of muscles to my left. Camilla's father—How did I know it was he? I don't know. It was he—hung head down from the rock wall, sticking to the surface of moist, mossy rock. Watching me.

His scaley surface was not as clean and opalescent as I'd kept Camilla's. Rot clung to the scabrous flesh. There were more teeth in him, and larger than Camilla's.

He came away from the wall with a sucking sound and dropped to the floor of the cavern. Then, without difficulty—and I am a large man—he extended two of his arms and took me by the collar of the mac and dragged me across the floor, toward one of the tunnels on the far side of the chamber, through the river of seawater that ebbed and flowed as the audience applauded against the cliffs of Bennane Head.

He dragged me through the mouth of the tunnel, and we passed chamber after chamber, a vast labyrinth of cave system—and I looked in on Camilla's family, inhabiting the rooms beneath the Galloway moors.

In one chamber I saw nothing but bones, hundreds of thousands of bones, pale green with their gnawed-clean curves and knobs, hollow where the marrow had been sucked out. Bones in mountainous heaps that clogged the chamber from floor to roof, and spilled out into the passage. He dragged me through the history of a thousand meals.

In another chamber were piles of clothing. Rags and garments, boots and dresses, shapeless masses of raiment that seemed to have come from a hundred eras. Plumed bonnets with moss growing on them, jodhpurs and corselets, leather greaves and housecoats, bedroom slippers and deer-stalkers, anoraks and cuirasses, masses of clothing thrown haphazardly and in a profusion that defied estimation, filling the large side-chamber like the clothes closet of a mad empress.

I cannot describe the drying and curing rooms, save to say that bodies and parts of bodies hung from hooks in the low ceilings. Men with their faces gone. Women with their breasts ripped away. Small boys without hands or feet or sex organs. A mound of dried, leathery babies.

And on, and on, and on.

I could not stop him, he was too strong, I was too weak and in pain, and I was able merely to turn my head as we bumped along. Turned my head to see horror upon horror in this seemingly endless charnel house.

Into a cavernous hold far back in the system, where I finally, after fifteen years, confronted Camilla's family. All of them. The children of Sawney Beane.

And there, in the bosom of her loved ones, was the woman I loved. My cool and beautiful Camilla, with a gobbet of human flesh hanging from her lipless mouth, her fingerless hands redolent with blood.

In the center of the chamber was a great stone bowl. And as I lay there, watching, first one, then another, of Camilla's brothers and sisters and nieces and nephews—all the products of incestuous coupling—kneeled before the stone crucible and drank slurpingly from the thick, clotted liquor. I knew the name of that terrible brew.

Camilla's father left me there and went to his wife and daughter. I knew at once who they were. The affection they showed toward one another, and the attention all the others lavished on them, indicated how pleased they were that the prodigal had, at last, returned. And bearing such a tender banquet as oblation to the family.

I saw the resemblance between mother and daughter.

And for the first time asked myself how old Camilla really was. I'd assumed she was young, but what did that mean in a lineal line where one hundred, two hundred years was only early maturity?

I was too terrified to move, and the nausea that swelled in my throat left me weak and empty.

Then Camilla came to me, and settled down beside me, and lifted my head and stroked my face with a bloody hand. And she kissed me. And I smelled the butcher shop on her lipless mouth. I almost cried: she still loved me.

What they spoke was barely a human tongue, a language that had been guttural and ancient when King James the First had tracked them to these caves, and dragged out Sawney and his wife, and eight sons, and six daughters, and eighteen grandsons, and fourteen granddaughters—forty-eight in all—but, ah, not *all*, as he thought—and shrove them all the way to Leith, and condemned all, without exception, to death; and, as the women watched, King James ordered that the men have first their penises, then their hands and feet, chopped off, and were left to bleed to death where they lay; and then he had the women hurled living into three great bonfires, where they, too, perished. But it was not the end of Sawney Beane's clan. For the caves beneath Galloway were deep, and many, and mazelike, and some survived. And literally went to ground, to breed anew.

I learned all this from the woman I loved, who spoke a second language. A tongue that was slick with terrible history.

And she told me that she loved me, would always love me. And she told me that it was cool and protected here. And told me that her family approved of her choice. And told me we could stay here. Together. In the bosom of her family. And not for a second did I see in her eyes the green, hungry glow in the eyes of her immense mother, who squatted across the floor all that night—I think it was still night—watching her intended son-in-law.

Camilla mewled and ran her tongue over me, and held me and rocked me. And spoke of our love.

Then, when I was able to stand, I ran. I turned and ran back the way we had come; and each of the horrors I had passed was a marker: the drying rooms, the hanging chambers, the rows of skulls in niches with tallow candles that had burned down centuries ago, the clothing room and the bone room, where I grabbed a femur and, hearing feet pounding along behind me, turned and swung the longbone as hard as I could, and shattered the head of a scion of the family of Sawney Beane, perhaps Camilla's father, I don't know.

I found the sloping passage, and jumped and went half into the hole, and some rough appendage grasped my legs, and I kicked out, and heard a moan, and scrabbled up the slope and kept going, up and up and up toward the night sky that was now gray-blue with passing clouds and moonlight.

I went up, for my life, with the smell of slaughter from Camilla's kisses fresh on my lips.

I lie now in this room where I awoke this morning. *Clair de Lune* drifts up to me from Atlantis. I lie here, having left this brief chronicle, thinking of what I must do. I know I will return.

What I do not yet know, as I think of my rootless life and the emptiness I knew before I found Camilla in that gully, is whether I will dive down that hole in the cairn bearing gasoline and gelignite and a flamethrower if I can steal one from some armory somewhere...

Or if I will go to taste again the kisses of the woman I love, the only woman who has ever loved me.

This I know, however: Atlantis never existed.

BEAN, Sawney (fl. mid-1400s). Scottish highwayman, mass murderer, and cannibal. Illiterate and uncouth, he lived with his wife and fourteen children in a giant cave by the desolate seacoast along the Galloway region in southwestern Scotland. For over twenty-five years the Bean family assaulted, robbed, and killed travelers—men, women, and children—on their way to and from Edinburgh and Glasgow in the north. Their depredations included cannibalism as well. Finally, an intended victim who had seen his wife knocked from her horse, her throat immediately slit, and her body cannibalized, managed to escape to warn the Scottish king at Glasgow. Some four hundred men and bloodhounds, led by the king, tracked down and, after a fierce battle, captured the Beans in their cave, in which were found numerous mutilated cadavers. Sawney and the rest were brought to Leith, showed not the slightest repentance for their crimes, and were promptly burned to death at the stake without a trial. It was estimated that the Beans' murder victims totaled well over a thousand persons.

Extract from DICTIONARY OF CULPRITS AND CRIMINALS
(George C. Kohn; Scarecrow Press: London, 1986)

She moved into the trailer with me and Derry. There have been times in my life when, smart as I think I can be, I am truly as senseless as a flagstone. Tighten the electrodes in my neck. So. It wasn't till Derry took me aside one afternoon as I was getting ready to pull an all-night KP for having committed some stupid infraction of Army rules, that I knew Charlotte hadn't changed. She's puttin the bee on me, The Tiger said. We used that phrase in those days. Today, I'd say she was putting a move on him, or she was on the make. Whatever.

Derry told me he was my friend, and he didn't want to get in my face about it, but he was extremely uncomfortable with the situation and, like tonight, when I was going to be away for the long duty pull, she made it very unhealthy for him. So he opted to move out. As much as both of us hated living like animals in the barracks, Derry did that for me, rather than cause a scene.

Midnight in The Sunken Cathedral

He walked the bottom of the world and tried not to think about how his father had died. Half a mile from the ivory sand beach, off the east coast of Andros Island, two hundred feet below the surface of the Grand Bahama Banks. Trudging through the warm, cool, warm translucency of the North Atlantic at latitude 24°26′ N, longitude 77°57′ W. A quarter of a mile from the island — about twenty-five miles southwest of Nassau—well within the 1,500,000 square miles known as the Bermuda Triangle—the ledge suddenly tips out and goes from 80 feet, drops out of all earthly sight, all human conception, to 2000 feet, maybe 3000, maybe more. Miles, incomprehensible miles down, where the pressure of pounds per square inch is tens, perhaps hundreds of tons. Nothing we know can survive at such depths. It is called the Wall of Andros, and those depths are known as the Tongue of the Ocean. In specially constructed bathyspheres, and once in the International Hard Suit unit called a Newtsuit, the abyssal deep had been penetrated to the depth most commonly found in the international maritime atlas, 1382 meters; 4533 feet; almost a mile straight down. They had seen only darkness below them; and the cataclysmic stress-creaking of tungsten steel and case-molded maxi-plastic had warned them to pry no deeper, to go back up, go back home where soft flesh things would not be reduced to a crimson smear.

Walking through gorgeous plant life and coral outcrops and the racing, darting animated movie of piscatorial chromatics, he pulled himself along in the ancient hardhat diving suit, grabbing a medusa handful of writhing tubers, clawing the long-handled sand-fork against a chunk of upthrust coral, stirring the silt bottom as little as possible, plodding ahead step by step toward the anomaly he had read on his sonar screen.

In the basement of the Bermuda Triangle, blue as the eye of the most perfect sapphire ever uncovered, 330 carats, the Star of Asia, he teetered ahead of his bubble-trail, angled forward at forty-five degrees, hauling his airhose and lifeline behind him like the great tail of a saurian.

And he tried not to think about the way his father had died.

His father—whom he had loved and admired more than he had ever been able to say, ever been able to tell the man—had been slammed to pulp between the upper and lower dies of a gigantic body-part hydraulic punch press in the old Poletown plant, the Dodge main plant, in Hamtramck, the east side of Detroit, in 1952 when Dennis was less than a year old. George DeVore Lanfear had reached into the four foot high opening with his left hand when the cold-stamped steel front door stuck in the press. He reached in with a long piece of pry metal, as he had done a hundred times before, knowing that the press operator had set the safety buttons that would protect him. The press was on hold, the clutch was locked; he extended himself into that empty space between iron jaws, sixteen feet deep, twelve feet wide, until the upper half of his body right to the belt-line was under a metal roof, resting on a metal deck; and the master button die setter was an alcoholic who was half-wasted from the night before, and the clutch didn't hold, and the safety failed, and the press automatically repeated the operation and the press smashed down with a roof pressure of one hundred tons, and infant Dennis Lanfear was without a father. Dead as table scraps, in the old Dodge Main on Joseph Campeau Avenue, on the East Side of Detroit, in 1952, before Dennis could tell him how much he loved and admired him. Which he came to understand, when he grew older, because of the stories his mother told him about his father, was a manifestation of his infinite, terrible loss.

Dennis Lanfear had grown to manhood without ever having been given the moment to embrace his father, and tell him how dear his memory had become to him. Could never tell him, not when he was fourteen and went to see the building in which his father had died (and got bad directions and hitchhiked out to Ypsilanti, where he wound up at the soon-to-be-closed Willow Run plant that had helped win World War II); not when he was twenty-two and joined the U.S. Navy to honor the service in which George Lanfear had served during the battle of the Gulf of Leyte; not when he was thirty-five and got his top security clearance and was assigned as First Sonar Technician at the clandestine listening station and torpedo test site here at Andros, the secret base most line-item military agendas listed only as "U.S. Navy Autec Range."

Nor could he tell his father, more than forty years gone, that he had been picking up something bewildering on his screens for quite a while now.

He had no way of telling George Lanfear that something wild and weird and possibly wonderful—like the secret dream of his otherwise mundane life—was going on in that absolute nowhere called the Tongue of the Ocean. Something that could not be named, and certainly could not be brought to the attention of his superiors...because it made no sense.

So now he walked. Having invaded one of the old shipyards on Andros, having "liberated" some old unassisted "hardhat" diving dress from rusted lockers, having repaired it and made it sound (it was gear dated 1922), and having adapted the gear to accommodate a synthetic mixture called heliox—which mix of helium and oxygen would allow him to exceed the two hundred foot depth this kind of hardhat gear usually permitted—he was nearing the spot indicated on his sonar readings.

He walked the bottom of the world, tried not to think that one slip and he would topple over the edge of the Wall of Andros, sink into the Tongue of the Ocean, and long before his airhose and lifeline pulled taut, he would be crushed by pressures easily as great as those that had slapped his father into oblivion. He trudged, he tried to avoid thoughts and he did not see the smooth shadow that undulated above him and behind him. But soon he would reach...

There!

There it was. But it made no sense. He stared through the thick faceplate glass of his helmet, and at first could not comprehend what he was seeing. Time passed as he stood there amid neon-colored swimmers, breathing heavily, trying to get his eyes to re-rack the size and meaning of what he was seeing.

Out there, perhaps twenty-five meters beyond the lip of the ridge, out there hanging over the abyss, was a gigantic waterfall. He ran the word through his mind once:

QED. It is a waterfall.

Perhaps a hundred feet above him, there was a dark, odd, faintly glowing opening in the underwater. It was enormous, a mouth of water that opened *into* water. As if a vacuum hole—the words were the best he could do—a vacuum hole had opened into this deep. And pouring down out of that aperture, into the bottomless deep of the Tongue of the Ocean, was a waterfall of rushing, plunging, foaming water, faintly crimson and solid as paving stones, cascading out and over and down like an otherworldly Niagara, here beneath the Atlantic, here in the Bermuda Triangle, here in front of Dennis Lanfear.

He was frozen in place, disbelieving, frightened, and unable to defend himself as the painted, serpentine creature that had been pacing him curled herself over and over around his airhose and his lifeline, snapping them, descending on him, grasping him in incredibly powerful, naked arms, and dove with him...

Over and over, off the ledge, into the bottomless darkness below the Wall of Andros, down and down, to five hundred feet where the pounds of pressure per square inch was over two hundred, and Lanfear found himself embraced with death, as he was dragged down and down, till the faint light of the ocean was extinguished, and so was his consciousness; and the last thing he saw as oblivion rushed in on him was the sweet, smiling, thousand-year-old face of the watcher in the abyss, the guardian of the portal, the mermaid who bore him to extinction.

Lanfear was dissolving in a world of red thunder.

It was dark, and cold, and he was held so tightly he could barely flex a muscle inside the diving suit.

> "...here was darkness...darkness complete;
> it was that sepulchral and terrible moment
> which follows midnight."
> **VICTOR HUGO** *Les Misérables*

He had never feared tight places, closed-in confinement. There were other terrors, small ones, left over from childhood—cinders in the eye, certain soft insects with too many legs—but not the dark clothes closet, not the chilly dark basement, not the cobwebby shadowland under the back porch. But this was the weight of the entire ocean. This was the dungeon at the bottom of the world. *Everything* was up there above him, as he was borne below in the gentle, unremitting arms of a snippet of mythology.

For the first time in his life, Dennis Lanfear felt the paralyzing fear of claustrophobia; no rapture, in this deep.

The sound of wind rushing down through a great tunnel, the faint background memory sound of a great assembly line, the clank of metal on metal, the heartbeat regularity of machinery impacting on bendable steel. Dark and cold, like eternal midnight.

The sweet and gentle mermaid's face that had appeared for an instant in the Perspex, the fogging viewplate of his highly planished tinned copper diving helmet...and then was gone...as unlikely crimson water and sucking thunder took him through to the *other* side of unconsciousness.

A place that was always midnight.

Where the altar was closed for repairs, and the place of worship was boarded up. Watery, deep, high-ceilinged with misty vastness stretching up, up beyond sight. But always out of reach, and always at that terrible moment which follows midnight.

Dennis Lanfear was dissolving in a world of red thunder.

He was out, gone, blanked and insensible; but his flesh continued to listen in on the secret messages of the deep.

Instinctively, as his airhose had been severed when she had wrenched him off the ledge of the Wall of Andros, he had knocked his head against the spindle of the regulating air outlet valve. The valve was usually made to be adjusted by hand but—like the Perspex faceplate that had replaced the original plate-glass built into the gun-metal frames when the "hardhat" diving suit was new in 1922—someone had re-rigged the valve so the spindle was extended through to the inside of the helmet, fitted at its inner extremity with a small disc. Instinctively, he had knocked the disc with his head, trapping what air remained in the deep-sea dress. He could breathe. Oblivious, descending, bright with delirium, his listening molecules followed the passage of the story of his deep fall.

In this aspect of the Bermuda Triangle the water was always Nassau warm. But as he spiraled deeper into the Tongue of the Ocean, pressed to the breasts of the woman-fish, it grew even warmer. Lying out in an August hammock warm. And the intimation of thunder grew louder. Perhaps hundreds of meters above them as they fell into infinite shadow, the great crimson waterfall roared as it spilled its raging body out of that impossible vacuum hole. But the thunder was not from the impossible avalanche of gallons above them. It came from below in the bottomless deep. Lanfear's listening DNA clocked every insinuation, every nuance. And then, when the fragile sack of blood that was his human body should have come unseamed and split, at a depth no surface creature could call home, he began to dissolve.

Dennis Lanfear, hands empty, mind clutching no more than muted memories of the crushed, dead father he had never been privileged to know, began to dissolve in a world of crimson water, a world of red thunder.

He had feared he would die as his father had died, in the jaws of unbearable pounds per square inch, but it was not to be. The self-fulfilling prophecy—will I outlive the years allotted to my father—he died at fourty-four, will I live to be fifty—the unspoken fear that numbs all men—was eluded.

Dennis Lanfear did not crush under the heel of the deep, he merely dissolved. Molecule by molecule, atom by atom, submicroscopic electrical pulse by invisible swimming flux, he was carried down in the mermaid's arms toward the twin of the booming vacuum hole far above...a quiet yet susurrating void as black and empty of identity as the matrix of a thresher shark's eye. His every instant was culled, harvested, codified...and sucked into the vacuum hole as the guardian of the portal, the watcher of the Bermuda Triangle abyss, who had hauled such cargo uncounted times in her thousand-year existence, released his mortal flesh in its puny diving suit fabricated in 1922 in a city of a nation that had not existed for one-tenth her life-span. She smiled, and swam away in the warm.

And the essence of Lanfear was carried away, into the dead emotionless vacuum eye of an abyss that lived, as the shark lives, only to feed.

The light that came to his skin from the end of the universe was white and pure and bright; but the water around him as he came to the surface of the great lake pool was a chromatic sibling of red and pink and amber that no eye on Earth had ever seen. It registered in that vast and desolate cerebral Sahara within the parietal lobe where nothing can grow. There, in the unfathomable desolation of the primary sensory cortex, whose functions are the Bermuda Triangle of the brain's potential, such hues and shades as composed the gently rippling waters as his throbbing head broke the surface, had meaning and identity. In that alien landscape of the mind, to which no human being had ever retained valid passport, the spectrum was wider, broader, deeper, and sang with a brighter resonance.

The copper diving helmet was gone. Dispensed with. Somewhere behind him in the passage through the thunderingly silent drain of the vacuum hole. Perhaps its atoms had been dispersed in a cloudy shower saturating the life-heavy waters off the Grand Bahama Banks. Perhaps they had been fired away in a narrow-focus stream, like a lightless laser beam, as he was disassembled, broken-down, deconstructed, unbuilt, as his molecules were being transported here—to this place of the lake pool and exquisite diamond-bright light and gently rippling water that seemed heavier than he remembered water to be, seemed able to hold him higher in its totality than he remembered water was able. It was not that he felt lighter, more buoyant, just that the water was more reliable, more fatherly, gentler. He trusted it more than when he had been—

—had been where? Had been in the water beyond Andros Island? Had been in the North Atlantic Ocean? Had been on the planet Earth? Had been in the year and the month and the day on the calendar in his office back at the Sonar station? Had been in his right mind, his right-brain mind? Where he had *been*: that much he knew. Where he was now, what had happened to bring him to this new place, by what impossible transport...he could not *begin* to fathom. The diving suit, too, was gone. Its atoms dispersed at the checkout counter of transmogrification. Stale-dated. Roundfiled. Recycled. Where the hell *am* I?

He looked across the crimson lake and saw ships.

Hundreds, perhaps thousands of ships. Boats, craft, vessels of all sizes and periods and origins. Arab dhows and Gallic currachs, Greek triremes and balsa-wood PT boats, Canton delta lorcha and lateen-sailed Portuguese trawlers. Whalers, warships, feluccas and frigates; hydrofoils, hagboats, pinnaces and Pechili junks. Siamese lug-sails, brigantines, galeasses, Hanseatic League cogs, sixty-oared papyrus galleys, Norse *drakkars* and dragon-prowed Viking longships called the Oseberg ship. Barques, yawls, packet boats, cigarettes, freighters, cabin cruisers, sampans, windjammers and luxury liners; Turkish tchektirme, Greek sacoleva, Venetian trabaccoli, Levantine caïque, and the German U-1065 pigboat alleged to have been sunk by R.A.F. Mosquitos in the Kattegat. Sailing ships that were little more than rough-hewn logs lashed into the shape of a raft with lianas, and twin-hulled catamarans of titanium and PVC pipe. The lake pool, harbor of last resort, Sargasso of lost ships, was filled with the oceangoing detritus of ten thousand years.

Yet it was hardly jammed. It seemed endless in its capacity to hold the castaways of the shipping lanes, but the lake was spacious and only dotted with a shape here, a bobbing four-masted brigantine there. Dennis Lanfear, treading water, turned slowly, looking and looking, amazed at the bizarre optical illusion made by a storehouse overflowing...that remained capacious and expectant.

He turned and turned...and saw the city.

It rose from the very edge of the lake pool. Slanting up as softly blue and gray as psalms ascending to Heaven, it was massive, enthralling, breathtaking in the complexity of its segmented faces. Walls so high they dizzyingly ran to a sky that could not be seen in the misty upper reaches. Walls that abutted at right angles—yet formed no central square. Walls that seemed ancient, yet downy with the breath of first birth. The cave dwellings of the Anasazi, the prehistorical hive dwellings of slope-browed pre-men, the filing cabinets for gothamites gone eternally condo...this was the City indeed, the City supreme. It towered over the harbor, and at first Lanfear saw no hint of human movement.

But as he stroked toward the quay, toward the low lip of polished blue-gray stone that would allow him to climb up to the walkway fronting the Great Walls, he saw one small figure, just one. No, there was a second person. Man or woman, he could not be sure...either of them.

He breast-stroked through the lovely crimson water, softly lapping at the stones of the quay, and paddled in to shelter. He pulled himself along till he reached something like a hemp cargo net hanging into the water, anchored out of sight on the walkway above. He pulled himself up, and stood, dripping heavy pink moisture, dwarfed by the immensity of the cyclopean walls that slanted away above him. He craned to see the sky, even to see a ceiling, but all was mist and the reborn antiquity of structures ageless and ever new.

He marveled that, if he were indeed somewhere beneath the Bermuda Triangle, in some impossible sub-oceanic world that could exist in defiance of the rigors of physics and plate tectonics and magma certainties, then this subterranean edifice was certainly the most colossal structure ever built on the planet. A holy sunken cathedral built by gods.

He stood there dripping pink, thick water, sanctifying himself in the first moment of true religion he had ever known.

And one of the two figures who had been walking beside the quay came toward him, and it was a man in his very late thirties or early forties, wearing a gray chambray shirt and casual chino slacks. He was a pleasant-looking man, and he walked toward Dennis Lanfear and, as he drew near, he smiled and said, "Dennis? Is that you, son?"

Dennis Lanfear came back from abstract visions of the City of God, the holy sunken cathedral, and looked at the man. Then he stared at the man. Then he *saw* the man.

Then he *knew* the man.

He had not seen his father since he had been ten months old. Now he was just over forty. He was older than the man in front of him, but he knew the face from his mother's photographs—the picnic at Crystal Beach, the wedding, the shot of him leaning against the Packard, the snapshot on the dock when he came back from the War. Dennis Lanfear stared into, and knew, the smile of his father dead four decades; the loving face of George DeVore Lanfear, come to beam upon, and pridefully acknowledge, the son he had never been allowed to see grow to manhood.

Dennis stood silent, the pain swelling up from his stomach to his chest and into his eyes. As his father embraced him, he began to cry. His father's arms went around him, the tough, corded arms that had worked so diligently until death in the auto assembly plant; and that strength bound Dennis as securely as had the arms of the mermaid who had brought him here, beyond midnight, to the sunken cathedral.

"Where are you? Who am I? What is this place?"

His father sat with him in one of the great rooms of the submerged city. They had eaten, they had talked endlessly, they had swapped stories of the past before Dennis had been born, and of the world since George DeVore Lanfear had died. They had caught up. They were father and son. And now was the moment of explanations, and of decisions about the future...because the journey was only half the destination.

"Atlantis," his father said gently. "You're in Atlantis."

Dennis shook his head in pleasant, startled incredulity. "The legend?" he said. "The great sunken continent, Plato, Minoan Crete, all that...is that what you mean?"

"Welcome to Mars," his father said, grinning widely.

"You said Atlantis."

"Welcome to Atlantis."

"I, I don't seem to..."

"The Atlanteans went to Mars, son. You were brought here the way millions of others have been brought here, for thousands of years, because you got too near one of the drains. Our recycling system. Hadn't you noticed the red water?"

"I—I—" He stopped. He held his head comically, and waggled it back and forth. "I'm not up to this, dad. You've given me too much to—"

"All right, more slowly, then. The Atlanteans absolutely commanded time and space, just as the tall tales tell. They looked ahead, and they saw what was coming, what the human race was heading toward becoming, and they left. They went to Mars."

"But there's no life on Mars, we can see that from the probes we've sent. It's desolate, unlivable. Are you telling me that we're *under* Mars?"

"Exactly. But not the Mars that hangs in the night sky of Earth's tele-scopes. They, the ones who will build the ships, they'll never reach Mars. Whatever red planet in their sky that they land upon...whatever it's called...it will *not* be Mars. Command of time and space, remember? Come on, tell me you remember, don't fall behind."

Dennis laughed, a mild amusement. "I remember."

"Excellent. It's almost as if either one of us is smart enough to under-stand this. What it is, son, is that even if the human race reaches 'Mars' it won't be *this* place. To *some* Mars, perhaps; but never to *this* Mars, this Atlantis, to which we fled. In fairness, they left the legend. Just to tantalize. It was a debt they felt, a debt we still feel. An even break, if you get what I mean. If the world changes—it hasn't, has it?—"

Dennis sighed and shook his head.

"Ah. Well, then...if the world *does* change, and people change, and the legend draws them to us, we'll take them in. We took *you* in, didn't we?" Dennis smiled. "But not otherwise.

"Otherwise...they'll have to shoulder their own destiny. If we could do it, why shouldn't they? We all come from the same egg."

He stared at his father, knowing all was not as it seemed.

The explanations were shimmering, insubstantial, missed a beat here and there.

His father looked at him with unbent affection, and said gently, "And I? Am I your father? Well, perhaps and perhaps not exactly. But I'll do. I am—really and truly—one of the many possible men your father would have become, had he been accorded the chance. I'm a good chance at your father."

"Am I dead?"

"Ah. *That* question. You ask it a little less quickly than most of the cargo she brings us. But...yes, *that* question again."

"Am I? Am I dead?"

"Not an important consideration. Probably not. But maybe you are. So what? Does it really matter a hoot in hell? Live, dead, you're in a warm place with wonderful things happening. We've got the opportunity denied us back where you came from, the opportunity to get to know each other. Isn't that something you've always wanted? Haven't you always cried in your heart that we never got to talk about everything that mattered?"

"Yes. But—"

His father spread his hands and gave him that spiffy smile. "Buts keep coming, Dennis. They never stop. And let me tell you a thing: even if you knew someone you loved, like your father, for instance, knew he was dying, and you sat by his bedside for six months before he passed on, and you said everything you'd ever wanted to say, tied off all the loose ends, made all the little wry observations, shared every experience you'd ever had, the both of you...and you got said every last thing there was to say, about love and family and how much you'd miss me...I promise you that the moment I'd closed my eyes and gone away, you'd think of something you left out, something desperate to be said, and you'd rue the moment for the rest of your life.

"But here, now, the two of us, father and son together at last, here on Mars, in Atlantis. We can talk as long as we wish. It's really fortuitous Dennis. Or do you prefer Denny?"

And there, in the sunken cathedral, far away in another sky, beneath a broiling sun, under a crimson ocean, inside a triangle that opened onto misty reaches, father and son walked and talked together. As it had been ordained. As it had never been ordained. By chance. By choice. By design. Happenstance.

At last Dennis Lanfear had all the time he would ever need to realize his dearest wish: to share, amazingly, all the aspects of the father he had never known. *Never knowing this:* that at the final moment of George DeVore Lanfear's life, as death plunged toward him from above, his last fleeting thought was that he would never see his kid grow up, never know what sort of man he was to become.

By chance. By choice.

Somewhere in the North Atlantic, a body bobbed face-down in warm waters, but that body might not have once been Dennis Lanfear.

Nor was there, for any reason, a howl in the halls of hell; not even in the halls of the gods.

When I got mustered out, on April Fool's Day 1959, and was going to make tracks for Chicago to work for Hamling at *Rogue*, I literally had to pull Charlotte into the car. She was high on busting my chops, pretending she wanted to stay in that crummy trailer, in E-town. Yeah, that'd happen. But after driving me buggywhipcrazy she came along. We got a nice apartment on Dempster Street in Evanston, I steamed the wallpaper and repainted, and we moved in all the new furniture. When Hamling and I went to New York for a distributors' convention, I asked her to open the new bank account with my salary advance of a thousand bucks. When I got back three days later, the apartment was cleaned to the walls. I filed two days later. It took eight, nine months for the divorce to be final. Now it's thirty-seven years later. She's a real bad, sun-faded memory. But it was, significantly, the first or second big slippage I had to deal with. And how's everything with you?